VIRTUOUS SONS

VIRTUOUS SONS

A Greco-Roman Cultivation Epic

Virtuous Sons
Book 1

Y.B. STRIKER

Timeless
Wind

First published by Timeless Wind Publishing LLC 2022

First edition

Editing by Silas Sontag and Paul Martin

Cover art by Macarious

Interior art by Hodge

Title page design by MiblArt

For the boys

Contents

Act I: Rosy Dawn

The Beginning

The 8th Olympic Century is nearing its end, and the Mediterranean is as peaceful as it can be. The free city-states have not engaged in all-out war with one another in decades, and at times, their relations can even be called friendly. Crops are bountiful and trade thrives. The barbarian nations of the far east and west are as they ever were, snarling beasts fighting for scraps at the foot of Olympus Mons. The life of a free citizen is a decadent existence.

Naturally, it is not enough. The climb to the peak of the divine mountain is one wrought with ruinous tribulations, yet men climb it all the same. Wealth and pleasure in outrageous quantities are all too often cast off like dead weight from a man's back as he reaches, perilously, for the next handhold. It is a mad thing. It is utterly against the will of the Fates.

It is cultivation. And it is what separates men from beasts.

Our story begins in the city-state of Álikos on the coast of the Ionian Sea, home to the Rosy Dawn Cult of Greater Mysteries. At its heart is the vast personal estate of the Rosy Dawn's kyrios. His name is Damon Aetos, and he is the father and head of the cult.

On this night, his honored son is throwing a party—a dazzling symposium with some of the cult's most promising initiates in attendance. The night sky is clear and bright with starlight, a half-moon bathing the courtyards in its silver glow. Spirit wine flows freely, and laughter fills the halls of the estate. The young men of the Rosy Dawn Cult are in high spirits.

Our story begins with a slave fighting for their entertainment.

Chapter One

THE YOUNG ARISTOCRAT

I accepted a fresh skyphos of spirit wine from a coyly smiling hetaira, reclining with my head resting on one hand while my cousin traded blows with a slave.

Jeers and taunts flowed freely from those in attendance, each of them initiates of the Rosy Dawn Cult and sons of respected citizens besides. The chambers were just small enough to see the whites of a man's eyes from across the way, an intentional design for nights like these—the young men of the cult lined all four walls.

As such, we all had a clear view of the spectacle in the center, as my younger cousin swung with all his might and missed his mark again. The slave ducked and thrust forward two hands clasped in a single fist, driving them into Heron's gut and knocking the wind from him. He pressed his advantage, bludgeoning my cousin with the manacles affixed to each of his wrists.

A chain linked the wretch's manacles together. He couldn't pull his hands far enough apart to throw a real punch, and yet Heron was the one spitting blood. I drank deeply of my spirit wine, savoring the taste and the sensation of it flowing down my throat and seeping into my core, where it mingled with my pneuma.

"Do you think this is the learning experience he had in mind?" the hetaira asked mirthfully, seating herself behind me and threading her fingers through my hair. A particularly vicious blow to the side broke bone, sending my cousin staggering sideways. "Somehow, I think not."

"A lesson is learned regardless." The fool had no one to blame but himself. His pankration was atrocious, the time he spent toiling between the legs of whores instead of the gymnasium made plainly apparent. In an ideal world, this would serve as a wake-up call. But I had known him too long to hope for that.

Heron's supporters had been the first to fall silent while the rest of the initiates and their companions heckled and cheered, but as the brutality mounted, even the drunkest of the lot grew quiet. The sound of my cousin's grunting filled the chamber, along with the dull noise of the slave striking his flesh.

Finally, my cousin's patience reached its limit. He swung furiously, forcing the slave back, and then he held an open hand out. Palm up. My eyes narrowed.

"Arrogant filth," Heron snarled, baring blood-stained teeth. "You think you're fit to trade blows with an initiate of my stature? You were called on as a *joke*." Light bloomed within his palm. That rosy glow crept, slowly but inevitably, to the tips of his fingers.

"But so be it. If you want to act like an initiate, I will treat you like one!"

My worthless cousin lunged forward, striking at a slave with the Rosy-Fingers of Dawn. Had it connected as it should have, I may have taken him to task myself for the insult. It didn't, though. It didn't even come close.

The slave lunged beneath my cousin's grapple with unreasonable speed, diving into his legs and sending them both to the marble. Those rosy fingers never found purchase, the slave riding him through every tumble and roll with undeniable alacrity. And then it was over. The slave took his back and wound the chain around my cousin's throat, hauling up and choking him.

Silence gave way to shouts of outrage as Heron scrabbled at the chain, his most ardent supporters among the cult coming to their feet. The slave ignored them all and wrenched harder, standing and dragging Heron up with him. My cousin's eyes bulged.

"That's enough."

For a moment, the slave did not respond. My pneuma rose.

Heron collapsed to the floor, staining the marble red as he heaved for breath.

"You dare?"

"Insolent trash—"

"You're tempting the Fates!"

My eyes rolled. The young men of the Rosy Dawn blustered and spat at a lone, bonded slave, no doubt feeling quite righteous about themselves. It took an embarrassing amount of time for one to pluck up the courage to actually approach him, and only then with the company of two others. The slave shifted his feet, hands flexing.

"I said that's enough." The three mystikos froze in their tracks, looking my way. I waved them off. "He's learned enough from my cousin, don't you think?"

The hetairai in attendance tittered and laughed, and only a few of the other initiates kept their silence on my cousin's behalf. The trio hastened back to their lounges and the comforting hands of their hired companions. The hetaira that had hitched herself to me chuckled softly, leaning into me so that her thighs were pressed against my back and her bosom rested over my head. Bold, even for a whore.

Heron recovered soon after, thunder in his eyes. His pneuma, pitiful thing that it was, roiled with murderous intent. I smothered it beneath my own, meeting his glare with dull amusement. For a moment, it almost looked like he would make something of it, perhaps call me out, but no. That would be too manly of him. Instead, he found his feet and stalked back to the lounge beside my own, shoving his prostitute from the bench and reclothing himself in stony silence. The chatter of drunken young men and women soon filled the chambers.

"It was a valiant effort," I offered my cousin. His jaw clenched. "You'd surely have won if his legs were bound too." He held silent, and that was the only credit I'd give him. The fool deserved the loss in standing. I drained the last of my cup until all that remained was the impure lees, closing my eyes and tracing the essence of the spirit wine as it coursed through me.

The hetaira's stroking hand stilled. I opened my eyes to find the slave standing in front of me. Looking at me.

Looking down at me.

My pneuma flooded the symposia chambers. Mystikos choked on mouthfuls of spirit wine while hetairai trembled and hid behind them. The whore behind me did not move, did not breathe. Even my cousin's rage gave way to immediate unease. I raised an eyebrow at the bonded man who had dared to place himself above me.

He was unfazed.

"How may I serve the Young Aristocrat?"

His tone, his bearing, his expression. They were all utterly unacceptable.

"I should kill you where you stand," I told him honestly.

"If that is your wish."

I considered him. He was worn and tattered, but not how you would expect of a lifelong slave. His body was muscled in the sculpted way of thinking men, and his skin was only lightly tanned. A product of conquest, then. His duties had not yet turned his body grotesque, made leather of his skin, or warped his frame. His eyes were defiant.

I lashed out with a hand, and he did not flinch from it. The chain connecting his wrists parted like a strand of silk.

"It is not my wish," I decided. "Leave us. You've had enough fun."

The slave dipped his head just enough to not offer insult. Then he turned and strode out of the chamber on bare feet.

Hours later, I stepped out into the courtyard, the midnight breeze a more than welcome reprieve from the symposia chamber. I inhaled deeply and then sighed, exhaling my frustration and impatience into the open air.

I could only entertain the other mystikos for so long before their sophistry began to grate. It was a duty that I couldn't ignore as the first and only son of the Rosy Dawn Cult's kyrios, and that was the only reason I suffered it. They were so dull. Their ethos, their discourse, and especially their cultivation. They were so far from Olympus Mons that I doubted they could even see it.

"Even you must be better company, slave."

The slave who had no business being in my father's courtyard did not look up from his work, though to call it that was a stretch. He was tuning a lyre. It was a crude thing, the arms and crossbar made of twisted reeds and the tuning pegs of carved bone. Certainly, nothing that a member of the cult would have paid for. I moved to get a closer look.

Our courtyard was of the same scale as the rest of the estate—that was to say, massive in every way. Where the average citizen might take pride in a small pavilion in the center of their home, we enjoyed a vast expanse of vibrant green gardens and marble statues carved with divine precision in the likeness of the Aetos family's past fathers, each standing proudly in a pool of crystalline water.

The slave had sat on the edge of one of those pools to do his work, and he had even gone so far as to dip his feet into its pure waters. Being in the courtyard like this for his own pleasure was already cause for a severe lashing, but that? That was cause for execution. Had anyone else found him, he would already be dead.

It was clear that he didn't care.

"How may I serve the Young Aristocrat?" he asked again, as unperturbed as before.

I was leaning against a pillar covered in winding vines before I knew it, looking over his shoulder while he tuned his crude instrument. Each plucked string sounded sweeter than the last.

"Play for me," I decided.

He did.

Minutes that had dragged on torturously slow in the symposia chamber flowed like water in the courtyard while he plucked his strings of sheep's gut. It was an instrument crafted from a slave's materials, but it was not a slave's hands that made it sing. For the first time in hours, I found myself smiling faintly.

"You're skilled," I told him during a lull. He only nodded as if my praise was to be expected. Perhaps it was. A suspicion that had been seeded in my mind earlier, the moment he arrived with the other slaves to deliver food and spirit wine, took firm root.

Fortunately, it was a simple thing to confirm.

"Tell me, slave," I said, looking up at the celestial glory, "were you born in this city?"

"No."

"Where do you come from, then?"

"The greatest city in the world."

"Ho? Those are fighting words." My arms crossed as I considered. "Go on, then. Let's hear the name of the great city."

The slave's jaw clenched.

"Rome."

I knew it.

The slave's music stopped, his shoulders tensing. He watched me from the corner of wrathful gray eyes. I was smirking, I realized. It hadn't been my intent. Yet, even so, I found myself going a step further and voicing the first thought that had come to my mind.

"I don't know any city by that name. Only a salted ruin."

The peasant's lyre shattered to pieces against the marble pillar where my head had been leaning a moment ago, the tortoise shell flying apart from the force. I spun from my crouch, putting the pillar between us as the slave surged out of the pool.

I inhaled deeply, feeling my pneuma race through my body. From the first blow, Heron should have recognized his mistake. He was a fool, but even fools had eyes. But he had insisted on treating his opponent like a bonded slave, even after his body felt the truth of the matter, and he'd paid for it.

This slave was no slave at all.

Clenched fists lashed out with deliberation and speed, each a potentially debilitating blow if landed. I weaved through them, tracking the motion of his hips as he drove me furiously back. Even outraged as he was, his movements were deliberate and brutal. His anger was cold. His pankration was not.

Pankration, the bonded art of striking and grappling, had as many styles and faces as there were stars in heaven. It was the first thing a cultivator learned and the last thing he mastered. It was not flashy, and it could not, by design, withstand an armed phalanx or a cavalry's charge. It was a simple art, yet it was infinite in its little complexities.

I caught a jab on raised forearms and lowered my shoulders,

driving forward and throwing us both into the pool. At some point, my smirk had become a wild grin.

The realm where pankration truly shined was in single combat. One man against another. There, it became something divine.

My pneuma flared and wound its way through my body, strengthening my muscles and enhancing their flexibility as we wrestled for control in the clear waters of the pool. It had been clear to me from the start that there was something off about this slave, something unique from the others. His performance against my cousin had just made it obvious.

Pneuma was the vital force that gave men their strength, the circulating breath that facilitated all life. It was present in all living things, even those that didn't breathe in the traditional sense. Only a select few could control their pneuma. Even fewer could focus it, concentrate it, and bid it to multiply.

A slave once bonded in chains could not even control his own destiny. How could he possibly control his pneuma?

I drove a forearm up under the slave's throat and flipped us both, winding one leg around his own and bracing the other against the bottom of the pool. I applied pressure that no common citizen could match, enhanced by my own vital life force. The slave twisted and bucked like a bull, snarling, until the slick marble at the bottom of the pool betrayed me, and my footing slipped. We rolled, water filling my nose and throat. I was laughing.

In the end, there could only be one word to describe that unique quality. That formless thing that had caught my cousin's eye, compelling him to call out a slave for a row in full view of his peers. That special characteristic that allowed a man chained and robbed of all control of his life to lunge fearlessly at a far stronger opponent.

To disdain me with his eyes and strike my face with his clenched fist.

"The audacity!" I exclaimed in purest joy, and I struck him right back.

We sat side by side, leaning back on our hands as we heaved for breath beside the filial pool. Its waters were tinted red.

"What's your name, slave?" I asked him. He grimaced and spat blood.

"Solus."

Of course. What else could it have been?

"King of nothing. King of no one. I'll call you Sol," I said, letting my head hang back. I was bruised and bleeding. I'd never felt better in my life.

"Call me Griffon."

Chapter Two

THE YOUNG ARISTOCRAT

"Tell me again, but truthfully this time."

I stifled a yawn. Suffering my father's attention was ever an unpleasant experience, but doing so half asleep and stiff from a fight was a special kind of torture. I'd been roused from a dead sleep at the break of dawn, only a couple hours after Sol and I had parted ways, and informed by a nervous slave that my father required my presence in the courtyard. His expression upon my arrival made his mood all too clear.

I'd known there would be consequences for the mess we'd made, but I'd hoped to get half a night's sleep first. As it was, I was still half-drunk on spirit wine.

"I'll tell you again, father, I was the first to leave the symposia. How am I to know what those burdens to the earth did with their whores in my absence?"

My father gave me a look. Nearly every slave doing morning maintenance of the gardens suddenly realized they had forgotten a crucial tool or alternative task that took precedence and hurried back into the estate. Feh. Cowards.

"Those burdens to the earth are your sworn brothers. And within these walls, they are *your* responsibility." My father's pneuma swept down on me, tightly controlled and utterly dominant like an eagle with talons spread. I winced as a migraine started to form.

Damon Aetos was imposing by any standard, and that was while in a good mood. Even seated with legs and arms crossed, his stature was imposing. At his full height, he stood head and shoulders taller than the average philosopher within the cult, who themselves were head and shoulders taller than the average citizen. His pristine white tunic with its scarlet trim did little to hide his powerful tanned build, a perfect match to any one of the sculptures within the courtyard. His beard was full, distinguished. His eyes were sky blue.

My father was a harsh man but fair. My earliest memories of him were lessons taught and re-taught until properly learned. Swift punishment for failure—and for success, new lessons. Every action he took was heavy with intent. To hear the elder philosophers of the cult tell it, it was his work alone that had pulled the Rosy Dawn Cult up from the brink of ruin decades ago, and his vision primarily that drove it forward each day to greater heights.

It was easy to believe them when Damon Aetos was a philosopher in the Realm of Tyrants.

"You didn't deny what I called them," I pointed out. Unfortunately for my father, I was his son. If I cowered at every sharp look or scowl he sent my way, I'd have never left my room as a child.

"Only a fool denies that the sun rises." He snorted. "And only a fool feels the need to point it out. The difference between you and the rest of the initiates is already clear. What do you think constantly referencing it will accomplish?"

"I enjoy their reactions," I said honestly.

"Finally a true statement." The talons of his pneuma released me, and I sighed in relief as the pressure behind my eyes relaxed. "Let's see if you can manage another. I'll ask one last time. Who dared to defile our filial pools with their blood last night?"

"It's a mystery, father." And so it was. We'd both been beaten bloody by the end of things, but who was to say when the bleeding had started and whose had stained the clear waters red? Could have been mine, could have been Sol's, could have been both. Truly a mystery worthy of the Rosy Dawn.

Damon Aetos was spectacularly unimpressed. "Ignorance is your answer, then. So be it." He stood and regarded the statue within the tainted pool. They were of a height with one another. "You'll clean this pool yourself. And all the rest while you're at it."

Son of a bitch.

"I should have hung you out to dry," I snarled, dunking a bucket into the soiled pool and dumping its contents into a larger clay jug. The slaves that had fled my father's presence had yet to return. That left me alone with the one slave that had been audacious enough to continue working in proximity to a displeased Tyrant.

Sol shrugged, filling his own jug.

Maintaining the courtyard was a daily ritual. The filial pools were drained and that water was used for the gardens. The marble pools were then thoroughly cleaned, each and every one, and refilled from the rivers that wound throughout the Rosy Dawn Cult's estate lands. It was a time-consuming process that was normally attended to by several sets of hands.

It was also slave work. Literally, anything else would have been a better use of my time. I could have been *asleep*.

"Pain in my ass. All because I pointed out that your city's a pile of salted ash—"

A clay jug filled with water shattered against my head, drenching me. I looked up, wide-eyed.

Sol hummed a soft tune as he went about his work sans jug.

My bucket soared on eagle wings.

Álikos, the Scarlet City, was a vast expanse of civil engineering that wound like a serpent through the valley gap between two mountain ranges in the southernmost reach of the Mediterranean. The city's wealth was reflected in its architecture, even the poorest sections boasting stone-walled homes with the distinct, scarlet-baked clay roofs that gave the city its name. Rivers ran like veins through the valley, dividing the city into districts bridged by stone arches.

The wealthiest districts of the city radiated outward from a central point—the Scarlet Stadium. It was a massive edifice, a half-dome carved into the earth that could seat tens of thousands of spectators. Gymnasiums, bathhouses, and wealthy estates alike rippled out like waves around it, each one built on smooth stone foundations and supported by columns of scarlet stone.

Be it for business, recreation, or simple living, every citizen coveted proximity to the grand venue where the city's finest gathered to compete.

Throughout the valley city, and especially on the banks of the rivers that cut through it, life flourished. Olive and fig trees abounded. Bird song was thick where the trees grew closest together, and cows, goats, and sheep were common sights, especially at the edges where the city brushed up against the mountains.

At the peak of the western mountain range, where the sun touched the earth as day turned to night, the Burning Dusk Cult's estate rose gaudy and proud on pillars of twilight stone. It sprawled across the top of the mountain, and in the moments before the sun vanished fully from the sky, its rooftops glowed like fire.

Perched atop the opposing eastern mountain range was the Rosy Dawn Cult. It was, naturally, superior in every way.

Regardless, it was still on top of a mountain.

The rivers were not.

"Tell me, slave—"

"Solus."

"Right. Tell me, Sol"—his eyes rolled—"who taught you how to fight?" I adjusted the yoke over my right shoulder. Eight clay jugs full of water swayed back and forth as we scaled the mountain path leading to the main estate. With any luck, it would be our last trip from the river.

"... My father, at first," Sol eventually said. He had a yoke of his own slung over his left shoulder. "Later, when I was ten, the legions."

"That young?" I asked, surprised.

"I wasn't serving—not at first. My father was called up and chose to bring me with him, and the legionaries thought I was amusing. They would offer to show me techniques and spar with me while my father was busy." There was something fond and wistful in his eyes as his eyes gazed upon something I couldn't see. It made him look like a different person entirely. "By the time my mother made it out to our camp the next summer and demanded that I return home, I had already decided the ranks were where I belonged."

"I didn't realize the legions knew how to fight," I mused. Then, before the touchy slave tackled me down the mountain, I amended, "Properly, I mean. Unarmed, man to man."

"The legions are roaming cities that exist to do war. Why would single unarmed combat be a priority?" There it was, that disdainful gaze. Like looking in a mirror. "Lack of need does not equate to lack of ability. There were always, at least, a few men looking for a brawl during leisure hours. Only, they didn't strip down and slather themselves in oil first."

"Ho, is the Roman looking down on me? My body is chiseled from marble, and it was my own hands that did the work. Why should I be ashamed of it?"

"Pride is a vice."

"Pride is virtue if your heart is true."

Sol frowned pensively. We scaled the mountain in silence, the midday sun beating down on our backs. I had missed two meals and a private morning instruction with one of the elder philosophers of the cult, but I found myself not caring all that much. Tending the pools and gathering water was slave work, but it was rigorous, and the company was good. Honestly, I might have preferred it this way.

The more we spoke, the more I was convinced that Sol was not just another cultivator from a far-flung barbarian culture. The way he carried himself, his upbringing, they painted a vivid picture. Our origins rhymed.

This slave was no slave at all.

He was a young patrician.

When we had nearly reached the top of the mountain where the rough stone merged seamlessly with marble steps, Sol finally spoke again, his gray eyes narrowed in confusion.

"But why the oil?"

Chapter Three

THE YOUNG ARISTOCRAT

Days passed. It was amusing, the places you crossed paths with someone.

At dawn, ducking into the kitchens for a morsel and encountering a surly Roman applying altogether too much force to the bread dough he was kneading, to the dismay of the slave girl trying to teach him. Glancing into an open bedroom on the way to the courtyard to see him fitting a sheet over a featherbed with meticulous precision. Paying the youngest of the initiates a visit during their leisure hours and finding them gleefully playing one of his legion dice games.

And here he was again, attending in the Rosy Dawn's gymnasium while mystikos of varying ages trained their bodies and minds under the gymnasiarch's watchful eyes. Sol, for his part, stared sightlessly ahead. Cloth towels were draped over one of his arms, and a jug of olive oil was cradled in the other.

His disgust with the situation was plainly apparent as I approached.

"Be honored, Sol," I told him, shucking my tunic and tossing it over his shoulder. His upper lip twitched. "It isn't every day a barbarian lays eyes on our divine cultivation in motion."

"Where is it?" he asked tonelessly. "All I see is bare ass."

"Lust is a sin," I chided him. He sneered fully. "Turn your eyes to the palaestra and try to control your urges, you just might learn something. Ah, first though." I spread my arms wide, nodding to the jug.

He didn't hesitate. "Never."

"The Young Aristocrat demands it."

"Allow this one to assist the Young Aristocrat!" a man in slave garb interjected. Sol's teeth clicked together, though I could guess as to the words that almost left his mouth. The older slave's frantic movement and tightly controlled terror as he rubbed me down with olive oil spoke volumes. He'd known it, too.

"Next time," I said, amused, and left him to his work.

To reach the palaestra, the marbled octagon where pankration was practiced and refined, one first had to pass through the central plaza where young men gathered to socialize and trade discourse. Mystikos called out cheerfully to me as I passed, some attempting to coax me over to talk or participate in whatever gymnastics they happened to be practicing. Most knew better, though. I accepted friendly slaps on the shoulder and exchanged greetings with initiates as I passed, but my sights were set.

I stepped onto the raised octagon and rolled my shoulders, surveying the current match.

No, that wouldn't do at all.

"Cease!" The two initiates froze. They were each younger than me but not by much. They'd been locked in the ground game when I spoke, the larger of the two struggling to submit his opponent with a leg wrapped around his neck and an arm pinned to his side.

"Old Perdix takes time out of his day to watch you two roll, and this is what you show him?" I waved a hand, and they hurriedly disengaged from one another, taking a knee in front of me. Each of them heaved for breath, sweat mingling with oil on their bodies as they awaited judgment. I supposed I couldn't fault their effort. Their form, though? Shameful.

Old Perdix watched on in amusement just outside the octagon. He was one of the cult's elder philosophers, a respected cultivator of advanced rank as well as the cult's gymnasiarch. The daily physical and mental training of the cult's young men was his responsibility, and within the gymnasium's walls, his word was second only to my father's. I waited until he inclined his head, and then I went to work on the initiates.

"Aktis and Sinon, correct?" The two nodded silently. "The palaestra is for pankration. If you've come here to rub up against one another like needy whores, the baths are over there." I hooked a thumb to the pools in question on the opposite side of the plaza, where a dozen mystikos were currently playing a ball game.

"We're here to fight!" the smaller of the two insisted. His partner nodded firmly.

"So you say. But are you here to learn?"

Their eyes lit up.

Cultivation.

It is said that there are as many paths to cultivating virtue as there are ways to climb Olympus Mons. Every path, followed with a clear mind and a virtuous heart, leads to the same place—the peak of the divine mountain, where men become gods and the Fates weave their threads. It is a simple progression. Of course, the climb is rarely straightforward.

There are four cardinal realms, each standing on the shoulders of those preceding it.

At the very base of Olympus Mons is the Civic Realm, where the vast majority of Mediterranean citizens live their lives. While ascension to the Civic Realm is a requirement for citizenship in every city-state, it is not a particularly difficult bar to clear—provided you are a free man and not a slave. Ascending past that, however, is a different story.

From birth until death, it is not at all uncommon for a citizen of the Scarlet City to never advance past the third rank of the first realm. It is called the Realm of Citizens for a reason. Harnessing the power of one's own pneuma, their invigorating breath, and bidding it to multiply is the deliberate work of a lifetime.

Cultivation is a race to heaven. It is the refinement of the tripartite soul, an ever-precarious balancing act between the three elements of self: cold reason, burning emotion, and ravenous hunger. It is commitment to a life spent tempting heaven's wrath.

It is no surprise that most choose to tend farms or sell wares instead.

For those that choose to tempt the Fates, and are talented enough to do so, there exists a second realm above the first. The Sophic Realm, where Philosophers toil. It is widely agreed that this is where the climb truly begins, and it is where the vast majority of cultivators languish until their dying days.

Within the Rosy Dawn Cult, every elder is a philosopher of advanced rank. There are even a few prodigies, too young to be true elders but sophists in their souls, who have ascended to the coveted second realm.

The third realm is one that the common cultivator never reaches. At this state of being the soul becomes an entity of its own, immune to the impositions of natural law, dazzling in its brilliance. Only men of the highest virtue and the most egregious audacity ever set foot in this hallowed realm. Officers, revolutionaries, and slayers of monsters.

It is the Heroic Realm, and its members are the subject of epics.

Above the third realm, where the heavens obscure all mortal sight with storm clouds and wrath, there is a fourth. After all, the officer is still a soldier following orders. The revolutionary is often put down. The monsters sometimes win.

The Tyrannic Realm is the pinnacle of enlightened cultivation. It is where rulers of men reside. It's where I'll be someday.

But cultivation is not the work of a single day or a single act. It's a thousand virtuous steps, and each one is a refinement of the body and the mind. It is impossible to have one without the other. A scholar is learned. An athlete is robust.

A cultivator is both. And as this wisdom was passed on to him, so is it his duty to pass it on.

Sinon grunted in agony as I pulled him over my shoulder and slammed him to the stone. He had tried to take me on while standing, but his striking form was as pitiful as his ground game, and I'd easily grappled him. Aktis had already committed to a running tackle by the time I turned, but the fool had lowered his head to avoid my fists. I slammed a knee up into his nose and sent him skittering back across the octagon. The sickening crunch of cartilage echoed as he quickly forced it back into place, eyes watering.

They were both fifth-rank Citizens. The difference between us—four steps within the Civic Realm—was already absurd without factoring in their appalling lack of technique. The former I excused as it was only natural that my cultivation surpassed their own. The latter, though?

"Reinforcement is not good enough!" I snapped. They wore their pneuma like armor and trembled behind it just the same. "We are not *soldiers*. We cultivate virtue, and virtue is performative excellence!"

Sinon regained his feet and rushed me, knowing better than to stop fighting just because I was speaking. I leaned away from a straight cross and slapped a right hook contemptuously aside, headbutting him viciously. He fell flat on his ass, dazed.

I stalked towards Aktis. He feinted a jab and then swung his other elbow at my temple. I caught it in one hand and threw it wide, sending him off balance. I jabbed him once in the kidney and swept his feet out from under him. He lay on his back and wheezed.

"I'm not using any more pneuma than you two right now, and yet look at the difference between us." I hadn't even started to sweat. "What have you been doing with your time here?"

"Perhaps they've been focusing on more *relevant* forms of combat."

Who dared?

I turned and beheld an initiate approaching the octagon, naked but for a belt with a sword strapped to it. He was tall, nearly as tall as me, with long, curly blond hair and sharply defined features. There was an eager smirk on his face.

His pneuma rose. Civic Realm, eighth rank.

Castor. I knew him all too well.

"You must be lost, junior brother," I said blithely. "This is where initiates practice true combat. The sword ring is over in the southwest corner."

"Senior brother is never there," Castor returned, unbelting his sword and rotating it in his grip. It was of medium length and had an edge on both sides. A duelist's blade. "It's been weeks since our last bout. Can you blame me for seeking your guidance?"

"Come, then," I invited him, even stepping aside so that he could climb up unobstructed. "Drop your sword and step into the octagon."

He made no move to do so. "Ah, but pankration isn't my path. That was made clear last time; I'm sure senior can agree. This lowly sophist seeks guidance in his sword forms."

"I am not carrying a sword," I pointed out. However, instead of procuring another one as I'd expected, he only smiled brightly.

"That is fortunate. I was hoping to practice against an unarmed opponent."

Aktis and Sinon stared at him, aghast, and they weren't alone. The palaestra naturally drew spectators within the gymnasium, especially when I was in the octagon. Dozens of initiates had already been watching my impromptu instruction of my juniors. Now they were waving over others in the plaza, hurriedly spreading the word.

"Excuse me?" I said quietly.

"It's common knowledge that the Young Aristocrat reigns supreme in the octagon," Castor said deferentially. "And in your own words, pankration is the pinnacle of martial combat. Is that not so?"

"It is."

"Then there should be no danger for you to humor this junior initiate in his attempts to broaden his understanding of the sword. Is that not so?" Castor looked to the gymnasiarch, who up until this point had pointedly not said a word. The old philosopher leaned against the side of the marble octagon, considering us both for a moment.

"If the Young Aristocrat deigns to accept, I will moderate," he eventually said.

Ah, now I understood. I was being called out.

I hated politics.

Through the press of the growing crowd of spectators, I spotted a flash of white cloth. A clothed figure in a sea of naked bodies. Sol remained in the same place I had found him upon entering, but he was no longer staring dully at the far columns of the gymnasium. His head was turned, looking to the crowd.

Looking at me.

"Come then," I said. Aktis and Sinon scrambled off the octagon while Castor ascended, an eager smile on his face.

"I thank you, senior brother."

I scoffed. "Take notes."

Castor's pneuma roared like a flame, and in an instant, he was beside me. His sword lashed for my throat.

I rolled my shoulders, waving off hollers and cheers as I crossed the plaza and grabbed myself a towel. It was poor form to enter the baths while covered in blood.

"You'll want to head over there once the crowd has thinned," I informed the slave. "I made a mess."

Sol hummed thoughtfully. "He wasn't very good."

"Few are," I agreed, scrubbing the oil and sweat from my hair.

"I'd have beaten him in chains."

A laugh burst from my lips against my will. I raised my hands to heaven, stretching and relishing in my victory, and I only laughed harder when I saw Castor staggering out of the gymnasium with the assistance of two other mystikos.

"Ah, that felt good," I said, feeling light with mirth. "I'm ready for a bath. Care to join me?"

"No."

Unfortunate, then, that he was standing where he was.

I kicked him into the pools and dove in after.

Chapter Four

THE CAGED DOVE

Life in the Rosy Dawn Cult was terrifying.

Athis knew it was an ungrateful fear. She knew that her fortune had been immeasurably good to be chosen for service in Scarlet City's premier cult of greater mysteries. It was said that a slave answered only to their master, but the reality of things was that slaves answered to whoever could freely command them. Forced to choose between insulting a stronger cultivator or parting with a slave, a weak master would always make the latter choice.

Fortunately, there was no man within the Scarlet City stronger than Damon Aetos. Unlike many female slaves, she would never be snatched off the streets in the midst of her work. No man was mad enough to spit in the face of the Rosy Dawn.

But that did not mean she was safe. It did not mean she could rest easy at night. The reputation of the Rosy Dawn's kyrios protected her from external dangers, but it could not protect her from the cult itself.

"It's alright," Pervicas whispered, peering out into the halls surrounding the courtyard. "They're gone." The faint jeering and laughter of young men echoed in the stone. Athis shivered.

She had learned all too quickly that she existed to Damon Aetos only as a tick on a ledger. If she was stolen or damaged by some external source, he would retaliate the same way he would if any trinket or possession of the cult was tampered with by an outsider. If it was one of his own, though?

Well, that was all too easy to overlook.

"Let's go before someone else comes by." Pervicas tilted her head and slipped out of the empty bedroom, and Athis hurried behind her.

They raced silently down the halls, clutching woven reed baskets filled with wool to their chests. They would be safe once they made it to the women's quarters, and with any luck, they would be busy spinning and weaving for the rest of the day. Moments like these were the most terrifying by far—traveling alone, without any higher authority to protect them from wandering eyes. Utterly exposed to the whim of any cultivators that might happen upon them.

"What's this? You're pretty for a slave."

Athis had been a slave to the Rosy Dawn Cult for three months, but it had only taken a week for her to see what happened to a bonded girl that caught an initiate's eye. She'd never forget it.

Pervicas raced up the stairs to the second floor of the estate, shoulder-length golden hair flying behind her. She was hardly panting at all, while Athis was struggling just to keep up. Pervicas had been a slave within the Rosy Dawn for over two years. She'd had much time to learn the ways of the estate. To learn how to navigate its halls and train her body to do so with speed. Athis didn't know where she would be if the other girl hadn't taken her under her wing. Likely nowhere good.

They rounded a corner, so that the gardens and pools of the courtyard were on their left. The women's quarters were at the end of the hall—a short sprint even for her. They traded relieved smiles, racing forward.

Two mystikos emerged from one of the rooms halfway down the hall, chatting animatedly with one another, and Athis' heart sank. They should have been at the gymnasium with the rest. Yet there they were. Pervicas knew the halls better than most, but even she couldn't account for bad luck.

Her friend smoothly transitioned from a dead sprint to an unassuming walking gait in the space of two steps while Athis skittered to a stop before hurriedly approximating a more natural pace. It was a pointless effort, of course. Pervicas knew it just as well as she did. These were cultivators, citizens who had won membership within a cult of greater mysteries.

Their only hope now was that they wouldn't care to stop them.

Athis' heartbeat thundered in her ears as they approached one another. She didn't recognize either of them, and if Pervicas did, it didn't show on her face. Her expression was serene. Had she not been looking for it, Athis would never have noticed the bead of sweat on her brow.

The initiates were discussing some recent lessons as they passed. She wasn't in the right state of mind to truly listen. One of the two glanced her way, and for a moment her heart stopped. Then his gaze slid past her and they crossed.

Athis sighed, shoulders sagging in relief.

"What's this?"

Oh, no.

Pervicas looked back at her with wide eyes.

"Turn around, girl. Let me get another look at you."

Oh please, no.

Athis forced herself to turn. The other initiate, the one she hadn't locked eyes with, was staring at her speculatively. His eyes trailed up and down her body, and she bit her lip as terror and memories from not too long ago of another girl in a similar position assaulted her. She forced herself to take a breath and speak.

"How may I serve, honored mystiko?" she asked, her voice tremoring only slightly.

"I can think of a few ways," he said. He glanced sidelong at his fellow initiate, raising an eyebrow suggestively. The other initiate shrugged.

"Not my type."

"You always did have poor taste," he said wryly. The other initiate scoffed.

Against her will, Athis found the image of the man burning itself into her mind's eye. He was taller than her by several palms, his body powerfully defined as cultivators tended to be. His hair was coarse and brown, the dark shadow of a beard tracing a strong jaw. His leering eyes were hazel with flakes of gold in the irises. Objectively, he was an attractive man. Athis felt her hands start to shake.

"Am I going alone, then? Make a decision," the other initiate said impatiently. *Go with your friend*, Athis silently begged him. Their eyes met. She saw his decision as he made it.

"Go on—"

"What are you two doing?"

Athis spun around, heart in her throat. A man was stalking down the hall towards them. She was saved. She was saved!

It was only when his eyes roved from Pervicas to her and no further, did she realize this was not a superior member of the cult come to chastise the two mystikos. Then she took him in fully. The state of his clothes, ragged and worn, without any of the cult's distinctive scarlet trimming. This man was far less than even a citizen. He was another slave.

In fact, she recognized his face. He was a new arrival, even more recent than herself. What had his name been? Sabas? No... Pelonus? Not quite. It was...

"Solus?" Pervicas whispered, confused. Solus. That was it.

"The others have been waiting for that wool," he said, tilting his head towards their destination at the end of the hall. "Enough talking. Go on. Make haste." Athis exchanged a bewildered look with Pervicas. Solus had never spoken directly to them before this moment. As far as she knew, he'd never spoken to anyone.

But she wasn't going to look twice at good fortune. Athis hurried to follow the command, Pervicas at her side.

Alas. Some things were too good to be true.

"Hold it, slave," the initiate with the leering hazel eyes snapped. Athis froze. "Who gave you the right to interrupt a conversation between mystikos? Do you have any idea who you're dealing with?"

Finally, Solus looked at the two cultivators in the hall. To her astonishment, there was no fear in his eyes. He did not quake with the sudden realization of the insult he'd just offered a sworn initiate of the Rosy Dawn. He merely eyed the initiate up and down and then shrugged.

"I do not."

The hazel-eyed initiate's lips peeled back in a snarl. His companion sighed.

"Of course he doesn't know you, Xuthus. He's a slave. He doesn't know anything."

She wished he hadn't said his name. It was so much harder to forget a face when it had a name to match it.

Xuthus scowled, striding up to Solus until they were finger lengths apart. Solus was taller than him by several inches. It only seemed to worsen his mood. Without looking, the cultivator reached out and ripped the reed basket from her arms, shoving it into Solus' chest. The taller slave didn't budge, though he did wrap an arm around the basket so it wouldn't fall.

"Carry the basket yourself. I've decided I want some company for the night."

"There are brothels in the city," Solus said blithely. "These two are needed on the looms."

The other initiate whistled as Xuthus' face twisted in outrage. Pervicas grabbed her by the shoulder to turn her away. The last thing she saw was Xuthus' arm rearing back and then lashing forward to backhand the intrepid slave.

Athis didn't see what happened next. She heard it, though.

There was a piercing, shattering crack. And then Xuthus screamed.

When she looked back, she could hardly believe her eyes. Xuthus had staggered several steps back and fallen to one knee, gripping his right wrist tightly. His right hand, the one that he had used to presumably backhand the slave's head from his body, hung limp and misshapen, bone bulging against the skin in several places. Somehow, impossibly, Solus hadn't moved an inch.

There was nothing to show for the slap except a faint red mark on his right cheek. The mystiko had shattered his hand against Solus' face.

Xuthus' friend crouched beside him, looking between his mangled hand and Solus with wary confusion. "What was that? What did you do to him?" he demanded. Xuthus groaned through clenched teeth.

"Nothing," Solus said. "I'd suggest a trip to the medico before the brothel. Would you like help getting there?"

They didn't.

"How did you do that?" Athis asked wonderingly as the two initiates fled down the hall, accepting the reed basket when he offered it back. Solus considered her. His gray eyes and dark features that she had found so intimidating the first time she'd seen him seemed, oddly, less so now.

He shrugged again, something faintly amused in his expression. "My mother always said I was hard-headed."

"*Why* did you do that?" Pervicas asked, perhaps more prudently. "You know what could happen to you, don't you?" Solus considered that for a moment. But only for a moment.

"I know his type," he said.

Then he was gone, striding down the hall towards whatever business he had been taking care of in the first place. That was her first experience with Solus. It wouldn't be the last.

Absurdly enough, it wouldn't even be the most memorable.

She found herself crossing paths with him more and more, after that. Or perhaps she was just more aware of it. Doing laundry, preparing meals, and tending to the children. Each time she found herself noticing some new little detail, some quirk she had been too wary to see before.

His wrists were shackled like many of the slaves within the Rosy Dawn. Pervicas explained that it was what one did to a slave that had already entered the realm of cultivation. The shackles prevented them from controlling their pneuma.

It was odd, though. She had seen many slaves within the estate with shackles of cold iron around their wrists, but she had never seen them chained together like his were. Pervicas wasn't sure as to the reason either. If the lack of mobility bothered him, it didn't show. He performed his duties easily enough.

Especially when it came to tending to the children. Child care was generally delegated to the women within the slave ranks, but at times, a firm touch was required. It turned out that Solus was adept at entertaining young, rowdy cultivators. He taught them games she had never heard of, showed them how to carve bone dice, and allowed them to practice on him the techniques they had seen their older brothers and sisters utilizing within the gymnasium. He bore it every time with that tolerant amusement of his.

It was during one of those occasions, when they were both minding a group of young cultivators, that he revealed he was a musician.

Athis closed her eyes and leaned her head back against the trunk of an olive tree, idly stroking a young girl's hair while Solus lulled her and the rest of the children to sleep with the soft sounds of a lyre. One of the boys had brought it with him at his mother's behest, and after a few minutes of tuneless plucking, he had declared it broken and cast it down in disgust. Solus had picked it right up and shown him otherwise.

An idea blossomed in her mind's eye as she listened to him play that afternoon. Pervicas thought she was mad for it and insisted up and down that she would have no part of it, but when Athis slipped away during water gathering the following day to catch a tortoise, it was Pervicas that helped her kill the animal and clean out its shell.

Assembling the rest of the components was the grueling work of days in-between her usual duties as a slave, and the final product was nothing close to the fine ivory and bronze instrument the young cultivator had so carelessly disdained. Even so, it played fine, and her heart swelled with pride when she presented it to him.

"I've wanted to thank you for a while now," she said. She'd grown comfortable with him since that time. In a way, she felt almost as safe with him around as she did in the women's quarters. Even so, she felt shy as he carefully accepted the lyre, his expression unreadable.

"You made this?" he asked, running a finger across the sheep's gut strings.

"I had help," she admitted. "But... the way you played, I thought it would be a shame to never hear it again."

Those stony gray eyes crinkled at their edges. It was a small, barely seen thing, but he smiled for her. Her heart raced.

"I'll play it tonight," he told her. "After dinner."

She couldn't wait.

• • •

Dinner came and went, but Athis never got to hear him play. The Young Aristocrat had decided to gather the Rosy Dawn Cult's finest young initiates for an evening symposia, and Solus had been conscripted for the dinner service. Pervicas and the rest of the girls were already settling in for the night when the party began, and she could only lay awake, waiting, for so long. She drifted off to sleep disappointed.

The crooning of a lyre woke her up. It was faint, drifting through the cracks between the doors like smoke. She lay still, holding her breath and listening intently. No, she wasn't hearing things. He was playing.

Athis carefully slipped out from under wool blankets, stepping silently over Pervicas and the rest of the girls between her and the door. She eased it open and peered out, making sure the halls were empty before stepping out.

It was only a few steps to the rail that looked down over the court-yard with its shadowed gardens and filial pools, and she crouched beside it, looking down. The pools all but glowed with reflected moon-light, clearly illuminating the two young men lounging by one of them. She recognized them both. For a moment, Athis couldn't breathe.

That Solus was in the courtyard alone for no legitimate purpose, that he had *dipped his feet in a filial pool*, was shocking enough. But what made her heart clench was the other young man leaning against a pillar and watching over his shoulder as he played. He was as unmis-takable to her as Solus.

Everyone within the Rosy Dawn knew the Young Aristocrat's face.

But as the slave continued to play and the cultivator made no move to stop him, it became clear that Solus wasn't in trouble. At least not for the moment. Athis watched them through the gaps in the railing, but as the minutes passed and her anxiety for him eased, the music took precedence in her thoughts.

He really was talented. Even her pitiful lyre sang like sweet doves in his hands. Athis leaned against the railing, closing her eyes and allowing the melody to fill her senses. Her awareness drifted.

A crash jolted her awake. Athis whipped her head around, looking up and down the halls, but they were empty. Then, realizing where she was and what she had come out here for, she looked down to the courtyards.

Terror overtook her as she watched Solus and the Young Aristocrat crash into a filial pool.

Her hands flew up to cover her mouth as they struck each other over and over. She nearly screamed when the Young Aristocrat wound arms and legs around him like a serpent and wrestled him down into the water. She couldn't believe her eyes. This couldn't be real!

Athis stumbled to her feet and rushed back into the women's quarters, just barely making it back to her spot on the floor without stepping on any of the other girls and curling into a tight ball beneath her blanket.

I just watched a man die.

She didn't sleep for the rest of the night.

The next morning Solus gave her a nod as he passed by, carrying a yoke laden with water jugs. The Young Aristocrat walked in step beside him with a matching load slung over his shoulder, carrying water and chatting away like he was just another slave.

Athis turned and watched them go, having stumbled to a dead stop at the sight of him. Alive and well. After striking the Young Aristocrat. He was—

Ah. She'd dropped the laundry.

Chapter Five

THE YOUNG ARISTOCRAT

"Am I boring you, young Aetos?" an old man asked me. He was a philosopher, eighth rank within the sophic realm, with a beard that hung down to his chest and bushy white eyebrows. He was in the midst of sorting a book's worth of loose papers spread across the table between us, each sheet covered in numeric equations and geometric formations. He was the cult's resident master of the Pythagorean virtues and had been a tutor of mine since I was a boy.

He was also, yes, boring me.

"You are," I told him freely. "I think I've had my fill of you for today."

For a man of such advanced cultivation, he was easy enough to read. He resented our time together. I'd known that much since I was a boy. He suffered from the same delusions that many of the cult's elders did—that they continued to exist for any reason other than my father's mercy, and they would ever contribute anything to the world that my father had not already mastered and internalized.

It made it hard to take any of them particularly seriously. This one was particularly surly about the private instruction my father demanded all his elder philosophers give to his son, to the point that he made even otherwise interesting topics miserable.

"Your father expects these forms to be finished by dinner," the elder warned. As much as I knew he'd love to send me on my way, within these walls the word of Damon Aetos was absolute.

"Naturally." So I swept the papers into a messy stack and rolled them up, utterly ruining the sorting he'd been doing. His expression tightened. His pneuma flickered, ever so slightly. Alas, he held his tongue. "I'll deliver them myself."

"If the work is not properly done—"

"It will be on my head," I finished, standing from the table and turning my back on him. "As always, your instruction has been invaluable. Truly, I had eyes before today, but now I finally see."

"The pleasure is mine," he said, a model of restraint.

They were all so dull.

"Slave, with me," I called without breaking stride. A dozen heads whipped around at the sound of my voice, but I trusted they had enough sense to know I wasn't talking to any of them. I continued down the hall, pondering the best place to finish my busy work and enjoy the sun while it was still bright in the sky.

Why did I not hear footsteps?

I stopped and looked behind me. There were a few initiates chatting with one another, leaning against the rails looking out into the courtyard, but no one else. I frowned, doubling back to the kitchen entrance.

"Slave."

Once more a dozen slaves looked up from their work in unison, radiating confusion and anxiety in varying amounts. All but one, stood over a table in the back with a mound of dough in his hands. Beside him, the same slave girl that I'd seen teaching him to knead dough the other day tugged frantically at his sleeve, eyes wide as she looked at me. He brushed her hand off absent-mindedly and drove his palms into the dough.

Men and women scrambled to get out of my way as I entered the kitchen. The girl watched me approach with naked terror.

"Slave," I said, softly, standing directly beside him. "Are you ignoring me?"

"I'm making bread," Sol responded.

"And that takes precedence over me?" I asked curiously.

"Evidently."

The girl sucked air through clenched teeth, looking for all the world like she wanted to leap past me and slap her hands over his mouth to silence him. The rest of the kitchen's staff stood frozen in their work, eyeing me like a goat eyes a mountain cat. I considered him.

"Fair enough," I decided, sweeping the rest of the table's contents to the floor and tossing down my papers. The girl and another slave scrambled to gather the materials up while I sat on the tabletop, picking a sheet at random and glancing over it.

"What do you know of the quadrivium?" I asked him, pulling a slotted stick of reed from behind my ear and filling in the papyrus sheet. "Rome has discovered numbers by now, hasn't it?"

"We prefer to use our fingers."

I snorted, picking up another sheet of papyrus. More arithmetic, this time couched in the logistics of a supply chain between Álikos and the Rosy Dawn. It was nothing I didn't already know. The elder knew that, which meant my father knew it too. Yet here I was wasting my time with it anyway.

"It's all the same work," I said, exasperated. "Work orders, internal disputes, negotiations with city vendors. Day in and day out. What lesson am I supposed to learn from endless repetition, other than that the life of a kyrios is miserably dull?"

"Strong foundations build tall cities."

"And many hands make light work." I flicked a few sheets over his way. He continued kneading his dough, but I was patient.

Sol could act as stoic as he liked, but at the end of the day, a cultivator needed more stimulation than a lump of dough and endless chores.

Soon enough he was leaning against the table, poring over a papyrus sheet with that same focused intensity he'd applied to making bread. Slaves cast furtive glances at us every now and then, especially the girl with the dark braided hair, but none of them spoke. The scent of fresh fruits and baking bread hung heavy in the room.

"This *is* light work," Sol mused, tapping the second reed stick I'd brought with me rhythmically against a papyrus sheet. "All arithmetic, as well. When do you do practical work?"

"When it pleases me," I said, setting aside another finished sheet.

Sol rolled his eyes. "Better a slave than father to a Greek." There came a crash and a panicked curse as someone dropped a dish. I only grinned.

"Enlighten this lowly sophist," I said mockingly. "What was your sublime cultivating regimen?"

He considered me out of the corner of his eye for a moment, then flipped the sheet he'd been working on and began writing on its blank side. A soldier's regimented schedule came to life on the page, down to the absurd portioning of time for things like maintaining armor and stretching before exercise. He may as well have been drawing a picture of a cell on the page.

"Numbers require theoretical and practical application in balance with one another," he said as he went. "The quadrivium is worthless if its four points aren't given equal attention. Musical practice in the afternoons, astronomy after dusk. Drills hone the body..."

"I think I'd rather be a slave," I admitted, watching him portion narrower and narrower blocks of time. Hmm. I leaned forward, tapping a block simply labeled 'dice'. "And how does this balance the soul?"

We went back and forth like that. Dinner came and went, and discussions of daily routines and the benefits of tightly scheduled leisure turned to the topic of military life in general. We ate at that table, and when the girl with the dark braid nervously asked if the Young Aristocrat would like anything else for the night, I waved her out with the rest of them.

It was nearly dawn when Sol flatly informed me that he had work to do in the morning and was too busy to entertain me all night and day.

I dropped the work forms off in my father's study as the rosy-fingered dawn breached the heavens. They were late. My tutor had surely been reprimanded for his negligence the night before. A tragedy, to be sure.

My bed was soft, the sheets cool and inviting, but I was still too invigorated for sleep.

"Too busy for me, eh?"

I gave up and went looking for my slave.

Chapter Six

THE YOUNG ARISTOCRAT

"You said we were going monster hunting," Myron, my littlest cousin, grumbled, petulantly swiping wheat stalks out of his face. "You're a liar. Lio the Liar."

Spring had turned to summer, and we were traversing one of the Rosy Dawn's many farms. Located on the other side of the eastern mountain range from the city, the cult's agricultural lands stretched nearly to the coast on the horizon, where the Ionian Sea loomed. Fields of barley and wheat and vast olive orchards made up the bulk of the cult's yearly crops, though there were small fig orchards scattered throughout the landscape as well.

The land was practically swarming with slaves and had been for weeks now. It was harvesting season, and this year was shaping up to be a plentiful one.

Idly, I smacked the back of my cousin's head for his cheek. He yelped and went stumbling into the stalks.

"My virtuous heart won't tolerate such insults," I informed him seriously. He pouted, shaking wheat seeds out of his curly blond hair. "Especially when the monster I promised you is just up ahead." He looked eagerly to where I was pointing, palming the little dagger he carried on his belt, only to groan.

"That's just a slave," Myron complained. In the distance, a crouching slave carved methodically through stalks of wheat with a sickle. A tall reed basket sat beside him, which he deposited the stalks into as he went.

"What did you think I meant by hidden monster, little cousin?" I asked, amused. His nose scrunched up as if I had just served him a great indignity.

"Something dangerous like a harpy or a chimera or—"

I waved a hand. He'd list every nightfire story he'd ever heard if I let him.

"You don't think he's dangerous?" I asked. By this point, we were close enough for even Myron to sense if there was any latent pneuma in the air. He focused intently on the slave, who either hadn't heard us approach or didn't care to acknowledge us. Myron's expression twisted in disdain.

"He isn't using any pneuma. I knew he was just a slave."

"Ho, then, by all means, strike him down. I'll see that you aren't punished for it." I waved a hand invitingly. Myron, for all his faults, was not his older brother—Heron wouldn't have hesitated, but he eyed the slave with sudden uncertainty.

"Kill him?" he asked.

"If you can," I said obligingly. "Unless a slave is too frightening an opponent for you."

He scowled. "I don't need to kill him to prove you're a liar. Watch me!" With that, he dashed forward.

Pneuma within the sixth rank of the civic realm propelled my littlest cousin across the earth at breakneck speed. The slave had paused in his harvesting to stand and stretch, and he turned at the sound of pounding feet just in time for Myron to leap with all the grace of an Olympic long jumper, bronze dagger whipping like a snake's fang towards the slave's shoulder. It wasn't a fatal blow, even with the strength of a cultivator behind it.

And then it wasn't a blow at all as the slave struck the blade from my cousin's hand with his sickle. Myron didn't have time even to voice his shock because the slave then palmed the boy's face with his free hand and dunked him into the tall reed basket.

42

We both watched silently as the boy's pale legs kicked wildly. I glanced at the hidden monster.

"Sol," I greeted.

"Griffon."

"How goes the harvest?"

"Well."

Myron howled in outrage, muffled by all the wheat stalks he'd been stuffed into. I wondered why he didn't just tear his way out of the basket. It wasn't as if it would require any particular effort on his part. He *was* a cultivator, after all.

I kicked the basket over, spilling my cousin and a sizable amount of wheat onto the ground.

"What was that act for?" I asked him, genuinely curious. Myron hacked and spat, glaring mutinously at me while he fruitlessly tried slapping his tunic clean.

"I wasn't acting," he said hotly. "I couldn't pull myself out!"

"Was the reed basket too strong for you? Couldn't break through?"

He rolled his eyes. "He's stronger than me. Why would I break his things?"

"Wise," Sol said approvingly.

"He's a slave," I chided my littlest cousin. "His things are our things."

"But you said he was a hidden monster! He countered my attack!"

"Those things are also true," I agreed. "But he's still a slave. Don't be afraid to treat him like one."

"Who is this?" Sol asked, ignoring my words with ease that came from months of practice. He knelt and gathered the scattered stalks back into the basket, then returned to work with his sickle.

"My youngest cousin, Myron Aetos," I introduced him, patting his shoulder. "I'm minding him for the day. You met his brother at the symposia." Sol acknowledged that fond memory with a grunt. "Myron, this is Solus. He's worth more than most of the other initiates here combined, but feel free to bother him if you're ever bored."

"He's *what?*"

"Someone trusted you with a child?" Sol asked doubtfully.

"Naturally. He's come up against a block in his cultivation recently.

My uncle asked me to help him through it." I went from patting his shoulder to patting his head, deftly avoiding his attempts to swat my hand away. "And if I must suffer this, I see no reason why you shouldn't suffer it too."

"Where does he stand?" Sol asked, and though he didn't look back, there was a note of interest in his voice.

"Civic Realm, sixth rank," Myron declared, frustrated. For a boy his age, only nine years old, it was an absurd level. But for Myron, it was not nearly enough, and it was especially not enough now that his growth had finally slowed to something resembling normal cultivation on the precipice of the seventh rank.

"What's your path?"

Myron looked down, fists clenching. "I don't have one."

Sol froze. He looked incredulously back at me. Unfortunately, the truth really was that ludicrous.

Men cultivated virtue, that they might cast off destiny's threads and ascend Olympus Mons. Each virtue was itself a path that a cultivator walked, a stairway to heaven that they built with their own heart and soul. If cultivation was the journey, then virtue was the guiding light of constellations in the night sky.

In theory, it was possible to set sail beneath a starless sky and arrive at the intended shore. In practice, though? It was a miracle that Myron had progressed as far as he had in such a short life. That he would eventually hit a block had been inevitable. The only question was whether he would be allowed to overcome that block in his own time, the natural way, or whether my uncle would step in.

Sol shook his head and stood, wiping sweat from his brow and running fingers through damp black hair. For some odd reason, he always kept it short, shorn on the sides nearly to the scalp and barely a finger's length on top. He shaved his face entirely. Romans.

"No wonder, then," he said, tossing his sickle underhand. Myron caught it deftly, eyeing the farming implement curiously. He switched his grip on it a few times, attempting to gauge the sublime technique that Sol had used to so easily disarm him. "It's just a sickle. Not a particularly good one, either. Now come here."

Myron looked to me for confirmation, and I shrugged. He hesitantly approached the slave, who crouched back down and motioned for him to do the same.

"You're young. No older than ten, I'm guessing?" Sol asked. Myron nodded, reaching out and grasping a few stalks of wheat and hacking at them with the sickle. Sol plucked the tool from his hand and demonstrated the proper form, then gave it back to him.

"When I was around your age, my father brought me to the legions, and I began to learn the way of the world in a way that I had not been capable of inside the protective walls of our villa at the city's edge." He took the sickle, demonstrated a faulty twist of the wrist in Myron's technique, and then showed the correct form before again handing it back. "There are an infinite number of things that a man can do to advance his cultivation, but there is a chaotic way to do things and there is an ordered way to do things."

"What do you mean?"

"Think of cultivation as a naval journey," I said, lying down on my side with an arm propping my head up while they worked. "Your undying soul is the ship and you are its captain. You can rig your sails to catch only the favorable winds, man your oars with the finest men, and chart the stars at night to track your path. Or you can disdain the oars and let the sails fly free, sleep soundly through the night, and trust the gods to deliver you to heaven."

"A cultivator follows virtue the same way a captain follows the stars," Sol explained. "When I was introduced to the legions and witnessed thousands of men following thousands of different virtuous paths, I was eager to join them. They were awe-inspiring, powerful, and determined in the way I had always wanted to be. But they would not teach me what I wanted to learn.

"Instead, they taught me how to play their games. They taught me how to properly maintain my body, how to hone my mind with discipline. They broadened my experiences, but they would not advise me in my cultivation. Not a single one."

"Why not?" Myron demanded, horribly frustrated. His experience had been much the same within the cult. I saw the thrust of Sol's point, though, and so I threw my own drachma down on the table.

"There is a saying that the elders are quite fond of," I mused. "A young man is like a puppy that only plays with an argument. He's easily convinced into and out of all opinions until eventually, he believes nothing at all."

"Your father won't guide you onto his own path, will he? Even though you've asked him many times." Sol didn't need to wait for Myron to nod. He already knew he was right. "He isn't trying to stifle you. It's the opposite. Philosophy is the study of virtue, and it is a poison to the mind if you don't have the life experiences to give it proper context. Your father doesn't want to stifle you by exposing you to these things before you're ready to decide your true path."

"Then what am I supposed to *do?*" Myron asked. "I can't progress anymore. I go to the gymnasium every day, I attend extra hours with the instructors, and it isn't good enough anymore! What am I doing wrong?"

"You're doing the same things you've always done," I said. Sol nodded, correcting Myron's posture as his frustration bled into his harvesting. "It's a miracle you've made it as far as you have, but this was bound to happen. You've been sailing without oarsmen or stars to guide you, cousin. Be thankful the winds have merely stopped blowing."

"The legionaries could not, or would not, stifle me by exposing me to paths I wasn't ready to walk. But they introduced me to new things. New aspects of life that I had never experienced before. Virtue is performative excellence. And there is excellence to be found in every action." Sol took the sickle and swiped it once, cleanly, through a bundle of wheat stalks. Myron blinked, sky blue eyes widening. "You've made it this far by achieving excellence in the tasks you were given as a young aristocrat. Now you need to try something new."

"We can't give you the answer," I said, amused. "But you can add a few oarsmen to your ship and start rowing until the winds return."

Chapter Seven

THE YOUNG MISS-TOCRAT

There were only so many indignities she could be made to suffer. Surely, at some point, the nightmare had to end.

"Absent again," Castor observed. Her brother, younger by a year, reclined on a couch to the left of her own, frowning as he rolled an olive between his fingers. "He really is shameless."

"I tell you every time," Heron said, on his own couch across the table, "he lost what little sense he had when that slave showed up, and it's only getting worse with time. Lio would rather spend time with garbage than us, his own family." His gaze was as thick as olive oil on her skin. His motives were as obvious as they'd ever been. So tactless.

"That's too harsh," Myron said, stirring a chunk of bread in his spirit wine. His older brother glanced sharply at him, but he glared mutinously back. Since he'd broken past his cultivating block weeks ago, ascending to the same seventh rank that Heron currently occupied, he had grown far bolder during their nightly dinners. Though, perhaps his cultivation wasn't the only thing to blame for that.

"What does it matter if he eats elsewhere? It's not like any of you went out of your way to invite him. Besides, I like Solus—"

"Do *not!*"

Myron's mouth shut reflexively, and though he tried to hide it behind a pout, his hands trembled at the weight of her pneuma bearing down on him. He may have been a nigh unprecedented prodigy for his age, but he was still only a boy.

And while his cultivation was a match for his older brother, it was not at all a match for hers.

"Do not say that name in this room," she said. Her voice brooked no argument. She waited for his sullen nod, and only then did she release her pneuma. Madness. Even here, it was seeping through.

It had long been tradition for the three pillars of the Rosy Dawn Cult to take their dinners together, and it was the same for their children. For as long as she could remember, the young pillars of the Rosy Dawn had shared evening meals in a private chamber separate from the other initiates. It served as an oasis away from the mob, a reinforcement of their status above it. They were the young aristocrats of the Rosy Dawn, elite among the elite, and in time they would be the ones that held the sun in their rising palms.

No matter what trials the day brought, she could always look forward to nights with her family. It was a time and a place where she could fully relax and indulge in the little things. Things like teasing her younger siblings, exchanging discourse with her cousins, and flirting with her fiancé. Yes, even though she was only recently fifteen years old, she had known her fiancé her entire life.

Lydia Aetos had been promised to Lio Aetos the moment she was born.

And now, as their promised wedding date loomed less than a year away, he was drifting away from her. From all of them, really. The boy with the wild grin and unstoppable vitality that had so enchanted her when they were children had slowly changed as years passed, and every one of the younger pillars was forced to grow into the roles their fathers had laid out for them.

The wild grin had dimmed, replaced by a leonine smirk that matched his mane of blond hair and rumbling tenor. His boundless energy and insatiable curiosity had gradually given way to the lazy grace of a predator that knew its place within its domain—above all the rest. It showed in the way he spoke to them—*all* of them, not just the unrelated initiates. It showed in his actions, the flippancy with which he treated subjects that had received his full focus in the past. These changes by themselves were far from unattractive, in her unbiased eyes, but they were only symptoms of a larger issue.

Lio Aetos had paced around the Rosy Dawn Cult like it was a cage for years. Watching, waiting. All those years she had wondered fruitlessly as to what he was waiting for, what she could do to satisfy him. To revitalize him and return that excitement to his eyes.

She still didn't know what it was, exactly, that he'd been waiting for. What she did know was that he had found it in a *slave*.

"Perhaps Myron is right."

Lydia turned, dismayed, to her younger sister.

"Even you, Rena?"

Rena Aetos winced, looking down into her cup. She ran the tip of one slim finger around its rim. "I don't think Lio dislikes us. I think he just doesn't realize how much we miss his company." Heron scoffed at that, and Castor sneered, but she pushed on. "If we invited him to join us, I'm sure he'd come."

"He would!" Myron agreed at once.

Lydia frowned fiercely. It was absurd that they even had to ask. Family was family, was it not? She was his future wife, *was she not?* That they would seek each other's company should have been a given.

Yet here she was, swallowing her pride anyway. When it came to Lio, she was truly hopeless.

"Fine"—she sighed, taking a vine of grapes from the table and settling back onto her lounge—"tomorrow, I'll extend an invitation."

Tomorrow arrived along with its indignities.

Lydia walked the mountaintop peaks with a retinue of the cult's most promising young women in tow. There was an electric, excited energy amongst the girls, and for good reason—the harvest season was reaching its end, and the Rosy Dawn was beginning to turn its attention to the processes of the cult's annual initiation.

The initiation rites of the Rosy Dawn were a tradition that traced back all the way to the cult's beginning when its founder rose to greet the first dawn and passed down his virtues to his children and his sworn brothers-in-arms, drank spirit wine from the same vessel, and contemplated the greater mysteries of the rising sun. Every year that followed, new blood climbed the eastern mountain ranges of the Scarlet City and submitted themselves to the Rosy Dawn, seeking enlightenment to one of life's greatest mysteries and membership within the strongest group of cultivators in the region.

Beyond admittance of new members, it was also a method for current mystikos to elevate their standing within the cult and compete for a chance at being sent to the Daylight Tournament within the Scarlet Stadium, come summer's end. Naturally, this was what excited the current initiates most.

During this time, the gymnasiums flooded with eager men and women hoping to advance their cultivation one last time before the rites, torches burned within the cult's libraries long into the night, and the mountaintop estates abounded with families from the city hoping to win their children a spot on the roster.

Lydia waved a hand, halting her fellow initiates while she moved forward, stepping deftly through perilous outcroppings of rock and tracing a path that only a few had walked over the years.

There was always something to be done, whether one was a slave or an honored elder philosopher. Even she had struggled to slip away from her duties to track down her fiancé and ask him to dinner.

It made it all the more galling to find him here, lounging in a depression carved out of the mountain's face by hand, such that you could be shaded while looking down upon Álikos in all its glory. She had known to search this place despite its isolation from the rest of the estate for a simple reason. They had carved it out together, all the cousins, years ago. It had been a secret location for them to gather during the day when they were too impatient to wait for dinner.

Now he shared it with a slave.

Her blood boiled. It was an insult that her virtuous heart could not stand.

"Lio," she said, her voice deceptively mild, "what do you think you're doing?"

"Cousin," he greeted, looking up at her. Normally, her heart raced when he looked at her with those scarlet eyes of his, so sharp a contrast from the sky blue that the rest of the family bore. But not now. She was too furious to be smitten.

"How dare you defile this place with that garbage?" She jabbed a finger at the slave.

The wretch didn't even acknowledge her. He sat beside her fiancé with his legs crossed, back against the mountain, and his miserable eyes shut. He looked for all the world as if he hadn't heard her, hadn't felt her pneuma sweep down and attempt to wring the life from his cursed neck the moment she saw him.

"That judgment is hardly fair," Lio chided her. Amusement made his eyes shine. "He hasn't even introduced himself. Go on, slave. Say hello to my cousin."

"Another one?" the slave asked, eyes still closed. He opened gray eyes, regarding her neutrally. "My name is Solus. How can I serve the Young Mistress?"

"You can die," she hissed.

"As you wish."

Before her disbelieving eyes, he stood and walked to the alcove's edge.

"Belay that," Griffon commanded, reaching up and grabbing a fistful of the slave's ragged tunic. He yanked him back from the edge. "Worthless Roman. No one thinks you're funny."

Roman?

"If you must know," he told her, "we were contemplating the celestial mystery."

It was a common form of meditation within the cult, one that Damon Aetos himself was said to often practice. The sun was just now descending from its zenith, still a vibrant gold. The view of it from the alcove was breathtaking.

"Why is a slave contemplating the mysteries when there is work to be done?" she demanded.

The slave nodded, eyes once more closed as he resumed his meditation. "I agree."

The impudence of this man. "Did I ask your opinion, slave?"

"No," he said, "but you received it."

"Haa?"

Lydia Aetos' frayed patience finally snapped. She'd had enough of barking dogs.

She threw forth a rosy palm, her pneuma lighting up the alcove with its terrible splendor as her technique surged from her virtuous heart to the tips of her fingers. She would put an end to this herself. Something about this slave had blinded her cousin, but she would help him see. He belonged by her side. He belonged with his *family*, not here in their old place with that miserable, cursed—

Griffon caught her wrist and pulled her tight to his chest. Her divine technique fizzled and died in her hand. She found herself staring up into curious scarlet eyes, unable to breathe.

"Why are you here, Lydia?" he asked her. *Ah. Right.*

"Will you come to dinner tonight?" she asked, her voice small.

"Of course"—he laughed, and she fell in love again—"we'll be there."

Rage.

Chapter Eight

THE YOUNG ARISTOCRAT

"I told you to focus! Look at what you've done—a block of the Rosy Dawn's finest marble, wasted!"

There was something profoundly comedic about watching a nine-year-old boy so flagrantly berate a boy older and larger than him, and then for that older, larger boy to cringe as if death itself was hanging over his head. There was sense to it, of course. The nine-year-old may have been younger and smaller, but his cultivation was also advanced beyond most initiates twice his age. The older, larger boy was hardly a cultivator at all. Certainly, he was no mystiko.

It was the final day of the qualifying week that prefaced the Rosy Dawn Cult's annual initiation rites, and hopeful cultivators of varying ages had been coming in droves from far and wide to test themselves before their would-be seniors.

"What do you have to say for yourself?" Myron demanded of the boy, who looked to be a few years older than him. Stout and muscled, he'd honed his body well. Alas, his cultivation evidently left much to be desired. "Well? Speak! I, your father, will decide your fate!"

The would-be mystiko shook, eyes darting frantically as he struggled to find an answer that would save his life. In the distance, amidst the crowd of parents and other relatives, his father took his sobbing mother into his arms and turned them both away. Myron's pneuma rose as the silence grew long, expression darkening with affected rage.

"Ho, the little kyrios is fierce," I said, planting a hand on my littlest cousin's head and ruffling his hair vigorously. I smothered his pneuma beneath my own, and the young applicant gasped in a breath.

"Lio!" he cried, embarrassed. "You're interrupting!"

"Is it not a senior initiate's imperative to advise his junior when he errs?" I asked rhetorically. Ah, the boy was still here. "Begone," I said, and he went sprinting back to his parents.

"I wasn't erring," Myron said, crossing his arms and glaring petulantly at the failed applicant's retreating back. "That's how father said seniors are supposed to handle failures. I was even letting him explain himself first."

My uncle had surely been thinking along a different path than my littlest cousin. In his own way, Myron had been attempting to help the would-be initiate by giving him a chance to explain himself. I could easily imagine him procuring a second marble block for the boy if he'd managed to explain his first poor performance. Unfortunately, my cousin underestimated the effect he had on his juniors.

"Have a seat, cousin," I told him, and he reluctantly obliged.

"Who would join the Rosy Dawn?" I called, and the crowd of hopefuls at the edge of the pavilion roiled and heaved. Another young boy was spat out, urged forward by his parents. He approached with visible anxiety.

I snapped my fingers. "Marble."

Sol stepped between us, dropping a block of marble the size of a man down in front of the applicant. The boy flinched as stone slammed against stone.

"You've come here to pursue one of life's greater mysteries," I declared. The applicant nodded as if it had been a question. "The Rosy Dawn Cult has neither the time nor the inclination to polish every filthy scrap of bronze that presents itself to us. Lay your hands on this marble block and chisel it in your image."

He forced himself to meet my eyes and knew I found him wanting.

"Let us see your soul."

The boy grit his teeth and stepped forward, pressing both hands flat against the block and splaying his fingers wide. His pneuma rose and pierced the stone, suffusing it from edge to edge. The boy's eyes clenched shut as he focused, whispering soundlessly to himself as he manipulated his life's essence.

"You didn't ask for his name," Myron whispered crossly.

I blinked, confused. "Why would I want to know it?"

The stone groaned and cracked, hairline fractures appearing on its surface and spreading like the veins of a lightning strike. The applicant gasped, eyes flying open, and all at once, a portion of the marble block simply fell away. Chunks and shards littered the ground around what now stood where before had been a formless pillar.

A statue of the applicant jutting proudly from the earth, the only immediate difference from the boy whose pneuma had carved it being that it was naked. Its expression, as well, was far more confident and assured, marble eyes staring wantonly up to heaven. It stood, back straight, one hand on its hip and the other clenched into a fist at its side. It was a strong pose, well conceptualized.

There were small inconsistencies, issues of refinement. The nose was not quite the right shape, and one ear was chipped at the tip. The musculature was off in several places. That being said, it was far better than the mangled wretch the previous applicant had managed.

"Crude," I observed, and the boy's shoulders fell. "But I suppose I'll accept it. Your fate is in the elders' hands, now. Take your spirit marble and go find someone who looks too old to be alive. Tell them the Young Aristocrat sent you."

The boy's face lit up, and he frantically thanked me before heaving the spirit marble over his shoulder with some effort. He moved deeper into the pavilion in search of a philosopher. In the crowd, his mother jumped up and down in joy while his father accepted clasped hands and words of praise from the other men around them.

The pavilion that the qualification trials took place in was the central point of the Rosy Dawn Cult, from which its gymnasiums, bathhouses, and various estates branched out along the mountaintop. It was built in the same style as the grand agora within the Scarlet City where citizens gathered each day to conduct the majority of the city's business and was of a comparable size despite seeing far less daily traffic.

Pristine stone steps on each side led up to a massive alabaster plaza, framed by pillars in the shape of the cult's greatest Heroic cultivators, each one gazing longingly up to heaven. Within the heart of the central pavilion was a grand fountain that gushed crystalline water from the open palm of a faceless man.

On an average day there might be a few dozen initiates and merchants scattered around the grand agora, but today it was packed full.

"Did you see the difference between us?" I asked my littlest cousin. He was watching me intently. "The senior initiates ridicule and threaten applicants because they can, because they were ridiculed and threatened when they were applicants. It's an assertion of what small renown they've gained since then."

"It's also an application of pressure," Sol observed, having stayed back to watch. He had that distant look in his eyes, reliving some memory or another. "There are parts of a man that you'll never see unless you push him to his breaking point."

I scoffed. "The Rosy Dawn isn't the legions, and these children are no soldiers." He shrugged, conceding the point.

"The trials are pressure enough as it is," I said. Myron nodded. "And you are a pillar of the Rosy Dawn, whose cultivation speaks for itself." Another, pleased nod. "So why are you barking like a dog?"

"I'm not! I'm just..." He frowned.

"Copying the other initiates, who are beneath you in every way," I finished.

"But Heron does it this way."

I raised an eyebrow. Myron looked away, chagrined.

"There is a reason why senior initiates are enlisted to screen applicants," I explained, sitting and picking up a stray chunk of marble the size of my head. I exhaled, permeating it with my pneuma. "It eases the burden of numbers on the elders, but not by much. The true purpose is to introduce future juniors to current seniors."

A fine stone powder drifted off the marble chunk as my pneuma wore it down. Within moments I held a fierce marble eagle in my hand, its wings spread wide. I tossed it to him.

"Today is the day that future initiates will pass judgment on your character," I told him. "So, since you are their superior in all things, act like it. Leave the barking to the dogs."

"And leave the preening to your cousin." Sol offered his opinion, unprompted as usual.

I sneered. "Fetch us another block, slave." He snorted but obliged.

Myron brushed down his cult attire and gathered himself. "I'll do my best," he declared.

"I know you will," I said, ruffling his hair fondly. I wandered off, and I heard him clearly as he called out to the masses.

"Who would join the Rosy Dawn?"

By dusk, the last of the year's applicants had been accepted or rejected and processed accordingly. Successful applicants were given time to bid their families a joyful farewell and then ushered into one of the outer estates where they would be living as fresh initiates. The beginnings of many sworn brotherhoods would be forged in those first few hours as soon-to-be initiates excitedly spoke to one another about the rites to come.

The rites began in the dead of night, hours before the dawn. The men and women of the Rosy Dawn, however, began preparations much earlier than that. It was an event that every single member of the cult took part in, from the lowliest junior initiates to the pillars themselves, Damon Aetos and his brothers.

Every cultist had a role to fulfill as the sun dipped below the western mountain range. Many took to the mountain trails in their ceremonial robes with ornate clay jugs in their arms, racing through harvested wheat fields towards the sea. Others lined themselves along the peaks of the eastern mountain range, torches burning brightly in their hands. The challengers, junior initiates looking to ascend to senior rank, gathered in a crowd amongst each other and exchanged barbs in tense anticipation. The estates were alive with shadowed motion and excited whispers.

The rites lasted for two full days, ending as the sun dawned on the third. Due to the confidential nature of the initiation, they were two of the most restful days a slave would experience in service to the Rosy Dawn Cult. Every single servant was confined to quarters for the entirety of the rites.

Most of them, anyway.

Dozens of men shouted and flinched as I kicked down the door to their quarters, woken from what had no doubt been blissful sleep. I grinned brightly, stalking across the room towards the one man who had the audacity to glare at me. The slaves in my path hurriedly threw themselves out of the way.

"What is this?" Sol demanded, his voice rough from sleep.

I dropped a leather sack over his head and cinched it tight, and then I threw him over my shoulder.

"Don't fight it!" I told him cheerfully.

Traditionally, the qualifying trials were a prerequisite for initiation to the cult. However, the pillars of the Rosy Dawn enjoyed the unique privilege of being able to sponsor one initiate of their choosing each year, regardless of cultivation or status, so long as they personally saw them through the rites. They could choose anyone.

Even a slave.

Chapter Nine

THE YOUNG ARISTOCRAT

The mysteries. Greater or lesser, they were the foundation of enlightened society as the Mediterranean knew it. The phenomena that eluded all explanation and drove men to maddening heights of cultivation in pursuit of an explanation. No man, no matter how sublime his cultivation, had ever found a satisfying answer to even the least of the divine mysteries. They were the questions that had plagued humanity for as long as there were written histories.

But we pursued them anyway. It was our hubris that drove us. Our fundamental audacity, that we could look upon the deepest complexities of creation and decide that they were within our understanding. To be *incensed* that there were things in this life that were not already known to our collective conscious.

Cultivators were nothing more and nothing less than stargazers reaching desperately up to heaven, trying to catch divinity in our hands. It was the only way to part the cosmic veil. The only way to know.

What lay at the peak of Olympus Mons wasn't something mortal eyes could see.

We stole the new initiates from their rooms as the moon fell out of the sky, covering their heads with leather sacks and coaxing them down the far side of the mountain range. More than a few panicked, stumbled, even tripped and fell. A senior mystiko was always close by to catch them, though they received an earful for the trouble.

It was a chaotic process, meant to disrupt and disorient the new blood. Several mystikos carried drums that they pounded as the new initiates staggered past, and a low chant was carried from the peak of the mountain all the way down to the harvesting fields. The chaos centered them. Forced them to focus on the rites, here and now, and not whatever delusions of renown they had been dreaming of after passing the qualification trials.

We walked them down the mountains and through the fields until the smell of soil and livestock gave way to the salty tang of the Ionian Sea. A line of fire stood out on the beach, senior initiates patiently waiting with torches in hand and clay jugs filled to the brim with seawater. Their eyes were bright, underscored with scarlet paint.

I dumped Sol into the sand, rolling my shoulder while he cursed. One of the senior initiates approached us, walking out of the ocean shallows and offering me their torch. I accepted it, kicking the back of Sol's knee when he tried to rise. He snarled another curse.

The senior mystiko, a man a few years older than me with scarlet-painted hair, hesitated. His eyes locked onto the manacles around Sol's wrists, the severed halves of the chain that had connected them coiling in the sand. He looked askance at me.

"Why is the morning tide sacred?" I asked him. His expression firmed.

"Because it is the first to greet the dawn," he said, and he tore the leather sack off Sol's head.

The irritated Roman hardly had time to blink before the senior's jug of saltwater was upended over his head. He coughed and spat, shaking seawater from his eyes.

"Son of a—"

"Repeat after me—"

"—*whore*."

"Repeat after me!" the senior initiate snapped. "I have fasted." Sol glared at him.

"Say the words, slave," I ordered him. "I didn't carry you down that mountain for nothing."

"I have fasted."

"I have drunk the kykeon," the senior initiate continued, procuring an animal skin from the folds of his ceremonial attire and holding it out. Sol considered it dubiously. I sighed, plucking it from the mystiko's hand and taking a long pull from its contents. The spirit wine was sweet and potent, heavily spiced.

I tossed it Sol's way, and he reluctantly drank the rest. His pupils dilated.

"I have drunk the kykeon."

"Then prepare to greet the dawn," the mystiko intoned and led us into the sea.

A man's first experience with spirit wine was always a memorable one. Doubly so if he had the mixed fortune of experiencing it during the rites.

Sol knelt in warm waves, transfixed, along with all the other new initiates as the scarlet sun breached the far horizon. He'd drunk all but the impure lees at the bottom of the wineskin, and I knew from experience that his every essence was alive in this moment, his pneuma coursing through his veins in a way he had never felt before. It was a powerful resonance even to the most undeveloped of cultivators.

For someone on his level, it was something truly profound. It was a shame about the manacles. I could only imagine how infuriating it must have been to feel his pneuma in such a state, begging to be unleashed, and having no way to reach it.

The dawn broke fully through the waves. The rites had begun.

"What makes you think I want to join your cult?" Sol asked, later, as juniors and seniors alike hiked back up the mountain. Rising clear-eyed with the dawn. His pupils were still dilated, but he had shaken off the haze that came with the overindulgence of the spirits. He was lucid enough to sneer.

"What makes you think you have a choice?" I countered. "Be

thankful. It's by my grace alone that you'll witness one of heaven's greatest mysteries."

He frowned, looking back and raising a hand against the rising sun. "What are we expected to do for two days straight?"

"The first day is more about the established members of the cult than it is about you." I withdrew my own wineskin from the folds of my ceremonial robes, dyed entirely red with white trim along the edges. The kykeon burned pleasantly down my throat. Sol eyed it warily, shaking his head when I offered him a pull.

"You've witnessed your first rosy dawn. Now we return to the pavilion, where you'll observe the cult's finest cultivators seeking renown before their peers. A truly inspiring sight," I said wryly. "There are three trials a junior can advance by, one for each element of the tripartite soul."

Trial by logos, thymos, and eros. Reason. Spirit. Hunger.

"What are these trials?" Sol asked as we crested the mountain.

I waved a hand. "See for yourself." He stopped short and stared.

The Rosy Dawn was at war.

There was no other description for the chaos that had overtaken the mountaintop while we were out greeting the dawn. Hundreds upon hundreds of mystikos, from the young prodigies to the fully grown seniors, were locked in a riotous melee that had originated in the central pavilion and quickly spilled out onto the pathways that connected the estates. Fine ceremonial tunics and robes were marred with dirt and blood as mystiko battled mystiko with furious zeal.

Two factions warred at the center of the mayhem. Sixteen men, eight on each side, heaved and pulled with all their might on a rope as thick around as their forearms. Helkustinda—the pulling war. The men of both teams snarled and gnashed their teeth, muscles straining visibly as each team struggled to pull the other's farthest member past the central point of the pavilion—the faceless fountain statue's open palm.

They were surrounded by a roaring crowd armed with jugs full of kykeon. When a man began to lose steam, the crowd doused him in spirit wine so that he might rally his pneuma. Meanwhile, man-to-man brawls raged along the pavilion's edges. Already, its pure gray stone was slick with blood and wine.

"This is mad," Sol said, wide-eyed.

"This is trial by spirit," I corrected. "Every mystiko within the Civic Realm is welcome to take part and test themselves against another cultivator of civic rank. The elders are watching, obviously. Advancement to senior status is decided by martial prowess, strength of will, and *stamina*."

Up on the pavilion, a flagging member of the pulling war's western team shouted in furious determination. He threw his head back, mouth open wide, and his fellow mystikos were more than happy to oblige him with a deluge of spirit wine. He gulped down as much as he could and shook himself like a dog. Eyes blazing, muscles flexing. His efforts redoubled.

Off to our left, a junior mystiko came hurtling through the air, flailing wildly with a dagger in each hand. Sol moved, snatching him out of the air and slamming him down on the stone steps. The boy choked, clutching his side in agony.

"That was hardly necessary."

"He approached me," Sol said, prodding the boy with a foot. The mystiko groaned and rolled pitifully away from it. I raised an eyebrow.

"He was thrown."

"He approached me," Sol repeated. He watched the other brand-new initiates stream past, rushing after their senior chaperones in search of safety from the chaos. "What of the other two?"

"*You!*"

And so he was answered.

"Trial by hunger," I supplied, amused, as Heron stormed through the press of combat to reach us. He was as of yet untouched, his ceremonial attire pristine. Though perhaps not for much longer. His pneuma rose precipitously as he laid eyes on Sol.

"Slaves are confined to quarters," he snapped. "Arrogant wretch. I should lash the skin off your back."

"That's no way to speak to a new initiate, cousin," I chided. His blue eyes widened in rage.

"You can't possibly be serious. You would taint your father's Rosy

Dawn with this *filth?*" Heron jabbed a finger into Sol's chest. The Roman didn't move, and he had no ability to flex his pneuma, but the look in his dilated eyes made clear his intent. My dear cousin was tempting the Fates. "Are you out of your mind, Lio?"

"I thought you'd be pleased," I said mildly. "With this, you can say it was a future mystiko that savaged you in chains."

At last, my cousin found his manly side. His face hardened. His hands burned brightly as he assumed a pankration stance, disdaining the slave entirely.

"There are certain privileges that a member of the Rosy Dawn is afforded as they gain renown," I explained for Sol's benefit, shrugging my shoulders out of my ceremonial robes. A belt of white cloth around my waist kept them from falling away completely. "Certain benefits. Certain *affections.*" Heron's expression didn't change, but his pneuma flared wrathfully.

"It's a man's nature to desire what he does not have. That is the trial by hunger. During the rites, he can take it by force. If he's able." I grinned savagely, throwing my arms out wide for my cousin.

"You want this status? Come try and take it."

Chapter Ten

THE YOUNG ARISTOCRAT

The Rosy Dawn was a cult that pursued the mysteries of heaven. Its purpose was wholly divorced from issues of blood-based hierarchy; by its nature, it valued performative excellence over filial ties. *And yet.*

Heron gagged as I buried my fist in his gut.

My father's line reigned supreme.

"You're familiar with the concept of social standing, yes?" I asked Sol, leaning away from a burning right cross and shifting my feet. I jabbed through my cousin's guard, breaking his nose with a sharp crack. "Even animals recognize hierarchy—surely, Rome has come that far." Sol squinted at me, no doubt weighing the pros and cons of joining the fight on my cousin's side.

"I'm familiar."

"Then you know that within every society, civilized or not, there is social order. When one man stands above another it's only natural that his word carries greater weight." Heron exhaled a seething breath, his pneuma spiraling around his right fist. Predictably, it was only a feint to draw my attention away from a left hook. I ducked the left and lunged in before he could turn the right into a true strike, planting my shoulder in his gut and lifting him off his feet.

"The Scarlet City is built upon the backs of four social classes," I explained, wrapping both arms around my cousin's head and twisting at the hips, slamming him to the stone. "Slaves are the lowest of the four, obviously. Freedmen are technically their betters, occupying the third rank. Metics, foreigners that have won citizenship, are second class. And then there are the true Álikons, the natural-born citizens."

Heron found his feet quickly, pneuma blazing as he advanced his virtuous technique to a higher level. Ho, that looked lethal. Striking your own cousin with those shining hands? How cruel.

"The slave covets the life of a freedman. The freedman covets the life of a metic, who covets the life of an Álikon. We're all united by terrible ambition."

"Stop talking!" Heron snapped, advancing with a flurry of punches that blazed like comets. They were burning hot as I diverted them.

"But there is division within the classes, too. A metic that works for an Álikon is lesser to the metic who peddles his own wares, is he not? A slave who works a trade to pay his freedom price is naturally above the slave that languishes in worthless duties, is that not so?"

"And a nephew to the kyrios is lesser to the son," Sol finished for me. I grinned, sweeping my cousin's feet and kicking him down the steps when he tried to catch his fall with a handstand.

"The citizen is lesser to the noble, and the noble is lesser to the heir," I agreed. "My cousins occupy a leading class within the leading class. The Aristos. Did your tutor ever teach you that word, slave?" Sol sneered. I'd take that as a yes. "I exist on a level even higher than that. Heron covets that space and resents me for occupying it. It consumes him."

"Difficult to blame him," Sol mused while I deflected Heron's blazing charge up the steps. His rosy cultivation had spread from the tips of his fingers all the way to his elbows now and seared any eye that looked upon them. "Bad enough that you were born to the ruling brother by chance. That you're insufferable on top of it? I'd be furious as well."

I barked a laugh, catching burning fists that would have shattered and immolated the body of any cultivator below the fifth civic rank. Our fingers interlocked as Heron strained against me with everything he had, soul blazing. I looked him in the eyes and tightened my grip.

"You misunderstand," I told Sol, without breaking eye contact. "Aristos is a word with two meanings. Best by birth, yes. But best by virtue just the same. My father was the oldest son of my grandfather, but he was also the strongest of the four. That's why he leads today."

Heron roared in impotent rage and then in pain as my grip tightened past the point his body could bear. He fell to one knee, straining against me with broken hands and flickering, dying light.

"The reason I exist above you is not that I had the good fortune of being born, cousin." I pressed down. His rosy light faded, and I told him the truth.

"It's because I am *better than you*."

"You don't even want it," Heron hissed, defeat in his eyes. "Any of it!"

I raised an eyebrow. "What does that matter?"

Finally, his body gave out. He bitterly conceded, and the trial by hunger ended.

His cultivator's soul starved.

Sol was pensively silent as we moved on to the next stage of the rites.

The third ascendant trial was the least physical but most arduous by far. The trial by spirit was a simple test of will and brute force, judged holistically by the elders and easy to pass. This was how the vast majority of junior initiates rose to senior status. The trial by hunger was brutally decisive, won and lost without any input from the ruling class. This was how personal vendettas and greed were settled.

The trial by reason was a test of virtue conducted by the pillars of the Rosy Dawn themselves. It was not a holistic process. There were correct and incorrect answers, made evident by the manifestation of virtue that was a cultivator's pneuma. The elders were known to favor certain initiates over others, and those biases were reflected in their judgments.

My uncles had no such weakness.

Fotios and Stavros Aetos, the twin eagle pillars of the Rosy Dawn, were men that other men paid to hear stories of. Built in my grandfather's image, they shared my father's massive frame as well as his dark curls, and their skin was burnished bronze. Their eyes burned an unearthly blue, their virtuous spirits lighting them from within. There was an unmistakable gravity that accompanied them, conveyed through their every word and motion.

They were both captains of the Heroic Realm. Legendary cultivators so far beyond the average cultivator that they were a separate existence entirely. It was said that even the lowest Hero was beloved by the Muses and reviled by the Fates. They were slayers of monsters, champions of humanity.

That these two had returned from their epic journeys alongside my father, two decades ago, and subjugated themselves to their brother in service of the cult only added to Damon Aetos' absurd renown.

On any other day, my uncles would have had far more pressing concerns than the business of mystikos, but during the rites, they were the arbiters of virtue for those who sought ascendancy through reason. Mystikos gathered in the hallowed gymnasium, normally reserved for Damon Aetos and his brothers alone, and presented their souls for judgment.

Unlike the trial by spirit, there was no upper limit to how high a member of the Rosy Dawn could ascend through reason. This was how honored philosophers were born. Every respected elder within the Rosy Dawn had at some point gathered in the kyrios' gymnasium and laid bare his soul. For this reason, and because meeting the twin eagles and being found wanting was in many ways worse than death, only the cult's absolute finest had gathered within the filial gymnasium to test their fate.

"What is the first virtue?" Fotios intoned.

"Justice."

"And what is justice?" Stavros prompted the mystiko.

"Justice is the providence of strength," the man said, back straight and proud as he stood before the twin eagles. "It is the unshakeable foundation upon which enlightened civilization is built. It is the unspoken contract between virtuous men. Vengeance against vice, light in endless night. Justice isn't something the eyes can see, but it can be felt in every corner of the soul."

The twin pillars closed their eyes in solemn contemplation. In reality, I knew my uncles well enough to know that they were restraining the urge to slap the young man across his face. It hadn't been a particularly good answer. Fotios reigned his irritation in first and spoke.

"Show us your justice, then."

The hopeful ascendant's pneuma rose, denser and more vibrant than any of the younger generation by orders of magnitude. Sophic realm. He held out his hand, palm up, and his pneuma spiraled into it. A ball of light formed, invisible to the eye but easily felt even on the fringes of the gymnasium where Sol and I were observing.

The mystiko inhaled sharply. The ball rippled and split apart into four shards, each warped and chaotic. He grit his teeth, sweat beading on his brow. My uncles watched impassively.

He exhaled, and his intent turned the four writhing shards of spirit light into blades. They fanned out around him, hanging in the air, unseen but lethally sharp. The mystiko gestured, and each blade flew through the room, following its own distinct trajectory as it weaved through pillars and initiates alike.

The mystiko's body jerked as the spirit blades were ripped from his control in an instant. My uncles, having plucked them from the air with their own Heroic pneuma, considered them briefly before dismissing them. They shared a glance, wordlessly exchanging profound judgment that could likely be vocalized as "these worthless children", and made their decision.

"The Rosy Dawn recognizes your virtuous heart, senior mystiko," Fotios said. He smiled faintly, a forced gesture. "You are not yet ready to join the ranks of the elder philosophers, but we commend your effort. The cult is glad to have you."

It was a kinder judgment than Stavros would have rendered. Frankly, it was a kinder judgment than I would have given. The trial thus ended, the mystiko immediately dropped to one knee and gave thanks to the twin eagles for their consideration, struggling to contain his dejection. Respects paid, he rose and fled the gymnasium with as much grace as he could manage. It wasn't much.

Another senior initiate swiftly approached.

"What is the first virtue?" my uncle asked.

"Courage."

"And what is courage?"

And so it went.

"What do you think, slave?" I asked hours later as we left the gymnasium. Precious few of the ascendant prospects had received favorable judgment—and for good reason. My eyes had glazed over more than once, listening to some of those sophists speak.

I was more than ready for the feasting and celebration. Those that had ascended by each of the three trials would revel in their hard-won renown for the night, telling stories to the new blood and basking in their starry-eyed praise. It would carry us through the night and into the dawn. Then, tomorrow, the initiation of the new members would truly begin.

"What do I think of what?" Sol asked. There had been something on his mind since I'd beaten down my cousin. Even now, he had that pensive air about him.

"What is the first virtue?" I prompted. Unsurprisingly, he didn't hesitate.

"Freedom."

I snorted. "So says the slave."

He shrugged.

"There are four cardinal virtues," I said, ticking four fingers off one by one. "Justice, courage, wisdom, and temperance. In every story worth telling of every man worth remembering, at least one has been present. Is that not so?"

"It is."

"But you say freedom comes first?"

"It does."

"Can a slave not be wise? Can they not be bold?" I asked. "Can your eyes not see justice while your wrists are shackled? If I offered you a cup of wine, would you not be able to restrain yourself from drinking it?"

"I'm capable of all of those things," he said evenly.

"And yet you are not free."

The slave tilted his head.

"Neither are you."

I'd never heard such an absurd thing in my life. My pneuma rose. "Excuse me?"

He was as he had always been. Since that very first day, in that courtyard under the stars. He weathered my wrath without hesitation, meeting my eyes without fear.

"What is the purpose of a man?" he asked.

"To climb Olympus Mon," I answered at once. "To challenge the Fates and win."

"When a man is born, the Fates weave his future and swaddle him in it," he recited. It was a common saying among the cults, the foundation of one of the greater mysteries. "Men cultivate virtue so that they can cast off that swaddling weave."

"If the Fates are defied, who else can tell a man to die?" I finished his thought.

"A man that other men tell stories about can be wise, brave, tempered, or just. He can be all these things at once. Or he can be none of them." His dark brows furrowed. "None of it matters if he can't control his own destiny. Glory is the product of action. Action requires agency.

"If you decided to leave this place, here and now, and never return, would you be able to do it? Would your father allow it? Would your *status* allow it?"

I stared at him, silent.

"No. It wouldn't, and you couldn't. Because you exist within this hierarchy just like everyone else. Your status doesn't matter. Renown is worthless alone."

Sol disdained me with his eyes and finally spoke the words he'd been thinking since the day we met.

"I may be a slave. But you aren't any more free."

Chapter Eleven

THE YOUNG ARISTOCRAT

The night passed in a blur of celebration, good food piled high on symposia tables and cups overflowing with spirit wine. This ordering of events was deliberate for the new blood. A saltwater shock to the senses to prime them, an introduction to the spirit and vigor of their senior initiates and the martial prowess that was expected of them, and now a night of reveling for those triumphant.

Life in the mystery cults of the Mediterranean was vibrant. But it was also intensely dangerous and cared little for those who couldn't handle the rigors of cultivation. The first day of the rites was a gut check. More than a few new initiates had withdrawn meekly down the mountain when they thought no one was looking, unable to handle the intensity of the trials. They were seen, obviously, but the mystikos let them go.

Better they leave on the first day. After the second, there was no going back.

"Mystikos!" a philosopher hollered, his voice easily carrying across the pavilion. He looked to be in his twenties but wore the attire of an honored elder. He cast a hand to the east and all eyes followed. "Rise and greet the dawn!"

Hundreds of mystikos all across the mountaintops rose and

cheered as the sun breached the far horizon, throwing cups of spirit wine and all manner of olives, figs, meats, and cheeses into the air. Nearly to a man they were all roaring drunk. It wasn't a state of being that the elders would normally tolerate. Today, though, it was encouraged.

Kykeon was an elevated spirit wine, a cultivator's drink, but it was still wine. It overpowered the senses in excess. The definition of excess, however, changed depending on one's familiarity with it. A tolerance could be built up to the more intense cognitive influences of the spirit wine with enough exposure.

For that reason, among others more obvious, it was a heavily restricted luxury. Only on nights like these were initiates allowed to truly indulge themselves. The absence of a built-up tolerance made the experience all the more spectacular.

I considered the dawn, sat at a long cypress table with a cup of kykeon in my hand. Sol sat across from me. His eyes were lidded and fatigued. The night had come and gone, and we hadn't exchanged another word.

Drums pounded as the rosy fingers of dawn reached across the sky. A low chant was taken up at the edges of the central pavilion, philosophers and senior initiates that hadn't taken part in the festivities advancing into the final stage of the rites. The new blood looked around in drunken bewilderment as their intoxicated senior brothers shouted and clambered from their seats in excitement. It was time.

A new initiate cried out in terror, pointing at the sky. Eyes followed, the new blood shocked and disbelieving while those who had lived through this day before watched in anticipation.

A meteor was falling from heaven.

The new blood, ranging from boys my littlest cousin's age to young men nearly grown, spilled out of the pavilion in a panicked tide as the ball of fire fell. The intoxicated juniors and seniors in attendance made way as well, but there was no fear in their eyes. The meteor hurtled down through burning clouds, and soon its low roar overtook the drumbeats and chanting of the philosophers.

Sol watched it fall in stunned wonder. I tilted my cup back, spirit wine spilling down my chin.

The falling star struck the central pavilion like the fist of an angry god.

"We're going," I declared once the world had stopped shaking. I stood from the ruined table, blown to shrapnel and shards save for the small section that I had reinforced with my pneuma. Idly, I brushed marble dust and small debris off my ceremonial attire.

"Going where?" Sol asked incredulously. He looked pointedly around.

The Rosy Dawn's central pavilion had been utterly devastated. The stone steps were shattered, the tables and benches blown clear off the mountain by the force of the impact. The pavilion itself was a cratered ruin, its once flawless stone crushed to pieces small enough for use in a mosaic.

The only structures left standing, miraculously so, were the marble statues of the Heroic cultivators that lined the outer edge of the pavilion. They stood as they always had, proud and tall, gazing up as if tracing the path of the fallen star back to heaven.

"Into the mountain to finish your rites," I informed him, striding towards the heart of the crater.

Where there had once been a grand central fountain with a faceless statue of a man standing in its waters there was now a yawning chasm. The falling star had punched clean through it and the mountain both, leaving a tunnel of stone that spiraled down through the mountain. Emanating from its depths, impossible for the eye to clearly see at this distance, a rosy glow illuminated the stone.

The rest of the initiates would be close behind us. Already, the sober mystikos and philosophers were herding the new blood and their drunken seniors into a manageable crowd, preparing them for their descent. It was a chaotic press of terror and excitement, but cultivators were experts at imposing order on chaos.

We reached the edge of the chasm. The meteor had seemingly struck the mountain at an angle, providing a steep but navigable slope down. Sol peered dubiously into it.

"Scared?"

He snorted. "You Greeks are mad."

Together we traversed the depths.

The rosy glow had long since faded, leaving us in pitch black with only the distant sounds of the initiates at our backs and our cultivators' eyes to guide us. The benefits of cultivation allowed us to see, even in oppressive darkness, but only just. We felt our way along the walls as we descended, the stone miraculously cool to the touch.

Eventually, a new light appeared. This was the dull orange flickering of torchlight, seemingly emanating from the walls of the mountain themselves. It wasn't until we got closer that their true source became apparent.

Stone hallways, carved out of the mountain on either side of the tunnel. Torches mounted to the walls illuminated their paths, winding and curving at a shallower decline until they both eventually turned corners out of sight. In contrast to the main tunnel, which continued seemingly endlessly downward, these were clearly man-made.

"All of that to open a path that was already here," Sol said. I hummed, confirming his suspicion. "A locked door would have sufficed."

"No," I said. "It wouldn't have."

I grabbed a torch from off the wall and continued down the main tunnel. Eventually, the dim noise of the drums and chanting behind us faded entirely as the initiates and their minders split off to follow the hand-carved halls.

"The initiation rites exist to convey something that's impossible to directly describe," I said, crouching and sliding down a particularly steep path of slick rock. "Think, slave. They're called *mysteries* for a reason. How could I explain the terror of drowning to you if you had no need to breathe? How could I explain the beauty of a woman if you had no eyes to see?"

"Indirectly," he realized. I nodded.

Even my father couldn't truly describe what lay at the heart of these mountains or how they came to be here. The greater mysteries of heaven were something even a Tyrant couldn't wholly grasp. He could show us, though. And so he did.

"The halls we passed wind through the entire mountain range," I explained. "The mystikos will be walking them for the rest of the day and through the night. It won't feel like it because they're all blind drunk on spirit wine and the rest of the cult is inside the mountains with us, carrying on the show."

"The show?" Sol echoed.

"The falling star was only the beginning," I said. "The walls of those man-made tunnels are inlaid with mosaics that visually approximate the genesis of the Rosy Dawn. There are staging caverns carved into the stone at intervals throughout, where initiates are waiting to act out the events for the benefit of the new blood. Members of the cult spend months perfecting virtuous techniques in preparation for their performances."

"Then why aren't we following those paths?"

"Because they're worthless," I answered easily. "There is value in my father cracking open this mountain like a tortoise shell. It imparts a sense of scale if nothing else. The acting and the wall art, though? The song and dance? It doesn't matter."

He grunted, annoyed. "What does?" he asked. I smirked and tossed my torch down the path.

Sol watched it careen down the mountain vein, nonplussed, and was about to speak when it suddenly plunged into a massive opening and vanished. In that moment, that split second before it was snuffed out, something was illuminated that stole his ability to speak. In the silence that followed I could almost hear the hammering of his heartbeat. My own was a rolling thunder in my ears.

We crept like thieves towards that gaping precipice. Tension and something else, something thick and overpowering, permeated the stone as we approached. When we finally reached its edge, looking down into a massive cavern that glittered with sourceless light, Sol hesitated. I slammed a hand down on the back of his neck and dragged him with me into the abyss.

The cavern was warm, the stone itself seeming to radiate heat. Those bizarre lights that we had seen from the edge of the tunnel were embedded in the cavern's floor and walls themselves—stones that I had no name for and had never seen above the surface. They converged in a spiraling pattern towards the center of the cavern, towards—

"What," Sol breathed, "is *that?*"

A bisected corpse. Sprawling, almost languidly, across a dais of shattered stone.

It was a sight I had seen exactly seventeen times before. One for each year of my life. And from the first to the last, each memory was as distant as the one that came before it. Indistinct, nearly formless. There were nights that I woke up and wondered if this place was a dream, an elaborate delusion. And then the rites would come, and I'd delve into the mountain, and I would *remember.*

But even here and now, crouched beside a shell-shocked slave, the details were slipping away from me as I observed them. My eyes traced the body, but it was utterly featureless.

The face—

Tan skin. Chiseled jaw, a high and defined cheekbone. Blond curls the color of the sun and an eye that *burned*—

—was eerily flat, smooth like the demolished statue within the pavilion's central fountain. The body—

Leanly muscled, perfectly sculpted. A constellation of stars tattooed across the chest, severed—

—was the same. Not a single defining feature.

The corpse had been severed cleanly down its center, from crown to groin. The right half was nowhere to be seen, though I suspected I knew where it could be found. The innards, in defiance of all natural forces, remained perfectly contained within their half of the corpse. Somehow, the organs—

—half a brain that crackled and flashed like the center of a lightning storm. A spine that had fractured as if it were made of marble, trailing threads of sensory veins that almost floated in the air, reaching. Something in the liver, written or spoken, or both or neither. And *the heart*—

I realized, with a start, that the cavern was suddenly full of people. All the initiates, new arrivals and juniors and seniors, honored elder philosophers, my uncles and cousins. How much time had passed?

How long had we been staring? They all looked upon the mysterious entity in the center of the cavern. My incomprehension was reflected in their own eyes. None dared approach.

None but my father.

Damon Aetos stood over the bisected corpse of the fallen sun god. He was speaking, had been speaking for some amount of time that I couldn't possibly name. But I only now heard him as he looked across the cavern at me. Me and my slave.

"Rise," he commanded. We rose. All of us, the Rosy Dawn. "Initiates old and new. For the third and final time, rise and greet the dawn."

And there, within the corpse's palm, light bloomed.

The sun rose.

Chapter Twelve

THE LITTLE KYRIOS

There was something wrong with his cousin.

Objectively, Myron knew that Lio had always been an agitator. His earliest memories of his cousin were acts of defiance—Lio had a bad habit of giving credit only when credit was due, and that naturally grated on some of the older mystes. It had led to more than one senior attempting to *educate* the Young Aristocrat in the early days when he was still refining his virtue, unerringly to their detriment.

But his attitude had always been tempered by a noble restraint, an unspoken acknowledgment that he was the one and only son of Damon Aetos, and with that came responsibilities. Lio did what was expected of him. He excelled. As a result, he knew he could get away with things that others could not.

Since the initiation rites, though, something had changed. It was a small thing. If asked, Myron wouldn't know how to describe it. But it was there. And it was growing by the day.

"Your mind is wandering." The cousin in question poked his forehead, and Myron flinched. He hated when he did that!

"It is not!" he denied, though it surely had been.

They were meditating in the courtyard, among the filial pools and the statues of the cult's past kyrioi. Lio had offered to give him a few pointers, seemingly on a whim, the day before. Myron had made a big show of deliberating heavily on the offer, not wanting to be teased for his excitement, but something told him he'd been seen through. Even without the allure of advancing his cultivation, Lio knew he'd never let slip an opportunity to spend time with his older cousin.

"Perhaps we've been at it too long," Lio mused, glancing up. The sun had been newly risen when they started. It was at its zenith now. "Let's call it a day—"

"No!"

Myron flushed, cursing himself for the outburst. Lio considered him with that scarlet-eyed amusement that all his cousins despised. It was a look that made you feel like an ant making demands of a lion. A look backed by arrogance that, somehow, had not once been humbled in seventeen years of life.

It was also, according to Lydia, maddeningly attractive. She'd always been a little strange when it came to him.

"I can keep going," Myron said, firming his posture and inhaling deeply. Lio chuckled, resuming his own meditative stance—though calling it that was an insult to the elders, really. He'd simply draped himself over the stone rim of one of the filial pools, head resting on the crook of his elbow as he circulated his pneuma.

Pneuma was the vital life force that fueled cultivation. It was virtue made manifest, and ultimately, its refinement was what drove cultivators. Each realm of cultivation, from civic to tyrannic, further refined the soul into something approaching divinity. Each realm revealed to the cultivator a new aspect of their soul—something always known but from birth forgotten. The refinement of that new element was key to ascending to the next realm. And so it went.

To enter the Civic Realm one had to first become aware of their soul. Manipulating your pneuma was impossible if you couldn't see it, feel it, or sense it in your blood. While every living thing possessed pneuma, that knowledge alone was not enough to make one aware of their own vital breath.

Myron had discovered his pneuma while riding on his father's shoulders, watching his oldest cousin set sail across the Ionian Sea with tears in his eyes. The Aetos family had all been present at the docks to see him off, even Lio and Uncle Damon. In that moment, the salty sea breeze filling his lungs and sorrow making his heart clench, Myron had realized exactly what the Aetos family was. He'd realized, dimly, the space he occupied within it. And that had been enough.

Once a cultivator could sense their pneuma, they were able to exercise it. The challenge of the Civic Realm was consolidation and fortification. A man could chisel himself a divine body with calisthenics and combat, and he could broaden his mind with philosophy and learning, but he could not bid his pneuma to multiply unless he did both. And even then, it was not always that simple.

Myron had reached the seventh rank of the Civic Realm after only three years of active cultivation. His tutors and peers called it an absurd feat. His mother cooed and called him her little prodigy. It was his father and his uncles that Myron gauged his success by, however, and they had only ever been *satisfied*. Never impressed. Never joyful. Only ever content with his progress.

He knew why. At his age, nine years old, his eldest cousin had already long reached the Sophic Realm. And here was little Myron, languishing in the Civic Realm without a virtue in his heart. It vexed him. It made him want to try *harder*.

So he did. Every day his pneuma grew. And every day he utterly exhausted it until he fell into bed without a spark of energy left. Some of the mystikos said it was counterintuitive to exhaust his reserves as he was trying to build them, but Myron was an Aetos. He knew the truth.

The soul was a muscle like any other. It had to be broken down before it could be built back up.

It was nearly evening when Lio decided he'd had enough. Myron followed him through a brief series of stretches, pondering the best way to broach the topic that had been on his mind for days now. When it came to Lio, direct was almost always the best approach—at least, it was the only approach that had a chance of getting an answer. But something, some gut feeling, told him that this wasn't the time to be direct.

Instead, he asked, "Have you started training for the games?"

Summer was nearing its end, and that only meant one thing to the mystikos of the Rosy Dawn. The Scarlet City's Daylight Games were nearly upon them. Now that the initiation rites were concluded, it was all that was talked about among the cult. Who would be chosen to represent the Rosy Dawn this year, who would be sent by the Burning Dusk Cult, and who was favored to ultimately win it all?

The Scarlet City's annual games were a spectacle like none other, and while, by their nature, they couldn't match the profound wonder of the initiation rites, they were still an incredible experience. Both the Rosy Dawn and the Burning Dusk pooled their resources with the city each year to throw a city-wide celebration for the winner, and during the games themselves, there were vendors of every kind come from far and wide to peddle their exotic wares. It was a non-stop spectacle, and without a doubt, it was Myron's favorite time of the year.

"Training for the games?" his cousin repeated, rocking back and forth as he stretched out his hamstrings. "Why would I do that?"

Myron gaped. He couldn't be serious. Even he had limits!

"You're representing the Rosy Dawn! You're our top contender!"

"And?" Lio prompted him as if anything else had to be said.

"You have to win!"

Lio tilted his head. "Why?"

"Because—" Myron struggled to formulate an answer to a question that should have been common sense. He was being teased, wasn't he? That was just like Lio. Still, he answered. "Because you're the Young Aristocrat! You represent the Rosy Dawn, but more than that, you represent Uncle Damon. If you lose, it'll look bad on him."

"Why should my father's reputation matter to me?" Lio asked curiously. There was an undercurrent of something in his voice. Myron frowned, uneasy.

"Because you're his son."

He didn't know how else to explain it.

"I'm his son," Lio mused, running a hand through his wild blond mane. It had long been a subject of gossip that the Young Aristocrat shared none of his father's defining features. Damon Aetos' dark curls and blue eyes were nowhere to be seen in Lio. His stoic glare was something his son had never cared to mimic.

But every so often, the heir to the kyrios did something that left no doubt as to his parentage. And as Lio turned away from him to look upon the statue of their ancestor, standing in its filial pool, his stance was its mirror image.

"I am his son," Lio said, almost to himself. "And I am a part of the Rosy Dawn, aren't I?"

"We all are," Myron said hesitantly. His cousin hummed.

"I suppose I have no choice but to win."

Myron clenched and unclenched his fists. He wasn't sure what to say.

It didn't matter. Whatever Lio had been deliberating on, he found his answer.

Myron watched, stunned, as his cousin stepped into the filial pool and walked through its sacred waters. He stood nose-to-nose with the marble statue, looking it up and down. And then he reached up around its neck and undid the clasp of its golden chain necklace. The pendant, a radiant scarlet gem, flashed where the sunlight touched it.

"What—" Myron whispered in horror. His cousin clasped the necklace around his own neck and strode out of the pool. He looked pleased.

"I won't be training for the games, cousin, but worry not." Lio ruffled his hair, and for once Myron didn't have the presence of mind to shake him off. The Young Aristocrat grinned fiercely.

"I'll win them regardless."

Chapter Thirteen

THE YOUNG ARISTOCRAT

It is commonly known that there is a gap between birth and the first conscious thought. During this infancy one simply exists, entirely at the mercy of the elements. Then there is a singular event, a spark of true thought, that every man and woman can recall as the moment the veil was lifted and they could finally see. The moment they ascended from the realm of animal instinct and into humanity. The inception of a cultivator is much the same. A spark, a lifting of a veil, and pneuma is revealed.

I experienced both in the same moment. I was three years old when I first witnessed the initiation rites of the Rosy Dawn. My father was holding me in the crook of his right arm, calling down heaven's wrath with his left. It was the impact that shook awake my sleeping soul. He held me in that arm as we descended alone into the depths of the Scarlet City's eastern mountain range. He held me as he approached the bisected corpse of the fallen sun god.

My father held me as the corpse reached up and laid its palm over my face.

"This is justice," he told me. *"Remember its face."* But I never could.

I'd decided to show Sol the city. It was as good a time as any for it. The streets of Álikos were alive with citizens, metics, freedmen, and slaves all bustling around in preparation for the games. Foreigners abounded, leading carts and waving cloth and ornaments enticingly to passing citizens. They were like a flood, streaming in from every no-name village within the geopolitical orbit of the Scarlet City.

Despite the press of bodies, Sol and I were given a comparatively respectful berth as we walked the street. I was well enough known among the citizenry that deference was a given, and Sol's freshly issued mystiko attire caught the eye long before his slave manacles did.

Naturally, he found reason to criticize it anyway.

"This isn't practical in the slightest," he grunted, yanking the trailing edge of his tunic out from under the feet of a passing Álikon. We were given more space than most, but in the narrower streets at this time of year, there was only so much that could be done. The female citizen fell to the street, already shrieking in outrage, only for it to die in her throat as she spotted the distinctive uniform of the Rosy Dawn.

"Wearing it properly is a skill," I said airily. The furthest edges of my cloth were pristine, unmarred even by the dust of the roads. He scowled as I shifted just so, avoiding a passing metic with careless grace. "You'll learn eventually."

He shifted his next step just enough to catch the edge of my tunic. Unfortunately, I'd known him well enough to expect it, and he missed by a finger's width. His scowl deepened.

"You Greeks make everything more complicated than it needs to be."

"Yes, because a toga is so much more practical," I said, rolling my eyes. "It's easy enough to criticize, but don't act as if you're any better. Half your city's greatest cultural achievements are the product of Greeks that happened to be passing through, and that's being generous."

"The best parts of Rome have never been touched by Greek hands," he said. It was likely a common saying among the legions. They had to tell themselves something to maintain morale, after all.

I sneered. "The best parts of Rome are salt and ash."

His expression darkened. Luckily for the public order, we'd just reached our destination. I slipped into a thermopolium, and with nothing in his hands to throw, the slave initiate had no choice but to follow me. He entered with eyes blazing but was immediately distracted.

Thermopolia were commercial developments, glorified bars where work-weary metics and freedmen could gather to drink and gorge themselves on poorly made food. A well-to-do citizen wouldn't be caught dead in one, and for that reason, they were ideal havens for scum and all manner of assorted criminals. If an elder were to discover a member of the Rosy Dawn had been patronizing such a venue, they'd be given a sublime lashing. It was that sort of place.

And this one, in particular, was even worse. It wasn't just full of low-class wretches and conniving thieves. It was also seething with foreign cultivators, come to challenge the mystery cults of the Scarlet City in the games.

"What are we doing here?" Sol asked in a low voice, assessing the room. More than a few unfriendly eyes were doing the same. Our attire was rather distinct.

"I told you. We're here to eat."

They were the usual suspects. Men from low-born villages on the edges of enlightened civilization, clothed in rags just a step above what our own slaves wore. Too far from the free city-states of the Mediterranean to regularly benefit from their patronage but arrogant enough to think that they could challenge us in spite of that.

The hue of their skin tended towards leather more than bronze. Their hair was often worn in locks or shorn off entirely. They were the children of poor farmers and fishermen, uneducated in all but the most plainly apparent matters of natural philosophy. Their cultivation reflected this. And their pankration was invariably *atrocious*.

"Grab us a few bowls of stew," I bid my slave and junior brother, nodding towards the masonry counter at the far corner of the establishment. "I have a hunger." He eyed me, still simmering over my comment, but nodded once and split away.

I walked up behind a seated cultivator and set both hands on the back of his chair. His fellows across the table glared murderously at me. They all wore wind-worn cloth, a faded yellow dye winding over their torsos in the symbol of whatever hovel they had sprung from. The two across the table wore their hair in locks. The one beneath my hands was shaved bald, with a powerful build and weathered skin that spoke to a life of hard labor.

"You're in my seat," I told him simply. He tilted his head back to look up at me.

"I don't see your name on it."

The audacity of these country dogs was something else. "What does that matter? You wouldn't be able to read it if it was."

The dog bared its teeth. "Go to the crows."

I swept the chair back, spilling him from it and stomping him down when he tried to rise. His sworn brothers shouted and lunged across the table at me, one tossing a half-full bowl of fish stew at my face while the other pulled an obsidian dagger of all things and threw it at my chest.

I leaned away from the flying stew and flicked the broad side of the knife, embedding it in the far wall. With my other hand, I caught the neck of the faster of the two and swung him viciously into his sworn brother, striking their skulls together hard enough to daze a bull. They both crashed through a nearby table and collapsed bonelessly. The residents of *that* table started shouting and drawing weapons over their spilled drinks. Off to my left, a group of what looked like regular patrons were eyeing me with vile intent.

My pneuma rose and everything stopped.

"I'll spare your dog life this once," I told the man beneath my foot pleasantly. The whites of his eyes were plainly apparent, filled with that wild fear of cornered prey. "Because even if you could read, you wouldn't have been able to see my name from here. You'd have to climb the nearest mountain and look down to see it written across this whole city."

It's said that as a man progresses through the stages of his cultivation, it is only natural that his renown and his hubris grow in equal proportion. Tribulations are heaven's way of reminding men that for all that they covet the stars, they will never stand among their number. Vice is as inherent to a cultivator's lifestyle as his virtue, and attempting to avoid it outright often leads to even worse retribution than the norm.

I've lived what most would call a privileged lifestyle. I enjoyed a position of power and influence that the vast majority of even enlightened citizens would never experience in their entire lives, even with the longevity that cultivation provided. That I coveted more on top of that? That I had chosen to trawl through dive bars in the city and scope out challengers to harass rather than prepare for the Daylight Games the correct way, the virtuous way?

That was cause for correction.

A man in a hooded cloak lunged from a shadowed corner of the room, pneuma blazing as he lashed out with a technique that I didn't recognize, could not predict the effects of. His cloak had obscured the color of his tunic underneath, the same faded yellow of the men I'd singled out. The intensity of his pneuma was such that his technique, many times magnified, was far too dangerous to block. I shifted on my feet, only for the cultivator I'd stepped on to wrap himself around my leg with a vindictive grin.

I watched what might have been my death approach. It is the way of heaven to strike down those who revel in hubris. It is an inescapable truth that men were born mortal and die mortal. The peak of Olympus Mons was nothing more than an ever-distant fantasy. The cultivator's eyes were a cold grass green.

Sol appeared in the empty space behind the cultivator and slammed his head through the stone table. He spasmed once and went limp.

Of course, we defied the heavens anyway. It was what one did.

"Ho, took you long enough," I said, stomping viciously on the bald cultivator's throat. He gagged and heaved, scrabbling at his windpipe. I righted the chair and sat down. Sol sat across, setting down two bowls of stew that he'd balanced in his other arm.

I've lived my life by the terms of the cult. Where were the edges of those boundaries, my father's will and that of heaven? How far could I push them?

When would my tribulations come?

It was time to find out.

Chapter Fourteen

THE CAGED DOVE

The relationship between Solus and the Young Aristocrat was something that no one really understood. It was perhaps the only matter in which the lowly slaves and the honored mystikos of the Rosy Dawn stood equal. Equally bewildered.

Athis had slowly eased into her position within the cult since those first few terrifying months, and Solus had been a large part of that. Pervicas, who'd been a slave in the cult's service far longer than her, hadn't seen anything like him before. He was undoubtedly a slave, but the way he carried himself and the way others responded to him, instinctively, was evocative of an honored citizen far more than a bonded man.

He was kind to the rest of them, if distant. Since their first meeting, Athis had done her best to overcome his intimidating aura and had soon realized that while he was peerless in certain realms, he was far from perfect. He'd never cooked a day in his life. He had little interest in maintaining the gardens, and he regularly took on disproportionate work from other slaves to avoid the task.

Athis had taken it upon herself to teach him what few things she could. Pervicas could crack jokes and make eyes at them all she wanted, but it was really just her way of giving thanks for everything he did for them. Truly.

Solus existed as a silent pillar within the enslaved class of the Rosy Dawn's brutal hierarchy. He was a bulwark against the whims of the mystikos, a safe haven for any females caught outside of their quarters, and a supporting hand to any males struggling beneath the weight of a day's punishing work. What he lacked in affability he more than made up for with strength of character. He was inexhaustible and utterly fearless.

Unfortunately, Athis was not the only one to notice this.

For weeks after that night in the courtyard, Athis had been terrified for her fellow slave. For a slave to speak out against an initiate was cause for severe lashing. To speak out against an honored philosopher was grounds for execution. To go beyond that, *to lay hands upon the son of the kyrios*, Lio Aetos himself? She had been utterly convinced that his fate was sealed and that all of the Young Aristocrat's interest in him was nothing but a long, drawn-out execution.

Yet he lived. Months passed, and he continued to defy the social order. The Young Aristocrat did not grow tired of him like Pervicas had worried he might. In fact, on the rare occasion that a mystiko had the temerity to strike him for some slight or another, Lio Aetos himself would suddenly arrive at the opportune moment to rebuke his junior initiate and whisk Solus away on some little adventure or another.

It was almost as if they were friends. But that was impossible. It was more likely for lions to mingle with wolves than for an Álikon to make friends with a slave. And more than that, there was something about the way they interacted the few times she'd seen it in motion. Like predators sizing one another up. Like dogs about to fight.

Athis wished he would stop. Whatever it was he was doing to draw the Young Aristocrat's eye, she wished with all her heart that he would stop it. They all did. It seemed like every day one of them had a story to share at dinner about some mad thing Solus had done—or would have done had they not rushed to stop him.

He'd quickly occupied a cherished space in their sorry community. It terrified them to see him tempt the Fates with such flagrant disregard. After all, a slave suffered tribulations just as well as a Tyrant.

But there was little they could do when each day only seemed to bind Solus and the Young Aristocrat more tightly together.

"Where do we sit?" Athis whispered, nervously brushing down her dinner attire. The cloth was soft and pure white, of a quality she'd never experienced in her living memory. It made her feel anxious just wearing it. The braids they'd done each other's hair in only compounded the feeling. She felt like an imposter.

There were many holidays that the Scarlet City celebrated, and even more that the Rosy Dawn Cult celebrated on top of that. The vast majority were days like any other to the slaves of the cult. If anything, some brought extra work. The initiation rites were a rare exception—a two-day respite that every slave relished.

The Kronia was another. It was a day of festival and celebration, and it went a step further than the rites. Slaves were not merely excused from their duties for the day. They were given fresh clothes of the cult's own make and allowed to run wild among the estates and recreational buildings. And come dinner, they were served by their masters and allowed to eat alongside them as equals.

It was a day that Pervicas and the rest of the senior girls had been speaking of excitedly since the rites had ended. When it finally came, it was almost as if Athis had woken up from a nightmare that had been plaguing her for years. She donned clean, comfortable clothes and walked outside freely. She enjoyed a relaxed morning, exchanging pleasant conversation with her fellow female slaves and even some of the honored daughters of the cult. She watched and cheered that after-noon as the boys among their number started an impromptu series of games, and she cheered even harder when a few mystikos joined in, and Solus handed them their heads.

Now it was time for dinner, where slaves would eat meals prepared by cultivators and dine with them shoulder-to-shoulder. It was a prospect that worried and excited her in equal measure.

The pavilion had been prepared in much the same way it had for the initiation rites. The horrifying damage that had been done to the central plaza had been repaired by the joint efforts of slaves and junior initiates in the days following, and the elder philosophers had worked such wonders on the finer details of the space that it looked as if it had never been damaged to begin with. Long wooden tables and benches filled with chattering slaves and mystikos abounded. The heroes of the cult stood their same vigil on their outskirts, and the faceless statue jutted up proudly in its fountain, sparkling waters gushing from its extended palm.

Already, initiates in fine scarlet and white robes were emerging from the kitchens with platters of food in their hands. They had to choose a spot, and quickly, before the choice was made for them. Equals for the day or not, Athis had felt more than a few sets of eyes on her during the day. She had no desire to find out who they belonged to.

Pervicas, who had been assessing the pavilion, suddenly lit up and waved her arm in the air. "Solus! Hey, over here!"

The man in question, easily spotted among even the cultivators of the cult due to his size, cocked his head their way and waved. Another slave was walking in step with him, a mess of red hair and a lush beard marking him as Tasos. He was older than them by a few years and had taken to accompanying Solus on certain tasks when he could. Or minding him, as he would say.

Athis and Pervicas hurried through the crowds to reach them, and Athis flushed as Tasos looked them both up and down admiringly.

"Those suit you," he said. Pervicas scoffed, but she was clearly pleased. Athis snuck a quick glance at Solus, but he was surveying the tables, looking for an open space for the four of them. For some reason that disappointed her, just a bit.

"Thank you," she said to Tasos. Then, shyly, she ventured, "You wear those well, Solus."

The attire of the Rosy Dawn's mystikos, pure white with scarlet trim, really did look all too natural on his imposing frame. It had been a terrible shock to see him wearing it the day after the rites ended. Even though the male slaves had insisted up and down that it was the Young Aristocrat himself who'd come and stolen him away in the night for the ceremony, she'd still been worried sick those first few days that some mystiko would take offense to a slave wearing their colors and strike him down. It had yet to happen, though.

Storm gray eyes glanced her way, and though he didn't admire her as Tasos had, he did favor her with a faint smile. "Thank you. It's a skill I had to learn."

A skill? Athis looked to Pervicas, confused, but she only shrugged.

"There's a space," he declared, striding forward. Throngs of slaves and initiates alike parted, most without real conscious acknowledgment of having done so. It was just what happened when Solus was around. Athis had long gotten used to it.

They sat together on the same bench, Pervicas nudging her meaningfully towards the empty space on Solus' left. Tasos sat down on his right, and Pervicas took the space to her left. There were already platters of olives, dates, goat cheeses, and other morsels scattered across the table. Solus and Tasos wasted no time, grabbing handfuls of everything and digging in ravenously. Athis, for her part, took a vine of grapes and popped a couple in her mouth, savoring their sweet tang.

They spoke idly of the games, the ones they'd played earlier and the true ones to come, and of the dancing and festivities that would carry on into the night after dinner. They savored good food and the good company of friends without obligation. Once again, the feeling of being awoken from a long nightmare suffused her. Her elbow bumped Solus' as they reached for the same hunk of cheese. He smirked lightly, offering it to her.

This was how life should always be.

Alas, all good things end.

A tanned, muscular arm came between them, holding a platter of roasted swordfish filets. It smelled divine as it was placed in front of them on the table, but Athis abruptly found herself without an appetite.

On this day, it was the duty of the masters to serve the slaves. That did not mean the pillars of the Rosy Dawn were to cook food and carry platters themselves, though. They sat as a family at a central table in the pavilion, perpendicular to the rest, and they entertained their personal servants with wine and food prepared and served by the rest of the cult. To expect anything more was pure absurdity.

So why, oh why, was the Young Aristocrat serving them fish?

"Only the finest for our diligent slaves," he said, setting down the platter in his other hand. This one was overflowing with mouthwatering slabs of goat's meat, seared and slathered with fragrant spices and herbs. "Now, allow this humble sophist to join you for a meal."

Lio Aetos laid scarlet eyes upon her, and Athis couldn't breathe. Terror locked her limbs up. Those eyes pierced through her, judging her and finding her hopelessly wanting. She had to get out of the way. She couldn't get out of the way. She couldn't *breathe*—

"That seat is taken," Solus said flatly, tearing off two chunks of fresh bread that another mystiko had just placed down and putting a slab of goat meat and cheese between them. Those scarlet eyes flickered away from her, dangerous and amused.

"Ho, you'd deny me a place at your table? Does your audacity know no limits?"

"Today, slaves are equal to masters," Solus replied simply, taking a bite of his sandwich. He closed his eyes, savoring the taste. Some distant, less terrified part of Athis wondered how long it had been since he'd eaten red meat.

"So they are, but you forget"—the Young Aristocrat leaned on Solus' shoulder as Pervicas's hand gripped hers under the table, and Athis squeezed it until her knuckles bled white—"you aren't just a slave anymore, Sol. A junior initiate pays respect to his seniors, don't you know?"

"You've never paid anyone respect."

"Naturally not," he said easily. "As I have no seniors. Now move, girl, or be moved."

Solus' eyes narrowed. *Oh no.*

"This seat is open!"

Lio Aetos raised an eyebrow as Tasos sprung from his seat, hurriedly excusing himself from the table. Athis watched him quickly move to another table, weathering jeers and catcalls from mystikos that had been watching, and wondered if she pitied or envied him.

She had her answer when Pervicas hissed, flicking her eyes at the central table. The Young Miss, Lydia Aetos, peerless marble beauty of the Rosy Dawn, was glaring furiously their way. Her brother and sister, Castor and Rena Aetos, were casting worried looks between her and their elder cousin. She looked like she was debating coming over and lashing them all. Then the youngest of the cousins, Myron Aetos, who had been idly picking at his food until that moment, finally noticed the trajectory of their gazes.

The young prodigy's eyes lit up, and he immediately excused himself from the table, making a beeline towards them. Then, to Athis' horror, it got worse. The Young Miss herself slammed her palms to the table and stood, stalking after her little cousin.

"You eat like an animal," Lio Aetos was saying, gathering olives and figs in one hand while he sorted through the platter of swordfish in search of the best cut. "You realize you won't be getting food like this again anytime soon. You should be savoring it."

Solus grunted, taking another large bite of his sandwich. "Work makes a man hungry. You wouldn't understand."

Athis *saw* the mystikos at their table wince, expecting the worst. And why shouldn't they? If any other slave had said something like that to the Young Aristocrat, they'd have been dead. If any other *initiate* had said something like that to the Young Aristocrat, they might have been dead. Yet Lio Aetos simply laughed, flicking an olive at Solus' face and cackling when he turned and caught it in his mouth.

They acted like belligerent brothers, and the effect was only compounded when the young prodigy made himself known, squirming into the space between them and grabbing eagerly for a pile of figs. The Young Aristocrat moved them just out of his little cousin's reach, a mischievous smirk on his lips that forced even Athis to admit that the whispers and gossip about his looks were more than warranted.

"Excuse me."

Athis looked back, heart hammering, and found the Young Miss looking down on her with piercing blue eyes. Up close like this, she really was ethereally beautiful. From her thickly lashed eyes to her full lips and the royal slope of her neck, she looked like someone had spent the best years of their life chiseling her from a block of marble. Not to mention the, ah, *fullness* of her figure. Athis felt the tips of her ears burning as she realized she was staring.

Lydia Aetos didn't comment on her roving eyes, though they'd certainly been noticed. Instead, she looked pointedly at the narrow space between her thighs and Solus' on the bench.

"Could you make room?" she asked politely. Athis hurried to oblige, shimmying sideways against Pervicas who hissed at the next slave down to move as well. They managed enough space for the Young Miss to sit, though their thighs were touching. It felt almost sinful.

"Lean back, junior, I can't see my cousins," she immediately demanded of Solus. He wordlessly obliged, offering her a platter of fresh bread. She gave him an ugly look but took a loaf and joined in on the conversation that Lio was having with Myron. Athis traded a look with Pervicas. In the end, there was nothing they could do but grab themselves some meat and bread.

They had dinner in the company of kings, going back and forth over wine and good food as if it was the most natural thing in the world.

For Solus, it simply was.

Chapter Fifteen

THE YOUNG ARISTOCRAT

Summer had come and gone, and the Daylight Games loomed on the horizon of tomorrow's dawn. It was the privilege of those that would compete to spend the day before the games resting and basking in the encouragement and adulation of their peers. Legends would be made tomorrow, and a new champion would don the laurel wreath.

I'd chosen to take a bath.

The Rosy Dawn's gymnasiums contained baths, as all proper establishments of its type did, but just as the pillars of the cult enjoyed a private gymnasium of sublime quality, so too did they enjoy an unparalleled bathhouse. The myriad pools, ranging from scalding hot to frigidly cold, had been carved out of the rock face of the mountain itself. The warm side of the grand Corinthian building was perpetually cloaked in steam, emitted from the mountain's own natural hot springs.

It was empty but for myself, my slave, and my littlest cousin. No one but an Aetos would dare pass through its hallowed pillars.

I hummed, elbows propped up on the cool stone of the hot spring's rim as I unwound. My head hung back, a warm cloth draped over my eyes. For all that it chafed, the life of a Young Aristocrat came with undeniable benefits.

"Tell me, slave," I murmured, "did they have baths as good as these in Rome?"

"The baths at the forum were better," he said, somewhere off to the right. Myron, who had gotten bored soon after entering and started splashing around, paused in interest. "What we lacked in natural springs we made up for with ingenuity. The greatest of them had rooms for steam as well as baths heated by hypocausts, mosaic floors, and fine marble walls. They were open to anyone with two denarii, and on holidays they were free."

"Sounds filthy," I said. "This place is for cleansing. Why should I share bath water with every wretch that has two silver bits to rub together?"

"You would understand if you spent time in your own city." He sighed. "There's pneuma in every living thing, and there's virtue just the same. The baths are one of a thousand ways to expose yourself to new aspects of life. Even the lowest of men can be wise."

"Like you," Myron declared.

"The little kyrios is too kind." Myron squawked at the teasing nickname. "The only thing I know is that I know nothing at all."

I lifted the corner of the cloth covering my eyes. There it was. That distant, wistful look.

"Tell me more."

He blinked. "More of what?"

"You said the baths were one of a thousand ways," I said. "You may not be wise, but you're worldly, aren't you? Tell me about your life. I want to hear it." He looked surprised. Ho, how insulting. Surely, I wasn't that bad.

"So do I!" Myron chimed in, kicking off from the far side of the spring and paddling over. "What were the legions like? How'd you get so strong? How many places did you conquer—"

"One at a time, cousin," I said, flicking a jet of water in his face. He shouted and splashed me back, only for Sol to dunk him when he wasn't looking.

"The legions," Sol said thoughtfully, while Myron coughed and spluttered. "I was young when my father was called up, and everything seemed so much larger than life. I'd only ever been to the forum a few times by that point and always under supervision. I lived my life ensconced in our villa until that day."

"Your father had some influence," I said. I'd known it, but saying the words gave them new weight. "Legionaries don't bring their sons to war."

Sol considered me. He knew. He'd known from the start, just as I had. Our origins rhymed.

"He was a captain," he finally said. "An infantryman from the moment he could hold a sword. When I was young, he'd tell me stories of his time in the ranks. The first century he was ever assigned to, the first men that he stood shoulder-to-shoulder with in combat." He smiled faintly. "The first centurion that handed him his head. He used to say that those were the cruelest years of his life but also the best."

"He married into money, then," I mused.

"He did," Sol acknowledged. He ran a hand through his hair, frowning. "It was like most marriages of its kind. Politically driven. Loveless. My father had gained enough renown in his service to warrant the match, but my mother's family and friends never let them forget his roots. It made her bitter.

"But it allowed him to climb the ranks. And that was what mattered."

"Where did he stand?" Myron asked eagerly. A common question when it came to cultivators. Where did he stand, among heaven and earth?

Sol hummed. "By your standards, he was at the peak of the Sophic Realm."

What?

"Oh," Myron said, failing to fully conceal his disappointment. The cloth covering my eyes hit the surface of the pool. I realized I'd sat fully up.

"Sophic Realm," I repeated, incredulous. "*Your* father?"

It didn't make any sense. The son was built upon the foundation of the father. To be at his level, at his age, with such a worthless father? It defied reason.

"My father was a good man," Sol said firmly. "He lived his life for Rome and for the legions that raised him."

"I'm not questioning your father's character," I said, waving an impatient hand. "I'm questioning—"

"He was a man that other men respected," the audacious slave continued, speaking over me without care. "Renowned for his tactics in war and his generosity in victory. Men followed him without question."

"So you learned from him?" Myron pressed, curious as I was to know how a man of such subpar cultivation could produce a son like Sol. Myron's father was a peerless Hero. Damon Aetos was Damon Aetos. It only made sense that we would excel. But Sol?

The slave and junior initiate was silent for a moment too long.

Ah. So that's what it was.

"I learned many things from my father," Sol seemingly confirmed. I settled back onto the rim of the stone pool, propping my head on one hand. "Until the day he died, he was always teaching me."

I watched Myron's excitement crumble. It was too easy, sometimes, to forget how young he was. Only nine years old. Excitable and easy to tease, yes, but learned far beyond any of his peers. Still a child, though. All this time, and he'd likely never once seriously considered what circumstances could have brought Sol here in chains to begin with. It was a child's naivety to expect only the best for those close to them.

And Sol *was* someone close to him. I doubted it was a conscious decision he'd made, to make friends with a slave. At some point, my littlest cousin had simply been pulled in by his presence. He was far from the only one.

"Did he teach you to shave the hair off your face?" I asked. Myron looked at me in shock. He was young. He had yet to learn that the only men who desired pity were the ones that didn't deserve it. Sol eyed my challenging smirk.

He scoffed. "Of course. A clean face is the mark of a civilized man."

"A clean face is the mark of a boy," I said mockingly. "Or a 'man' who can't grow a proper beard."

"Any pleb can grow a beard," Sol said, sneering. "What differentiates men from beasts is our ability to refine ourselves."

"A beard is natural."

"So is shitting."

I frowned.

"I suppose it's understandable that a Greek would prefer a luscious beard," Sol mused. "They hide a weak jaw rather well." Myron looked between us, wide-eyed.

Gray eyes met mine. "You're tempting the Fates, slave." Slowly, I smiled. "Myron, fetch me a knife."

He hesitated. "Lio—"

"Now."

He leapt from the pool and was out of the bathhouse in seconds. I considered the audacious Roman across from me.

"Back then, when you first met Myron, you knew exactly what ailed him because you'd experienced it yourself. A terrible ambition, restrained by a father who cared," I spoke casually. The humor in his eyes immediately died. "You told him it was a father's love that stayed my uncle's hand."

"I thought that sounded right, but I personally have no experience in such an upbringing. From the moment I was born, the path that I'd walk to heaven was already decided." I raised a hand from the water, palm up, and light bloomed between my fingers.

"Justice."

Sol stared at me, silent.

"But the odd thing was," I continued, in the very same tone, "you spoke of the consequences of premature virtue with just as much confidence. You warned him off the way a ruined drunk warns a boy off his first cup of wine. And that, I *did* have experience in. So tell me, slave, because my knowledge of your legions is admittedly deficient. Who stands above the captain?"

He didn't speak. His eyes were haunted.

"My father forced justice upon me," I said, walking through the water until I stood nose to nose with him. "Who forced you, and upon which path? Who made you what you are today?"

Myron chose that moment to come rushing back in, bare feet slapping against stone tiles in quick step. He slid to a stop beside the pool, panting lightly, with something like fear in his eyes. There was a sheathed blade in his hands. The kind used by members of the cult for ritual sacrifice.

"He was just teasing you, Lio," Myron tried one last time, desperately. "You don't have to do this." How cute.

"No, cousin. I'm afraid I do," I said, pulling the blade from its sheath.

I flipped it in my grip and held it out to Sol, handle first. They both stared at it in bewilderment.

"I have an important day tomorrow, and I would hate to look anything less than divine," I said pleasantly. "Shave me."

Sol took the knife, turning it over in his hand. "You can't be serious."

My silence spoke for me.

There would be consequences, of course. The Rosy Dawn's Young Aristocrat arriving at his first Daylight Games with a shaved face? That was an embarrassment that couldn't be ignored. My uncles would be absolutely furious, and Lydia may well fall out of love with me. The elders would surely suffer deviations in their cultivation, or at least their daily bowel movements.

It became harder to care with every dawn. The knowledge that there was another world out there, shaping men like Sol from the basest materials while I languished up on this mountain? It made me wonder. It kept me awake.

I was stagnating while others thrived. It was enough to drive a man mad. Enough to make demons of his soul.

My virtuous heart would not allow it.

Chapter Sixteen

THE YOUNG ARISTOCRAT

We awaited glory in the silence of the night. The pit sand was cool beneath our feet. A pre-dawn breeze crept across our naked bodies, raising bumps on our skin. We breathed slowly and deeply, each searching for our tranquil center. No one spoke. No one moved.

Daylight broke over the eastern mountain range, and fifty thousand spectators erupted in cheers.

The stadium steps had been filled to capacity since the night before, of course. Admittance to the games was first come, first served, with only the usual vagrant provisions enforced. I had no doubt that more than a few up on those steps had been holding their seats for days. Beyond, at the rim of the massive crater in the earth that was the Scarlet Stadium, thousands more stood looking down, mingling with food carts and merchant stalls.

The residential rooftops of those citizens influential and fortunate enough to have land close to the stadium were likewise packed with wealthy viewing parties. And I knew that somewhere, up in those mountain ranges, the initiates of the Rosy Dawn and the Burning Dusk would be watching eagerly while their elder philosophers provided narration.

The pillars, naturally, enjoyed pride of place within the stands. This respect was afforded to both premier cults of Álikos, although the Rosy Dawn was the only one of the two that truly deserved it. Nonetheless, there at the western edge of the stands, on the fourth tier of the steps, the kyrios of the Burning Dusk sat with his arms crossed. He was flanked by his wife and three of their four children. The fourth was down in the pits with me.

On the eastern side of the great oval steps, Damon Aetos sat in the fourth tier with his brothers and all five of my adorable cousins. I raised a hand against the sun's glare, smiling brightly up at my family.

Naturally, my uncles were furious. Uncle Fotios was without a doubt the more kindly of the two, and even he looked like he wanted to lay a few good smacks across my newly shaved cheeks. Uncle Stavros looked simply murderous. Heron wasn't far behind his father, face turning scarlet with the sun. Castor was stunned, and Myron sat consoling a mortified Rena, who'd buried her face in her hands.

Lydia stared at me with wide eyes, lips parted in shock.

Damon Aetos raised an eyebrow as we locked gazes. As ever my father was unimpressed, but I'd expected as much. Not every war could be won in a day.

The clarion cry of a salpinx split the air. The cheers of the masses redoubled.

The Daylight Games began.

The Daylight Games were an institution that had existed for over seven hundred years within the Scarlet City. They were a series of trials that any man or woman could compete in, should they meet the qualifications set by the city, testing every element of human athleticism. From sprints and discus and javelin throwing all the way to martial combat of every type. Every year, men and women tested the limits of their virtuous souls in pursuit of that laurel leaf crown.

Of course, these games were only an approximation of the real thing. Each of the eight sovereign city-states of the free Mediterranean hosted their own yearly games, but these were only substitutes for the true competition. The event that drew men and women of sublime cultivation from the farthest reaches of the Greek Isles to compete beneath the eyes of gods and men for supremacy.

For three years, the free city-states sharpened their athletes to a fine edge with local games. But on the fourth, they all paid their respects to the supreme crucible of virtuous men.

Among heaven and earth, the Olympic Games were king.

But these games were not those, and the stakes were far lower. Rather than humanity's renown and power overwhelming, men and women competed in the Daylight Games for things such as citizenship, political influence, and most of all, bragging rights between cults. Certainly, they dressed it up as filial duty and harped upon the economic implications of the Rosy Dawn losing standing to the Burning Dusk, but none of it *mattered*.

The Burning Dusk had not been a relevant threat since the day my father returned home from his journeys. On that day, he'd subjugated Álikos in its entirety beneath the Tyrant's fist. Just as the sun rose in the palm of a bisected corpse god, in my father's palm rose the Scarlet City.

So long as Damon Aetos drew breath, no game would ever change that fact. It made it difficult to truly care about the reputations at stake. So I didn't. I'd watched these games seventeen different times from the vantage of those stone steps. This time, I wasn't going to be watching. I was going to be competing, and I was going to enjoy every minute of it.

"Oil," I called, and three separate civil volunteers came rushing over with jars of olive oil. I disdained their attempts to rub me down themselves, taking a handful of the spirit oil and massaging it into my skin.

The games were run sequentially, beginning first with the sprints. The vast pitted track that lay at the center of the Scarlet Stadium was large enough for even the strongest Sophic cultivator to heave a discus from one side and never hit the other—provided there was no pneuma involved—but that did not mean it was large enough to conduct every game at once. There were dozens upon dozens of competitors and games spanning all pursuits. The equestrian events alone would have dominated most of the track.

The sprints were conducted tournament style, in heats of eight, whereupon each heat's victor would compete in a champion's heat. And on it would go until a single competitor stood out above the rest. Already, the first heat was being assembled. Naturally, the competitors from the Rosy Dawn and the Burning Dusk were given pride of place, just as their spectators were.

I would compete in the first heat, and the Young Aristocrat of the Burning Dusk would compete in the last. The rest of our two cults' competitors would be evenly spread between us. It was undoubtedly an unfair advantage. But it was one that the city had no choice but to award us.

"You know," I said idly as I passed a certain initiate of the Rosy Dawn. He was nestled amongst citizens and wealthy metics alike on the first level of the stairs, at eye level with the competitors. "Citizenship is granted to any man who wins a laurel crown. Tell me, slave. How would you like to be free?"

The chaotic noise of the stands was such that none of the nearby competitors or spectators heard me. But he did. I could tell. While wealthy citizens shouted and reached out to touch me, lavishing me in praise and words of encouragement, he sat stock-still. Speechless.

"It's not too late," I said, holding a hand out. He stared at it like it was a living snake.

The war trumpets sounded for the first heat. The commencement speeches had ended. For a long moment, I stayed exactly where I was. Even as the spectators began to panic, urging me to go take my place at the starting line, I watched the storm gathering in those gray eyes. There would be real consequences if we did this. Tribulations. I realized I couldn't care less.

Those eyes flickered away. For the first time since I had known him, Sol avoided my gaze. My outstretched hand clenched into a fist.

"Coward," I snarled and walked away.

Seven men crouched beside me in the sands. The sun rose behind us, beating on our oiled backs. Rage made my blood thunder in my ears, stole from me my senses. I didn't hear the call to run. I only saw seven men tear off in a dead sprint, gaining four steps before I finally had the presence of mind to go. An insurmountable lead.

I moved.

"Lio Aetos!"
Thunder.

"I've been waiting for this, Aetos," spoke the Young Aristocrat of the Burning Dusk Cult.

Gianni Scala, son of Yianni Scala, crouched beside me among six other victors. The knuckles of his fingers bled pure white as he pressed them to the sands. Every muscle in his body was taut, begging to move.

"Have you?" I asked, distracted. I was still furious. My mind kept wandering back to those shifting eyes. I had known. I hadn't believed it, hadn't wanted to believe it, but I had known. That fucking *coward*.

"You've coasted on your father's laurels your entire life and no one has denied you it. You even came here with a shaved face. Insulted everyone in attendance! But no longer." He bared his teeth, burning determination in his eyes. "Today the Burning Dusk retakes its scarlet throne!"

"Fool." None of this mattered. Nothing would change.

The officials raised their flags.

"Lio Aetos!"
Ovation.

After the sprints came the discus.
"Lio Aetos!"
After the discus came the javelin.
"Lio Aetos!"
The horse races.
"Lio Aetos!"
Jumping.
"Lio Aetos! Lio Aetos! Lio Aetos!"

The officials cried out my name, again and again. They may as well have been up in the stands with the rest of the city. Athletes all over the pits gnashed their teeth and pounded the sand with their fists. Cultivators from the Burning Dusk to the farthest reaches of the city's outskirt villages watched in hateful envy as I took from them what they'd spent their entire lives dreaming of without any particular effort. Without any particular care.

Why hadn't he taken my hand?

Bronze trumpets let fly their clarion calls. The sun had reached its zenith. The athletic games were over, and now came the martial trials.

Myron charged out onto the sands with a wrapped blade in his hands. He offered it to me with the same concern that he had offered the ritual knife the day before. A glance up to the stands showed that he wasn't the only one.

"Are you well, Lio?" my littlest cousin asked quietly. I closed my eyes. Inhaled deeply.

What is the first virtue?

"I will be," I said and accepted the blade.

First, the armed trials.

"Lio Aetos!"

Then, pankration.

Chapter Seventeen

THE YOUNG ARISTOCRAT

"It isn't fair," Gianni Scala said bitterly, circling me in the pit. His blade, a finely wrought bronze that shimmered in the setting sunlight, hissed quietly through the air. "Why should heaven reward you for disdaining all that you've been given? You treat this life like a joke, you always have, and you're rewarded for it at every turn!"

As the Daylight Games had progressed, the Young Aristocrat of the Burning Dusk had fallen further and further into despair. He was a diligent student of his cult's teachings. A fierce athlete. Had I not been present, he would have dominated nearly every single event.

But I was present. And so he lost and kept losing. My jumps, both long and high, were superior. My discus and my javelin, superior. My sprints and my horse races, superior. In every way that mattered, I was superior. We were the perfect reflections of our fathers.

I grimaced and spat.

"We are filial sons!" he kept on. "It's our duty to bear the torches of our fathers!" Despair had all but taken him, but still, he attempted to distract me with self-righteous scolding while he searched desperately for an opening. The martial trials were entities in and of themselves within the games. Triumphing here would bring him more than enough renown.

We had each conquered three opponents in armed combat to reach this final match. Gianni, to his credit, had not suffered a single scratch. Blade work had always been his specialty as far back as I had known him. As well as I knew that, he knew that pankration was mine. He had no hope of victory in the unarmed events to come. This was his final chance.

He surged forward, having apparently found his mark. His blade caught the light of the falling sun and erupted in blood-orange flames as he swung down, from heaven to earth.

It was an obvious truth that not all cultivation techniques were created equal. They were manifestations of a man's virtuous soul, shaped by his unfaltering will and the experiences that had molded him throughout his life. Intent and execution were the dual forces that determined a technique's overall quality, but it was also possible for the origins themselves to be a contributing factor.

It was a well-kept secret among the two premier cults of the Scarlet City that our foundational techniques were tied to our mysteries. The Rosy-Fingered Dawn was a technique that waxed and waned in strength as the sun blazed its way through heaven. It was strongest at the dawn when the sun's first rays breached the far horizon. At the zenith of midday, it was as weak as it could be. Because at that point, the Burning-Edged Dusk began to gain in strength.

That the non-combative events had been portioned for the first half of the day, when the Burning Dusk Cult's foundational technique was at its weakest, was no coincidence. The Burning Dusk had long enjoyed a position of disproportionate influence within the Scarlet City, and the structure of its Daylight Games reflected this.

Could Damon Aetos have changed these orders, restructured things in favor of the Rosy Dawn? Without question. Such a thing was well within his power. He'd simply chosen not to.

The Burning-Edged Dusk was at its strongest when utilized with a falling strike, in the light of the setting sun. Gianni brought his blade down upon me with every ounce of strength in his body, steam seething through his clenched teeth. My own blade rose to meet it. The Rosy-Fingered Dawn was strongest when it climbed, in the light of the rising sun. At this time of day, I could only fulfill one of those two conditions.

Unfortunately, a technique could not triumph on origins and mysticism alone. Execution was king. Damon Aetos had not bothered to alter the city in pursuit of cheap advantages because he had no need for them.

My waning blade of dawn struck his sword and shattered it.

"Lio Aetos!"

"Have you ever left this city, Gianni?" I asked, idly rolling my shoulder. My rival, laughable as that statement was, glared silently as we circled one another.

The games were nearly at their end, now. After armed combat had come wrestling and then boxing, both of which the heir to the Burning Dusk had abstained from competing in. In average circumstances, it would have been a terrible loss in standing to do such a thing as his cult's leading athlete, but I doubted anyone would hold it against him, given his inevitable opponent. It was understandable that he'd save his body for the final event, the only one that mattered. Pankration.

Perhaps unsurprisingly, I had found myself slowly unwinding as I progressed through the wrestling and boxing trials. They soothed my raging soul, provided a balm to my heart. Unarmed combat had always been my style. How conflict ought to be. It was simple. It was profound.

It was *free*.

Gianni ducked and lunged forward in two quick steps, attempting to box me out of the ring. I blocked what could not be avoided, met his raised knee with my own, and relished the crunch of bone striking bone. Gianni winced, faltering ever so slightly as he tried to pivot on that wounded knee, and I shoved him back with two palms to his chest.

I could have done more, obviously. But instead, I paced around him, wondering.

"I'll take your silence as a no," I said. "But surely, you've thought about it. Pretend for a moment the cults did not exist. If you could go somewhere, anywhere in this world, where would it be?"

"Nowhere," Gianni spat. "My place is here."

This sanctimonious *liar*.

"You would go nowhere," I repeated scornfully. "You would see nothing? Where is your curiosity? Where is the passion of your soul!?"

I struck him once, twice, a cross and a right hook to the kidney that folded him over my fist. The crowds screamed and raved, having known from the start how this would go. I swept his feet out from under him and rode him to the sand. He thrashed and kicked, flipping like a beached fish in an effort to escape my hold. His hands were alight, his foundational technique at the height of its power as the scarlet sun touched the peak of the western mountain range.

It wasn't even close to the fight Sol had given me with shackles around his wrists. Ah, there was the rage again. I snarled and drove my right forearm into the back of Gianni's neck, pinning him to the sand.

"Have you never wondered what life is truly like? The real thing, not this caricature our fathers made for us. Don't you wish your first Daylight Games had been *real*? A competition attended by real cultivators and not these handpicked dregs? You know as well as I do that we were the only athletes that mattered today. You know that it was by design, not by virtue!"

He struggled out of the press and flipped himself onto his back, wound both legs around me, attempting to put me in a counter hold. It was sloppy. It was *weak*. I smashed my forehead into his nose, breaking it.

"I pity your father," Gianni wheezed. "That you are his son."

I sneered. "And I pity the slave that praises his master."

This time, I didn't allow him to escape the press of my choke. He struggled and spat until his last conscious breath, but he had never had a chance. The Fates had decided things for him long in advance, and he'd thanked them for the privilege.

"LIO AETOS!"

The noise was deafening. I stood up, tall and triumphant in the last light of the setting sun, and looked up at my family. Grudging approval from my uncles. Vibrant cheers from Myron and Rena, nearly enough to bring a smile to my face. Lydia was nearly aglow with pride. Even Heron and Castor could do nothing less than applaud me.

I locked eyes with my father. Damon Aetos nodded once. Nothing more. There was no pride, no joy. After all, I had only done what was expected of me.

I stood there and accepted the praise and adoration of fifty thousand men and more beyond the stadium's rim. I accepted laurel leaf crowns, one for every event that I had won, which was all of them. I played along to the crowd, piling each of them on top of the other until they toppled off my head and into the sand. I offered them to the second and third place athletes of various events, and when they stiffly declined, I shrugged and wore them around my neck, my biceps, everywhere they would fit.

Dusk finally slipped into night, and torches were lit up and down the aisles of the Scarlet Stadium to illuminate the closing ceremonies. Their flickering light made shadows of the spectators, fifty thousand faces obscured and featureless. I realized that it made no difference.

I basked in their orchestrated worship. And I understood.

They were all slaves. Every single one of them. And so was I.

This city was the chain.

My pneuma rippled and burst inside my soul, expanding past the limits that had constrained it for the past year of my life. That nearly forgotten rush of ecstasy pounded through my veins, filling me with joy. My virtuous heart swelled in my chest.

I ascended from the ninth rank of the Civic Realm to the tenth.

My cousins went wild in the stands. The spectators were even worse. I strode out of the victor's circle clothed in laurel leaf crowns, head held high and proud like the good little heir that I was. I passed a thousand grasping hands, each one reaching out from the torch-thrown shadows to touch my oiled skin. To catch triumph with their worthless fingers.

"That's it?" a slave asked me as I passed, his dark features illuminated by the torch in his hand.

He looked how I felt. Lost.

"I guess it is," I said and kept on walking.

Chapter Eighteen

THE YOUNG MISS-TOCRAT

Lio Aetos was returned to them.

For weeks Lydia could hardly believe it. She'd been certain that his victories in the Daylight Games would only drive him further away from his family, deeper into the company of his favored slave. Yet there he was. Back as suddenly as he'd left. Eating dinner with them, night after night. Attending sessions in the gymnasium and engaging properly—as he used to. Spending time with her as a fiancé should.

It was as if she had been awoken from a nightmare, and every day that followed was bliss. Castor had been the one to propose an explanation after the third night in a row that Lio had shown up for dinner. As soon as it had been said, Lydia berated herself for not realizing it sooner. It made perfect intuitive sense.

Lio Aetos had been stuck at a bottleneck in the ninth rank of the Civic Realm for over a year. Interacting with the Roman had been his way of breaking through that bottleneck. A radically different life experience to broaden his cultivation. Now that he had broken through, there was no need to continue humoring the slave.

It was easy to forget that Lio could struggle with his cultivation as much as any other mystiko within the cult. He had harnessed his pneuma at an unprecedentedly young age and ascended to the upper ranks of the Civic Realm at a breakneck pace, cementing himself early on as a prodigy, but he had never reached their eldest cousin's heights. That his progress had slowed to such a degree would normally have been cause for great concern. Indeed, had Lio Aetos not been Lio Aetos, her father may have called his status as heir into question himself.

But Lio was himself. It was said that strong foundations built tall cities, and Lio's foundations were perhaps the strongest of all. It was an absurd prospect in all but the most niche circumstances for a citizen to triumph over a philosopher, whether inside the marble octagon or the symposia chambers, and yet Lio's was an absurd existence.

He did not hesitate to punch above his station, and he never, ever lost. Whether it was an exceedingly keen eye that allowed him to pick only the battles he knew he could win or some higher providence, no one knew. But his results spoke for themselves.

So yes, it was easy to forget that for all his triumphs, her fiancé had been languishing in the ninth rank of the Civic Realm for an untenable amount of time. That didn't mean it had not been bothering him, though. She only wished she'd known it sooner.

It had resolved itself in the end. He stood now as a captain of the Civic Realm, the tenth and final rank before ascendance to the Sophic Realm. Champion of the Daylight Games. Summer turned to fall, and fall turned to winter. It was as if the Roman had ceased to exist to him.

Things made sense again.

"They're losing their minds," Lio said, amused, as slaves ran wild through the central pavilion. They were walking back from their hidden place, the alcove in the mountain's face that the seven of them had carved out so many years ago. They'd spent the afternoon watching light snow fall across Álikos, just the two of them.

"It was rather short notice," Lydia said, watching with bubbling excitement as the Rosy Dawn's servant class rushed to prepare the estates for a celebration the likes of which had not been seen in over a decade. Damon Aetos had given the word to his brothers a month ago, who had passed it on to their children. It was all they could talk about since.

A young pillar of the Rosy Dawn was getting married. The prodigal son of the Aetos line had found himself a girl in the course of his journeys and was returning home to properly introduce her to the family that had raised him. Then, with his uncle's blessing, he would wed her.

Nikolas Aetos was coming home.

"My, my. Look at you," a Heroic beauty murmured, leaning against the archway that connected Lydia's room to her younger sister's. Her mother looked her up and down, something nostalgic and wondering in her eyes.

"What about me?" Lydia asked archly, checking her appearance in a polished bronze mirror. She'd chosen a white silk dress for the occasion, bound at the shoulders by carved bronze eagles, and a scarlet sash was draped diagonally across her chest as a symbol of her status. Her hair had been finely braided by a pair of slaves and wound into a bun at the nape of her neck. It was the color of spun gold—a trait she'd inherited from her mother.

Chryse Aetos crossed the stone tiles and took Lydia's hair in hand, touching up the braids with deft fingers. Those fingers could cave in bronze plate with little effort, but they were gentle and unerringly precise as they undid and redid the braids in her eldest daughter's hair.

"You went and became a beautiful woman while I wasn't looking," Lydia's mother said. "Who is this marble swan that's taken the place of my little ugly duck?" A tinkling laugh spilled from her lips as Lydia swatted at her. "Wasn't it only yesterday that you were begging me to attend lessons in the gymnasium with the boys?"

"Perhaps if you spent less time behind closed doors it wouldn't come as such a shock," Lydia said, with no real heat. Nonetheless, her mother feigned a wounded expression, reflected in the bronze mirror.

"My daughter inherited her father's cruelty. Truly, I am reviled by the Fates."

Lydia rolled her eyes, fighting a smile. "If anyone is reviled it's father. He received you for a tribulation, after all." She yelped as her mother sharply twisted her ear.

"You're still far too young to be getting cheeky with me," her mother chided her. Her sea-green eyes glowed merrily, backlit by the flames of her Heroic soul.

Chryse Aetos was a woman whose presence captivated and intimi-dated in equal proportion. Lydia had inherited most of her defining traits from her mother, sans the color of her eyes, and it showed in their bronze reflections. Chryse was taller than her by a forearm's length, taller than most men, the product of a pristine bloodline and her own advanced cultivation. But they shared the same long, lusciously powerful legs. The same smooth skin, the color of polished marble despite the years her mother had journeyed beneath the Mediterranean sun.

Her mother's arms were muscled in a way that hers weren't—one of the few signs that she had lived an entire life before her daughter. They could have passed for sisters, standing there before that bronze mirror. Timelessness was a given when one reached her mother's level of renown.

Lydia had always been awed by her mother. She was gorgeous, yes. Ethereally so. But she was *powerful,* too. She was no coy maiden or cringing wallflower. She was married to one of the most powerful men in the Scarlet City, one of the more powerful men in the known world, and she stood by her father's side as an equal. They had traveled the Mediterranean together. They had cultivated virtue together. And they had triumphed, as one. Together.

She'd long admired her mother, and it was for that reason that her opinion was the most difficult to ask for. Still, though, Lydia had never been a coward. She swallowed her fears and raised a hand to grasp her mother's fingers, lowering them from their work. She stared at her mother's curious reflection in the bronze.

"Mother," she said, slowly. "Am I...ready?"

The fire in her mother's eyes flickered. But when firm hands turned her around, Chryse Aetos was smiling with pride.

"More than I ever was," her mother said, rubbing her thumbs tenderly across the knuckles of Lydia's hands. "Already, you are more than that boy will ever deserve."

"Mother!" she exclaimed, pushing away. "I'm serious!"

Her mother pulled her back with strength that could not be denied and wrapped her up in a tight embrace. Lydia resisted valiantly, but she may as well have been fighting against the ocean tides. Finally, she huffed and surrendered herself to it.

"So am I, my ugly duck," her mother whispered. "So am I."

It was not her wedding day, not yet, but it felt nearly like it as she walked through snow-covered fields to join her fiancé at the docks.

Lio greeted her with a faint smile and did not question her when she slipped her hand into his. His hand was large, tan, and calloused. She squeezed it once, searchingly, and her heart leapt in her chest when he squeezed back. She smiled brightly up at him, and he chuckled.

"Our wedding won't be long from now," she said casually as the rest of their family gathered at the docks. The pillars were all in attendance, her mother and aunt chatting animatedly about the upcoming wedding while her father and uncles stood at the edge of the dock, towering symbols of the Rosy Dawn's might. The rest of her cousins had yet to arrive.

"Not long at all," Lio agreed, gazing wistfully at the sea. They were all eager to see their eldest cousin again after all these years. "We might as well make it a dual affair. Get both marriages out of the way while things are set up."

Lydia smacked his arm, and he laughed.

"Our wedding will be about *us*," she said imperiously. "And it will be better than Niko's wedding in every way, or you will feel this mommy's wrath. Do you understand?"

Lio looked fondly down at her, his features somehow more pleasing than they had been before he started shaving. The tips of her ears burned. That, Lydia had decided, was one habit he'd picked up from the slave that she would allow.

"Of course, cousin," he said. "Anything you want."

Lydia nodded firmly, doing her best to conceal how warm she felt, and turned to watch the horizon with him. Soon enough, a ship appeared.

The prodigal son returned.

Chapter Nineteen

THE YOUNG MISS-TOCRAT

Nikolas Aetos disdained a gangway, not even waiting for his ship to near the docks before leaping from the deck at an absurd distance and landing adroitly before the three pillars of the Rosy Dawn Cult.

"Uncles," he greeted warmly, arms spread wide.

A truly amazing sight followed. Lydia's own father laughed, breaking formation with his brothers to wrap his nephew up in a tight embrace. Uncle Stavros was not far behind, wrapping him up and slapping his back with a fierce grin and a rib about his nephew's slender frame. The ever-stone-faced twin eagles radiated joy.

And then something even more unbelievable happened. Damon Aetos himself stepped forward and clasped forearms with his nephew, a fond smile on his lips. In her living memory, Lydia couldn't recall ever seeing such an expression on her uncle's face.

"Welcome home, nephew," spoke the kyrios.

Nikolas returned the smile, crinkled eyes burning sky blue with the light of his virtuous soul. He stood tall, of a height with Lydia's father and Uncle Stavros, and rippling with muscle despite her uncle's jokes. His hair was cropped short at the sides, black as night, and his skin was heavily bronzed. He bore a burnished chest plate over a red tunic and stylized greaves as easily as he would a silk robe.

His pneuma rolled off him like heat from a flame. If his eyes hadn't been a clear enough sign, the intensity of his presence left no doubt. Their eldest cousin had left as an unprecedented prodigy with an indomitable determination to win glory.

He had returned to them as a Hero.

Watching the four of them trade greetings was an eerie thing. Lydia wasn't the only one to notice it, either. Her mother and aunt stood entranced by the sight. Nikolas Aetos looked like he belonged among his uncles. For a moment, it was as if the fourth Aetos brother had never died.

It felt that way, too, when his gaze moved past his uncles and settled on them. It was a powerful sensation, all too similar to the one she felt whenever her father or uncles felt the need to flex their presence. But all thoughts of pressure and intimidation fled her mind when she saw that familiar shining grin, the one she remembered from her childhood.

"Look at you two!" Niko exclaimed, striding excitedly past his uncles. Lydia wanted to rush forward to meet him, but she couldn't bring herself to pull her hand from Lio's. It didn't end up being an issue. Niko swept them both up in his arms, squeezing them tight. "Who told you to grow while I was gone? Where did my baby cousins go?"

Lio snorted, clapping his cousin's back. He was nearly as tall as Niko, his feet still firmly on the docks while hers dangled in the air. Lydia, for her part, wrapped her free arm around her eldest cousin's neck and returned the hug with all her strength.

"Who told you to leave?" Lio returned wryly. "You've missed all the fun."

"Without a doubt," Niko agreed, lowering her back to her feet and giving them a conspirator's grin. "But the wider world has its own appeal, too. It's one thing to hear the stories and quite another to live them for yourself."

Lio smiled lightly. "I wouldn't know."

"You will," Niko promised, gripping his shoulder. He glanced her way mischievously. "Provided you keep our little swan happy, of course."

They exchanged a few more pleasantries before Niko's aunts descended on him, the marble beauties of the Rosy Dawn cooing and fawning over their eldest nephew while he tried valiantly to maintain his Heroic bearing. The other cousins were soon to follow, Heron and Myron pounding down the docks with Castor and Rena not far behind. It was a joyous reunion. Even if it was only a temporary thing, the Aetos family was whole again.

Lydia watched fondly as Niko swung a giddy Myron through the air, marveling at how much he'd grown. She squeezed Lio's hand again, glancing up at him. His head was tilted to the side, scarlet eyes looking back at the approaching ship.

No, not the ship.

The sea.

Niko had arrived a week ahead of his wedding. He used that time to re-familiarize himself with the cult and all that he'd missed in his absence from it, to catch up with old friends within the ranks of the mystikos and the honored philosophers both, and especially to make the rounds and introduce everyone to his blushing bride-to-be.

Iphys Rosi, soon to be Iphys Aetos, was a rose worthy of her name. She wasn't as tall as Lydia's mother or her aunt, but she was no less striking for it. She wore her hair in a long braid the color of harvested wheat, tied with multiple strips of blue silk. Her eyes were a kind hazel flecked with gold, even as her Heroic soul lit them like a flame. Rena had immediately found a kindred spirit in the woman, and it had warmed Lydia to her immensely to see them interact.

More than even that, though, Niko had done his level best to spend as much of his time as he possibly could before the wedding with his cousins. They ate all their meals together, attended the gymnasium together, and shared stories long into each night. Somehow, Niko was as eager to hear their banal tales of life in the cult as they were to hear about his Heroic adventures. To that end, he insisted that for every story he told, each of them tell one in return.

Myron complained that such a ratio was far from fair, but there was little he could do to persuade a Heroic cultivator. Besides, Lydia knew that he enjoyed the praise that their eldest cousin heaped upon them. He was just too proud to show it.

The only one truly reluctant to share was Lio.

"Come now, cousin," Niko finally insisted, three days before the wedding, "how can the Young Aristocrat stay silent while his cousins take all the glory? I've been here four days, and I don't know you any better for it."

They sat around a fire in the shadow of the eastern mountain range, telling stories after dark. Iphys was up in the main estate with her new aunts and a bevy of slaves, undergoing preparation for the wedding. Lydia's father and uncles were handling their own preparations, though they'd stolen Niko away more than once over the last few days to discuss things that Niko wouldn't speak to.

"There's little to say," Lio said. He was laid out across the fire from his eldest cousin, head propped up on his palm while he gazed lazily into the flames. "We're all familiar with life in the Rosy Dawn. I'm more interested in hearing about the lands across the sea."

"I'm familiar with *my* life in the Rosy Dawn," Niko said, leaning forward. "I want to hear about *yours*. Surely, you have a few tales to tell. I refuse to believe Uncle Damon's son has not been living an interesting life."

Lio smiled faintly. Something about it made Lydia's stomach lurch with unease. It bid her to speak.

"Lio won the Daylight Games."

Niko blinked, surprised. An unspoken tension in the air suddenly eased. "He did? Which event?"

"All of them," she said, pride warring with her concern. "He went undefeated."

"And it wasn't even close," Myron added. "They gave him so many laurel crowns that he had to wear them on his arms!"

"He was incredible," Rena said softly.

"He could have done worse," Heron grudgingly admitted. Castor, sitting beside him, chuckled and draped an arm across his shoulders.

"Now, now, it's alright to be honest. Our senior brother brutalized the competition."

"Is that so?" Niko asked. Lio hummed, neither confirming nor denying it. "You cheeky brat, I only won three events when I competed, and you mean to tell me you swept the whole lot? Tell me all about it!" For some reason, Lio didn't puff up with pride as any of them surely would have. The knowledge that he had triumphed so absolutely where even their prodigal cousin had struggled didn't seem to fill him with any particular joy.

His eyes only narrowed. That faint, gnawing dread compounded.

"We competed in different games, cousin," Lio finally said. Modestly, almost. Since when had Lio become modest? "You'd have won just as easily. More, even. Even back then, your cultivation was far beyond what mine is now."

"Nonsense," Niko said, waving a hand. Myron and Rena exchanged nervous looks. "The Lio I remember was never too far behind me. He wasn't modest about it, either. Where do you stand now, fifth rank? Sixth?"

"Tenth."

Niko's eyes flickered in honest shock. "Captain of the Sophic Realm? Already?" Lydia's eyes clenched shut.

"Civic," came Lio's mild reply.

Silence.

"... Ah, I see. So it's like that." Niko sighed, leaning back. "You know, you have nothing to be ashamed of. Captain of the Civic Realm at your age is impressive by any metric. Especially under these conditions."

Please stop talking, Lydia silently asked.

"What do you mean by that?" Heron asked.

Stop.

"Well, there's only so much you can do on top of a mountain, no matter what the elders say," Niko reasoned. "My time abroad has exposed me to things I had never even heard of in my childhood days here. Our uncles provide the best education they can, and I can't think of anywhere else I'd have liked better to grow up, but at a certain point, an eagle has to spread its wings and fly."

Enough.

"Some men feel the itch worse than others. We call it wanderlust," Niko said, winking and nudging Myron with an elbow. "But you'll all get a chance to scratch it soon enough. The business of a cult like the

Rosy Dawn is endlessly demanding. I'm sure Uncle Damon is just waiting until you hit the Sophic Realm to send you out, Lio. How long have you been at the tenth rank?"

"Four months."

He didn't wince. He didn't have to. "Soon enough, then. How about we exchange a few pointers before I leave? I may be able to offer you some insight."

"Of course, cousin," Lio said. He smiled, scarlet eyes glinting in the firelight. "Now, I think it's your turn. Tell me about your time in the north."

Niko accepted the cue for what it was, and the storytelling continued late into the night. Slowly, one by one, they each drifted off to sleep. Myron was the first to go, his age asserting itself as he splayed across Rena's lap. The poor girl wasn't far behind, and after a few more hours of valiant struggle, Heron and Castor gave in as well. Lydia was the last to drift off, wrapped up in Lio's arms with her back to his chest.

The last thing she saw before sleep claimed her, glancing up, was his eyes. Raptly focused on Niko as he spoke.

Growing colder with every word.

Chapter Twenty

THE YOUNG ARISTOCRAT

The eve of Nikolas Aetos' wedding arrived with snow flurries and songs. Spirit wine flowed freely, and freshly butchered meats abounded. Mystikos spent the morning conducting their own mock games for the entertainment of our guests, while the honored philosophers traded discourse with the young heroes in the afternoon. When evening came, they all gathered to enjoy a feast with my elder cousin's companions.

This entire day was itself a celebration in preparation for the ceremonies tomorrow. The only portion of the cult not present for the pavilion feast was the Aetos family itself. Instead, we were to welcome the newest addition to the family with a grand symposium, hosted in the main estate.

I'd cleansed myself in the bathhouse with my cousins and donned my finest cult attire for the occasion. The quiet slap of my bare feet against the marble floors of the hall was the only sound to be heard as I made my way to the symposia chambers. The pavilion feast was already well underway. My own would begin soon enough. Then, tomorrow, the wedding. After that, farewell to Nikolas once more. Then...

I paused. In the low light of the sunset, I saw something truly ludicrous taking place in my courtyard. My legs carried me into the gardens and pools of their own volition.

"What are you doing?" I asked the slave tending to one of my ancestors' filial pools.

"What does it look like?" Sol asked. I tilted my head.

"It looks like you're draining the pool with a spoon."

And so he was. As I watched incredulously, the slave dipped a shallow silver spoon into the filial pool and deposited its meager contents into the clay jar beside him. There were seven more jugs off to the side, and three of them were full. How long had he been doing this?

"Why are you doing this?" I asked when it became clear that he was letting his actions speak for him. He glanced up at me, storm gray eyes flickering with something that was almost annoyance, almost amusement.

"Your cousin's orders."

I blinked. "Heron?" Sol nodded, and I found myself laughing. Once it started it didn't stop. I gripped his shoulder as a brace, nearly doubled over in mirth. "He made you use a spoon?" I finally gasped.

"He did."

"And you're actually doing it?" This was too much.

"It was an order from on high." He shrugged and dipped his spoon back into the water, depositing another few drops into the jar. "Besides, what else is there to do?" My laughter died down to low chuckling and then faded to a thoughtful silence. I considered the filial pool and its sunkissed waters.

What else was there to do?

"Tell me something, slave," I said, dipping my spoon into the pool. Sol hummed. "How long do you plan to suffer this?"

"Suffer what? Enslavement?"

"Obviously," I said. He stared at me for a moment, lost for words. "Has it not lost its luster yet? Or is it the kiss of the whip that gives you pleasure? I knew Romans were deviants, but still."

"You're still upset about the games?" Sol asked. I snorted, dipping my spoon. It really would have been faster to just use our cupped palms.

"What am I, a woman? No, I'm genuinely asking. There's only so much a man can do to punish himself before it becomes gratuitous. If you keep this up there won't be anything left of you for the Fates to torment."

His expression shuttered, right on cue. "You don't know what you're talking about."

"No, that's where you're mistaken. I'm the *only one* who knows what I'm talking about." I grabbed one of the full jars and dumped it back into the pool. Sol glared murderously at me, but really, what else was there to do?

"Day in and day out, we're all just staring up at heaven. Waiting for the sun to rise and thinking to ourselves that this is the day we'll finally catch it in our hands." I filled my spoon with water and deposited it in an empty jug, then grabbed another full jug and dumped it back in the pool. "We cultivate virtue so that we can someday break bread with the gods, but what does cultivating virtue *mean*, really?"

"You're about to tell me," Sol muttered. I bared my teeth in a grin and flicked a spoonful of water at his face.

"We exist, body, mind, and spirit. The philosophers preach that the tripartite soul is a balancing act, that we must restrain with reason the hunger in our souls if we are to ascend. Disdain our heart's natural passions in the pursuit of virtue. Why? For what purpose? Is it our filial duty to be *dull?*"

"Temperance is virtue," Sol said.

"Virtue is performative excellence," I corrected him. "We agreed before that a man's purpose was to ascend the divine mountain and throw off his destined threads. Whatever path leads him there, by default, is a virtuous one. Isn't that so?"

Sol eyed me.

"Results are all that matter. Cultivation is all that matters. If I strangled you here and now, drowned you in this pool, and in so doing ascended to the Sophic Realm, the act would become virtuous by default. *Isn't that so?*"

"No."

"Explain yourself."

Sol tapped the fingers of his free hand against the pool's marble rim, his manacle's severed chain swaying to and fro. "A man is more than just a number," he said.

"More than just a rank," I added. He ignored me. Continued to play dumb.

"It isn't enough to be blessed by heaven," he said. "Cultivation only makes us more of what we already are."

Therein lay the issue. There was a reason that some men rose to perilous heights on the shoulders of virtue while others languished in the lowest realms despite living as they should. Heroes and Tyrants were the product of epics. Beloved by the Muses and reviled by the Fates, they were all connected by a common thread. Wicked or kind, monstrous or just, they were *interesting*. Nikolas had given himself fully to this concept. Enslaved himself to it.

"My cousin would disagree," I informed Sol. He only shrugged.

"Why should I care what a Grecian thinks?"

I laughed. "Exactly! Who cares what they all think? Who cares what heaven has to say? We exist in three parts, and each of them is king inside our soul. Why should we disdain one for the other? Why should we cultivate virtue at the expense of our dignity?"

He was the only one that understood. The rest of them were too deeply immersed in it. They'd been born into this world, had never thought to wonder what existed beyond it. It was only natural they would respond as they did.

"My cousins think I'm jealous," I said, resting an elbow on the rim of the pool and fully facing the slave. "They think I covet Nikolas' advanced cultivation. My aunts and uncles think I envy his circumstances."

"Do you?" Sol asked.

"Do I envy him for having a longer leash than I do? Of course not. He's still a dog." Silver spoons dipped into crystalline water. At some point, the sun had given way to the stars. It was a dead moon night. "My cousins pity me for my bottlenecks as if they were the disease themselves and not merely the symptom. My aunts and uncles scorn me for my impatience as if these token journeys my father hands out are what I actually want."

"What do you want, then?" He paused in his own spooning, looking at me. For a moment even his faint, ever-present contempt gave way to honest curiosity.

"I have no idea."

Sol rolled his eyes.

"My virtuous heart can't lie," I told him, grinning. "But I know that whatever it is, it's not something a slave's eyes can see."

"Seems you'll never know, then." Ho, how cruel.

"And what about you?" I asked. "What does the son of Rome desire?"

"Nothing," he said. "Nothing at all."

I frowned, propping my cheek up on my free hand. I stirred my spoon idly in the pool, flicking small streams into an open jar with unerring precision. "That right there. I despise that about you."

This was why he hadn't taken my hand in the Scarlet Stadium. This was why he suffered the daily indignities of a slave, never once bothered to sell his skills for coin. He had no intention of paying his freedom's price. He had no desire to be a citizen of the Scarlet City. Because even if he was, it wouldn't matter.

"Most slaves only serve one master. But not you," I said. "Even if my father let you go, it wouldn't make a difference to you. Would it?"

He shook his head once.

"You can't wallow forever." I watched his fist clench, his jaw flex. Pathetic. He was so close. And yet here he was. *Pathetic.* "You had aspirations before, didn't you? There's an entire world out there, lands that enlightened eyes have never seen before. Don't you ache to see them? To experience everything this world has to offer?"

"For what purpose? Why?" he demanded, frustrated not because he didn't feel that desire but because he did. Because his hunger was at war with his spirit, and his reason was lost. He was drowning, but his tripartite soul would not let him die.

"Because this world exists," I said simply. "Because we can."

What other reason did a man need?

· · ·

We talked about the places we would go, the things we wanted to see. We drained those filial pools with our spoons, and when the sun rose, I left him to join my family in a joyous ceremony. My aunts and uncles were furious with me for missing the symposia, of course, and my cousins weren't far behind. But there were more important things to focus on.

The wedding was beautiful beyond words. The bride and the groom joined hands around an ornamented blade and sacrificed their first animal as husband and wife, to the cheers of their companions. A grand feast followed, with the men occupying one set of tables and the women occupying another, and after that came all manner of wedding games.

When the time finally came to consecrate the marriage, to lift the lover's veil, the bride and the rest of my eldest cousin's companions were treated to the memorable sight of a star falling from heaven to earth.

Their Heroic pneuma blanketed the mountaintop, virtuous hearts rising to confront the threat, but they needn't have bothered. Nikolas Aetos held his wife steady and watched fondly as Damon Aetos blew a hole in the eastern mountain range, revealing the path to the greater mystery of the Rosy Dawn Cult.

It was only natural that an Aetos' wife would be inducted into the cult, after all.

Nikolas swept his veiled bride into his arms and went charging down into the yawning abyss, calling for his companions to follow him. They didn't hesitate, eyes blazing with excitement as they descended into the abyss. My aunts and uncles followed suit. My father was the last to go. He sealed the chasm behind him, leaving the rest of the cult to their afterparty.

I turned and left the pavilion, accepting a jug of spirit wine from a mousy slave as I did. By the time I found him it was empty, and my pneuma was aglow.

"How would you like to be free?" I asked, and Sol looked up from tuning his lyre. Somehow, this one was even uglier than the last.

"Don't you have anything better to be doing?" he asked, annoyed.

"I don't," I said confidently, and I gripped his manacles in both hands. My pneuma drove into them, warping them until they cracked apart. That was all it took. "And now neither do you."

Sol stared at his wrists uncomprehendingly. The manacles were utterly ruined, joined only by the thinnest slivers of iron. All he had to do was take them off.

"From this moment on, your life is your own," I told him. "If you're still a slave tomorrow, it'll be because you chose it."

He would come with me or he wouldn't. Either way, I wouldn't begrudge him his decision. My heart was singing. The ocean called.

Freedom was a distant shore.

Chapter Twenty-One

CAPTAIN OF SALT AND ASH

I watched my father burn to ash. The salt of the sea coated my tongue.

Fourteen years old. Too young to stand shoulder-to-shoulder within the ranks, to have been there to make a difference. Too old to ever forget the sight of him carried in on a bed of broken shields. Tears blurred my vision, smoke and sea breeze mingling unbearably on my senses. I refused to sob. The men bore it in grim silence, watching their captain and countless brothers burn to ash. I would do the same.

Captains led from the front. It was the way of the legions, the first virtue of the Republic. It was the first lesson that my father had taught me, and he had matched his words to action time and again in his service. The men of the fifth legion loved him for it. They moved mountains for him because of it.

And when he died and entered the great beyond, they followed him there, too.

The mournful bellows of the legions' war trumpets blanketed the camp, legionaries breathing their souls into their horns for the fallen captain and his men. Some men wept silent tears. Others stared vacantly into the flames, their minds still in the thick of the fight. Most, though. Most were simply grim.

"Dry your eyes, young Solus."

Instinct moved me. I snapped to attention, dashing tears of grief, salt, and smoke from my eyes. A wave of sound swept through the ranks, hundreds of men slamming clenched fists to their hearts in respect. Belatedly, I did the same.

The general of the western front dropped a hand onto my shoulder, and I staggered under the weight of it. It was not a physical thing. It was his presence alone that nearly drove me to my knees. The general looked upon the mass funeral pyre, with my father at its center. There was sorrow in his eyes. But no tears.

"We don't weep until the battle is won," he told me. His resolve was a quiet thing. Yet it shook the earth beneath our feet. "Your father accepted death before defeat. It's up to us to honor that resolve with action. Dry those eyes until we've swept his enemies into the sea."

The words were for me, but they carried as easily as the war horns. Legionaries shouted and hammered their fists to their breast-plates, slamming the butts of their spears against the earth. It was the nature of a Roman general to command unfaltering loyalty, but it was the providence of the man that led the western front to command devotion overwhelming. No man in the entire Republic was so beloved.

He turned me away from the pyre, away from the ash and salt, and urged me back to camp with his hand on my shoulder. I might as well have tried to resist the turning of the seasons.

"Your father was a fine husband to my niece and a finer captain in my legions." My great-uncle led me through the camp, with its weath-ered tents and siege materials. The earth beneath our feet had long been pounded to mud. "What I owed him, I now owe you. A boy your age needs a hand to guide you. I'll have to suffice."

He parted the command tent's flap and ushered me in. Inside were men that appeared to be no older than my father but possessed the bearing and scars of men far older preserved by cultivation. The logisticos of the western legions laid eyes upon me, and the pressure of their notice nearly drove me to my knees.

I grit my teeth and stood to attention, and though I had no breast-plate to strike, I slammed a fist to my heart anyway. They eyed me appraisingly.

My great-uncle entered behind me, and those monsters rose and followed my example before the general of the west.

"At ease," he said, allowing a legionnaire that had been waiting just inside the tent's entrance to remove his heavy crimson cloak. He kept his armor, taking his place on a simple bench at the head of a wide sand table. The logisticos relaxed, retaking their seats and returning to their prior discussion.

One of them, though, glanced curiously at me. I hadn't moved. Hadn't dared to leave the position of attention.

"Gaius," the logistico said. "Who is the boy?"

My great-uncle glanced back at me, and his expression made my heart clench in my chest. I'd mastered the tears. But the taste of sea salt and funeral ash remained.

"This is my nephew, Solus," he said. "His father brought him here to show him how the virtuous men of Rome live. Now, I'll teach him how to lead them."

He gestured, and I joined him on the bench. The farthest western reaches of the Mediterranean were arrayed before us on the sand table, with all their armies. My eyes immediately sought out one set of pieces, in particular. My great-uncle shook his head once.

"We have a long campaign ahead of us, nephew." He pointed elsewhere. North.

"First we take the Gauls."

"What is the primary quality that a man must have to lead?" my great-uncle asked me. It was a rhetorical question like most he asked. His bright gray eyes swiveled across the field, searching for something only he could see. "It is not strength alone. Neither is it wisdom. A man doesn't need to be superior to those he leads in any particular manner, but for one."

"What is that, Uncle?" I asked dutifully, resisting the urge to roll my shoulders in the unfamiliar armor I'd been issued. Still too young to stand shoulder-to-shoulder in the ranks, but neither could I ride at the general's side in plain clothes.

"Men, in general, are quick to believe that which they wish to be true," Gaius spoke. "It is the burden of the Republic to shed light on every shadowed nation. We are besieged on all sides by barbarian states. In circumstances like these, a man desires a guiding light above all else. To make that man believe you are someone worth following into the screaming hordes, someone worth dying alongside. Worth dying *for*. That is the minimum that you'll need to lead."

His eyes burned as he found what he had been looking for in the press of battle.

"Watch me," he commanded, and he urged his horse into a sprint.

The western legions were joined in vicious combat with the Gallic hordes. They had tried to hide behind the walls of their settlement, but Gaius' officers had shattered them with cultivation that shook my senses. The barbarians that spilled out were massive, larger than all but the greatest of legionaries and far more numerous. Thousands upon thousands had come charging out of the walls, and then the buccinators among the legions had raised their trumpets and sounded the alarm as more came howling up the rear.

We were caught in the middle. The only way out was through. I watched the general of the west run his horse headlong into the fray, and I watched the disrupted ranks of the legions reform themselves, as if by magic, where he passed.

Shield walls slammed together. Century lines dug their heels into the mud and held, where before they had been pushed back. Legionaries who had been shouting in anger and fear, or in simple exhilaration, went silent. Focused. Gaius shot through the lines like an arrow, and in his passing left them silent and dangerous as a knife.

He plunged that blade into the Gallic army's screaming throat.

I gripped the gladius at my side tightly, aching to join them. Every fallen legionnaire was a life I could have saved. A father that would burn on the pyre because I hadn't been there to cover him in the press. But I mastered the desire. I observed. And I promised myself that someday soon, I would be as my great-uncle was. The light that guided.

Gaius drove through the Gallic tides and found his mark. The general of the west met the Gallic king, and their clash rocked me off my mount. I scrambled for the reins while the war horse reared up and screamed its defiance to heaven. Even the beasts gave their hearts for Gaius.

It was over as quickly as it had begun. The Gallic armies gave way like they were made of sand, a cascading retreat that started from both fronts and was soon spilling over to their farthest back lines. They were held up as precipitously by their king as the legions were by their general, and as Gaius drove the Gallic king into the earth, it was clear who stood greater among heaven and earth.

The legions let fly their eagle standards, clarion calls of war trumpets splitting the air. The Gallic king clutched a gaping wound in his side, and before the eyes of legionaries and barbarians alike, he slowly knelt.

Lightning struck the general of the west.

Horror stopped my heart. The bolt fell out of a clear blue sky and was followed in the next instant by another. Then another. Dozens, in the blink of an eye. Hundreds. Barbarians caught too close were vaporized by the pillar of light. Legion shield walls were raised in turtle formation as the general's men formed ranks against heaven.

After what seemed like an eternity and yet no time at all, the lightning storm ceased. At the epicenter of its destruction knelt the Gallic king, a smoking ruin of a man. Still alive, still kneeling, but only just.

Gaius sat tall on his horse. His pneuma unfurled like an eagle standard across the battlefield, and where it passed, men fell to their knees. A rolling thunder of noise passed through the legion ranks, thousands of fists slamming to armored chests in salutes.

My legs shook with the urge to kneel. My basest instincts begged me to submit. But I stood tall and proud, a fist to my heart. And when my great-uncle looked back across the field at me, there was pride in his eyes.

From that day on, my path was set.

The general of the west returned home for his Triumph. The Gallic king was paraded around the great city, and for days Rome celebrated her favored son. It was a dizzying experience. I felt utterly out of place in the city that I had once so arrogantly prowled like a hunting cat.

My armor now felt more natural than the soft cloths and togas I'd worn as a boy. My blade was more familiar to my hand than any cup of wine.

When my great-uncle presented me with a girl and declared her to be my wife, I had no idea what to do with her. But I was my father's son. I offered her my hand and she took it. Her skin was soft, the color of fresh cream. She looked coyly up at me through long lashes. I decided I didn't like the schemes behind them.

So I pulled her tight to my chest and kissed her soundly. The men of the fifth legion cheered and laughed. When we parted her chestnut braids were disheveled, blue eyes startled.

"No games," I told her, "and I'm yours."

Slowly, she smiled.

I had just turned seventeen. The western front was a ruin. Crows blackened the skies, and ash rolled like mist through the countryside. Where the enemy went, they burned and they salted.

"We have no choice," my great-uncle said grimly. We were arrayed around the sand table, logisticos and officers of every legion gathered to hear the general speak. He moved ivory pieces through the sand, corralling a tide of obsidian stones. "Our internal conflicts have weakened us, and the enemy allows us no time to consolidate. We split them here and drive them into the sea, or we are lost."

Officers were given marching orders each, in turn, slamming fists to hearts and striding out of the command tent to round up their men. The legions were weary. They were worn. But they were sons of Rome, and they would march until the fight was won.

Soon only the logisticos remained. Gaius spoke to them for hours about the lands that lay between us and the enemy, the advantages that could be manufactured for our forces along the way. I stood by his side all the while, eyes roving over the sand table. My armor was cold. Heavier than usual on my shoulders.

"What do you see, Solus?" he asked me, sometime later.

"We outnumber them," I said. My fist clenched.

"Yet they ravage us like crows." He nodded, taking an ivory piece in hand that stood taller than the rest. He rolled it between his fingers, contemplating. "Wars are won in the hearts of the men fighting them. Men have to believe they can win. Triumphing against greater numbers builds that faith." He didn't explain what happened in the opposite case. He didn't have to.

"These stories we've been hearing..."

"Don't matter. Our objective is unchanged." He waved a hand, dismissing the logisticos from the tent. When they had gone, he brought that hand down and divided the ivory legions. He set his piece with the western forces. "I'm entrusting the fifth legion to you."

"You can't!" It was an immediate response. Instinctive. The Tyrant of the west raised an eyebrow at me. "Sir, I'm not ready. I'm not strong enough—"

"What have I told you?" Bright gray eyes burned. They measured me, the same way they had measured every enemy to fall at the Republic's feet. "Strength alone is not what matters. You are my nephew, who has cultivated my own virtue. The men of the fifth legion love you as dearly as they loved your father. You *will* lead them."

"Is there no one else?" I asked, a heavy weight in my stomach.

"None that I can spare. You will have advisors and logisticos, and three thousand shining Roman souls to carry you through. All you must do is show them the way."

I inhaled deeply. My fist rapped against my breastplate.

"I won't fail you, Uncle."

"Father," he corrected me, smiling faintly at my confusion. From a fold in his robes, he produced a roll of papyrus. He offered it to me. I unfurled the document and read in growing disbelief.

It was a declaration of adoption.

"Fight, my son," he said, rising and clapping my shoulder. His gray eyes burned fiercely. "Fight until the last man falls. I, your father, will handle the rest."

The enemy was unlike anything the fifth legion had ever seen. They surged across the battlefield like a midnight tide. Like a living nightmare. When they clashed against our shield walls, their howls shook the earth.

Within minutes our formations were shattered. They swept us away from our sister legions, the only sign as to their location being the wheeling murders of crows that darkened the sky. In the distance, lightning struck the earth over and over as the men of my adopted father's legions pitted their souls against the enemy and ascended. It was chaos. It was a nightmare that had no end.

I'd seen enough men die. I dug my heels into my horse's flank, and the midnight war stallion reared up and screamed defiance.

"Sir, you can't!" one of the advisors that Gaius had allotted me cried out, reaching for me. A life in the legions had sharpened the man's cultivation to a knife's edge. Without question, his life's essence was stronger than mine.

But strength alone was not enough. My pneuma rippled out from me in a wave. Gaius' virtue slammed the man down into his saddle.

"A captain leads from the front," I snarled, and my horse leapt into a gallop across the field.

It was worse to see the enemy up close. They were an impossibility. A perversion of nature. Worse, they wore the armor of a dead nation. An empire that could not exist.

Carthage had been burned and salted long ago.

"For Gaius!" I bellowed, charging into the nightmare's teeth with naught but a blade and my defiant soul. "For Rome!"

"Gaius!" the men of the fifth legion screamed. **"ROME!"**

I pierced the storm as the tip of the spear.

"Sir." The first spear stood at attention. I had dismissed everyone else from the tent.

The messenger eagle cocked its head, eyeing me curiously as I read its missive. Awaiting a reply that I could not give it because there was no one for the bird to deliver it to. No 'where' to return.

"The city of Rome is lost."

The first spear was an older man. Weathered and scarred despite the preserving nature of cultivation. He had been at war for longer than I had been alive. When I recited the news, he only closed his eyes in grief. I dropped the letter onto my cot. My hands were shaking, so I clenched them into fists.

"Do you have a family, First Spear? A wife?" I asked.

"Aye, sir," his voice rasped. "And three boys your age."

I tried to recall the taste of my wife's lips. Funeral ash and sea salt were all that remained.

"Those dogs burned and salted the city of Rome," I said. "They scattered her legions to the four corners of the Mediterranean and backed us into hostile lands. Tell me our options, Centurion."

The first spear answered without hesitation. "Fight and die, sir. Drag them down to Tartarus."

I stood, and the first spear straightened to face me. His grief mirrored mine, but it was something he'd mastered long ago. I would have to do the same.

A captain leads from the front.

"What are you waiting for, then?" I asked, a fire building in my soul. "Gather the men. Let's make them bleed."

The first spear slammed his fist to his chest.

Fight. Until the last man fell.

Carthage came for us in the night, and we met them screaming.

We set fire to our tents, that they might light the field. At my command, centurions bawled out the order to fire, and up and down the lines archers loosed their flaming arrows. Their lights arched high and long and were swallowed by the advancing horde. I led the charge with the first spear and the prime cohort at my side.

We clashed in thunder and blood. The warriors of Carthage raked us with clawed fingers that parted bronze like spider silk. They howled loud enough to make men bleed from their ears and snarled hatefully as they tore into us and were torn into in turn. I drove my spear through a Carthaginian breastplate and caught the retaliatory swing of a broadsword on my shield. The impact numbed my arm instantly. The enemy glared at me with caustic yellow eyes as it died.

They were wolves in the shape of men, the smallest of them taller than the tallest Gaul, walking upright on legs that were jointed like a hound. They bore the arms and armor of the fallen Carthaginian Empire, warped and stretched grotesquely over their monstrous frames. They were demons.

They could cultivate.

A whip-crack of sound and light stunned the men of the prime cohort. Links of chain lightning ripped through our shield wall in the blink of an eye, locking up limbs and staggering men for precious moments. The dogs howled and dove into our ranks with heavy spears and bronze blades. Men were torn apart, run through, and burnt out from the inside as the forces from Carthage drove lightning through their blades.

I grit my teeth and snarled against the lightning in my veins. I took my spear in both hands as three of the beasts lunged towards me and slammed its tip into the earth.

My virtue rocked the battlefield. Every arrow in the sky changed its course, careening through murders of shrieking crows to bury themselves in canine flesh. The wave of arrows drove back the first line of dogs for precious seconds. I shouted up and down the line. The ranks reformed around the dogs that had pierced through our formations, and legionaries of the prime cohort hacked them apart.

It only gave us time. It wasn't enough. Couldn't possibly be enough. They had overwhelmed the best of our legions when we outnumbered them four to one. We didn't have the advantage of numbers anymore. And we didn't have the greatest general in the Republic, either. The fifth legion only had me.

Centurions roared up and down the lines. The shield wall shifted as men moved up from the back to relieve the men up front, fresh blood to face the beasts of Carthage. I tore my spear from the earth and leveled it at the enemy. I panted harshly, my pneuma thundering through me.

But they didn't throw themselves mindlessly into our shields and spears. They fell back, and they parted around a single beast. The creature stared at me with burning golden eyes. Its lips peeled back from stark white fangs, and it snarled once. A word.

The vanguard dogs fell back, and hundreds more seamlessly took their place. Practiced. I watched in dread as the new arrivals closed ranks with one another and raised massive shields affixed to tree-trunk arms. Shields joined with shields, and the demons of Carthage vanished behind the largest shield wall the Mediterranean had ever seen.

A battle is lost the moment the men lose hope. I had known from the beginning that there was only one end to this fight. The first spear had known it. The officers. But the men of the rank and file, the infantry, had placed their hope in me. They'd trusted in me as they'd trusted my father, trusted my adopted father, to lead them through the bloody crucible alive if not whole. In all its years, the fifth legion of the western front had never once lost faith.

In that moment they did. And the battle was lost.

The captain of the Carthaginian demons snarled again, and their shield wall advanced. I saw terror in the eyes of my officers. I saw men twice my age look desperately to me for some command, some yet unseen miracle. I felt the cold breath of Tartarus as it breathed down my neck, wrapping its fingers around my throat.

A captain leads from the front.

I hollered in fury and plunged into the shield wall. My pneuma exploded from my soul, shattering through the front of their line as I ascended.

The world dissolved into the thunder of colliding shields, flashing blades, and snarling muzzles. I shattered shields with a spear that could have been used to pick their jagged teeth, driving through the beasts until I caught sight of the captain. It raised a man's hand, the skin thick and padded like a dog's paw, and lightning erupted between the tips of its clawed fingers. I slammed my spear through the dirt, driving my virtue into its depths. Beasts howled and yelped, thrown from their feet in a wide circle around me. The captain planted clawed feet and weathered it.

"You want my sons of Rome, dog?" I shouted furiously. My pneuma ran wild, spirit and hunger overwhelming reason in the throes of my ascension. "You can't have them! So long as I remain, I won't let you take a single one!"

The captain spoke.

"Then in hunger, this dog of heaven shall devour you."

It pulled a blade of obsidian stone from its sheath and coated its length with lightning. Then it moved, and I lunged forward to meet it.

Fight. Fight. Until the last man falls.

Fight. I drove my spear through a hound's yellow eye. **Fight.** I weaved my virtue through my fingers and crushed a dog's skull between them. **Fight.** I threw my spear with all my strength at the captain's retreating back, but a shield was raised against it. It pierced through the shield and the dog behind it, but not the one I wanted. And now I had no spear.

Fight. Men died. In numbers I couldn't track. In magnitudes that made my heart ache. Men that had raised me. Men that had taught me how to throw dice, how to hold a sword. They screamed, and they choked on their own blood as they died. The lightning took some. Swords and spears took others. Most, though, fell to sheer monstrous strength—fangs and clawed fingers.

Fight. I caught a beast's arm as it swung, twisting and slamming it over my shoulder. It arched up, and I stomped it to the earth. Its breastplate caved and shattered, and so did its chest. I heaved for breath, steam billowing from between my clenched teeth. It felt as if I was in a chariot careening down a mountain. My pneuma wouldn't stop, couldn't stop. When it did, I would die. I felt it deep in my bones.

"Rome," I breathed, catching a descending sword swing on my bare palms. The blade bit into the bone but could not sever. I wrenched it out of the demon's grip and swung the pommel into its skull like a mace, shattering it. "Rome!"

No one answered the call. I looked around. I saw corpses and crows, hundreds of prowling beasts. The stares of dead men drilled into me. They accused me. They judged me and found me wanting.

I was all that remained.

Fight.

A brassy cry split the heavens, and a sea of bronze struck the wolves of Carthage like a javelin. I stared, uncomprehendingly, as the beast legions were driven howling from the field by men in feathered helmets and shimmering bronze greaves. Their banners and tunics were scarlet. Rome's color. For a moment, I dared to hope.

Foolish.

They forced me to my knees before the Álikon captain, shackling and chaining my wrists. The man, tall and cruelly strong, rendered judgment upon me in the tongue of my childhood mentor.

"Son of Rome. Your life—"

"—is your own," Griffon told me. In his scarlet eyes, I saw the sun. "If you're still a slave tomorrow, it'll be because you chose it."

My pneuma, locked away for so many months, seeped through the cracks in my manacles. It brought everything with it. Pneuma was the essence of the soul. It was joy. It was grief. It was three thousand men, dead because I couldn't lead them home.

My eyes stung, and for the first time in a year, I tasted ash and salt on the wind.

Dry those eyes, young Solus. We don't weep until the battle is won.

I grit my teeth and stood.

Chapter Twenty-Two

THE SON OF ROME

Nothing was ever simple.

"Lio?"

Griffon's youngest cousin stood just outside the room where I'd hidden away to tune my lyre. Half-concealed by a marble pillar, he stared bewildered at my ruined manacles. I'd grown fond of Myron Aetos during my time as a slave. He was a powerfully gifted boy, yet still so young. Trusting. His sky-blue eyes looked first to me, then his cousin.

"What's going on?" he asked. "Why'd you leave the feast?"

"Sol and I are taking a walk," Griffon said easily. Utterly shameless, as always. "Care to join us, cousin?"

Myron visibly relaxed, suspicion giving way to curiosity. "Where are you going?"

"Olympia."

It was cruel, forcing a boy into this position. He could have lied. It was well within Griffon's ability to give a plausible excuse, send his cousin away. But that wasn't in his nature. His virtuous heart wouldn't tolerate such a thing. I rolled my wrists, considering my broken manacles. My pneuma was trickling in through their cracks, slowly, but not enough to manifest. I would have to tear them fully off.

Salt and ash. I clenched my fists and dropped them.

Myron looked like a deer before a lion. He backed up a single step.

"That's not funny," he whispered.

"No," Griffon agreed. "It's not."

Myron took off running, feet slapping against the marble floors of the junior mystiko estate as he fled. Griffon made no move to stop him, only glancing at me, raising an eyebrow challengingly.

"Well? It's now or never again." He strode out of the empty room, content with the audacity of what he'd come here to do. I hesitated, glancing back at the room's bed and its mound of woven wool blankets.

I lifted them carefully and met Athis' wide-eyed stare.

"Are you going with him?" she whispered. My heart lurched in my chest. Three thousand dead men whispered through the cracks in my manacles.

"I don't know."

Yet, even as I said it, I was picking up the lyre that I'd dropped and placing it on the bed. She reached desperately for my hand, her fingers slender and calloused by slave work. I squeezed her hand once and let it drop. Before I had consciously decided to do so, I was jogging down the hall to catch up with the arrogant Young Aristocrat of the Rosy Dawn.

"They'll never let us go," I said. My pulse pounded. The estate was all but empty, save for the slaves like myself and Athis that had disdained sleep but couldn't attend the party.

"Naturally. But tragedy of tragedies, my father and all my uncles and aunts are currently at the bottom of this mountain, inducting our honored guests into the greater mystery of the Rosy Dawn." He flicked his right hand, shooting rosy streamers of light through the air. "I trust you understand what that means."

Memories of glittering light and a bisected corpse with no face, not a single defining feature. Time slipped through my fingers like sand as I stared into the rising light held in its palm. The dawn. Every legendary cultivator on this mountain, and the patriarch himself, would emerge only after the rites were concluded. We had until the dawn.

"There are dozens of philosophers in this cult," I warned him. The elders of the Greek cult were men that could have been officers in a typical Roman legion or senior legionaries in those led by the Tyrant of the west. They *weren't* soldiers, of course. Not even close. But they had strength of heart to spare.

"Ho, are you scared?" Griffon asked jeeringly. My virtuous heart throbbed. "Where's your courage? Where's that *audacity?* We're on the precipice of adventure, and you're worried about a few old men?"

It was the prerogative of a cultivator to tempt the Fates. And, in return, it was the prerogative of the Fates to strike them down for their transgressions.

"*Stop.*"

An elder cultivator appeared at the end of the hall. He was tall, ornately clothed in layered robes of philosopher threads. His beard was long, bone-white, his eyes a dull blue that spoke to blindness yet intently traced every detail of us. His body was strong, if not tan or rugged. And as his eyes fell upon my manacles, his pneuma flooded the marble hall.

"Young Aetos!" he thundered. "What have you done?"

"Nothing at all, honored elder!" Griffon called, never once breaking stride as he approached the philosopher. I felt a tension long-buried reassert itself in my soul. I heard the marching drums. "This lowly sophist was just fetching his junior brother for the wedding festivities."

"His shackles are broken!" The philosopher stalked towards me, thundering retribution in his steps. "This is beyond audacity! There are limits, Young Aetos, even for you. Be assured that your father will be hearing about this, and as for *you*—"

He wasn't given the chance to finish. Griffon lunged forward with pneuma flaring, closing the remaining five steps between them in a single bound.

Cultivation was an odd thing. Throughout the known world, there were nearly as many interpretations of man's relation to heaven and earth as there were cities and kingdoms. The barbarous Gauls had their own primitive understanding of the virtuous realms that lead up to heaven, as did the Celtics and the Numidians across the sea. The Greek interpretation was in many ways similar to the righteous path of the Republic, but even then, there were notable differences.

I couldn't intuitively grasp the immensity of the gap between a captain of the Civic Realm and an elder several ranks deep into the Sophic Realm. These were not my cultural touchstones despite the efforts of my old mentor. My tongue may have been fluent in their chosen language, but my soul was not.

Still. No matter the culture, some things were simply absurd.

The elder reacted with speed far beyond the mortal limits of a man his age, and it was not enough. Griffon slipped his grasping hand with a snake's grace. His clenched fist rose, burning with the mark of his cult's foundational virtue, and drove up into the elder's gut.

Audacity wasn't a strong enough word to describe it. The elder gasped in disbelief as much as pain, and his pneuma exploded in a wordless virtue. Wind howled through the halls, his dull blue eyes flashing as he drove an open palm down onto Griffon's outstretched arm. My sense for pneuma was still restrained, but through the cracks in the shackles, I could feel the immensity of the force behind it. It was a blow that would shatter bone.

It missed.

Griffon had already withdrawn from the blow, already driven his knee up to meet the palm strike. An invisible thundercrack of force rocked the hall, rending the marble beneath their feet. The Young Aristocrat was no faster than the elder—if anything he was slower—but he moved as if their fight was choreographed.

He stomped his raised leg down onto the elder's foot, pivoted to avoid an attempt at a grapple, and latched onto the elder's outstretched arm. He exhaled sharply and slammed the philosopher over his shoulder. The old man's back struck the marble.

Griffon fell with him, driving the weight of his body and soul into his elbow and smashing the elder philosopher's head through solid stone.

For a moment no one moved. The elder because he was unconscious, maybe dead. Griffon and I because the immensity of what he'd just done required a moment of proper appreciation. We locked eyes.

"Now we run," he decided.

. . .

Drumbeats and the pounding noise of a thousand dancing feet hit us in a wave as we came charging out of the junior mystiko estate. The layout of the Rosy Dawn Cult was such that we could have disdained the central pavilion entirely, skirted its edge, or simply doubled back around the estate we'd just left and descended the mountain into the city of Álikos. Griffon had other plans, though. He ran headlong into the masses, countless initiates celebrating the wedding that was being consecrated beneath our feet in the heart of the mountain.

Flickering torchlight and stars lit the ruined mountaintop. The initiation rites had been outrageous enough the first time I'd experienced them, but watching hundreds upon hundreds of men and women, young and old, dancing without a care across a shattered pavilion that had been struck not an hour ago by the fist of a falling star defied belief. *Greeks.*

I threaded through the crowds at a less frantic pace, tracking the Young Aristocrat as he speared through. He moved with confidence, and when grace failed him, he adapted quickly. A woman in fine cult attire bumped into him as he passed, and he turned the collision into a graceful spin, twirling her into another initiate's arms and swiping her cup of spirit wine in the process. He downed it in one mouthful, scarlet liquid spilling past the corners of his mouth and trailing down his throat. He didn't once break stride.

My waxing senses traced the initiates around me, but there were too many cultivators packed too closely together, and I was still too restricted by my shackles to meaningfully distinguish between them. I couldn't feel the ire of any approaching enemies, but that did not mean they weren't there.

My eyes were drawn to the center of the pavilion where the falling star had struck. Where there should have been a yawning chasm, there instead was the fountain, reconstituting itself stone-by-stone in a bizarre example of passive cultivation. A faint mist hung around it, moisture being drawn out of the air itself and into the basin of the fountain in thin, spiraling threads.

The faceless statue had yet to reform. Instead, the fountain was filled with dancing women. As the drumbeats rose and the chanting wedding song rose to a new peak, they whirled and spun through its waters, kicking up waves. I counted nine before a shout drew my attention away.

Griffon waved an arm from the edge of the crowd, lips moving silently. I read them easily enough. *With purpose, slave.*

I burst out of the crowd, sprinting after him.

"Can you hear it?" he called over his shoulder. "The call to adventure screaming in your ear? It's deafening!" His mania was infectious. I opened my ears, casting out for such a sound.

All I heard was howling.

We sprinted through the mountaintop trails that connected the various estates to the central pavilion, pounding up the marble steps of the Aetos estate. Past its grand columns, the night horizon was slowly lightening to gray. Pre-dawn was giving way, the dead moon falling unseen from its peak. We were nearly out of time.

"Why through here?" I shouted as we blew through the halls of the main estate. The courtyard with its gardens and pools flashed by on our right, the past patricians of the Rosy Dawn standing timeless watch in their pools.

"I forgot something!"

Worthless, thoughtless *Greek.*

We ascended the steps to the second level of the estate and sprinted down the shadowed halls. Past the room that I knew to be Griffon's own quarters. Past the chambers of his male cousins and those of his uncles. He planted his feet and slid across the marble as we reached a room with a heavy wooden door at the end of the hall, and as he reached it, he reared back and kicked it off its hinges.

The office of the cult's patrician, Damon Aetos, was militantly furnished. It evoked memories of Gaius' personal quarters while on campaign, those simple tents with their cots and unadorned trunks. Shelves were carved into the smooth pale stone of the wall, filled end to end with rolls of papyrus and clay tablets. A desk of rich dark wood was central in the room, a dining table balanced on three legs and a reclining dinner couch next to it positioned in the far-right corner with an open terrace showing a view of the central pavilion. Tapestries hung on the walls, depicting battles and landscapes that I had never seen or heard of. Carved into the side of the desk itself was a scene of four men, three locked in furious combat against one.

Griffon disdained the desk, and whatever its contents may have been, and ignored the tablets and scrolls in their shelves. Instead, he crossed over to the far wall, where a sheathed blade was mounted between two tapestries. He lifted the blade off its hooks and gripped the sheath in one hand, the pommel in the other. Gently, he eased it just slightly out of its sheath.

I saw a sliver of bronze that burned even to my dulled senses, and then he slammed it back fully into the sheath and hooked it to his belt.

The sound of running feet drifted through the broken doorway.

"It seems we are found out," Griffon said, rolling his shoulders. He stepped up beside me, shoulder to shoulder. "Is it time for the Son of Rome to show what he's made of?" I clenched and unclenched my fists. I couldn't bring myself to tear those shackles off. I dreaded what would come next too much.

Griffon snorted coldly. "Perhaps he already has."

He walked past me.

"Lio!"

The Fates were truly cruel.

Myron hadn't simply run off. Of course, he hadn't. He'd known his limits well enough to understand he couldn't stop his older cousin alone, so he'd enlisted help. The young generation of the Aetos family had come to stop their wayward cousin.

Lydia Aetos' gaze slid from Griffon for a bare moment when I exited the patriarch's study, sky blue eyes flashing hatefully. They refocused in the next instant.

"Lio," she repeated, softer. "Tell me Myron heard you wrong. Tell me the things he said were lies."

She stood in the middle of the hall back the way we'd come, with Myron and her younger sister, Rena. The other two, Heron and Castor, were currently sprinting around the other side of the rectangular second floor to prevent us from running the other way. Castor had his blade, Myron's hands were fidgeting on his daggers, and the Young Miss herself held a spear longer than she was tall in one hand.

Griffon tilted his head, amused. "Seems you already know that's not the case."

"Don't do this," Lydia pleaded. "You only have to wait a little longer. We'll travel the world like Niko did, like our parents did. *Together.*"

"Lio," Heron seethed, skidding to a stop just a few feet behind us with Castor at his side. "This isn't another one of your games. There's no coming back from something like this!"

"Think of what you'd be throwing away," Castor urged. His eyes flickered, meaningfully, to his older sister. "And for what? A privilege you'll be given anyway in a few years? All you have to do is be *patient.*"

"Who says I want to travel with any of you?" Griffon asked curiously. My eyes narrowed. The impact of his words was a visible thing. Myron flinched like a kicked dog. Rena's expression crumpled in grief. And Lydia...

"You son of a bitch!" Heron lunged forward, but Castor caught him under the arms and wrenched him back. "You don't deserve any of what you've been given! None of it—"

"Enough!" Lydia snapped, pneuma lashing through the hall. Heron's teeth clicked together, even as he continued to glare. The Young Miss sighed explosively, mastering herself into something resembling calm. "Lio," she said, one last time. "I won't let you throw your life away for a slave."

"For a slave?" Griffon echoed, confused.

"Don't be coy!" Lydia leveled her spear at me. "You've been obsessed with that wretch since he arrived here. I don't know what it is about him that fascinates you, and I don't care either. Whatever it is, it's not worth throwing us all away!"

Griffon... laughed.

"You think this is about Sol?" He shook his head, untenably long hair waving with the motion. His shoulders shook with mirth. "How could a slave have anything to do with it? I've hated this city since I was a boy. I've spent every day of my life watching the horizon and wishing I was on the other side of it, anywhere but here.

"I won't suffer another day with you. My virtuous heart won't tolerate it."

Griffon told the truth, as he always had, and in doing so, he lied.

I watched the shock, the hurt, and the fury rippled through the sons and daughters of the Aetos line in grim resignation. It was delivered with no particular heat, no emotion. Matter of fact. Spoken by the man that had ascended in cultivation out of pure spite for the city he lived in and then chose to suffer that city for another four long months thereafter. The same man that had spent every waking moment of those four months in the company of his cousins, in some way or another.

That man told them the truth, that his cultivator's heart could not bear another moment of this life. But in so doing he lied. And they believed him.

I'd known from our first encounter that Griffon possessed a terrible charisma.

His cousins moved as one. Heron roared a curse and rushed past me with fists of burning red, Castor's sword flying from its sheath as he leapt clear over my head. Myron rushed in low with his knives, teeth grit in frustrated grief. Rena moved in his shadow, her fingers curved like claws. Lydia came at him head-on, without any attempt to feint. Her eyes were resolute, her spear blazing with pneuma that whirled in a helix of light around the tip.

Griffon didn't reach for his new blade. His pneuma rose, his scarlet eyes blazed, and he exploded into motion.

Heron was the first to reach him and the first to be struck. Griffon whirled and laid the heel of his foot across his cousin's face, staggering him against the wall. He lashed out with both hands, diverting Castor's descending blade with the back of one palm and burying his other fist in the young man's gut as he fell, driving the breath out of him. He pivoted, gripping Castor firmly by his wedding attire and slamming him down on top of Myron.

Rena was just far enough back to avoid the tangle of limbs. Everything I had seen of the girl, shy as she was, spoke to the kindly nature of a mother. But that was all gone as she dove into Griffon's guard with —*clawed fingers, crackling with beast lightning*—elongated nails enhanced by her pneuma. She raked furiously at him, moving with a fluidity that could only come with practice.

With that same fluidity, he deflected each and every swipe, turning her aside with a blow to the temple and then sweeping her feet so she fell on top of her brother and cousin.

Griffon leaned sideways, and the cyclone of light and heat whirling around Lydia's spear singed a few golden hairs as it thrust past.

"Good!" He grabbed the spear and drove a knee up into Lydia's stomach. When she twisted her hips and blocked it with her thigh, he swung the spear and her with it, tossing her into Heron as he approached. The rosy light coating the young man's hands flickered and died out so he could catch her.

The Young Aristocrat tilted his head to the right, dodging one thrown dagger and catching the other between two fingers. Myron was already midair as he did, body a blur as he spun into a roundhouse kick that Griffon had leaned his head directly into the path of. Scarlet eyes flashed, and Myron slammed sideways into the wall.

"Even better!" Griffon exclaimed, stepping through a whirling series of coordinated strikes between Rena's claws and Castor's blade. He diverted one into the other, laying a kick into Castor's side when he yanked back to avoid skewering his sister. "Show me what the young pillars are made of!"

Griffon turned and backhanded Heron across his face, sending him spinning through the air.

"I won't suffer another day in this life, so take me by force!" He dodged back as Lydia laid into him with quick, shallow jabs. Not far enough for him to grab anything but the flaming tip. She swept it from side to side, herding him back into the others. "Give me all you have!"

"So be it!" Lydia snapped. Her pneuma rippled and flared around the tip of her spear, a searing point of light gathering at its tip.

The other four followed suit. She'd herded Griffon into the middle of them, and as one their pneuma rose like a tidal wave. Five separate virtuous techniques flared like the dawn, on steel blades and clenched fists.

They moved together. Griffon sucked in a breath.

External manipulation of pneuma is the mark of the truly advanced and the even more truly gifted. Shaping the vital essence of the self into a physical thing, something that can be touched and felt, is a lesson in frustration. A cultivator must catch their breath and mold it like clay, must wrestle it into shape with their will alone, make order of it where it had once been nothing but formless chaos.

When properly done, a man could manifest through intent alone a blade, a spear, even arrows. The best could manifest many at once and control each individually. Swords of Intent. Spears of Intent. Arrows of Intent. What a man chose to shape his soul into said as much about him as any words could.

Griffon exhaled, and his Pankration Intent flooded the hall.

Ten arms of purest pneuma burst from the sea of his soul, noticeable even through the haze of my manacles, and struck each of his cousins mid-technique.

They grappled. They punched, slapped, and elbowed. They gripped Lydia's spear and forced it up, where it discharged its pinprick of light in a beam that shot up to heaven. They struck the thinner bones of Castor's wrists and shattered them, forcing him to drop his burning blade. They locked grips with Heron, pushing him down the same as they had before, in the Trial by Hunger.

Myron was wrestled down, and Rena's shining claws raked ineffectually at arms that could not bleed. Griffon walked out of the circle untouched, one hand on his hip and the other resting negligently on the pommel of his stolen blade. His cousins struggled and thrashed in his wake, fighting against the manifestation of his unwavering soul.

"You can't keep watching forever," he said. He glanced back over his shoulder, a single scarlet eye leveling me with his contempt. A single arm of his intent lashed out at me across the hall.

I caught it in my hand and crushed it.

"So strong," he said mockingly. "I can feel your soul straining against those shackles. Desperate to run free. When will you allow it? For how long are you going to run from your failures? How much of your future will you throw away for your past?"

I grit my teeth, fists clenching and unclenching. They were too heavy to raise. Salt and ash. *Salt and ash.*

"ENOUGH!"

A hurricane pillar howled up from the courtyards below, and on its winds rose four more cultivators. But these ones did not wear the tunics of junior mystikos, or even the fine scarlet clothes of seniors and favored children.

They wore the philosopher threads of elders, every single one. From the eye of the hurricane emerged a fifth, the same one whose head Griffon had planted through the marble floor. His nose was a broken ruin. The man was *livid*.

"This ends here!" the elder philosopher roared, and the hurricane followed his voice as it carried down the hall. "Your father was always too lenient with you. Come, vile boy, I will teach you the way of things in the real world you so covet! *Attend*."

The pneuma of all five elders flooded the estate. Griffon's eyes flickered back and forth, the hand on the pommel of the patrician's blade tensing. He drew it, just a sliver, from its sheath. Then he snorted and slammed it back home. His cousins slumped and gasped as the arms of his pankration intent withdrew, whirling around him.

Griffon glanced back at me.

"So you were a slave after all."

He dismissed me, turned, and advanced into the tide of rosy light and hurricane winds.

What does it take for a man to lead?

The children of Aetos, each in the process of recovering, slammed flat against the floor. The marble groaned and cracked, spiderweb fractures fanning out across its length.

What is it that calls others to him?

The head elder's hurricane virtue guttered out, dispersed, and was reformed. It whirled, like a cyclone, around a new central point.

*What gives them **faith**?*

Griffon grinned victoriously as my shackles clattered to the stone.

"*I knew it.*"

I raised an empty hand and clenched it.

Gravitas.

Five elder philosophers staggered beneath the gravity of the captain's virtue. Two of them fell entirely to their knees, unable to resist the pressure of my will. My pneuma did not rise. It did not pierce, thrust, or harry. It fell like a blanket across every shoulder and pressed them all down. Three of the philosophers, and somehow Griffon himself, remained standing. But it was an effort.

I cast forward my empty fist and opened it like I was throwing a knife. Gravity changed, sending Griffon's cousins tumbling and driving the five philosophers back across the marble. Griffon planted his feet, ten arms of pneuma gripped every banner, column, and railing they could to hold him in place. He laughed wildly.

My virtue carried down the hall, past the philosophers, and struck the farthest wall. It groaned and cracked and just barely held. I narrowed my eyes and flicked a finger.

The eastern wall of the Aetos estate screamed as it flew apart.

"What—" Lydia gasped as I passed her on the floor. She struggled to rise against my gravity, shoving a trembling arm beneath her. A few feet away, Myron had managed to come to one knee, barely. "What *is* this?"

I kicked the end of her spear, flipping it up into my hand.

"This is virtue."

I raced down the hall, and Griffon threw himself into a sprint alongside me. He grinned like a madman all the while as we weaved and leapt over and across one another in the press of the fight. His pankration intent was a storm of fists that shattered every guard, his own hands bloodied and scraped as they drove into the bones of men with bodies enhanced far beyond his own. I whirled my stolen spear with Gaius' virtue affixed to its tip, drawing virtuous techniques into it and away from us as it swept through their ranks.

Scarlet light bloomed on the horizon, visible through the gaping hole I'd blown through the wall. Griffon and I locked eyes, and words weren't needed for what came next.

I planted both feet and reared back my spear. It was too long to be thrown like a javelin, unwieldy and poorly balanced. It didn't matter. I shouted and threw it with all my strength, and gravitas led it straight and true. It struck one philosopher and produced a shockwave that threw him into another. In the same moment, all ten of Griffon's pankration arms swarmed the final elder that stood between us and the end of the hall, dragging, beating, and grappling him through the air. Griffon cast him bodily over our shoulders, into the two elders behind us.

And the path revealed itself.

"Lio, please! *Don't go!*" Lydia cried out. There were tears in her eyes.

I was the only one that saw the moment he hesitated.

But this choice had been made for him long ago. His cultivator's soul would accept nothing less. "It's Griffon!" he shouted joyfully and took off in a dead sprint. I matched him every step of the way.

We reached the precipice together and leapt out without hesitation.

The sun breached the Ionian Sea. The rosy-fingered dawn reached out across the heavens.

Griffon spread his arms against the wind, laughing in pure and honest joy as we plummeted through open air, off the mountain entirely. His pneuma rippled and pulsed. His soul rejoiced, and in the light of the cresting dawn, the wings of his pneuma flew wide for the first time. He ascended.

My own pneuma rushed back to me in a flood, everything that had been locked behind chains since that day. I felt it all in excruciating clarity. The memories. The funeral ash and the sea salt. The corpses. Crows. Three thousand men laid hands upon me, clawing, pulling, dragging me back to the mountaintop. Back to enslavement.

I wouldn't let them. Not yet.

The battle was yet to be won.

Interlude: Selene

"Take care, cultivator. Your heart is not your own."

Selene cast off her golden veil, rising before a broken man. The whisper of shifting cloth and his own ragged breaths were the only sounds to be heard in the temple. Her shawl fell away from her shoulders, revealing an armored breastplate of purest gold. An ornately crafted spear came to her hand, its shaft a bone-white wood inlaid with carved prophecies and its head a glimmering bronze.

The cultivator's fine tunic was drenched in sweat, his traveling cloak draped over his hunched body like a funeral shroud. He had attractive features, as most powerful cultivators did, but they were made grotesque by his anguish. His gold was scattered across the floor between them—he'd barely had the strength to dump it out of his purse.

"I beg the Oracle," he gasped, pupils quivering. "I will pay any price. Just make me whole again."

In the beginning, when the first man was molded from clay by a titan with no face or name that could be remembered, order was made of chaos. The titans and their children, the gods of Olympus, were the first ordered existence to emerge from the primordial sea. Humanity, then, was made in their image. An imposition of order on the earth mother's materials.

To cultivate virtue was to make order of a chaotic soul. It was humanity's long march towards the light of enlightened civilization reflected in a single man's journey. Cultivators rose on the principles that had built the strongest empires of history, and they fell in just the same way.

Internal strife had toppled more than one great empire. If she did not step in here, it would soon topple another.

"Have hope," Selene told the cultivator, smiling softly. "You're not alone anymore."

She drove her spear through his chest and dove into the sea of his soul.

Virtue was a winding mountain path. A man could walk it in the light of day or the darkest night and never stray from it, and he could just as easily be lost. Or, if he was truly unfortunate, driven off it. By wind, by rain, or by virtuous beasts. It was an easy thing to lose course in the slightest of degrees. Over time, those minute diversions might not amount to more than a few grains of sand slipping through cupped palms.

But it was a cultivator's nature to seek greater heights and ascend Olympus Mons. With every ascending step, a cultivator became more of what they were. Their every essence grew exponentially. Those grains of sand became stones, and those stones became boulders. Even the greatest cultivator could only carry so much weight up the divine mountain.

Souls deviated in those small moments. That is how heart demons were born.

The souls of cultivators were said to be grand things, marble edicts built by their unwavering virtue. A soul plagued by a heart demon, though, was a ruin. Selene stepped into the cultivator's soul and looked upon a devastated landscape. Broken pillars and crushed marble were all her eyes could see. The parthenon of the cultivator's heart, the central edifice of his cultivation, had been torn down to its foundation and set aflame. The demon of the cultivator's heart watched with satisfaction as it burned.

"*You*," the cultivator said, suddenly at her side. Here, within the sea of his soul, he stood unhindered by the agonies that had incapacitated him in the waking world. Not for much longer, though. Even now, sweat beaded on his brow. His hands faintly tremored.

"Me?" the heart demon echoed, turning away from the vast conflagration. He was a mirror image of the cultivator, save for a scar that ran from the bottom of his square chin to the corner of his right eye. It was a wound that his cultivation had long ago healed externally. Superficially.

"Demon of my heart," the cultivator seethed. "I've come to kill you."

"Of course, you have." The heart demon sneered, strolling down the parthenon's broken steps on light feet. The smoke and miasma of the burning wreckage whirled and coiled into his palm, forming a blade that matched the one in the cultivator's white-knuckled grip. "It's what you do, after all. Man, woman, or child. The old men snap their fingers, and you go hunting like a dog."

The cultivator bared blood-stained teeth. "Vile imposter. A man of the cult does what he must. I refuse to accept that any part of me could be as cowardly as you."

"And we are *brave*, aren't we?" the heart demon mused, whirling his dark blade in hand. "These hands of ours built such a fine monument. Any of the free cities would have been proud to lay claim to such a monolith. What a tragedy that it fell so quickly." He smiled faintly. "The foundations always were weak."

The cultivator shouted and leapt forward, locking blades with the demon of his heart in the ruin of his soul. Before his deviation, he had been a man of wide renown for his martial prowess. It showed in the ferocity of his bladework, the intensity of his pneuma.

But to call it an even fight would have been far too charitable.

"Here he comes, the butcher with his blade!" the heart demon taunted, parrying lightning-quick strikes with horrible ease. "It's been some time since you've faced an opponent that could fight back, hasn't it? It shows!"

The heart demon lashed out, once, and opened up a gouge across the cultivator's face. From the bottom of his chin to the corner of his right eye, a perfect match to the heart demon's own. The significance of the wound staggered the cultivator as much as the pain of it. The memory likely hurt him more.

"Don't lose heart now," the heart demon spoke, advancing with his grimacing smile. "Remember your virtue, dog. Remember the path you made slick with blood. What was it the old men said?"

The cultivator gripped his blade with both hands and snarled, swinging with all his strength. The heart demon blocked it with one hand on his sword. With the other, he took the cultivator's throat in hand and lifted him from his feet.

"**Courage,**" the heart demon snarled. "Courage until the job is done—"

The demon choked. He looked down at the bronze-headed spear buried in his gut, confused. For the first time, he seemed to see her. And then the burning light in his eyes faded, and he slumped over the bone-white shaft of her weapon. The cultivator fell to the ground, choking and clutching his face, while the demon of his heart slid slowly off her weapon.

"Is—" The cultivator coughed. The heart demon's grip had left bruises on his throat. "Is it done?"

Selene looked sadly down at the corpse. She shook her head once. "Cast the body into the fire, cultivator, else it will rot inside your soul."

He grunted and forced himself to his feet, dragging the twin corpse over his shoulder and trudging up the steps of the burning parthenon.

The cultivator heaved the corpse of his guilt into the flames.

"There is nothing else I can give you? Truly?" The cultivator was on his knees before her, back in the temple that housed the Oracle. His eyes were shining with relief. "This lowly sophist swears he'll fulfill any wish, no matter how steep!"

It was terrible, watching them fall back into the same habits that had brought them to her. Selene only smiled and donned her shawl and veil of gold, obscuring her features more than the mists already did.

"Focus on the wishes of your own heart first," she advised him.

Most didn't listen, of course, but that didn't mean she would stop trying. "Live so that I never have to see you again."

The cultivator bowed his head deferentially. Almost as an afterthought, he pulled another purse from the folds of his traveler's cloak and dropped it at her feet. It chimed, drachma against drachma, as it struck the marble. A small fortune, but to a cultivator of his renown, it was hardly a day's labor.

"Then you have my undying thanks," he said. He rose to leave, hair matted to his skull and still drenched with sweat, but already he looked stronger. Healthier. The only lasting remnant of his near-death were the strangulation marks around his throat and the gouge across his face. Selene hoped he'd let it scar. Some things needed to be remembered.

The cultivator hesitated at the temple's entrance. She waited patiently for the question he was trying his best not to ask.

"... Honored Oracle," he finally said, "have you seen my fate?"

"I'm sorry, cultivator," Selene said. "You know the gods don't speak to us anymore."

The cultivator sighed, nodded, and left.

Selene sat on the sacrificial tripod of the temple of the Oracle and closed her eyes. The echo of the fallen sun god's death throes were deafening in her ears.

The free cities of the Mediterranean had long forgotten the names and faces of the Greek pantheon, and the gods no longer whispered prophecies in their ears. But that didn't mean the oracles stopped listening. It didn't mean there was nothing left to be heard.

That night Selene dreamed of a war that would shake the heavens and a serpent with the sun in its mouth.

Act II: Raging Heaven

Chapter Twenty-Three

THE SON OF ROME

The *Eos* was a ship built for speed. Her hull was sleek, and her scarlet sails caught the wind like eagle wings, driving her through the waves at speeds that belied all common sense. It was a beautiful day for her to sail.

It was my first time on an open sea. The taste of salt on the air was all too familiar, but the cresting blue waves, the vast empty horizons, and the steady rolling of the deck beneath my feet were all entirely new experiences. I'd had my doubts when Griffon had suggested sailing—and, in particular, sailing this ship—but most of my concerns had quickly been put to rest. It was an exhilarating experience.

Still, there were complications to consider.

"They're going to be furious," I said, leaning on the rail at the bow. The Ionian Sea stretched out endlessly ahead, clear blue and shimmering in the sun.

"Will they?" Griffon asked behind me, and I could hear the roll of his eyes. "I hadn't realized. What other profundities does the son of Rome have to offer?"

He'd stacked every single rowing bench on the ship into a bizarre approximation of a throne and now lounged in it while the ship's oars and favorable winds steadily propelled us forward. I'd allowed the absurd display as he was doing the hard sailing. His pneuma intent had grown alongside the rest of his cultivation when he'd ascended, and where there had been ten arms before there were now twenty. Each arm of pure intent heaved on the oars of the *Eos*.

"More than they would have been if we hadn't stolen their ship," I clarified, turning to him and leaning back against the ship's rail. "Why did you feel the need to slap every face you possibly could on your way out the door?"

The faint cries of sea birds and the rolling slaps of waves against the *Eos'* hull hung between us while the former Young Aristocrat of the Rosy Dawn considered his answer. His right cheek rested on his fist, scarlet eyes glittering with the satisfaction of a lion that had just eaten its fill. He'd slipped his scarlet and white robes off his shoulders early on into the voyage so that they hung down around his belt, leaving his torso bare. He looked utterly content.

For now.

"Tell me something, Sol," he said. "Are you familiar with the hero's journey?"

"Vaguely." Faint memories of an old man in weathered Álikon cloth, afternoons spent in the vineyards discussing everything under the sun.

"There are an infinite number of paths to the peak of Olympus Mons, but it's a fact of life that some are more often tread than others," he explained. "Every man likes to think he's unique, but all too often we're just echoes of those that came before us. We all labor within the divine framework. As such, there are certain constants that any man can expect to run up against in the race to divinity."

Griffon lazily raised his free hand, lifting fingers one by one. "Bottlenecks. Deviations. Trials."

"Tribulations," I said. Lightning falling from clear blue skies. Griffon inclined his head.

"It's the nature of the Fates to decide our lives for us from the moment we're born. As we draw our first breath, they know. Which among us will be Tyrants, and which will be slaves. It's why they hate men like you and me." He smiled, something vicious in the quirk of his lips. "They know that their only choice is to kill us in the cradle because we will never, *ever* submit.

"To cast off destiny's threads a man must first live an utterly audacious life. No one is born a Tyrant, and there are no shortcuts to the peak of the mountain. How is it, then, that men ascend at all? The Fates know us fully at the moment of birth. Intuitively, there are only two possibilities—that the Fates *can* be defied or that ascension is a lie, and we're all just dancing to our graves while heaven beats its drums."

Griffon shrugged. "I choose to believe the former. And because I believe it, it is so. Until the moment I die my life is my own, and so I'll always be reviled by the Fates. Tribulations are inevitable. Why cringe away from them?"

"So instead," I said incredulously, "you welcome them with open arms."

"They're the best part of the journey, after all."

My heart and soul for a companion with sense.

"If that's the case, Olympia is where we part," I decided. He laid a palm on his bare chest, eyes closing in mock hurt. I snorted. "I have enough madness ahead of me without throwing you onto the pile."

"Oh? What sort of madness? Is it the kind that howls?"

For some reason that I still wasn't quite sure of, I'd told him the story of my time in the legions as we ran through the fields of the Rosy Dawn towards the docks. I'd told him as we rigged his cousin's ship and cut it loose, and as the sun fully rose to light up the Ionian Sea, I'd seen in vivid clarity the hunger in his eyes as he listened.

"It is," I decided.

"And how is one son of Rome going to tear down an empire of demons?" Griffon asked curiously. "Your legions are dead and gone."

My fists clenched and unclenched. "How does any man stand against an empire?"

"And you call me mad." Griffon chuckled. His arms of pankration intent withdrew into his soul all at once, the *Eos* coasting to a steady halt in the calm waves. "How can a Roman ever hope to raise an army of Greeks against anyone but himself?"

"The legions of the Republic were the finest in the world," I said, and before he could make a smart remark, I continued, "We triumphed over superior numbers and individuals of absurd cultivation as a matter of course. That those dogs drove us from our provinces, flushed us from our city, and tore apart our legions? With *smaller numbers?*" I snarled and spat over the side of the ship. "They're dogs, but they're war dogs. They were built for this work.

"If they only wanted Rome, then fine. I'll climb that fucking mountain and bury them under the sea with my strength alone. But if they're the kind of animals I think they are, they won't stop at just one. They'll be at your father's door next, and then I won't have to raise the army. Damon Aetos will do it for me."

One way or another, I'd tear that captain's throat out and eat his beating heart.

"That's my kind of plan," Griffon said approvingly. "But there is *one* flaw in your reasoning, and as your blood brother, I can't help but point it out."

I sneered. "We aren't brothers."

"Worthless Roman, we have been from the start." He leaned forward, elbows on his knees. His pneuma was alight. "And as your brother, I must ask the hard questions. First and foremostly, what makes you think that these dogs of Carthage will pose a threat to my father? Just because they thrashed your glorious Republic? The same Republic that never once dared to war with our free city-states?"

"After Gaul, you were next," I informed him simply. He smirked.

"I'm sure we were. But even if I were to believe that, there's another flaw in your plan."

I raised my own pneuma, flexing muscles that had gone unused for months on end. The waves around the *Eos* shuddered and pulsed.

"Enlighten me."

"You're under a delusion," Griffon informed me, "that anything you do will make what's to come any less mad, any less ruinous. We were marked by the Fates from the beginning, and you've already begun to suffer their attention. Run from me if you'd like. It won't make a difference."

I made to answer but was interrupted by the sound of beating wings. An eagle's cry split the air, and from the sky dove the predator itself, talons spread wide. I raised an arm, some instinct holding back my pneuma, and it landed roughly on my forearm. Its talons sank into my flesh, would have shredded it if not for the reinforcement of my cultivation.

I stared, lost for words, at the messenger eagle of Rome. It tilted its head left and right, watching me expectantly. It had no scroll on its leg.

"The poets like to say that the Epic doesn't start until a man ascends to the Heroic Realm," Griffon mused. The eagle cocked its head and whistled sharply at him. "But the truth is, the winds have been blowing for a year now. The Muses are already watching. How can we do anything but give them a show?"

On the horizon, a ship appeared. It was a light, shallow-bottomed vessel. Its sails were ragged, its oars pumping furiously against the waves. As it breached the far horizon and we became as visible to it as it was to us, its course changed at once.

"Pirates?" I whispered, watching it come for us.

"Heaven beats its drums," Griffon said, rising from his throne and stretching. "Are you ready to dance?"

I stared at him for a silent moment.

Gravitas.

Griffon laughed as the captain's virtue threw him from the ship. The eagle on my arm shrieked and took flight as twenty arms of pneuma latched onto me and dragged me over the rail with him.

Chapter Twenty-Four

THE STARK BLADE, NIKOLAS

Slayer of monsters.

It was a title Niko had been given the day he ascended. A title most cultivators within the Heroic Realm received, sooner or later. A natural consequence of the lives they lived. He took pride in it—as he knew his wife and companions did. The life of a Hero was fraught with dangers, both internal and external, but that was part of what made it so rewarding.

Celebrating success was important. It wasn't always the case that the monsters lost, after all. He'd seen that particular reality for himself. Lived it since he was a boy.

There were some monsters that even Heroes couldn't slay.

Damon Aetos stood in the gaping entry to his office. His door had been kicked cleanly off its hinges. The force of the conflict that had taken place in the hall had carried through the open entry, shattering the dining couch and table entirely. The contents of the wall-carved shelves were scattered around the room—some had been blown clear off the terrace, into the central pavilion outside.

The Tyrant of the Rosy Dawn stepped into his office and righted his desk. It had been thrown up against the back wall, but unlike the other furniture, it had weathered the blow. Lacking a proper seat, he leaned back against it, arms crossed.

"Enter."

Niko entered the ruined office with his bride at his side, a bracing hand on the small of her back. She was tense, understandably so. The initiation rites were a bewildering experience, even to a cultivator of her stature, and the mystery at the bottom of the eastern mountain range baffled the mind no matter where you stood among heaven and earth. Niko had wondered, as they descended, whether it would be different now that he'd reached the same realm as his aunts and uncles, if there would be any greater clarity. But no. It had been just the same.

Then they'd exited the mountain, reeling from the mystery of the bisected corpse of the fallen sun god, and found the cult in chaos. It hadn't been hard to guess who was behind it.

Niko's stomach sank as his cousins slunk into the office like beaten dogs. They had the marks to match their posture, too. Bruises, split lips, and black eyes abounded. The entire right side of Heron's face was already darkening into an ugly purple bruise, leftover from a vicious backhand. Poor Rena's left eye was almost entirely swollen shut. Castor gingerly cradled a broken wrist, and Myron walked with a noticeable limp.

Lydia was the worst by far. She had escaped with the least physical damage, but her expression was haunting. She looked utterly lost. As the five of them knelt in front of the kyrios, she was the only one who didn't look shamefully at the floor. She stared straight ahead.

"What happened here?" Damon asked. His voice was level. Iphys inhaled quietly, circulating her pneuma. Niko shook his head. She glanced at him, hesitated, but released it.

If it came to that, it wouldn't matter anyway.

"I saw Lio leave the pavilion," Myron said. The other three cousins that were paying attention to the conversation visibly relaxed. "He'd been acting strange since Niko arrived, so I followed him. He went looking for Sol—"

"Sol?" Damon interrupted. Myron swallowed.

"The slave, Uncle. The one that Lio sponsored for initiation."

"Why do you know this slave by name?" Damon asked.

"We used to spend time together, the three of us," Myron admitted.

"And why were you spending time with a slave?" It was asked with no particular inflection. Even so, the dread it invoked was palpable. Heron gritted his teeth, warring with himself, but he was beaten to the punch before he could speak up on his younger brother's behalf.

By Myron himself. "He's skilled, Uncle. I tried to ambush him when we first met, and I couldn't touch him, even in chains. He's wise, too. He and Lio helped me get through my bottleneck over the summer. And... Lio acted like he used to when he was with Sol. It was fun."

Not for the first time since returning home, Niko marveled at the boy his youngest cousin had become in just a few short years. Only nine years old and already facing challenges that his elder cousins balked at. He was growing at a prodigious rate, and it was clear that it hadn't gone to his head. Though perhaps there had been another hand involved in that.

"I see," Damon said. His nephews and nieces waited nervously. "Continue."

Myron exhaled. "He went looking for Sol. When he found him, he broke his manacles. I asked what they were doing, and he said—"

"Olympia," Lydia murmured. "He said he was going to Olympia."

Myron nodded miserably. "I should have tried to talk him down, at least stall for time until the rites finished, but I panicked. I went and found Lydia, and then we split up to get the others. I found Castor and Rena while she went after Heron. By the time we joined back up, they'd already made it here."

"So you tried to fight him," Damon stated. Nods. He hummed. "Elders, a moment."

Five honored philosophers of the Rosy Dawn entered the kyrios' office with what dignity they could. For all that they dwarfed Niko's cousins in rank of cultivation, they had been savaged far worse in the escape. Three of them, philosophers Niko had not personally known before he departed from the cult, were covered in the inflamed red skin of coming bruises. The fourth was cradling a broken jaw. He was a younger man that Niko remembered vaguely as being a senior of his back when he was a mystiko. Was it Dymus? Pollio, maybe?

The fifth philosopher was a man Niko knew all too well. Old Chersis the uncharitable. The infamously surly tutor that every young pillar of the Rosy Dawn had to suffer at some time or another. Niko had been the first to receive his wisdom, and it had not been a pleasant experience for either of them. Before he'd left, Lio and Lydia had just started their lessons with the old philosopher.

He supposed the broken nose summed up Lio's opinion of his tutor rather succinctly.

"Who did this to you?" Damon asked the wise men of the cult.

Niko liked to think of himself as a virtuous man, on his good days at least, and his wedding day was better than most. Still, there was a not insignificant part of him that enjoyed every single moment of old Chersis struggling to explain how the little lion of the Rosy Dawn had thrashed him not once, but *twice* in the span of an hour. There was some pride there as well. It was a complicated feeling.

When the story was fully told by all those involved, Damon closed his eyes in silent deliberation. Tense moments passed. He sighed.

"In summation, my son defeated the five of you alone and unarmed, simultaneously," he said, addressing the children. "Then," he continued, "he made a mockery of the elders that this cult holds in such high regard, that are showered with resources and renown in exchange for their competence and wisdom. Not once. But twice."

"Lord Damon," Chersis protested, "I did not expect him to do something so..."

"Bold," Niko offered. His old tutor looked sharply at him.

"*Cheeky*. I did not expect the son of the kyrios to so brazenly strike at his own tutor. The second occasion he was not alone."

"Ah, yes," Damon said. "He had a slave."

"He was no ordinary slave, Lord Damon," one of the horrifically bruised philosophers insisted. "His pneuma was in the Sophic Realm at least, and his virtue was incredibly potent—"

"Potent?"

Ah, there it was.

The tyrant's fist.

Niko held his bride firmly to him, lest she crumple to her knees beneath the weight of Damon Aetos' pneuma. She reached back and grabbed his hand tightly. Her eyes were wide and intent, the way they always were before a fight, but her grip was white-knuckled with panic. Iphys was strong enough to know just how far beyond them the kyrios of the Rosy Dawn cult was. It was an all too familiar feeling for Niko.

"The slave's virtue was too potent for you," Damon repeated. "And those bruises, those were his work as well? He did that to you with his spear?"

"No, Lord Damon," the unfortunate philosopher said through gritted teeth. His head bowed, as surely as the sun set, before the kyrios' pressure.

"Who, then?"

"The Young Aristocrat," Old Chersis bit out. "It was a joint attack between them."

"I believe I've heard enough excuses," Damon said quietly. The philosophers shut their mouths and awaited judgment, and in that moment, they looked little different from the children kneeling on the floor. "Return to your estates. Do not leave them for any reason until I've come for you myself. And, if you so choose, take this time to contemplate tonight's events."

His smile was an executioner's blade. "It might be wise."

The philosophers fled the room, and the tyrant pulled back his fist. Niko inhaled slowly, marveling at the sudden lack of pressure. How long had it been since a cultivator's sheer presence had driven his soul into such a corner like that? How long had it been since anything, monster or man, had filled him with such unshakeable dread?

Since he'd first ascended to the Heroic Realm, Niko had been walking on glass. He was still acclimating to the changes in his tripartite soul, still worried even when interacting with his cousins who were all deep into the Civic Realm. They still felt like baby birds in his hands. He couldn't trust himself to rough house with them like he used to, let alone truly spar. He'd become far too strong in too short a time.

Was that how a Tyrant felt, to look at a Hero? At what point did the entire world feel as if it was made of glass?

"Nikolas." Niko straightened. There was something in his uncle's eye. "I'm sorry. He took your father's sword." Iphys looked back at him, concerned. She knew the story, of course. He'd told her.

"I see," he rasped.

"That impudent child," came a voice from the hall. The twin eagles of the Rosy Dawn and their wives entered the office. Niko's aunts went to their children at once, raising their faces and checking them for serious or disfiguring injuries. Stavros Aetos placed a hand atop Heron's head, his expression a storm as he locked eyes with his brother. "We warned you for years. Years, Damon! How many times has that boy spat on the name of the Rosy Dawn while you sat back and watched him fondly? How many times has he shirked his duties as heir? And now *this?*"

Damon's eyes narrowed. "You want to do this now?"

"He took Iskander's blade." Fotios Aetos stood beside his brother, rigid with outrage. "He beat our children like dogs and discarded my daughter *three months before their marriage!* We're doing it now!"

"What would you have me do?"

"I want him disowned!" Fotios snapped. Niko had never seen him so furious. Watching Aunt Chryse attempt to console Lydia, still slumped on the marble floor, he found it hard to hold it against his uncle.

"Never," Damon said immediately. Fotios' expression darkened, and Niko wondered if this was the day he'd see a tyrant fight. But Stavros clamped a hand on his brother's shoulder, stopping him before he said something he couldn't take back.

"Disinherited, then," Stavros said. When Damon didn't immediately respond, he went on, "Look at our children, Brother. Look at what your son has given them in return for their love. A kyrios' hands didn't leave those marks. This isn't *justice.*"

Damon stared at his younger brother for a long moment.

"Chryse. Raisa. Take the children, please."

Niko's aunts looked worriedly between their husbands and their brother-in-law but ultimately complied. Niko whispered assurances to his cousins as they passed, squeezing Rena's shoulder and pulling Castor into a quick one-armed hug. Then it was only the pillars and them. Niko decided that was still two too many and quietly ushered Iphys towards the door.

"Stay."

He looked back, confusion and a low dread in his gut. "Uncle?"

"My brothers demanded we do this now, so we will," Damon said. And then, simply, as if observing the weather, he declared, "As of now, my son is disinherited. I have no other children, so the burden of the kyrios falls to the next best candidate among my nephews and nieces."

The dread rose.

"What does that have to do with me?" Niko asked, though he already knew.

Damon smiled faintly. "Congratulations, nephew."

Niko looked to his other two uncles for help. Both of them had sons. Surely, they'd rather one of them take on the role? But no, while Stavros and Fotios were both scowling ferociously at the blatant snub, when they met his eyes, they only nodded in agreement. No, no, *no*. He didn't want their blessing! He didn't want *this!*

In that moment, he understood perfectly what his little cousin had been feeling. And he decided he was going to do exactly the same thing about it. As soon as his uncles entered their closed-door cultivation, he was going to jump in his ship and sail far, far—

"Niko!" a Hero's voice carried from outside. The fastest of their companions leapt up and through the gaping hole in the eastern wall of the Aetos estate, sliding down the hall in the blink of an eye and catching himself roughly on the door frame. He was heaving for breath, his eyes wild. The Heroic cultivator held up a length of severed rope.

"They took the *Eos*."

Son of a *bitch*.

Chapter Twenty-Five

THE YOUNG GRIFFON

Twenty arms of pankration intent pulled me from the sea, a crawling mass of grasping hands heaving me up and over the bow of the encroaching ship. I spat seawater and raked a hand through my soaked hair, surveying the deck.

The galley was a shallow thing, hardly fit for trade—a proper trireme would have dwarfed it. Even the *Eos* was a bit larger. It was a vessel built for speed and agility over deep waters and shallow coastlines both. A beautiful racing girl despite her ragged sails and sparse oars. Her keel had been lashed by rough strokes of white and blue paints, and up at the front, I could see her figurehead. No woman or beast. Just a single grasping hand.

A shout went up and down the deck as my presence was noticed. There were ten men at the oars, five on each side, and all of them twisted and jerked on their benches at the sight of me. There was a pitiful mix of terror and hope on their grubby faces as they tried to get away. They couldn't move far, unfortunately. They'd been shackled to their oars.

The slavers in charge of the vessel pounded down the deck towards me. I leapt fully onto it, rolling my neck and striding forward to meet them. The wings of my pneuma unfurled, blanketing the vessel.

The *Eos* was still a distant blot on the horizon. It was only just barely possible to make out the silhouette of a man crouching on the ship's figurehead.

The *Eos* dipped sharply, rocking in the water, and the man was gone.

"Well now, this is hardly fair," I said, spreading my arms wide. "I don't even have a blade!" Indeed, my late uncle's sword was still in its sheath back on my cousin's ship. I was utterly defenseless before these sea thieves.

The pirate closest to where I boarded the vessel growled a curse in a language not my own, a curved *kopis* in his right hand and a braided lash in his left. He cracked the whip in an effort to disorient me, the edge of the cord kissing my nose, and swept in with his sword.

The backs of twenty palms struck his cheek at one moment, throwing him spinning into the ocean.

"Have any of you been to Olympia recently?" I asked, continuing forward while the rest of the pirates staggered to a stop. They eyed me warily. "I'm on my way to visit, and I want to make the most of it. Any suggestions?"

Unfortunately for me, they didn't get a chance to respond. A shadow passed over the ship in that instant, and two of the pirates looked up just in time to be smashed flat against the deck by a falling Roman. The slave galley rocked as Sol discharged his virtuous technique at the point of impact, arresting his momentum and driving the two hapless pirates cleanly through the wood. He stood, rolling his shoulders.

"My uncle said that two things were universal when it came to pirates," Sol said, holding out an empty hand. His virtue called, and a blade leapt to his palm, courtesy of one of the thieves he'd just flattened. "They cheat at dice no matter what and hunger endlessly above their station. One is a symptom of the other. The punishment for both is the same."

"You kill people for cheating at dice?" I asked, confused.

"No. We crucify them."

The deck groaned and cracked beneath the weight of a gravity that had not been there before. The remaining slavers, seven strong and armed to the teeth, fell to their knees. The slaves slumped over their oars, unable to bring any pneuma to bear in defense against the Roman's virtue. Their eyes rolled wildly in their heads.

"You crucify people," I repeated, "for cheating at dice."

One of the pirates spoke furiously, struggling to raise his head.

Sol frowned. "What did he say?"

"Just bring your own dice and they can't cheat," I reasoned.

"They said that?"

"No, *I* said—"

Hngh.

I looked down, surprised, at the bolt protruding from my stomach. Where had that come from? I touched it experimentally, wincing at the sharp stab of pain it invoked. It was real. I heard seven slavers roar and lurch across the deck at Sol, hoping to overwhelm the lone cultivator while I was stunned. I squinted at the bolt. It had entered through my back.

Behind me, a loose plank slid near soundlessly back into place. I inhaled, eyes rolling back into my head. *Ow.* Twenty hands of pankration intent smashed through the deck of the ship, pulling a thrashing young boy from underneath. He wiggled like a fish, fruitlessly trying to kick and bite the arms of my soul. He was small, around Myron's age if I had to guess, and he was clutching the most bizarre bow I'd ever seen.

I pressed him to the deck and slapped his face twenty times with my pankration intent, leaving him stunned. I took the bow in my hand, and when he lurched up with it like a barnacle, I gave him another twenty slaps. He fell back, clutching his face and moaning. I laid a kick into his ass for good measure, inspecting his weapon.

It was a bow and yet it was not. It had been mounted to a shaft, and at the shaft's end, there was a curved brace with wooden handles on either side. The string was attached to a sliding mechanism which the brace at the end of the handle was used to prime. I recognized the design. This was the first time I'd ever seen such a thing in person, though. It was a crude, inefficient weapon for a cultivator. The Rosy Dawn cult had no need for such a thing.

Though it clearly had its uses, I tossed it into the sea, ignoring the boy's protesting cry, and I reached behind my back. I snapped the back of the shaft, took another breath, and pulled the arrow out from the front in one swift motion.

The boy shrieked as my pankration arms rained slaps upon his face.

Wood shattered, and the ship rolled dangerously beneath my feet, doing wonderful things to my wound. Worthless Roman. If you wanted to sink the ship, you should have just done so to begin with. I stalked across the deck, catching a pirate with pankration arms as he hurtled through the air, planting him through the boards.

Sol was either taking his time or was atrociously bad at fighting on a moving ship. He wielded the pirate's unfamiliar blade with admirable dexterity, parrying and casting aside multiple blades at once, but his opponents were wily on the deck. They moved between the shackled oarsmen, striking only with short, weaselly chops and stabs.

They were all too susceptible to the Roman's virtue, but so was the ship.

"It occurs to me—" I paused, coughing blood. Embarrassing. I seized a man that was inching towards Sol's blind spot and hurled him bodily over the ship's rail. "We never asked these men what their intentions were, or if they were even targeting the *Eos* to begin with. For all we know, they're perfectly friendly slavers."

"*Beardless boy whore!*" one of the pirates spat in their vile language, lashing a whip at me. I caught it around my own flesh and blood arm, rolling my wrist and gripping it tightly. The pirate had the good sense to let go when I yanked back, but it didn't do him much good. I whipped him with the handle's end and shattered his teeth, sending him tumbling into the lap of an oarsman.

I rolled my eyes. "Never mind."

We wrapped the rest of them up in short order, and Sol promptly started breaking chains. I reclined on a bench, eyeing our captives. The man I'd thrown overboard had clambered his way back onto the ship and been swiftly pummeled into submission, and I'd caught the red-haired boy before he could jump *off* the ship in turn. It wasn't hard to guess his intent. He'd been diving in the direction of the *Eos*, the cheeky wretch.

The rest of our captives were either fully unconscious or near enough to it. I kept them in the corner of my eye anyway—I'd already been given a kiss for my hubris. I wasn't eager for another.

"Who gave you that, by the way?" Sol asked, nodding to my wound. I'd tied the excess cloth hanging around my waist about it, stymieing the worst of the bleeding. A little salt water to cleanse it and I'd be healthy and whole tomorrow. My robes, though...

The pirate child flailed as I laid a dozen pankration slaps across his face. At this point, his cheeks were about as red as his hair.

"A boy?" Sol asked. His lips twitched.

"A gastraphetes," I corrected him sourly. "The boy just happened to be holding it. He was hiding under the deck."

"I see," he said, taking another set of chains in hand and snapping apart the links. His expression was stoic. I saw the mirth in his eyes, though. "Bad luck, I suppose." I snorted, fighting my own smile.

When the last of the slaves were set loose, Sol crossed his arms and looked to me. I raised an eyebrow.

"I don't speak their language."

"And what do you want me to say to them?" I asked, curious. We'd broken the back of the slaving crew and likely consigned them to death by releasing the oarsmen they'd been whipping like bulls for who knew how long. As far as I was concerned, the work was done. Our path to Olympia was clear once more.

Sol looked over the assembled oarsmen. They bowed their heads as his eyes fell upon them, murmuring thanks and prayers in a different tongue than the slavers had been using.

"Tell them where we're going. Ask if they'd like to come."

"I'm not taking my throne apart," I informed him. "They'll have to stand." Sol rolled his eyes, waving me on. I obliged, raising my voice in their tongue. "*Hear me, slaves. My brother and I sail for Olympia. Which of you dogs wants to be free?*"

Ten men were added to our number...and one struggling boy

pirate. We left the slavers with their ship—they wouldn't be rowing after us anytime soon. As we swam the distance between the slave galley and the *Eos*, my captive spluttering and cursing as my pankration arms dunked him beneath the waves more than was strictly necessary, I addressed the Roman swimming beside me.

"Over dice?"

Chapter Twenty-Six

THE SON OF ROME

"*Ego desoptron een, opos aee vlepis mi,*" called an oarsman who was heaving at the sea.

"*If only I could be a mirror, so that you would always look at me,*" Griffon sang, his voice smooth and sweet as honey. Nine more voices rose in nearly as many languages, belting out their foreign tongues in the same cadence.

"*Ego heeton genimin, opos aee foris mae!*"

"*If only I could be a robe, so that you would always wear me!*"

Griffon sat upon his throne of piled benches, somehow translating a Thracian sea song in such a way that every man on board could parse it regardless of their primary language. Including me. The oarsmen stood and pulled rhythmically, working with the practiced ease of men that had been forced to endure far more punishing paces for vastly longer periods of time.

"*Idor thelo genesthe, opos se hrota looso.*"

"*If only I could be water, so that I could wash your skin.*"

"*Opos, opos, opos se hrota looso!*"

"*So that, so that, so that I could wash your skin!*" Griffon leered at me across the ship while our new oarsmen echoed him in song. When I'd asked him why he wasn't manning the oars with his pankration arms anymore, he'd shrugged and asked why he should do such a thing now that there were proper sailors on the deck. Since then he'd simply lounged in the sun, bare above his waist but for a golden necklace with a scarlet pendant and a pair of laurel crowns that he was still, for some reason, wearing around his biceps.

"Are you not singing because you don't understand or because you don't care to?" I asked the boy pirate beside me. Bundled up by rigging lines as he was, he couldn't do much but growl and spit in reply. "I see."

The boy was exactly what I'd imagined a pirate to be, only smaller in scale. My boyhood mentor had described redheads as foxes and thieves, bereft of virtue and most often consigned to life at sea— because, of course, civilized society would not have them. My great-uncle had described pirates as irreverent vagrants, cheaters, and sneaks.

The boy was certainly guilty of all charges. Even after the thrashing Griffon had given him for his surprise attack, he'd still struggled like a demon to escape overboard long after his slave galley had disappeared behind us. Eventually, he'd switched tactics to mutiny. Unfortunately for him, all he got for his troubles were a few more slaps and a swaddle of rigging rope. Since then, he'd settled for sulking and making a nuisance of himself.

I wasn't sure what had possessed Griffon to take him with us, but the former Young Aristocrat seemed content to smack the pirate around when he got out of line and otherwise let him stew. For now, I'd let it be.

There were more pressing things, after all. Olympia loomed in the distance.

The city was hardly more than a lash of color on the horizon, now, but we'd be upon it soon enough. Then the journey would begin in full. My days had been numbered since that day a year ago, but looking at the far shore, it felt all too real. My fingers drummed along the rail of the *Eos*. I was leaning beside the ship's figurehead, a woman clad in flowing wood-carved robes, with both hands cupping her own cheeks. We both contemplated the landmass of Greece proper as we approached.

"Why don't you work those lungs of yours instead of brooding?" Griffon asked, leaning next to me on the rail. The red-haired pirate boy swore in a language I didn't know and lurched sideways, snapping at his ankles. Griffon kicked him across the deck. "We could use another baritone."

"I don't sing."

"Like fuck you don't sing. What kind of man knows how to play the lyre but doesn't sing?"

"The kind with a voice ill-suited to it," I said wryly.

"It would mean a lot to Khabur," Griffon prodded. He tilted his head at the Thracian, who was currently in the midst of belting out another verse. The rest of the oarsmen sang along, but without Griffon to translate, they were just mimicking his words as best they could. "Just look at him. His heart might well break if you, his father, don't join him for a verse."

"Ke sandalon genimin monon posin pati mae!"

Griffon snorted a laugh. I glanced at him, but he only shook his head. "Deviant old bastard," he muttered, chuckling.

"How do you understand them all?" I asked, unable to contain my curiosity any longer. I immediately regretted it. Griffon smirked at me, joyous at knowing something I didn't. "Never mind, I don't care."

"None of that," he chided. "No man knows everything. It's nothing to be ashamed of."

I rolled my eyes. "You're relaying lines a Thracian is saying, and somehow, every man on this ship understands you well enough to repeat them back in their own language. I know for a fact it isn't Álikon, and I don't know any other tongues besides Latin."

"How do you know I'm not speaking Álikon?" Griffon asked, curious.

"I've been trying to talk to the boy. He doesn't speak it. He's following along with what you're saying anyway."

Griffon glanced back over his shoulder at the bound pirate, currently struggling to stand up on the rocking deck with his limbs all bound together. The oarsmen watched him with varying degrees of vicious amusement. None of them had tried to strike the boy as of yet, but that was likely because we were present more than anything else.

"Maybe the little asshole just didn't want to talk," he offered.

"And maybe you're a liar," I said.

"My virtuous heart won't tolerate accusations like that."

"Your virtuous heart can pound sand. Keep your secrets—it doesn't matter to me."

Griffon ran a hand through windswept hair, scarlet eyes intent on the far shores of Olympia. "What do you really know of Greece, Sol?" he eventually asked. "You had a mentor of some kind that spoke Álikon, but what did they teach you about this world you're about to strike out into? You say you'll split from me as if it's really so simple when you can't speak the tongues and have no idea of where you're going. For someone who cultivates virtue to defy the Fates, you're trusting an awful lot to them."

For a long moment, I didn't respond. It was easy to become complacent around the former Young Aristocrat, to fall into his irreverent rhythm and forget that behind the veil of casual arrogance was something resembling an astute mind.

"My mentor was from Olympia," I finally said. "He taught me what he could in the time he had, but my father took me to the legions before he could finish the work. I know... enough. But if I can find him here—"

"—You can fill in the empty spaces," Griffon said, nodding. "And after that? Was your mentor so great a man that his full teachings will give you the strength to wipe out all of Carthage?"

My silence was answer enough.

"Assuming this man still lives here or is even still alive, what makes you think he'll have the time to tutor you as he once did? I assume he wasn't doing it for free back then."

I frowned. My fists clenched and unclenched.

"What will you do if he won't teach you, or you never find him? Join another mystery cult and leech off them for cultivation resources? Wander the free Mediterranean alone until you're miraculously strong enough to defy the heavens and strike down all your enemies? Join the local boy house, maybe?"

"And how are you any different?" I asked sharply. "How is

wandering in search of freedom any better? We're both vagrants at the end of the day."

"Absolutely," Griffon agreed. "But I'm a vagrant that's having a good time."

I scoffed.

"I asked you if you wanted to see the world back then," he said. I remembered starlit pools, draining them with spoons and then dumping the water back in so we'd have an excuse to keep talking about the lands we'd never seen. "Now that you have the opportunity to, now that you have the chance to be *free*, you're throwing it away for duty to a city that no longer exists."

"No."

He glanced at me. "Ho? I'm wrong?"

"Not to Rome." Rome had been the responsibility of men like Gaius, the tyrants of the Republic. Mine had been far smaller in scope. "Duty to my wife and to three thousand legionaries."

Griffon blinked. "You have a wife?"

"I had a wife."

Salt and ash.

A tanned and muscled arm settled across my shoulders. I tensed but didn't throw it off. My teeth grit, fists clenching and unclenching. Griffon didn't make any smart comments, no allusions to freedom from a different sort of slavery as I'd half expected him to. I think I'd have torn the ship apart if he had.

"I've been thinking about it since that day." When I spoke, my voice was raw. How pitiful. The Greek lifestyle was getting to me, it seemed. "Even in chains, I was thinking about it. What I would do, and how I would do it. But I'm so *weak*." I slammed a fist to the rail, the wood groaning even without the weight of my pneuma behind it.

"I have no family, no resources, no comrades in arms. My city is gone. I have one connection to this nation, and he may not want anything to do with me if I can even find him at all. I am alone in this world. I am *lost!*"

"No."

"*No?*" I snarled, rounding on him.

"You were lost," Griffon said simply. "But I found you."

I stared at him, at three thousand different faces imposed over his own. Men that had trusted me, that I had failed. I couldn't do it again. I couldn't let another one down.

I pushed his arm off, but Griffon only threw arms of pankration intent across my shoulders, bearing me down to the rail. My eyes narrowed, gravitas gathering in my hand.

"There's an entire world to the East," Griffon said, scarlet eyes bright and intent as we drew ever closer to Olympia. Details were slowly emerging on the horizon. A mountain, and what looked like an oncoming storm. "And just because I have nowhere I *must* go, it doesn't mean I have nowhere I *plan* to go. I have a thousand-thousand things I want to see, Sol. I want to learn everything I don't know, and once I've done that, I want to learn everything I never knew I didn't know.

"It's only natural that I'll become powerful in the process. It's simply justice that I'll gain unprecedented renown over the course of my life. And you'll be the same."

Griffon grinned boyishly at me. "Son of Rome, your future is hopelessly grim. Why not enjoy your life before it comes calling?"

"*Monon, monon, monon posin pati!*"

Chapter Twenty-Seven

THE YOUNG GRIFFON

Olympia. The holy city, where heroes became champions and oracles came to die.

The oarsmen eased the *Eos* into the city's dock town with careful precision. My cousin's vessel was sleek and agile, well-suited to just about any maneuvering, coasting through bobbing forests of merchant vessels without issue. She slid smoothly up onto the beach sands, and the oarsmen scrambled off the ship to start pushing her the rest of the way.

I vaulted the rail and landed in knee-deep seawater at the stern of the *Eos*. I laid both hands upon her rear, and twenty hands of pankration intent joined me to heave the *Eos* fully onto the beach. The oarsmen whooped and hollered at the display.

"What do we do about the ship?" Sol asked, landing adroitly in the warm white sands. He still had a conflicted air about him, but he'd stopped brooding for the moment.

"Do?" I asked. "We don't *do* anything."

The winter waters of the Ionian were deliciously cool, so I gathered them up in twenty pankration palms and flicked droplets at my body from every angle. Sol watched with furrowed brows as I basked in the refreshing shower. Envious, no doubt.

"It'll be gone in a day," he finally said, glancing up at the *Eos*. She was a beautiful vessel, I'd give her that much. From her scarlet sails to the sleek curve of her keel, she was a vessel fit for a Heroic crew. A shame that we'd stolen her. "Surely, we could pay to have her kept."

"We could," I agreed, "if we had the funds. Tell me, Sol, did you bring your drachmae with you? Any denarii from your final legion remittance? Myself, I didn't bring anything but the cloth around my waist." I had a thought and called out to our crew. *"Dogs! Your father needs coin. Who among you is the richest?"*

Ten hands pointed up at the ship's deck. Ah, right. The child. Sol and I leapt back onto the deck, and while I wrestled the boy down, the Roman went questing through the ship itself.

The pirate boy spat in my face. Pankration arms spiked him into the shallows of the beach, and I dove in after, dunking him mercilessly.

"Nothing," Sol said, landing beside us. "You said your cousin and his companions were all in the Heroic Realm, yet the ship might as well be empty."

"Of course it is." The vile little redhead reared up out of the water, gasping. I dunked him back down. "Cultivators at that level have other ways of storing their possessions. We're lucky one of them didn't store the *Eos* whole into a fold of their tunic."

"What about the boy? What does he have on him?"

I pulled the little pirate out of the water. He choked and gasped for breath, unable to put up more than a token resistance as I slapped him down for coin. Predictably, the vagrant child didn't have a fleck of gold on him. I shook my head, tossing him up onto the beach.

"So we're utterly without funds."

"We have a ship we could sell," I pointed out.

"You told me your father and his brothers built this ship," Sol said, incredulous. "And you want to sell it?"

I considered the *Eos*. She really was a pretty thing.

"Selling her *would* be cruel," I mused. "I suppose there's no choice. We'll have to return her to Álikos and find another way."

Sol sighed.

. . .

Olympia was a gathering place. It was the home of the Olympic Games, the cradle where champions of the Mediterranean were born and nurtured, and it had been so for nearly eight hundred years. Throughout our most tumultuous eras, it had stood as a beacon, untouched by war and universally coveted. It was where living legends came to test their might against one another. It was where epics began and were mercilessly concluded.

It was also home to the most powerful cult in the free Mediterranean.

The Cult of Raging Heaven was an institution that every man and woman with even the faintest spark inside their soul dreamt of one day joining. Vastly influential and boasting Heroic and even Tyrannic cultivators in absurd numbers, the Cult of Raging Heaven was as much a place of elite congregation as the city itself.

The cult's influence over its host city, from what I had been taught, was nearly as complete as my father's own control over Álikos. There was a suggestion of separation, of course, a citizen class that had nominal control through democratic rule. But the masses were easily swayed, and it was only natural that the best orators would come from the strongest grouping of cultivators in the city.

On the surface, Olympia and Álikos were vastly different entities. The former was the heart of the free Mediterranean, the place that all Greek citizens with the means to do so flocked to during Olympic years. The latter was a simple colony nation, isolated from the rest of the enlightened world by the Ionian Sea and pressed up against the barbarian state of Rome.

It was perhaps only natural that a cultivator of sufficient renown would take the Scarlet City in their hand to ensure its prosperity, with only the heartless sea and a horde of barbarians as their neighbors. That my father was one of only *two* Tyrants in the Scarlet City said enough about its strength relative to Olympia—or even most of the other eight city-states.

Still, something told me it wasn't quite so simple. That beneath the surface of the skin, the bones were all the same. That in the end, their offal smelled no better than ours.

Perhaps I'd been listening to my father for too long. Cynical old bastard. Regardless of any alleged political influence, though, the Cult of Raging Heaven had left an undeniable mark on the city. On the entire world.

As the sun set on the sanctuary city of Olympia, Sol and I beheld one of the world's eight wonders.

It was a statue, in so much as such a thing could be called a statue. Ensconced in an open-faced temple, beneath a sloping roof, sat an entity in the shape of a man. The statue was large beyond anything I'd ever seen, lounging on a throne of ivory and gold and only just fitting beneath the temple's roof. Were it to stand, it would break through entirely.

The male statue was carved from the same ivory as his throne, inlaid with the same gold, and the detail chiseled into his bare torso was utterly sublime. He wore around his waist a tunic of solid gold, decorated simply with gemstone roses. His legs were crossed at the ankles, ivory feet wrapped in fine golden sandals.

The curls of his hair were accented with gold, and a crown of emerald laurels sat proudly atop them. Every detail was so finely wrought, it made the statue's utterly blank face all the more jarring.

Sol stared, awestruck, at the statue as it glistened in the sunset lights. It was covered in olive oil—a precaution against the elements, among other reasons. As we looked upon it, that olive oil dripped off the giant in small streams into a square pool at his feet, surrounding the base of his throne. The pool was painted the deep blue of clear skies, its walls inlaid with gemstone mosaics, depicting men and women dancing and frolicking without care. Each of them was without a face.

"Who is this?" Sol breathed.

I smirked lightly. Only heaven knew the answer to that question. Still, I gestured for him to follow me and ascended the marble steps up to the temple.

In the hour of coming dusk, the temple was nearly empty. Metics and freedmen, noticeably poor, hovered in the gaps between columns and the corners of the temple, gazing reverently upon the seated king. But there was no press, and we were unimpeded as we approached the king's dais. A low whisper hung in the air as we drew close.

Carved into the sky-blue stone of the pool upon which he sat was the king's name.

I, Your Father

"They say the founder of the Cult of Raging Heaven constructed this wonder alone over the course of eight years," I said, my voice carrying low through the temple. "They say he gathered its gemstones, its golden plates, and its ebonies, all from the parthenon of his own cultivator's heart."

The chryselephantine king held a vast golden scepter in his left hand, nearly as tall as he might have been standing, topped by an eagle with folded golden wings. In his left hand, raised to eye level, stood a golden woman with ivory wings. Whether or not this woman had a face was impossible to say. A smaller set of ivory wings covered it.

"This is..."

"Incredible?" I finished, gazing up at the great king's splendor. A single look from afar was all it needed to take my breath away. This close, it was as if all my earthly troubles were falling away.

"Well, yes." Sol frowned, considering the king and his scoured face. "But it's also familiar."

"Ho, so you have eyes after all." I chuckled and turned away from the king in heaven, bare feet padding silently across the stone floors of his temple. Sol, after one last lingering glance, followed.

"What we saw during the rites," Sol said in a low voice, his eyes troubled, "that wasn't unique to the Rosy Dawn?"

"I don't know," I admitted freely. "I've never been within the walls of another mystery cult, let alone participated in their rites."

"But what do you *think?*" he pressed. I smiled, barely restrained excitement making my heart and pneuma thrum.

"I *think,*" I said, drawing out the sound, "that the cults of greater mysteries exist for a reason. I think they are a reaction to an event, or many events, and their aftermaths can be seen. Can be *felt.*"

I lifted an arm and pointed, into the far distance, at the home of the Cult of Raging Heaven.

As we'd approached the coastal edge of Olympia earlier that day, it had appeared as if a storm was coming from the east. The truth was something far more bizarre.

There was a storm, alright. A storm that the Raging Heaven's mountain wore like a crown, shrouding its peak in ruinously dark clouds. It did not bleed naturally through the heavens as a storm was meant to. It hung in the air above the Cult of Raging Heaven, tightly packed and seething with lightning.

"I think if what you're imagining exists, it's at the heart of the cult."

"Is that why you wanted to come here?" Sol asked, gray eyes locked on the Storm That Never Ceased. "To see it?"

"Not at all."

Sol blinked and looked at me, surprised. "For what, then?"

I laid a hand upon the pommel of my uncle's blade, running the other through my hair. There was a long trek ahead of us and night was nearly here. We didn't have a single chip of silver between us, and we'd given our only other asset to a motley group of slaves. Still, our spirits were high and our bodies strong. We had all that we needed.

"How else do epics begin?" I asked rhetorically, striding for the city.

I was here to see the Oracle.

Chapter Twenty-Eight

THE SON OF ROME

"You're an observant one, Solus."

"Thank you, Uncle."

"I wasn't finished."

"Sir."

"A keen eye is a virtue, but only if you know where to look. What to look for. Some things won't reveal themselves to wandering eyes. And some things reveal themselves only through the observation of others."

"Sir?"

"If you want the truest measure of a man, observe the world when he dies."

Gaius' Triumph was a ludicrous thing. It was decadence and ecstasy made manifest, a marching adulation that wound through every street in the great city of Rome. Impossible to ignore, and who would want to? The entire city turned out for the celebration. Music and cheers were abundant, military buglers and musicians of the citizenry achieving a miraculous synchronicity. As if the Muses themselves played through them.

My great-uncle's pneuma swept through the streets in a flood, declaring his return to all who had eyes to see and inexplicably revitalizing those of us in his procession. We marched as tirelessly on Rome's stone roads as we did the marshes and swamps of the western front. Legionaries specially chosen *for their valor in battle threw fistfuls of glimmering silver denarii into the crowds of plebs.*

There were more riches, of course. Far more. Gaius had his best tribunes parading them through the streets, precious metals and jewels the size of a man's clenched fist, enough to fill cart upon cart to their furthest limits.

Triumphs were already events that every Roman, from pleb to patrician, anticipated as much as any holiday. They were city-wide celebrations that lasted long into the night, awarded only to those that shed the light of the Republic on shadowed lands.

A man could bask in the adulation of the great city only if he first added to its borders. Made it greater than it had been before.

Today, Gaius celebrated his fourth Triumph in as many days.

"We know the men we lead," Gaius said. He sat tall on his personal mount and nodded graciously to the masses. A chariot was traditional, but the general of the western front had opted for his warhorse. "It's the least that can be expected of us—to know their names, who they are in their hearts. They're the blade, after all. How can victory be possible if you don't know what's sheathed at your hip?"

Walking beside my great-uncle's horse, at his hip, I considered the question. Rhetorical as always.

"You'll acquire this skill in time," he said to me. Not an assurance but a fact as if he could speak it into being. Maybe he could. "For now, observe what happens when a good man dies."

Gaius whistled a high and clear note, and the triumphal banners rose.

The vast sounds of the crowd rose higher as depictions of our efforts in the west were proudly presented on eagle-topped standards. Centurions of Gaius' favored legion carried them with stern faces, but their eyes were aglow.

Four sets of banners to match four days of triumph. On the first day, the battles for the Gallic lands had flown to riotous applause. On the second, the conquest of the savage Britons and their miserable island. Third, the bloodied snow plains of northern Germania.

Gaius paraded a toppled king around the city each day, one for every nation. They were warriors that could alone crush armies of lesser men with little effort, yet they weathered insults from patricians and plebs alike. They were spat upon by men that they could have killed with a cold snort, if not for the shackles around their wrists. And at the end of each day, they were beheaded to resounding applause.

Today, though, there were no kings to mock. When the banners rose to depict the fourth and final triumph of the general of the western front, the rising tide was not of adulation.

The people of Rome cried out in anguish.

*My wife's fingers tightened around mine. She pressed herself against my side as citizens and freedmen shouted. Hollered. **Wept.** An old woman up on her terrace wailed, clawing at her own wrinkled face as if to draw it away from the many banners.*

I looked back at the leading banner, the most gruesome by far. It was the first time I'd seen it. I knew at once what it was depicting, the news that my great-uncle had received with such fury out in the field.

Painted in shades of cinnabar and vermilion, the Young Wolf tore out his own innards while his son and servants fought to save him.

"The people of Rome know that I alone command the western legions," Gaius said as if we were still sitting around the sand table in his command tent. *"They know that I am more powerful than they could ever hope to be. My opinion of them matters. My status is a beast they can not afford to provoke. **And yet.**"*

The people of Rome called out against Gaius.

"This is the legacy of a good man," he said, cool gray eyes sweeping over the citizens of the Republic as they grieved. There were many banners today. *"It doesn't yield. Doesn't cower. Among heaven and earth, his character is undeniable."*

A memory. My great-uncle, hunched over his sand table. A papyrus missive crushed in his fist.

I grudge you your death, as you would have grudged me your life.

"Why celebrate it at all?" I asked quietly. My wife looked fearfully at me, her grip on my hand crushing. It was madness to question the Tyrant of the West.

"The first three days were celebrations," he said. His eyes were horribly old. *"Today is a statement."*

I looked upon a Republic in mourning. Understanding came, and with it dread. The people of Rome cried out in despair for their fallen sons. But they did not rise.

"You can be a good man, nephew," he offered me.
My jaw clenched. "Or I can lead them."
Gaius nodded.
"Never both."

"Something's wrong," Griffon mused. He strode barefoot through streets littered with pulverized stone and all manner of detritus, one hand propped on the pommel of his stolen blade and the other swaying at his side.

It was an egregious understatement. The outer limits of Olympia were a ruin, homes and roads torn up and scattered to the four winds as if by a furious god. As we ventured farther in, closer to that distant mountain with its perpetual storm, the damage slowly diminished. It was more to do with the quality of the architecture than anything else, though. The closer we drew to the heart of Olympia, the better her homes and monuments had been able to weather the apparent disaster.

Yet even as devastated slums gave way to battered residential districts, and then to smooth streets of baked scarlet clay, we hardly saw another soul. There were vagrants, yes. Urchins and slaves as well. But citizens were few and far between, and the few we did see rushed out ahead of us with torches and wrapped bundles in their arms.

"It's fresh," Griffon continued, scarlet eyes roving over the shadowed ruins. "But the atmosphere is all wrong. The citizens are in a rush while the mongrels are loitering."

I flexed my right hand, near the naked blade I'd stolen from a pirate. It was an ugly, ill-wrought weapon, without even a sheath to house it. It was all I had for the moment.

"The free cities don't hold standing armies," I said quietly. "They conscript their citizens when they go to war."

"Not likely." Griffon frowned, tilting his head as if a different angle would reveal the answer to him. "Olympia is the nexus of the free Mediterranean, a sanctuary state. Any city that decided to wage war with her would be torn apart by seven sets of teeth before they breached her walls."

Light bloomed in his swaying palm, the rosy fingers of dawn illuminating the path ahead. I tracked a female citizen's path as she leapt off her terrace, three floors up, and landed adroitly on the red stone road. She was dressed in fine indigo robes and had a wrapped bundle in her arms. She spared us a quick glance before turning and rushing down the street. Her sandals clattered with every step.

"It's not panic." The stragglers were in a rush but not frenzied. "They have somewhere to be."

"The whole city?" Griffon asked. "At this hour?"

"Maybe the Raging Heaven is conducting its rites," I suggested.

Griffon scoffed. "Don't be absurd."

"Absurd?" I echoed in disbelief. "Your father pulled a *star from the sky*, and you think a hurricane is absurd?"

"Onto his own cult, yes. He didn't level the whole fucking city."

I grunted, acknowledging the point.

We continued on, and the closer we got to the heart of the city, the grander its architecture became. Theaters, bathhouses, and all manner of grand residential estates abounded. Signs of calamity were everywhere, but the buildings themselves had weathered the storm without issue. And still the streets were empty of citizens.

It wasn't until we saw the torchlight that I finally understood. It was a distant glow at first, hardly brighter than the light in Griffon's palm, but as we drew closer, it grew larger and brighter. It became a sea, bobbing waves of torch flame streaming into the city's central pavilion. Thousands upon thousands of citizens gathered in the agora as the moon peered through the storm clouds wreathing the Raging Heaven's mountain.

Eerie silence gave way to cries. To shouts. To mournful chants. And I understood.

"This is a funeral," I said. Griffon's eyes widened as he made the connection.

My mentor had taught me about death as the Greeks understood it. When a man died his vital essence left him in his final breath. One last gasp, easily missed. This principle held true for cultivators just the same. But the scale differed. Cultivation makes a man more of what he already is. It enhances everything he does, for better or for worse.

Olympia hadn't been attacked. It *had* suffered a natural disaster, but not in the traditional sense. The truth was written on every weeping face and in every wrapped offering. The people of Olympia, cultivators from every corner of the Mediterranean, gathered in the battered agora to pay their respects.

A Tyrant had died.

Chapter Twenty-Nine

THE YOUNG GRIFFON

Sooner or later in life, you ran up against the feeling of being unwanted. Some time, in some place, by some person. It was only natural that man could not please every soul among heaven and earth. Even a man like me.

Especially a man like me.

It was a palpable sensation, something that could be felt if you had the sense for it. A formless blade that could slip between your ribs alongside a smile and pleasant conversation. Humanity was infinitely complex. Our little interactions with one another were the same. I didn't have to tell a man that I hated him for him to know. I didn't even have to strike him. I could do it with a glance.

The conveyance of contempt was an art that every Young Aristocrat mastered early in life. As a prodigy of that art, I had a keen eye for the contempt of others. I knew when I wasn't wanted. I knew when someone was trying to hide that fact from me. But as Sol and I weaved through the crowds of mourning citizens, I noticed a distinct lack of unwant.

Most paid little and less mind to us as we moved past them, my Rosy Fingers of Dawn raised like one of the countless torches congregating in the city's agora. The eyes that did take notice of us lingered, but that only made sense. Sol stalked through the crowd like he was going to war, a storm in his eyes—never mind the fact that he was always like that.

And I was myself.

Drawing attention was natural, but the lack of contempt was surprising. The *uninvitation* that I had expected wasn't there, and that told me a few things about the man that had died.

I'd connected the dots moments after Sol. The sanctuary city of Olympia looked like it had been hit by a hurricane. But the docks hadn't shown any signs of such a thing, and those would have been hit the hardest. The other possibility was a cultivator's work, but that was even less likely. To strike at Olympia was to strike at the heart of the free Mediterranean. There wasn't a dog nation on this earth with the courage to do that.

But if the cultivator in question wasn't an invader? If he was inside the sanctuary city when he struck, and his attack was no attack at all?

Any man's dying breath can stir the hearts of his family. Perhaps it can even scatter an anthill. A Tyrant's dying breath can stir the hearts of an entire city.

And level it.

"It's easy to forget"—slipping past a pair of crying women in purple slips of cloth, I noted the perfect affectation of their sobs, their skin lustrous in the torchlight—"for all their strength and influence, for all the cities they scatter in their wake, even Tyrants die someday."

"*Thus always,*" Sol murmured.

I glanced at him in askance, but he only shook his head, frowning.

"We need information," he said instead, scanning the crowd. His eyes settled on a throng of men with youthful features and gray beards, commiserating with one another. Their torches illuminated ornate tunics and glimmering rings and armbands.

I caught him by the arm when he made to walk their way. Sol looked back at me, annoyed.

"Those aren't the men we want to talk to," I explained, raising an eyebrow. "Haven't you noticed? There's no one worth listening to out here on the fringes."

Several heads turned at that, ugly looks and whispered threats.

Some of those ugly looks died as soon as they laid eyes on me. Citizens, no matter how wealthy or respected, knew they had no business even looking unfavorably upon an initiate of a greater mystery cult. Their clothing and ornaments were finer than mine, but a cultivator's tattered attire would always be worth more than a citizen's finest silks.

The gaggle of vain old men and the sobbing sisters I'd brushed past were reflected in a thousand faces, a thousand different styles. An important man had died, and every able body in Olympia with two drachma to rub together had come to claim their place in the spectacle. Like flies swarming a lion's corpse. It was the way of things.

"We can do better than flies," I told him, flicking a rosy finger at a glaring man with more ire than sense. He cursed and flinched back from the flying embers of my pneuma. "If you want to talk to scavengers, at least find yourself a crow."

"Cultivator or not, it doesn't matter," Sol said, shrugging me off. "I only want to know what we're walking into."

He moved through to the group of youthful graybeards. The crowds parted naturally around him as he did. It was faint, nearly drowned out by the press of so many different souls, but now I could feel that formless aura of his that caused it, whereas before I could only infer it. One of the benefits of my new standing.

I waited patiently while he spoke to the old men. From the looks of it, they were all too happy to share their thoughts.

"You shouldn't be walking around like that tonight, young man. It's disrespectful." I blinked, looking down at an old woman. She looked her age, all snow-white hair and wrinkled, weathered skin. There were laugh lines around her eyes, though she was currently scowling.

I tilted my head. "Did I ask for your opinion?"

Her pneuma rose and lashed out like a serpent, striking my arm. She slapped me with her soul. It was a pitiful thing, due as much to the lack of real heat behind it as to the difference in our standing. For all her years, she was still only in the Civic Realm. Oddly enough, she didn't seem to care. I flexed my pneuma once. She scoffed.

"Rude boy," she said, removing one of several embroidered shawls draped over her shoulders. "So what if you're stronger than a crone. I'd offer you a laurel, but you already have two." She pressed the pure white shawl with its fine gold embroidering insistently against my bare chest. "Put this on. This is a funeral, not a bathhouse."

I considered the shawl. "This isn't really my style," I told her. She grumbled and pulled a couple more off her shoulders, each a different color, and presented them to me impatiently.

"Quickly now, take one. You're a strong young man, surely you can pick your clothes without your mother's help?"

"I don't have a mother," I informed her.

"That explains it." She squinted in the low light of the torches and my own rosy fingers. Then, nodding once, she took the white and gold shawl from my hands. She replaced it with one that was entirely gold, though a shade darker than the embroideries on the first. "This will suit you nicely. Make you look presentable, though there's nothing I can do for that arrogant face."

"You're an audacious old woman," I said, amused. The shawl, which had nearly touched the ground when she wore it, was just large enough to cover my torso. The material was light and comfortable on my skin, and it parted easily when I shifted my arms. "I suppose I'll wear this. What do I owe you?"

"Some respect," she said, reaching up and patting me firmly on the cheek. "You boys always forget, this world is larger than any one man. Tonight is proof enough of that. Worry less about *standing* and other such nonsense and more about your manners. They're a virtue too, you know."

With that, she wandered off into the crowd. I watched her go.

"You were right," Sol admitted sourly, a trio of young citizens moving absently from his path as he returned. "All they know is that a cultivator has died. They didn't have anything meaningful to say."

I hummed. "No, I think I was wrong, too."

Sol looked me up and down. Admiring my new shawl, no doubt. "Who did you mug for that?"

"A crone."

"No, really."

I smirked faintly, moving deeper into the crowd.

. . .

Each stage of cultivation was an opening of the eyes. The Civic Realm was the first ascension, where cultivators initially perceived their pneuma and the pneuma of others. It was a crude sense, obviously. My father described it as a blind man sticking his hand into a fire to see that it was hot. It didn't allow for nuance. Though when I'd asked what sort of nuances I was missing, my father had only brushed me off to my studies.

Stepping into the Sophic Realm had come with several benefits, and one was a new depth of perception. I hadn't noticed it in the days that Sol and I spent alone on the *Eos*. I'd felt the first wisp of it when we raided the pirate vessel, but I hadn't been able to fully grasp it then. It was only here, in this crowd of thousands, that I couldn't help but see.

There was a new dimension to the pneuma I felt in the air. Before, as a Civic cultivator, I'd been able to sense the quantity of a cultivator's pneuma and little more. The intensity, *maybe*. Now, I was sensing... eddies.

Like whirlpool tides, I could feel the brush of swirling wind as the pneuma of those around me reacted to my own. It was a passive, innocuous thing. Citizens parted around me as I advanced deeper into the crowd, but their pneuma moved first. Before they even noticed me, I could feel their pneuma reacting to mine, shying away.

There was an added layer to it when it came to Sol. Citizens moved only after they noticed me, oblivious to the eddies of my soul, but for Sol it was different. Men and women moved unconsciously from his path, stepping in synchronicity with their pneuma as it shied away.

I'd noticed it from the beginning, the way people gravitated to and from him without any conscious intention. Now, I could see the ripples of that formless quality in motion.

"I wonder," I said, tracing the eddies of a few souls scattered around us. Advanced cultivators of the Civic Realm, and a few from the Sophic Realm. "Will I always feel this blind?"

I'd always been able to distinguish between the Civic and the Sophic Realms, and I'd expected my Sophic perception to be a simple refinement of that. Instead, I noticed now that of the two advanced cultivators closest to my right—one at the eighth rank of the Civic Realm and the other at the third of the Sophic Realm—the junior cultivator's pneuma had the larger presence. It parted the waves of vital energy more aggressively than the Sophic cultivator's pneuma despite the gulf between them. I had my ideas as to why, but that's all they were. Ideas.

I could see more than I ever had before, but I felt twice as blind.

"My mentor used to tell me that no man really knows anything," Sol said contemplatively. "All his years of learning just clarified that fact to him. Maybe this is the same."

"Maybe that's why all the gods have blank faces," I mused, only half-joking. "They're the blindest of us all."

"How profound," cawed a crow. A Heroic cultivator's pneuma pressed against mine like a tide, urging me back. I observed it thoughtfully as it broke like waves against a rock.

He was young, not much older than us if I judged it right. How much of that was true youth and how much was the boon of cultivation was always a coin flip, especially in the higher realms, but I was confident it was the former. It showed in how he carried himself. As he drifted our way through the crowd, he moved the same way Nikolas had in the days leading up to his wedding. Carefully, as if the people around him were made of eggshells.

He wasn't used to his new standing. A newly minted Hero, his control over his own strength was still unsteady. Sol shot me a warning look. In some ways, a fresh Hero was more dangerous than men like my uncles. To a junior, anyway.

They weren't very good at holding back.

The Heroic cultivator planted his feet and stood before us, blocking our path deeper into the agora. He was slightly shorter than both of us, but that didn't stop him from looking down his nose at us. It would have been as amusing as when Heron did it, if not for the weight of his presence. An entire realm's difference wasn't so easily ignored.

"I admire your dedication, cultivating virtue even here when Olympia has gathered to mourn," he said, making it clear that he didn't. "But there is a time and a place for stretching new muscles. This isn't it."

"Apologies, friend," I said easily. "It's difficult to tell where the symposia ends and the funeral begins."

The Hero's expression darkened, looking past us to the masses of gossiping citizens and lesser philosophers. Something in his pneuma pulsed, pressing more insistently on those around him. Interesting.

"Shameful as it is, I can't disagree with that," he admitted. Dark brown eyes flashed as they turned back to us. "A man has died, and most of the people here don't even know his name. They just know he was powerful, and that's enough for them to show. They can hardly even pretend to care."

"What sort of dogs show up to a stranger's funeral uninvited?" Sol asked, without a hint of irony. The Heroic cultivator studied us both for a moment. I carefully did not smile.

"You'd be surprised," he finally said, his stance relaxing. He plucked irritably at the green-gray material of his cult attire, revealing a short blade at his hip as it shifted. "Even a dog can be loyal. These people, though..." He shook his head.

"But that doesn't mean we should sink to their level," he continued firmly. "If you're here to mourn, then mourn."

"Of course," I said and threw an arm over his shoulder. The Hero stiffened. Sol closed his eyes, resigned. "But mourning is best done amongst friends, isn't it? Unless these new eyes of mine deceive me, it seems you're here alone."

"... I am," the cultivator admitted warily. I smiled winningly, striking the perfect balance between sympathy and camaraderie. In my periphery, Sol looked faintly ill.

"Tell me, who was he to you?"

Chapter Thirty

THE SON OF ROME

"... Truthfully, it's impossible for someone like me to have *known* a man like him," the Heroic cultivator said, winding down his somber recollection. "In the end, all I can offer tonight is my gratitude for the kindness he showed me, in those few moments that we crossed paths."

Griffon made some polite noises, said a few empathetic words, but he was looking at me out of the corner of his eye. His pupil shook faintly. Was it excitement or tightly leashed fear? The former, knowing him, though the latter would have been a more sensible reaction. The Heroic cultivator had spoken only briefly about his connection to the man of the night, but it had been enough.

Olympia laid more than just a Tyrant to rest tonight.

The kyrios of the Raging Heaven Cult was dead.

"What about you two? How did you know him?" the Hero asked, gathering himself. His brow suddenly furrowed, the flames behind his eyes flickering. "No, before that. Forgive me, I've forgotten myself. My name is Scythas." His name was bestowed, not gifted—with an expectation of return.

"Griffon," said the former Young Aristocrat without hesitation. Scythas' burning eyes turned to me.

"Sol."

"Well met," he decided.

"Agreed." Griffon's arm was somehow still slung across the young Hero's shoulder. He jostled him a bit as he waved between the two of us. "As for us, our paths crossed with the kyrios the same way yours did."

"Is that so?" Scythas asked, with interest and skilfully masked suspicion. His ploy had been clear from the start, describing his own circumstances here in Olympia in only the vaguest of terms. Even his acknowledgment of the kyrios' identity had been reluctantly given— and without a proper name. Something told me he'd only given up that much because he'd felt he had to.

To prove himself. It was a gut instinct, but Griffon had clearly come to the same conclusion. Scythas was feeling us out. Testing our legitimacy while proving his own. But why bother validating himself? A Hero had no reason to justify himself to a pair of uppity philosophers. The difference in our standing was clear as day.

Unless it wasn't.

"Don't pretend you can't tell," Griffon chided. "It's written all over your face—a challenger recognizes a challenger. We've come to take part in the games, just like you."

It wasn't a lie. Griffon didn't tell lies. But that only made the statement more absurd. I clenched my right fist, the one not in the Heroic cultivator's line of sight. What did he think he was doing?

Scythas looked to me, searching. He didn't deny Griffon's guess. Not just a Hero, but an Olympic athlete in the making.

Griffon cocked an expectant eyebrow. Unfortunately for him, he was no longer the Young Aristocrat of the Rosy Dawn, and I was no longer one of his slaves.

"*He* is taking part," I said, stressing the distinction. If he thought I'd play along with his schemes forever, he was sorely mistaken.

I only had a moment to savor Griffon's irritated glower. Scythas actually *relaxed* a fraction after I answered as if I'd just cleared up a discrepancy in the story rather than openly contradicting it. Griffon noticed it, too, irritation turning to satisfaction in a split second.

"Sol is too modest," he assured Scythas. "He may not be competing directly, but I wouldn't be here if it wasn't for him."

Worthless Greek.

"Your mentor?" Scythas asked, genuinely surprised. There was a wisp of sensation, that formless *something* that Griffon had been describing before Scythas interrupted us in the first place.

There had been too much happening when I ascended. Even looking back on it now, with my pneuma unfettered, it was impossible to separate any one sensation from another. Moments, seconds, minutes, and hours. They all bled together. It had been a vague impression in the Rosy Dawn when the shackles fell away and I called upon the captain's virtue. I'd felt its effect on the people around me more clearly than before.

Now, I felt the brush of a Heroic cultivator's influence against mine. Instinctively, I knew he wasn't gauging my pneuma. He'd already done that from the start, and we'd done the same. He was looking for something deeper than what that spiritual handshake could convey.

I flexed the captain's virtue once, experimentally, and watched in fascination as the grasping hands of his influence slammed to the dirt.

Scythas pulled back, staring at me.

I was implicated in that moment. Griffon radiated victory, and all I could do was pretend that my actions had been intentional.

"Stare into the sun and you'll go blind," I said mildly. Griffon chuckled. Scythas, for his part, shuffled in place. He smoothed out his cult robes in a nervous gesture.

It was madness for a mere Philosopher to masquerade as a Hero. The gulf that separated them was the difference between heaven and earth. Even so, I stepped towards him, appraising him as if he wasn't my senior in age and cultivation both.

"You haven't been here long," I said, looking him up and down. The soft sounds of mourning enveloped us. Men and women alike sobbed or spoke in low, solemn tones to one another. The kyrios had passed too soon. What were they to do without him? "This is your first time competing."

"And if it is?"

His hair was too long. It curled around the nape of his neck, a shade of blond just darker than Griffon's. My officer's instincts stirred, buried beneath salt and ash, and they rose to the surface of my thoughts. He was projecting all the wrong things. His hair, his posture, the state of his clothes. His pneuma didn't lie—he was a Hero. But he was failing to truly show it.

I offered Scythas my hand, and he didn't hesitate to take it. I held back a wince when he crushed mine in his—he thought he was the junior here, the underdog that needed to establish himself. It was only natural that he would show me his strength. I met his eyes calmly, and just before the fine bones in my hand broke, I invoked this new whisper-quiet version of the captain's virtue. Scythas jerked back.

"Apologies," he murmured.

"I've been in your place before." It was even the truth. I set my shoulders, nodding when he unconsciously mimicked me. "Stand proud. You're strong."

His spine straightened and his spirit—the ever-present fire that burned in the eyes of all Heroic cultivators—flared in pleasure. I knew immediately that he wasn't a man with many friends in this city. He reminded me of some of the younger legionaries in the fifth, the ones who'd joined up because they had nowhere else to go. In fact, if he cut his hair...

No. None of that.

"Why haven't I seen the two of you around the cult?" Scythas asked, lingering suspicion warring with genuine curiosity. He glanced at Griffon, sizing him up as a competitor now where before he'd been a potential... threat? Imposter? Was this even an exclusive event? It seemed like every cultivator in the city had turned out for it.

"I couldn't stand my *own* cult's politics," Griffon said, shrugging one shoulder. "I'd rather not trade one for another."

"You—what? Are you out of your mind?"

"He is," I confirmed. "In fact—"

My nose wrinkled.

Griffon said something in response to my comment, feigning offense, but I didn't hear it. I inhaled slowly. What was that scent? It was faint, cloyingly sweet like campfire smoke drifting on the wind. But there was something about it.

I held my breath and pinched my nose, ignoring the looks Griffon and Scythas gave me. The permeating stench of city scum and sweat brought by the crowds vanished.

The smell of sweet campfire smoke remained. I could taste it on my tongue.

"You don't smell like mint either," Griffon told me, and this time he actually did look offended. Scythas turned his head discreetly, sniffing his cult attire.

"Is something burning?" I finally asked. It wasn't a funeral pyre. It tasted like burnt cypress. Griffon and Scythas shared a look. Scythas held up his torch. "Never mind."

Griffon took it in stride, returning to the topic of the Raging Heaven Cult and his decision not to join its ranks. Scythas had already been led to believe that we'd been offered initiate status but declined it, and Griffon was happy to follow him down that path. What resulted was a heated discussion about the pros and cons of the greater mystery cults. He was thoroughly caught up in Griffon's rhythm now.

I listened with half an ear, responding to leading comments Griffon made about the Rosy Dawn but otherwise tuning the rest of it out. Scythas was as vague with the details of his home cult as he was with the Cult of Raging Heaven, though he was easing out of his wariness towards us moment by moment. Instead, I focused on that smoke, tracing it as it wound through the crowd.

It didn't follow the breeze like true smoke. There was intent behind it, and that became obvious as I followed its path with my own senses.

Where the smoke gathered, my Sophic sense grasped men and women of power. Smoke cycled around them in such dense clouds that I was surprised they could even breathe. It settled into their pores, leaving remnants of itself before moving on through the crowd in search of other powerful cultivators. When I reached for Scythas with my Sophic sense, I found nothing different about him. But the remnant of that scent was there. Not on Griffon, though, and not on me. Whatever this smoke was, it was marking Heroes in the crowd.

Scythas stopped mid-debate with Griffon, glancing curiously at me.

Ah. He'd felt it.

I'd just tagged every notable cultivator within shouting distance.

"It's true that there are benefits to joining an institution like the Raging Heaven," I said, carefully resisting the urge to start running. "Socialization, for one. There are certain things a peer can teach you that I never could."

"See? Your mentor agrees," Scythas added, smirking victoriously at Griffon. I could *feel* the question Griffon wanted to ask me, but instead, he tilted his head in acknowledgment. Scarlet eyes flickered in the light of his Rosy Fingers.

"I suppose getting to know the competition wouldn't hurt," he mused in mock reluctance. He leered at Scythas. "What do you say, friend? Care to introduce this lowly sophist to the others?"

"No need," I said.

In response to their wordless confusion, I let my Sophic sense, my new influence, settle on their shoulders like a pair of Griffon's pankration hands. It urged them both to turn west, and when they did, they saw a woman pushing her way through the crowd towards us. Her otherwise flawless skin was riddled with deep scars like a master had sculpted her from a block of marble and then handed the chisel off to a child.

Farther beyond and farther west was a man approaching at an even faster pace. He was massive, his stature alone clearing people from his path, and he wore a skinned crocodile as a mantle and cloak over his cult attire.

There were others, converging on us from every direction. Converging on me.

"I took the liberty of gathering them myself," I said blandly, committing to the act. My memories of the mentor that had done his best to make an upstanding man of an arrogant young patrician were faint, but I would never forget his tone.

It was a hunch, but I was confident in it. They were Heroes, all of them, wearing cult attire of varying colors. Not native citizens of Olympia, and not afraid to shoulder past those who were. They were young, strong, and raring for a fight.

After all the grief I'd given Griffon, I was the one who'd cast us to the wolves. Naturally, Griffon's expression lit up as he realized what I'd done. Somehow, that made it worse.

Griffon stepped forward to meet the scarred woman as she shoved through the last few Sophic cultivators between us, pulling Scythas along with him. The wariness that had all but faded from the shorter Hero was back in full force as they greeted one another. Whatever was said, though, was drowned out in the next moment by an echoing boom.

The funeral drums began to beat.

Chapter Thirty-One

THE YOUNG GRIFFON

The thunder of funeral drums drowned out all else. Around us, men and women of lesser constitution cried out soundlessly, gripping their ears and collapsing in the streets. It was a pitiful sight. Idly, I dragged two fingers across my right ear, frowning when they came away bloody.

"This seems excessive," I told Scythas. He looked at me like I was simple, waving his torch at his own ears and shaking his head. "What sort of worthless cultivator can't read lips?" Scythas gestured at his ears again, frustrated.

A calloused, marble-white hand planted itself against my chest, and the woman I'd been in the process of greeting shoved me aside. I felt the stone of the street crack beneath my feet, Scythas sent staggering as I went skidding back. The cultivator walked right past us, mouthing something to Scythas. He couldn't read lips, of course. But I could.

Out of my way, trash.

I couldn't physically hear the crack of my pankration hand slapping her face, but my imagination filled in the gap.

The woman went deathly still, her face turned only a fraction to the side by a blow I had used to throw a pirate clean off his ship days prior. Scythas looked between us, leaning on his back foot and gripping his torch so tightly I could see the shaft of it splinter. The drums changed their cadence as if by my own design, rising to a kinetically charged pace. **Boom, da-da, boom, da-da,** *boom da da da boom.*

You dare? the woman mouthed. Something told me that even if the drums were gone, it would have been impossible to hear her. It was that sort of deadly whisper.

The Heroine finally gave me her full attention. She was marred by deep scars, from her sandaled feet to the tips of her seemingly delicate fingers. They were a shade lighter than her skin, which itself was marble-white, to the point that they looked nearly translucent. Each scar was a smooth line without any jagged edges. One, curving from the nape of her neck up to the bridge of her nose, was currently creased by a furious expression.

I felt *danger* as she advanced on me. Her eyes were the color of desert heat, an earthen shade approaching orange that was backlit by the flame of her soul. Her Heroic spirit was raging.

I strode forward to meet her. She tried subduing me with her presence alone at first. Two of my pankration hands struck out at the eddies of her influence, parting them like a swimmer parted the waves. The fire in her eyes rose, and her left hand settled on the pommel of a blade that hung naked at her hip, made entirely of bronze.

No, I spoke, silent beneath the drums. Furious desert-flame eyes read my lips. **You dare. Laying your mongrel hand on me as if you were worth the time it would take to kill you.**

Her grip on her sword shifted. The hairs on the back of my neck rose.

You don't know who I am, do you? she asked. As if it was the most natural thing in the world that I would. We were close now, at her preferred sword striking distance if I had to guess. I leaned in, staring her down. I whispered an oath in the mad thunder of the funeral drums.

You're the woman who ruined my favorite shawl, I told her. *You could break your back working for the rest of your miserable life and it wouldn't amount to half this relic's value.*

The Heroine looked down at the golden shawl that an old woman had given me an hour ago. There was a small tear in the fabric where her nail had caught while shoving me. She stared at it for a moment, and I felt the currents of her influence ripple around it, examining it.

It's a rag, she said confidently. It only took her most of a minute to realize.

I sneered. *You have eyes. Tell me, then, where is Olympus Mons?*

I noticed Scythas backing away in my peripheral vision, his eddies pressing against me in a wordless warning. I shrugged it off as I had before. On the other hand, Sol's influence was not so easily shaken— more riptide than current. I forced it away with a few hands of pankration intent. Obnoxious Roman, I could handle myself.

In the moment between drumbeats, the Heroic cultivator drew her blade and lashed it at my face.

I caught it with nineteen overlapping hands of pankration intent, and even so, it almost killed me. My eyes crossed, heart hammering in time with the funeral drums as I watched the bronze edge quiver just short of my nose. My pankration arms couldn't be cut like true flesh, but the blade bit into my soul. I tasted the blood that hadn't been spilled.

A flicker of something other than rage appeared in the Heroine's expression. That same intense appraisal she'd focused on my shawl she now focused on me. She considered me, not withdrawing her blade or the force behind it. Her head tilted, chestnut ringlets of hair falling across her face.

Is this your limit? she mouthed, the ghost of a challenge.

Smiling, I slapped her with my twentieth pankration hand.

Several things happened at once.

All eight funeral drums boomed simultaneously, with powerful finality. Every torch in the agora flared up, from those held aloft like Scythas' to those guttering out on the stone streets, having been dropped by the weaker attendants when the drums first started beating. Smoke and embers whirled into the air, flowing in streamers overhead to coalesce in the center of the agora, only a short sprint away from us. We'd gotten closer than I thought.

At the same time that every torch in Olympia gained second life, so did the fire in the Heroine's eyes. That sense of *danger* doubled and redoubled, confirming what I'd suspected the moment she struck me with her blade. She had only been feeling me out before. Attempting to confirm or deny my standing among heaven and earth.

I'd performed well enough to throw it into question, and then I'd slapped her across the face and all but dared her to give me her best. And now she would do just that. It wasn't the brightest thing I'd ever done. A wiser man would have ignored the perfect opening she'd presented and deescalated a violent situation with a clearly superior opponent.

I am who I am.

All twenty of my pankration hands fanned out in front of me, moving far too slow in comparison to the technique the Heroine was preparing. In the clarity of an instant, I knew that I wouldn't be able to predict the trajectory of her attack quick enough to react with full force. I also knew that even if it was only as powerful as the first cursory blow, I wouldn't be able to divert it with anything less than the full force of my pankration intent.

Unbidden, I remembered something my father had once told me. An offhand comment, made in that courtyard with its filial pools on an innocuous day of my childhood. I'd done something ill-advised again, though I couldn't remember what it was now. In place of punishment, he'd passed on an old mentor's words to me—like a curse.

There is no great genius without some touch of madness.

I lunged into the Heroine's strike. Her sword, an uninterrupted blade of forged bronze, weaved effortlessly through my pankration hands. She tied knots in the air with a single strike that took less than a heartbeat, and this time when the blade found my face there were no pankration hands to stop it.

But I still had two more hands.

[The sun rises.]

Searing heat lashed through my right cheek. My true hands surged up, alive with the light of the sun, and struck the flat underside of the blade. In the dusk that precedes the dawn, with both hands ascending, the technique was nearly as powerful as it could be. It knocked the blade up off its trajectory, tearing it out of my cheek before it could do more than cosmetic damage.

The scarred Heroine easily compensated for the interruption, pivoting on her feet and bringing the blade back around—

[The dawn breaks.]

Twenty hands of pankration intent became visible to the naked eye as the light of the Rosy Dawn ignited along their edges. The Heroine's eyes widened, desert-flame flickering as she transitioned into a defensive technique. All twenty rosy fists hammered into her from different angles, and all twenty were deflected by shimmering bronze.

The twenty-first hand, one of real flesh and blood, caught her sword as it whipped around. I grinned savagely when it only cut shallowly through the light of my technique into the flesh of my hand. I'd watched her move through her defensive sword form and picked the motion with the least stability, the least power behind it. For a cultivator of her standing, it was like predicting where a raindrop would fall. But I'd done it. *And I'd been right.*

I twisted at the waist and gave her the twenty-second palm.

The palm strike hit her in the center of her chest, sending her skidding back. Her feet dug furrows through the stone. Her teeth grit, realization in those desert-heat eyes. I'd given her first careless shove right back to her. Heroic pneuma rose. I inhaled deeply, blood thundering through my veins.

Sol struck her with Gravitas, and through the lens of my new Sophic sense, it was like a tidal wave simply washed her away. She went flying through the crowd, howling a curse that I suddenly realized could be heard in the absence of the drums.

For a moment I didn't move, frozen in my stance. I felt eyes on me, but not as many as there might have been. The drums had stopped, but most of the people around us were still dazed in their absence. Overeager Philosophers and arrogant Citizens who had flown too close to the sun huddled on the ground, hands clapped over their ears in agony. I straightened up, exhaling slowly. I felt *good*.

I threw Sol a sly grin as he walked over. He had that storm in his eyes, the one that meant something exciting was coming.

"I thought I'd have to twist your arm," I told him, swiping a thumb across the cut on my cheek. It wasn't deep enough to scar. Somehow, that was disappointing. "But you're starting the fights for me."

"I'm not the one who slapped her," he said, annoyed. His gaze was distant, focused on things I couldn't see. "For this next one, there's a new technique I want you to practice."

"Ho? By all means, *master*. This lowly sophist is here to learn."

"It's an ancient virtue, passed down to me from my father, and to him from his father."

Despite myself, I was interested.

"This one awaits your wisdom," I said formally. Sol hummed, measuring his next words with that riptide gravity.

"It's called *diplomacy*."

I snorted, shoving him away from me. He glanced at me with storm-gray amusement before focusing fully on the cultivator currently approaching us. The Hero wearing the crocodile. I flexed all twenty-two of my hands. The two flesh hands stung, bleeding slowly from shallow cuts. The twenty of my soul's intent stung too, and I spat the taste of their blood from my mouth.

"You didn't draw your sword," Scythas muttered. He was looking out over the crowd, in the direction the Heroine had been sent flying, but the words were for me.

"Of course not," I said, ignoring the fact that I'd almost died three times. I laid a bleeding palm on the pommel of my uncle's blade. It hummed like lightning. "She wasn't worthy."

The giant of a Hero emerged from the crowd, stepping over a cringing family of cultivators all wearing matching indigo tunics and huddling away from the lingering echo of the drums. His skin was lightly tanned but weathered. His jaw was square, chest broad and strong. His hair was nearly as dark as Sol's but longer and shaggier. He wore ocean-blue robes beneath his crocodile cloak, bleached nearly white by the sun.

Unlike the Heroine, he made no move to attack. He considered Sol and me, and Scythas beside us.

"It's rude to start fights during a funeral," he finally said.

Sol and I shared a look. He mouthed *'diplomacy'* as if I'd been the one to call them to us.

"Agreed," I said, offering him a bloody hand. He took it. He was only about a head taller than Sol and me, but his hand dwarfed mine.

And the strength of his grip matched the size. I matched him grip for grip, smiling cheerfully through the pain.

"My name is Griffon, and this is Sol. What's yours, friend?"

A chant began in the center of the agora. The smoke and embers gathered there rose into the sky, taking the form of colossal fingers. An ashen hand reaching futilely up to heaven. The funeral entered a new phase.

Chapter Thirty-Two

THE SON OF ROME

If the chanting was any quieter than the funeral drums, it was impossible to tell. Eight voices carried as one from the center of the agora, at a volume that was difficult to believe. In all my life, I'd only ever experienced a few things as loud as that concert of voices.

I couldn't understand a word they were saying, of course. For all that my childhood mentor had taught me the smallest intricacies of Álikoan, he had neglected to mention that the Greek cities each had their own dominant language, and within each language its own varying dialects. Hadn't cared to mention it, or maybe just hadn't had the time.

Whatever was being said, it was compelling enough. Griffon, Scythas, and the new arrival in his cloak of crocodile skin watched raptly as the funeral rites progressed. Their eyes traced the coalescent form of a smoking hand, reaching perilously for the heavens. Their gazes were hungry and wanting—whatever was being said, and whatever the hand was meant to convey, they valued it far more highly than the scrap that had just taken place between Griffon and the scarred Heroine.

A citizen of Olympia, resplendent in his indigo tunic and precious stone jewelry, cringed away from me as I knelt. His hands were pressed against his ears, leaking blood the same as my own. If I'd needed any further indicator that we were closer to this event than we had any right to be, the punishing volume of the funeral rites was it.

I grabbed the man's hands and pulled them away from his ears. There were tears in his eyes. He avoided my gaze shamefully. It was one thing to be struck down in a fight, but another altogether to be reduced to this by a simple drum beat. His family was beside him, his wife and two girls that couldn't have been any older than Myron, crouched in similar states of shock and pain. The younger of the two girls was sobbing loudly while the other rocked back and forth on the balls of her feet, shaking her head as if to dislodge the noise from her skull.

"This isn't the place for you," I told him quietly. His eyes followed my lips but there was no comprehension there. Either he couldn't read lips or he didn't speak Álikoan. Regardless, there was a language that every man understood. I pulled him to his feet, nodding meaningfully to his daughters.

The noble-looking man gritted his teeth and scrubbed his ears with sleeves of fine indigo cloth, clearing what blood from them that he could. Then he scooped his daughters up in his arms, shushing them and making for the thinner edges of the crowd. I picked his wife up, an arm under her knees while the other supported her neck. She was stiff in my arms.

The father looked back, and there was something tragic in that look. Outrage, disgust, and a terrible acceptance. The daughter that had been rocking back and forth saw me holding her mother, and she started to scream. It couldn't be heard above the thunder of the funeral chants. Something told me that it wouldn't have mattered anyway. The mother wept silent tears as she watched them go.

I had always known there was a difference between those who cultivated strength and those who did not. But seeing the gap in motion was always unpleasant. I watched the father tuck his daughter's face against his shoulder so that she wouldn't see what was happening to her mother. He walked faster still, away from the agora, stepping over other suffering citizens as he went.

This small family—merchants or politicians of some kind, not warriors of any renown—had shown up to attend what they thought was a simple state funeral. More likely than not they lived in the heart of the city already and had walked out into the streets to observe with everyone else. It likely hadn't been an intentional power-play on their part the way it had been for Griffon, coming this close. Yet, even so, they had been swept up in the business of cultivators. Caught the wrong eye. And now they paid the price.

I followed swiftly after them. The father was terrified now. He had a hand on each of his daughters' heads, pressing their faces firmly into his neck. He thought I was going to take one of his daughters, too. Perhaps even both. A cultivator's appetite was insatiable, after all. His wife was shaking in my arms now, such was the force of her sobs.

I stopped and set her gently on her feet.

We were far enough now from the noise that I trusted them to make it out safely. Even the citizens of low cultivation had kept their feet at this distance. If and when the funeral drums returned, they'd be alright.

I inclined my head slightly to the father and then to his wife. She was staring at me, frozen. As if a sudden movement would be the end of her.

"Take care," I said, a warning in two parts. I turned and retraced my steps, returning to my idiot companion and his gaggle of new friends.

With any luck, they'd all be dead by the time I got back.

The drums returned. They melded seamlessly with the chants, a deafening dread coupling that assaulted the senses.

I'd stopped along the way to shepherd several other hapless citizens out of the immediate danger. Some had gratefully accepted the guidance. Others had been too wrapped up in their own senses to notice. Most, though, had reacted in the same vein as that first family —with tightly leashed fear of the cultivator whose whims could not be predicted or denied.

Unfortunately, Griffon and his friends were still there when I returned. The Heroine was back as well, and from the looks of it, she had tried to pick up where she'd left off with Griffon. For whatever reason, though, the hulking cultivator in the crocodile skin had decided to step in. He was currently holding her back with a massive forearm wrapped around her throat. It wasn't a cruel hold, but try as she might, she couldn't break out of it.

They'd even picked up a new addition. Standing on the opposite side of Griffon and Scythas, another of the Heroic cultivators that I had accidentally tagged with my awareness was staring up at the undulating cloud of torch smoke. He was whipcord lean, dressed in robes of fuchsia and ebony trim, with a bow as tall as him slung diagonally over his shoulder. He was the spitting image of every bowman I had ever known in the legions.

The archer wore armor of nicked and faded bronze beneath his cult attire. The fine robes were worn almost as an afterthought, parted at the chest and only negligently belted around his waist. Worn because they needed to be, and for no other reason.

He didn't seem aggressive, and as I approached, he didn't pay me any mind. He was riveted on the smoking silhouette that hung over the agora. As the chanting reached an apex, Griffon and the Heroic cultivators winced as one. Even the Heroine stopped struggling just long enough to grimace up at the sky.

"What are they saying?" I asked Griffon, moving up beside him and speaking directly into his ear.

He didn't look away from the smoke. It had changed its shape at some point—it was no longer a hand reaching futilely up to heaven. It was a towering blade now, and its edge was ember flames.

Griffon's lips moved silently, but I read them easily enough.

"It's a eulogy. These were his final moments."

"How did he die?" I asked.

Griffon smiled wonderingly as the smoke changed shape once more. A pair of smog-soot wings spread wide over the agora of the city of Olympia. Their feathers were ash and embers, and their wingspan stretched from horizon to horizon. They beat against the air once. The weight of tribulation fell upon my shoulders.

"He challenged the heavens."

A bolt of lightning fell from a clear night sky and struck down the apparition of smoke and flame.

Citizens, Philosophers, and Heroes alike all flinched back from the heavenly tribulation. I saw silent cries of disbelief and horror ripple through the masses. I was sure we were all thinking along the same lines.

Was the kyrios really dead? What was more absurd, a Tyrant faking his own death or the heavens taking offense to his funeral? What sort of man was so reviled by the Fates that they would spit on his eulogy?

There had only been one bolt of lightning, if such a thing could be considered in terms of "only". The searing after-impression of light that it had left behind, burnt into my eyelids when I blinked, was the only evidence it had happened at all. Relative silence settled like a blanket over the agora.

Screams and curses were smothered as people realized that the funeral rites had stopped. No, not stopped. The drums were still beating, and the men were still chanting, but the chants were now murmurs, and the drumbeats were bare thrummings now.

In the ringing aftermath of the post-mortem tribulation, the Heroic cultivators surrounding Griffon and I seemed to suddenly remember why they'd gathered here in the first place. I met the challenging eyes of the archer in bronze and ruffled fuchsia cloth. He looked me up and down, appraising me, but the tribulation had stolen most of the heat from the gesture.

"You're the one," he spoke into the yawning silence. "Marking us all like that. Jerking us around like dogs. Either you're an idiot or you're out of your mind—why did you call me here?"

I appraised him the same way he'd appraised me, made a show of it, and then shrugged.

It was an impossible question to answer because the truth was that it *had* been a mistake. But to admit that now was to admit to at least one hostile Heroic cultivator that Griffon and I were pretenders. That we really were exactly as we appeared to be. That was unacceptable. So instead, I took a page out of Griffon's book and spoke the truth in the most disingenuous way possible.

"I wasn't the one marking you," I told the Heroic archer honestly.

The smell of cypress smoke on his skin was faint now, but it was still there without a doubt. "I only made you aware of it."

It was the right thing to say. The archer stared at me searchingly and slowly paled when he found no deceit.

"What are you trying to say?" he asked. I didn't respond. Somehow, I knew that silence was the best answer now.

"Who are you two?" the Heroine demanded.

"You don't know?" Griffon asked her as if it was the most natural thing in the world that she would.

"You're from the Rosy Dawn," the man in the crocodile skin said. Somehow, the atmosphere became even more tense.

It was understandable that they hadn't noticed until now. The classic attire of the Rosy Dawn, the fine crimson and white robes that all initiates wore, had been thoroughly defiled by the time we came to shore in Olympia dock city. Griffon's scarlet robes were torn and bloodied, and he had used parts of them to wrap the puncture wound to his gut that the little pirate boy had given him. The faded golden shawl he'd picked up about an hour ago only further confused his allegiance.

For my part, I'd long ago soiled my cult attire with the unpleasant duties of slave work. There were some stains that didn't wash out, and I'd lost what little bargaining power I had within the cult when Griffon lost interest in me following the Daylight Games. A fresh set of robes hadn't been an option for me, and I hadn't cared enough to press the issue.

"You're from the Broken Tide," Griffon returned. The larger cultivator inclined his head in acknowledgment.

"After all this time, they finally send a competitor." The archer fingered the string of his bow, frowning. It was glossy in the torchlight. Spun gold, I realized. "And when they do, they sneak you in like thieves in the night. They douse your heart flames and smother your virtues."

"Something stinks," the Heroine said, a ferocious scowl on her lips. She tapped the large cultivator's forearm twice, and he let her go. She flicked her pure bronze blade back through the loop on her belt. She wasn't raring for a fight now, but she looked even less pleased than she had before.

Griffon shifted his stance, just slightly enough for his shoulder to bump mine. We shared a glance in the corners of our eyes, and it wasn't difficult to guess what the other was thinking.

We'd passed the point of no return about three Heroic cultivators ago. The only way out now was through.

"You can't possibly think they're connected," Scythas protested. For all the good it did. Scythas may have been our superior in cultivation, but he was the runt of this particular group. The looks the Heroine and the archer gave him only cemented it. "They wouldn't move now, not so soon. There's a limit to shamelessness!"

"Careful now," the archer said, his tone an uncomfortable mix of airy and tense. "They have eyes and ears that we can't perceive. Whether or not these two are involved, he said it himself. We've been marked."

"They wouldn't," Scythas insisted. "Not now. Not while the body is still warm."

Griffon realized something—I saw it in his face. I braced myself.

"The whims of Tyrants aren't moved by such petty concerns as propriety or filial duty," he said blithely. The cultivators surrounding us flinched.

I tasted salt in the air. It coated my tongue, in the same manner as the cypress smoke.

Someone was watching us.

"You haven't been here long, have you," the cultivator in the crocodile skin said. It wasn't a question.

"You won't be for much longer," the Heroine said. It wasn't a threat.

"Is that so?" Griffon asked, pearl-white teeth glinting in the low light of his cultivation technique. "What a shame. I think I'm starting to like it here."

The taste of salt on my tongue doubled and redoubled. It became overwhelming, worse than any over seasoned ration that I'd been forced to eat in the legions. There was sudden movement in my peripheral vision. A flurry of motion on the western edge of the crowd nearest to the agora, by the alleys that wound through one of Olympia's business districts.

"You're tempting the Fates," the archer promised us both. "Some things aren't meant to be said."

"Ho? I thought it was our providence to be reviled by the Fates?" Griffon planted a hand on his hip, the other bleeding palm still negligently resting on the pommel of his stolen sword. "Are you Heroes or not?"

"Enough of this," Scythas snapped. He glared, first at Griffon, then at his fellow Heroes. "The elders are the elders. This isn't the time nor the place to guess at their motives. The kyrios is *dead*. Can we not set aside petty politics for a single night? In his memory?"

His resemblance to the young soldiers of the fifth, and the truly frustrated grief in his voice, made me hesitant to speak up. But I couldn't ignore what I was seeing forever.

"It seems not," I said. When he turned his glare on me, I flicked my eyes to the western edge of the crowd.

At the edge of the funeral, where the fringes of Philosophers and Citizens in low favor gathered, one of the presences I had noted earlier was being dragged into an alleyway by a pair of similarly monstrous existences.

A Hero was being kidnapped.

"Crows!" Scythas snarled. He took off sprinting through the crowd. His fellow cultivators made no move to follow, nor to stop him. A sensible choice. No wise man ran full tilt into an ambush.

Scythas raced into the alleyway, and I followed at his heels.

I am who I am.

Chapter Thirty-Three

THE YOUNG GRIFFON

Sol and Scythas vanished down an alleyway in pursuit of a kidnapping. A beat passed.

"You're not going after them?" the cultivator with the bow asked me. He was less cautious now, tension easing out of his posture in Sol's absence. I glanced at the Heroine and the cultivator in the crocodile skin and saw them relax as well. My nose wrinkled in irritation. I'd done all the work, yet in their eyes, I was just another competitor. Meanwhile, Sol was my perceptive and dangerous mentor.

Twice the renown for half the effort. Worthless Roman.

"Why should I?" I asked, miraculously not spitting blood in my annoyance. "I may be a western savage, but even I know that it's rude to leave a conversation unfinished."

"This conversation never should have started in the first place," the Heroine declared flatly. The desert heat in her eyes was only embers now. The tribulation, Sol's nebulous comment, and the apparent kidnapping of another cultivator had thoroughly doused her competitive spirit, it seemed. A shame.

"How cruel," I said. I tilted my head, absently rubbing the cut she'd given me on the cheek. "You know, I still haven't gotten your name. You started a fight before I could properly introduce myself."

"*I started*—" A muscle in her scarred jaw throbbed, but the larger cultivator placed a hand on her shoulder, and she sighed, relenting.

"Elissa."

"Griffon," I replied in turn. "Well met."

Elissa spat at my feet.

"And you, friends?" I asked the other two, ignoring her.

"Kyno," said the man in the crocodile skin.

"Eleftherios," said the archer with the gold-strung bow. "Most call me Lefteris." That was fortunate because I would have shortened it anyway.

I struck out with three hands of pankration intent, and to their credit, all three of the Heroic cultivators surrounding me reacted instantly. Heroic pneuma rose and heart flames burned as three warriors, each individually capable of wiping me from the earth, prepared to defend themselves from my attack.

Each of my pankration hands slapped against their own and gripped tight, giving them a firm shake.

"Friendship seals our fates," I said brightly, savoring their reactions. "So tell me, friends, what sort of games are at play here? What vile political maneuvering does the Cult of Raging Heaven get up to behind closed doors?" Or in the middle of crowded pavilions, as it were.

"Nothing beyond the usual," Kyno said when it seemed the other two would be too uncomfortable to speak. "The strong wish to be stronger, and the weak are caught up in their schemes."

"It was inevitable that there would be a... question of succession," Lefteris said. "The cults of greater mystery are institutions that shape entire generations. The opportunity to lead one and decide what that future will look like? That sort of renown is something cultivators work countless natural lifetimes to achieve."

"Something like this could never be peaceful," Elissa said, eyes shifting minutely as she surveyed the crowd, looking for more thieves in the night.

"I don't know about never," I mused. "The Rosy Dawn's transition of power was fairly simple, I'm told."

The three Heroic cultivators looked at me as if I'd just said something incredibly dim.

"The Rosy Dawn is the Rosy Dawn," said Lefteris.

"Damon Aetos is Damon Aetos," Kyno amended.

Ho, so my father had admirers even here.

"Then you're saying the fight for the throne has already begun." I radiated disapproval despite not caring much at all—a skill I'd developed early in life to keep my cousins honest. "And before the funeral has even ended. Scythas was right. These elders truly are shameless."

"*Quiet!*" Elissa hissed. "Do you want to die?"

"Not particularly." I then continued on, finishing my thought, "The question now is: which elder do you three answer to?" There was a moment of heavy silence, punctuated by meaningful looks shared amongst the three of them.

"We're here to compete," Lefteris said as if that was answer enough.

Admittedly, it may have been. My knowledge of the wider world wasn't yet what I wanted it to be. I knew precious little about the internal dynamic of the Raging Heaven Cult, or any of the mystery cults aside from the Rosy Dawn and the Burning Dusk. I didn't have any of the context that was taken for granted among my "peers" in this circle.

I knew that the Raging Heaven was unique among the greater mystery cults, in the same way that the sanctuary city of Olympia was unique among the free city-states of the Mediterranean. As the nexus of all civilized cultures, the cult's initiates were the finest of the finest, the most elite cultivators from all over the free world.

I knew that among these elders, each of whom would be on the level of my uncles at the bare minimum, only a few would have been born and raised in this city. The majority of the candidates for the kyrios position were foreign-born. Men who had been born and raised in far-flung city-states, with far-flung priorities and ideals. It was only natural that they would disdain propriety in the pursuit of those ideals. Home first, Olympia a distant second.

What I *didn't* know was how an Olympic competitor's status fit into that. Kyno seemed to see my confusion and elaborated in his rumbling tenor.

"Every four years, the entire civilized world converges in this city to witness people like us compete. For glory, for standing, and ultimately, for the title of Champion."

"The Champion stands supreme above all other martial cultivators," Lefteris said as if reciting a prayer.

"The Champion is their own existence," Kyno explained. "Free from the trappings of filial obligation. Immune to any higher authority."

"We crossed mountains and deserts and seas to catch lightning in our teeth," Elissa said proudly. "Why should we involve ourselves in the squabbling of politicians?"

I knew I liked these people.

"Why involve you in this at all, then?" I supposed it wasn't necessarily the case that the cultivator being kidnapped was another competitor, but it felt right. The way the three of them had been acting since they'd arrived was all too telling. Even after Sol left, there was tension in their souls. He'd confirmed something that they had been suspecting already, and it wasn't difficult to guess what it was.

They were jumping at every shadow. And every pankration handshake as well. They were targets tonight, and they knew it.

"The Champion's accomplishments are their own and can be no one else's," Lefteris finally said. He frowned, eyes shifting towards the center of the agora. "But there are some who claim a portion of the glory regardless."

The crowd had rapidly thinned around us, all that remained being those powerful enough to withstand the sound of the rites. Through the diminishing haze of smoke and embers, I could just see an outline of some sort of raised platform. There was movement within, but it was impossible to discern anything further.

Kyno's arms crossed over a broad chest. He frowned darkly. "It isn't uncommon for matters of promotion and other rewards within the cult to be predicated on the success of a city's representative in the games."

"And what greater promotion than to the mantle of the kyrios?" I asked rhetorically, nodding along. They were eliminating the competition, sabotaging the athletic talents of the opposing home cities. It was just the sort of indirect attack that usually made me sick.

Somehow, though, the execution made up for the intent. The funeral rites continued to sow chaos in the ranks of the citizenry, and the remnants of ember and smoke that had been struck down by the heavens circulated through the crowd, obscuring sight and smell. In the confusion, I witnessed another kidnapping.

The eddies of my Sophic sense brushed against their kicking feet like low tide waves. They were younger than me, wearing fine lavender robes and boasting the pneuma of a Sophic cultivator, fifth rank. For all the good it was currently doing them.

I couldn't hear them scream, but the sight of them thrashing in the arms of two masked assailants carried loudly enough. In a flash of motion, they were gone, dragging into a residential building and condemned by a front door slammed shut. It wasn't just the competitors being targeted, it seemed.

"This is vicious," I said appreciatively. "They're not even bothering to hide it."

"Why would they?" Lefteris's lips twisted, working over a bitter taste in his mouth. "They're all doing the same thing. And they know none of the others will dare to interrupt the funeral rites. They'd be crippling themselves."

So it was the elders conducting the funeral. I'd suspected it already, but having it confirmed was nice as well. A Tyrant seen off by Tyrants. A jealous affair, to be sure. I started walking towards the thinning miasma in the center of the agora.

Elissa caught me by the arm. Her hand gripped tightly around the laurel leaf crown I wore on my bicep, my own champion's token from the farce my father had put on for me.

"What do you think you're doing?" she asked in a quiet, deadly tone.

"Introducing myself to the wise men of the cult." What else?

"Not now," Kyno said. I cocked an eyebrow, but he only shook his head once, with solemn finality. "Interrupting a man's funeral is cause for retribution. Interrupting a Tyrant's..."

240

"If the heavens opened up for a second time tonight and struck you down where you stood, it would be a mercy," Elissa promised me. How sweet. She was concerned about my health. As if sensing the thought in my head, she scoffed and shoved me away.

I smiled wryly, shrugging with twenty-two arms. "I'll defer to my seniors." I'd still do it if the opportunity presented itself, of course. I had nothing to fear from the heavens. If I was struck by tribulation lightning for my hubris, I would simply not die. "Are we to mourn while our fellow sophists are snatched out from under us, then? I have to admit, we handle the passing of friends differently in the Scarlet City."

"The elders are the elders," Kyno echoed Scythas' sentiment from before. "The actions of others can have no impact on our duty tonight. No matter their standing."

"A great man died," Lefteris agreed as if remembering. "The greatest I've ever known. To do anything less than mourn for the length of his eulogy would be to insult his epic."

"You respected him quite a bit," I observed.

"We respect him still," Kyno firmly corrected me.

"Of course we do," Elissa said, in that way of hers. Like it was the most obvious thing in the world. "He was one of us. One of the best of us. A breaker of chains."

"Leader of men," Lefteris added.

"Slayer of monsters," Kyno murmured.

"Olympic Champion," I realized. They each nodded.

"Epics like his can't be told in a single story," Lefteris said somberly. "Among heaven and earth, it's common sense that men reign supreme over beasts. It's even more obvious that cultivators reign supreme over lesser men. But the kyrios. The kyrios stood above us all. His very existence laid siege to the heights of Olympus Mons."

I hummed. "But he failed."

They didn't react as I expected them to. There was no outrage, no *You dare?*s or *You're tempting the Fates!*, and no blood spat. The flames in their eyes only dimmed, and their divinely sculpted bodies slumped ever so slightly.

"He failed," Kyno agreed.

Elissa looked bleakly up. "So what hope do we have?"

In the aftermath of a great man's failure, while our fellow sophists were pilfered in the night by the grasping hands of greedy old Tyrants, we considered the legacy of the kyrios of the Raging Heaven Cult. A great man, who, in the end, had been only that.

A man.

Chapter Thirty-Four

THE SON OF ROME

In the time it took my heart to beat twice, Scythas had covered a distance that contained hundreds of citizens and lesser cultivators. I followed as fast as I was physically able to, but the difference in our cultivation was undeniable. Two more heartbeats passed, and I reached the mouth of the alleyway.

Scythas was already rounding a corner, piercing deeper into the unlit bowels of the sanctuary city. I plunged into the darkness myself, the screams and wails of injured citizens and those still grieving fading to echoes that rebounded through the latticework of alleys.

I followed the sounds of Scythas raging.

"Cowards!" he hollered. "Unfilial sons! Rotten, scavenging *Crows!*"

I heard a powerful impact, and then a suffocating sensation enveloped my senses. Hands in the dark, reaching insidiously for the tattered edges of my cult attire. *Wearing it properly is a skill*, Griffon's airy voice reminded me. I pivoted, stepping adroitly past the grasping hands and then leaping into the air. I caught the rail of a terrace on the third floor, jutting out over the alley, and swung myself up and over the limbs of shadow intent.

The nameless technique, or perhaps simply the murderous intent of the Crows we were chasing, pursued me down the alley. The sounds

243

of vicious struggle carried from around a corner, off to my right. I slid down the stone face of another building and bolted for the conflict.

I nearly died in that moment.

A man that stank of shadows lunged at me as soon as I rounded the corner. He had a filthy, rusted knife in his hand. The sounds of conflict I'd been following vanished all at once. I'd been tricked, guided into a trap by false sounds and his own vile intent.

The knife—an assassin's weapon, all red rust and filthy, chipped edges—tickled the skin of my throat.

Gravitas.

The weight of command slammed him against the wall, pressing his knife hand flat against the stone. It only lasted a moment, the overwhelming heat of his Heroic spirit burning through the captain's virtue in the time it took me to plant my feet and lurch forward.

I drove a fist into the Crow's gut. I'd have been better off punching the stone wall behind him. The third knuckle of my right hand cracked nauseatingly against his stomach, and he wasn't even winded. The knife came back around. I only just ducked it before it could take my left eye. I drove a knee up into his crotch and viciously headbutted his face, and this time we both reeled. Even still, he managed to wrap five fingers around my throat like a vise.

Gravitas.

The pressure to lead drove the masked cultivator through the stone wall entirely, tearing his hand away from my throat in the process. A woman shrieked from inside, and as I bolted through the new entryway to the residential building, I saw her scrambling for the door while the Crow pulled himself from the rubble.

I didn't give him the chance. A Heroic cultivator's speed was too much for me, that much was clear. The only chance I had was to disorient and dispatch.

Gravitas.

The captain's virtue threw him sideways through the rubble, punching through another wall into a room filled with colorful threads and bolts of cloth, a loom in its center. Another woman, older than the first, cowered in the farthest corner of the room, visibly fighting the urge to scream.

My foot missed its legion-issue boot as I drove it into the Crow's stomach. Silver threads of pain shot up my calf, but this time the cultivator gagged from the force of the blow. Even now he was faster than me, whipping around like a snake and letting fly his rusted assassin's blade. Fortunately, I already had my pirate blade in hand. I deflected the thrown knife—

And my sword shattered.

I didn't have time to gawk at the impossible interaction. The knife had been knocked off course, but now I was without a weapon, and the cultivator was regaining his feet. So I returned his projectile with my own, viciously throwing the empty hilt of my broken sword at his face. He flinched back, just for a moment, and I pressed down on him with the captain's virtue.

Gravitas.

The Crow's skull hit the marble floor with an ugly crack. By the time he'd regained his senses, a moment and an eternity, I had the loom in my hands, raised up above my head.

The lady of the house winced and covered her face as I shattered her loom on the Crow's face.

When all was said and done, my hands were a bloody, bruised mess, and my shoulders ached beneath the weight of so many consecutive uses of the captain's virtue. I picked the unconscious cultivator up and threw him over my shoulder, retrieving his knife as well. As an afterthought, I pulled the midnight hood off his head. I didn't recognize the man's face beneath, obviously, and wouldn't have even if it wasn't as battered as my hands. I committed his features to memory anyway.

"Apologies for your loom," I told the woman crouched in the corner. She stared at me. Apparently, she didn't speak Álikoan either. I sighed and left her home the same way I'd entered.

I'd already fallen far behind Scythas, and now I'd wasted precious moments fighting. The Crow naturally didn't have the courtesy to be light in my arms, either. I shrugged him into a more comfortable position and raced down the opposite alley at my best pace. I followed new sounds of conflict that I could only hope were genuine this time.

Shouts, flesh striking flesh, and the whistle of projectiles cutting through the air.

Scythas' pneuma suddenly flared like a beacon of light in the narrow corridor, and another hooded cultivator came hurtling out of the darkness.

I twisted at the waist, heaving the unconscious Crow over my shoulder and throwing him at the airborne cultivator with all the force I could muster alongside the captain's virtue. The Crow flew out of my hands like a rock from a sling and hit the approaching cultivator with punishing force. My aim had been true. They both went flying through an open terrace into the apartment beyond. Panicked shouts and vitriolic curses sounded from inside.

Scythas was next, flying out of the shadows and slamming back-first into a stone wall a few feet away. The breath exploded out of him, and he sank to the cobbled street. He had another Hero in his arms.

"You took your time," he gasped, struggling to regain his wind. "There were two more, did you—"

"They'll be coming back," I said. I wasn't optimistic enough to think otherwise. Scythas nodded and spat blood, wiping his mouth with a grimace.

"That one is strong," he said. *That one*, it turned out, was a rapidly approaching pneuma that reeked of blood and unkept promises. The kidnapped Hero grunted urgently, shaking his arms. A wad of damp cloth had been shoved in his mouth to prevent him from calling for help, and a deceptively thin metal cord had been lashed several times around his wrists. He didn't have the strength to break it. Bound by iron, his cultivation was suppressed.

Scythas struggled with the cord, trying fruitlessly to find the leading edge of it. The hostage grunted with increasing panic as the bloodstained pneuma drew closer. Following an instinct, I pulled the rusted dagger that had shattered my sword from a fold in my cult attire and slid its edge between the Hero's wrists and the metal cord. He hissed in pain when it touched his skin, but the cord parted like silk when I drew up on it.

The Hero immediately pulled the damp cloth out of his mouth and spat the taste of it onto the ground, scraping his teeth across his tongue in disgust.

"They took me by surprise," he said gruffly, nodding to me in thanks. "They won't have such an easy time of it—"

Before he could finish his posturing, the third Crow exploded out of the shadows of the far alley. At the same time, the shadow intent of the Crow I'd beaten unconscious along with another, unfamiliar pneuma of similar intensity exploded from the upper residence behind us. They were awake again, and they were ready to fight.

I pointed a finger at the strongest of the three.

Gravitas.

Stone shrieked and flew apart from the walls and street both, but the Crow had already leapt back into the shadows the moment I made the gesture.

"Show me then," I demanded. "Take care of the subordinates. I'll handle this one." Before I could actually think about what I was doing, I rushed forward into the darkness to meet the strongest of the three. Behind me, Scythas and the other Hero shouted a challenge and leapt straight up, meeting the other two kidnappers in midair as they vaulted the terrace.

Rusted blades clashed in the dark. I couldn't see my enemy, but I could feel their breath against my face. I felt the hands of their influence gripping mine, pushing me back, sliding my stolen crow's knife away from theirs so they could punch it through my throat.

I was as thoroughly outclassed as Griffon had been against the scarred Heroine. The only difference was that I didn't have him here to bail me out of my fight.

So I taunted them. "You're not very good at this, are you? A real throat cutter is never seen unless they choose to be."

A flurry of shadow motion made my senses scream. I crouched, jerking our crossed blades aside. Invisible knives buried themselves in the wall where my head had been. Dagger intent. Each one was dripping with poison that my eyes couldn't see, that had no corporeal form, but it was clear as day to my pneuma sense. Poison, synthesized by their soul.

We exchanged a flurry of blows that I wouldn't have been able to visibly track even if there had been light to do so. I operated solely on instinct and my other senses, reflexes hammered into me by my mentors and by war, allowing me to block and deflect most strikes. I caught a stab at my temple with a forearm, and I bit down on a thumb attempting to gouge my eye out with full force. I felt a tooth crack before the skin broke.

The blood of a Heroic cultivator was far too hot. It burned, literally, and when I spat it out it caught fire in the air. For just a moment, I saw the cultivator's silhouette before *she* bounded up the wall of the nearest building, vile green light flaring from the flames behind her eyes. Her Heroic pneuma rose.

Gut instinct told me I'd die if I tried backtracking now. There would be no regrouping with the other two. There was no one here to help.

But that was fine. Hopeless fights were the domain of legionaries, against enemies of superior numbers, superior arms, and superior stature. To be expected, always, and good fortune if the gods granted you a fair fight.

It was all business.

The inferno of the Crow's poisonous green eyes lit up the alley, and I watched as an impossibility was writ bold on reality. The blades of her dagger intent, coated in the poison of her soul, forced themselves into true existence. Real and corporeal. They whistled through the air, flying fast for my throat, and in their after images, new daggers of dagger intent spawned like fingers unfurling from a clenched fist. Three became twelve, twelve became forty-eight, until the entire alley was filled with her intent.

I brandished my rusty knife, knowing it wouldn't be enough. I needed more.

They say that in the Legions.

They say that in the Legions! Three thousand dead men roared in my memories.

"The life is mighty fine." It came through clenched teeth. I deflected the first of the corporeal daggers, the fastest of the three.

The life is mighty fine!

"You leave your home for glory." The first dagger spiraled off to my right, spawning new blades of assassination intent in its wake. Each one spun unerringly towards me, but unlike the daggers bolstered by the Crow's Heroic spirit, these were susceptible to my own influence. My new Sophic sense batted them away disdainfully.

You leave your home for glory!

Two more impossibly real daggers swerved at unpredictable angles on their approach. I didn't bother trying to deflect them. I knew I'd fail. And I knew I'd look weak in the attempt. In a place like this, in a fight like this, with allies like these, appearing weak was worse than *being* weak. I couldn't fail to deflect them, and I couldn't be cut by them.

Or could I?

"To Caesar you're assigned!" I called cadence, taking a lash of poisoned intent across each of my shoulders as the two blades flew by. I slapped aside the dozens of pneuma blades that followed, diverting their paths just enough to not be cut.

To Caesar you're assigned!

I stood stock-still, frozen. The poison coating both blades tore through my body in seconds, flowing like lava through the channels of my tripartite soul. Breathing became difficult, the insidious poison targeting my vital breath first. Without breath, there was no cultivation. Without cultivation, there was no surviving an invasion like this.

My muscles locked up next, clenching in sudden agony. My limbs refused to move, joints grinding like rusted hinges. Through the haze of horrible sensation, I felt as much as saw the Crow swooping down on me like her namesake, descending for the kill.

"They say that in the legions," I breathed.

THEY SAY THAT IN THE LEGIONS!

Gravitas struck her from the sky. The Crow somehow kicked off from the air itself, heart flames flashing, and managed to avoid the brunt of the blow. It glanced off her right shoulder and sent her spinning to the ground just ahead of me.

If I could call cadence, I could breathe. If I could breathe, I could cultivate. If I could cultivate, I could march.

And if I could march, I could fight.

"The meals are mighty fine," I informed the cultivator trying to take my life.

"What?" she asked, baffled.

THE MEALS ARE MIGHTY FINE!

"Eat leather if you're hungry," I explained further. She lunged up at me with a blade in each hand, ebony edges blending with the shadows cast by her eyes. She attacked head-on, with the confidence of someone who knew that their target couldn't move to stop them. I had countered her dive, but I still couldn't move my body. My rigid posture spoke for itself. She could likely feel her poison winding through me, body and soul. Paralyzing me entirely.

EAT LEATHER IF YOU'RE HUNGRY!

Unfortunately, she had failed to account for one thing.

"Drink poison like it's wine!" I said sharply and uppercut her.

Something as banal as lethal poison was no excuse for a legionnaire to stop marching.

DRINK POISON LIKE IT'S WINE!

Breath exploded out of her from the force of the punch. Delivered in cadence, it struck her harder than anything I could have normally produced. She arched up above my fist, hovering in the air for a bare moment. I forced my body to move again before she could recover. I lashed out with my other hand and grabbed the back of her neck.

"*They say that in the legions!*" I shouted, slamming her to the stone.

THEY SAY THAT IN THE LEGIONS!

"The pay is fine it's great!" I kicked her up against the wall, feeling a crack that was either my foot or her ribs breaking. Maybe both.

THE PAY IS FINE IT'S GREAT!

"For every coin you gather!"

The kidnapper-turned-assassin recovered faster than I'd have liked, planting her hands against the ground and throwing herself up into a backflip that brought a slipper-clad foot a hair's breadth away from kicking my head off my shoulders.

FOR EVERY COIN YOU GATHER!

She twisted her body in midair and lashed out with a rigid hand, slapping the knife out of my grip. In response, I caught her by the ankle and swung her into a wall with all the remaining strength of my poisoned body, the captain's virtue, and my own furious influence.

In cadence.

"*The captain gathers eight!*"

For the second time in as many minutes, I threw a Heroic cultivator through a building.

THE CAPTAIN GATHERS EIGHT!

Eight poisoned daggers clattered to the stone at my feet, shaken free from the folds of her clothing. I heard a soft huff, the sound of a pouting woman, through the hole in the wall. Utterly disproportionate to this reaction, I felt a sickening wave of poisonous pneuma surge up and out of the rubble. It rushed towards me, grasping and ravenous. The sensation alone burned like acid on my skin. If it touched me directly, I'd drop dead in seconds.

Light and heat blossomed like the petals of a flower behind me, illuminating the alley in full. The short hairs on my arms and the back of my neck sizzled and curled, burning. Coiling streamers of flame careened over my head, colliding with the wave of poisonous pneuma and erupting into a noxious cloud of steam that made my eyes water and my spirit gag.

The Crow was gone when it cleared. I turned, every muscle in my body protesting the motion, to greet the Olympic athlete walking up behind me. I didn't let the pain show. A captain never did.

"So it was a wolf after all."

She had laughter in her eyes and a javelin in her hand. She wore the finely woven tunic-dress of yet another mystery cult, this one a pristine onyx that I had never seen before. She approached me silently on slipper-clad feet, and her influence brushed over me in bare fingertip caresses. Careful, but inquisitive. They finally settled on each of my shoulders, where the poisoned daggers had cut me. The cultivator's touch was feather-light, but it still felt unbearable on the wounds.

"I'm sorry I didn't come sooner," she said, all feigned remorse and naked interest. She idly twirled her bloody javelin. "I heard you howling, but I had my hands full at the time. What did you want to say to me?"

I was too poisoned for this.

"My name is Solus," I told her. "I'm hunting Crows." The Heroine tilted her head, midnight ponytail falling sideways with the motion.

"Of course you are," she said, a slow smile stealing across her lips. "Shall I join you, then?"

There was a clamor of noise and movement on the opposite end of the alley as Scythas and the other Hero came rushing to my defense. Scythas stopped short when he saw us and then saw the Crow-sized hole in the building beside us. I watched in real-time as his estimation of me rose. Wonderful.

"Sol," Scythas finally said, looking between me and the Heroine with poorly masked unease. "She's—"

"A fellow hunter," she said, beaming at the disgruntled look he gave her. "You two seem to be in good shape. Still, would you like me to give you a look? Just to be sure."

"Absolutely not," the kidnapped Hero said without hesitation. Scythas only shook his head, looking faintly pale in the light of his own heart flame.

"If you're certain." The Heroine dismissed them from her notice, turning to me with anticipation. To my dismay, Scythas and his rescue followed suit. Three cultivators, each individually strong enough to wipe me from the face of the earth, looked to me for a cue. A familiar weight settled on my aching shoulders.

My body ached so fiercely that I wanted to die. Every time I spoke and blood didn't come out in place of words, I was surprised. I wanted a skin of water, a hearty meal, and a dark room with a soft bed more than anything else in the world at that moment. If I was lucky, I'd get the water.

That was fine, though. Buried in every lie was a shade of the truth. I may not have been hunting Crows before, but there was a part of me that didn't mind the thought of it now. Those three, at least, had been kidnappers and assassins. Their tripartite souls had borne the stains of their work eternal. If the rest of their ilk were the same? Well, I could suffer a few more hours of poison and shadow stalking.

After all, I had everything I needed laid out in front of me.

Every officer knew the only cure for an ill soldier was more marching.

Chapter Thirty-Five

THE YOUNG MISS-TOCRAT

She didn't know what to do.

After Lydia's uncle dismissed them from the study, her mother and Aunt Raisa took the five of them back to Raisa's suite within the estate. The two Heroic women sat them down on lounging couches with large painted cups of spirit wine, sweet and warm and heavily spiced. They asked them, gently, to go over the events of the night again, in greater detail.

Heron, in contrast to when Uncle Damon had been asking, supplied most of the details. Castor and Rena added small details here and there, nursing their cups of wine. Myron didn't say anything more than he had in the office, shrugging his mother off when she attempted to pry into the time he'd spent with Lio and the slave.

No. Not Lio.

Griffon.

Lydia's mother did her best to coax answers out of Lydia. Anything at all, really. But she didn't know what to say. So she didn't say anything at all.

After the debrief came the consoling. Castor's wrist required setting, though fortunately, it was a clean injury. Their mother muttered furiously while she wrapped it, vowing that if Griffon hadn't been so lucky in delivering such a fine break, she'd have hunted him down herself. Somehow, Lydia knew luck had nothing to do with it.

Lydia's mother moved on to treating Rena's swollen left eye as soon as the wrist was set. Meanwhile, her aunt was carefully prodding Myron's right leg, her expression darkening every time he winced. Heron sat beside his little brother, on the same dining couch, a wet cloth pressed against the ugly bruise on his face. Every so often he spat blood into a jar on the floor. Griffon had knocked out two of his back teeth.

Of the five of them, only Lydia had escaped the encounter unscathed. She wasn't even bruised.

Chryse and Raisa did their best to convince them that it wasn't their fault as they worked. It quickly turned from assurance to ranting, though. Griffon's actions were entirely his own, her mother assured her. They were only the natural result of a character that had been flawed from the start. Weakness of spirit made manifest. Heron agreed emphatically, and surprisingly, Castor did too. Rena didn't say anything, staring into her cup of spiced wine miserably.

Myron only scowled and shook his head each time his mother, aunt, and male cousins tried to convince him that Griffon had always been selfish. They said some things to Lydia as well. Lydia didn't bother hearing them.

Their fathers joined them. Uncle Stavros was furious, of course, but his anger couldn't compare to Lydia's own father. Fotios Aetos was a man of powerful restraint, but in that moment, he looked fit to kill a man. He stopped only briefly to cup Rena's swollen cheek and to inspect Castor's wrapped wrist before kneeling in front of Lydia.

"He was a worthless boy from the moment he could walk," Lydia's father spoke fiercely, taking her hands in his and gripping them tightly. "And now he's a worthless man. The world can have him. I'll find you a husband that's better than him in every way, I promise you that."

Her father pulled her into a tight embrace. Lydia didn't feel the tears as they fell, but when the hug ended, there were damp spots on his robes where her face had been pressed.

"Of course, you can do it!" Griffon assured her, a hundred feet up the rock wall, clinging to the steepest face of the eastern mountain range. Only

eight years old and already fearless. He held out a hand as if she could simply reach up and take it. His scarlet eyes were bright. "Where I go, you go. You're going to be my wife, aren't you?"

She didn't want a better husband.

They gave up trying to comfort her after some time, moving on to their other children and nephews. When Heron sat beside her and tried to tell her that this might have been for the best, Lydia gave him such a poisonous glare that he didn't say another word. When they left her aunt's suite, Lydia returned to her own room without a word. They let her go.

She sat on her bed and stared at a small bronze mirror. Her reflection was empty, almost confused. How had it happened so quickly? Had he been acting the entire time? Since the Daylight Games? Since that slave had arrived? Or from the beginning.

Had Griffon ever cared for her? For any of them?

At some point, the sun set and night fell. Castor and Rena brought her dinner and pulled up two dining couches next to her bed so they could eat with her. They picked at their food in silence after a handful of aborted attempts at conversation. Lydia didn't touch the plate they'd brought. They left it there with her.

Later, in the middle of the night, the door to her room cracked open. A shadowed silhouette slid inside before shutting it silently behind them. Lydia was still awake, of course. She hadn't even bothered trying to sleep, instead dragging a dining couch out onto her terrace and contemplating the heavens. She looked at her intruder, vitriol on the tip of her tongue.

Leave me alone.

The scathing comment escaped her when she saw who it was. Myron limped quietly across her room, sitting beside her on the bench and leaning his shoulder against hers. For a while they sat there like that, just watching the stars.

Finally, he found his voice.

"I should have stopped him. I'm sorry."

It was the most absurd thing he could have possibly said. He was the youngest of them all, and Lydia's junior in cultivation besides. To say nothing of how he compared to Lio—to Griffon. For her youngest cousin to take personal responsibility for something all his elder cousins had failed to do was beyond all reason.

Lydia tried to tell him this, but all that came out was a choked sob. She found herself hunching over, burying her face in the crook between his shoulder and his neck, sobbing and sobbing. It hit her all at once, everything she'd been trying not to feel. The grief, the agony, and the betrayal.

Myron whispered soothingly to her all the while, forcing himself to stay strong for her sake. But his voice trembled with every word.

Niko arrived the next morning.

Myron jerked away at the creak of the opening door, falling entirely off her bed. They had both fallen asleep, thoroughly drained, just before dawn. Lydia looked blearily first at the newly risen sun and then at her eldest cousin. There was some mirth in his eyes as he watched Myron just barely catch himself on all fours, but it was subdued.

He'd brought breakfast with him, three simply adorned platters balanced on his left hand and a pitcher of fresh water in his right. He set it all wordlessly down on Lydia's dining table and set down to eat. Lydia considered telling him to leave, or perhaps rolling over and going back to sleep, but Myron made the choice for her by stumbling to his feet and joining Niko at the low table. Lydia threw her sheets aside.

"I'm not hungry," she said, just so he'd know.

"Neither am I," Niko said, popping an olive into his mouth. He washed it down with a long pull of clear water.

Reluctantly, Lydia started to eat. The food was simple and filling. Niko spoke to them as they ate.

"Uncle Damon spoke to the elders last night," he said, leaning an elbow on the table. There was a different air about him without his usual travel clothes. For the first time since he'd returned for his wedding, Nikolas Aetos wore the cult cloths of the Rosy Dawn. Specifically, he wore the predominantly scarlet style that Griffon had always worn. The attire of the Young Aristocrat.

"What did he decide to do with them?" Myron asked.

"Oh, nothing too severe." Niko shrugged. "A few of them will be losing their seniority within the cult. One tried making excuses to the very end, apparently, so he'll be getting a beating and some mandatory closed doors cultivation. As for Old Chersis, Uncle Damon decided the broken nose Lio gave him was enough punishment and told him to let it heal naturally. You can imagine how pleased he was about that."

Myron cracked a smile at the mental image, but it was a fleeting thing. Lydia picked methodically at a vine of grapes on her plate.

"Speculation is running rampant through the cult, unfortunately," Niko continued, giving up the attempt at humor. "It'll be that way for a while. They weren't very subtle on their way out the door."

Lydia drank deeply from her cup, hoping it would wash the sour taste out of her mouth. It didn't. She tried eating a grape, but it only made it worse. She wondered if this was what a deviation felt like.

"I spoke to the others earlier this morning," Niko said. "Rena is taking it hard. Castor is still a bit shocked, I think. An injury like that is always frightening for a sword artist, no matter how easy it heals. Heron is putting on a show and acting glad, but I can tell he's struggling as well."

"It's not a show," Myron muttered. He picked at a small block of cheese with his thumb, breaking it into crumbles. "He's always hated Lio."

Niko frowned. "You shouldn't think that of your brother."

"It's the truth," Lydia whispered. "Our parents, too—they couldn't throw him to the wolves fast enough. Like they'd waited years for this moment."

"That much is probably true," Niko admitted. "But Heron is only taking cues from his parents. Don't be too hard on him."

Neither of them replied. Niko sighed.

"Uncle Stavros and Uncle Fotios told me the two of you were taking it the worst," he said. "I know it's still fresh, and it hurts, but you *have to* understand that this wasn't your fault. If anything, the blame lies with me."

Lydia remembered the look in Griffon's eyes that night around the campfire as she'd drifted off to sleep in his arms. How cold they'd been. She'd never seen him like that in her entire life. And she'd done nothing about it. Stupid. She was so stupid.

"I should have known that he was feeling the itch." Niko ran a hand through his hair, frustrated. "And I should have known better than to taunt him with stories of all the things he couldn't have. Patience has never been his virtue, and I should have *known that*. I knew it before I left. I got too carried away reminiscing with all of you, and I pushed him over the edge."

"It would have happened anyway," Myron said, looking far too weary for his age. Lydia reached over and took his hand in hers, squeezing it. "Something happened to him after the initiation rites last year. Ever since then..." He shook his head and repeated, "It would have happened anyway."

"Lio is—" Niko hesitated, considering his words. Finally, he decided to go through with them. "Lio is a wanderer. I've met his type, over the course of my travels. He was always a little thrill-seeker growing up. When I saw how subdued he was at the dock, I thought adulthood might have mellowed him out. But he's still the same Lio. Always chasing new experiences, even at the expense of himself and the people he cares about. It's who he is.

"Heron and Castor told me what he said to you, at the end. I want you both to know that he didn't mean it."

"Lio doesn't lie," Myron said at once.

Niko smiled faintly, bitterly. "He may not have lied, but he didn't tell you the truth either."

A fine sentiment, but it wouldn't allow her to forget. She'd heard those words in her dreams.

I won't suffer another day with you.

"Niko," Lydia said, tracing a pattern in the wood of the table with her fingertips. "Could you tell us another story?"

"Of course," he said quickly. "Any story you'd like. What did you have in mind?"

"Tell us about Olympia."

His eager acquiescence vanished in a moment. Niko leaned back on his elbows, considering them both. "You really want to know? Right now?"

"Not knowing is worse," Myron said. Lydia nodded in agreement. "What are they getting themselves into?"

258

Against his own instincts, Niko obliged them.

"Olympia is the cultural epicenter of the Hellenistic world. It's the home of the Olympic Games, as you know, but even during off years, it's a melting pot of Greek civilizations. Its poorest districts are far beyond anything we have here in the Scarlet City.

"It's known as the Half-Step City, or the Plateau, because it's the second-most divine place in the world. Just short of Olympus itself. It's where our world's most powerful cultivators congregate, and it's where champions are born."

"But only Heroes can compete in the Olympic Games, right?" Myron asked. The obvious question in his mind was something Lydia herself had been thinking about all night.

"That's right," Niko agreed, smiling wryly. "Lio may be exceptional for his age, but even he can't pass as a Hero just yet. He won't be competing this time around."

"Then why go?" Myron pressed. "Just to see it happen? Lio's never been a spectator. And why tell me in the first place?"

"It may have been a misdirection," Niko suggested. "Something to throw any pursuers off their trail. He may not be headed there at all."

"Griffon doesn't lie," Lydia said, echoing Myron. Both of them looked at her blankly.

"What did you call him?" Niko asked, confused.

"It's…" Myron paused, glancing her way. "It's what Sol calls him."

"It's the name he chose for himself," Lydia quietly corrected her littlest cousin.

"I see." Niko sighed, processing that, and then moved on. "There are as many things to do in Olympia as you could think of. They honor every holiday of every city-state, and more of their own making. It's an old joke that the citizens of Olympia holiday as often as the rest of the world works. The revelries are constant, and business is exceedingly lucrative no matter the trade. It's a city of abundance."

"What are the people there like?" Myron asked. At this, Niko perked up despite himself.

"Incredible! By and large, anyway. I've met many good friends there, even a couple of my current companions. It's a nexus for cultivators of every kind, you see, but especially for those of great renown. It's not at all rare to meet a Tyrant in the course of your daily errands. The city is teeming with outstanding people."

He leaned across the table, nudging Myron slyly. "I met my Iphys there, too. People say there are as many fine marble beauties in the Half-Step City as there are stars in the sky."

"I see," Lydia whispered.

Niko winced.

"Not that any of them could hold a candle to my beautiful cousins," he quickly amended.

"I don't need your pity," she said, unable to summon any real heat to the words. "Why wouldn't he want a woman from such a fantastic place? I'm sure he'll find someone there who can stand beside him."

"Don't say that!" Myron cried, slapping the table. Such was his passion that when it split down the middle he didn't immediately apologize for the lapse in his control. "Lio cares about you. That's not why he left, and that's not what he's looking for."

Niko said nothing. The fact of the matter was, he'd been gone for too long. He didn't know enough to say one way or another. Lydia scowled, glaring at her littlest cousin.

"You don't know what you're talking about," she said sharply. The anger was slow to come, but when it did, it *burned*. She felt her eyes grow hot again, but she refused to cry. Not in front of Niko. "You're too young. You've never experienced something like this before."

"I don't have to be old to see Olympus when it's right in front of my face," he shot back. "Lio made a mistake in the heat of the moment. He got impatient, that's all! If we bring him back, I'm sure we can make him see reason!"

"Bring him back?" Lydia asked, incredulous. "How can we bring him back? He beat us like unruly children, all at the same time, and that was *without* the slave's help! We're too *weak*."

"We can get stronger," he insisted.

"You saw the difference between us," Lydia said, her voice rising precipitously. "He isn't going to be standing still while we rush to catch up!"

"So you just want to let him go?" Myron asked in disbelief. "But you love him."

"Of course, I love him." The anger and passion fell away from her in an instant. Lydia shook her head softly. "But it doesn't matter. Loving him isn't enough. It never has been."

"You're both too pessimistic," Niko said.

They looked sharply at him. He tilted his head, Heroic flames flickering behind thoughtful eyes.

"Catching up to him is far from impossible," he explained to Lydia. Then, to Myron, he added, "And you won't be going after him alone."

"Do you mean..." Myron trailed off hopefully. The grinding sound of nails digging through wood alerted Lydia to the fact that she was gripping the table's edge hard enough to carve furrows into its surface.

"Can the two of you keep a secret?" Niko asked in return, leaning in.

They nodded frantically.

"You can likely tell from what I'm wearing, but your fathers both demanded that Lio be abolished as heir to the Rosy Dawn as punishment for his actions. Uncle Damon agreed and made me the Young Aristocrat in his place.

"I may not be as bad as Lio, but I'm certainly not ready to stay here for the rest of my life. My time abroad has spoiled me too much, and I still have too many things that I want to do before I settle down. Gods know my wife would be furious, and I just got her. So in the interest of killing many birds with one stone, and possibly even reclaiming my ship, I intend to track him down myself. If the two of you are up for it, I can bring you with me."

"You're telling the truth?" Lydia demanded, fearful that she would wake up at any moment.

"I am," he said firmly. "It will take time, but I'll find a way to convince our uncle to let me go. We'll bring him home, kicking and screaming if need be, and make certain he does things in the proper order for once in his life. I know the boy that he used to be, and I saw a glimpse of the man he is today. He may have been troubled here, but he didn't hate it, and he certainly doesn't hate any of you. He's at a turning point in his life, and he needs guidance. Now more than ever."

"When?" Myron asked—the only question that mattered. They

both leaned forward, three heads huddled together over a broken table and three plates of forgotten scraps.

"Sooner than later," Niko promised. "There are a few things I need to do if I'm to get Uncle Damon's approval. They'll take me some time, but that will give the two of you time to get up to speed for the outside world."

"How much time?" Lydia demanded.

"Months at the most, weeks if we're fortunate." Niko poked her forehead. "Relax. We'll find him."

"*Relax.*" She gritted her teeth. "He's on his way to the most powerful city in the Mediterranean, we might not be able to follow him for *months*, and you're telling me to relax? Forget months from now. I'm worried about him *today*."

"You shouldn't be," Lydia's eldest cousin chided her. "Lio is many things, not all of them good, but he's always been resourceful. He knows how to conduct himself in a dangerous environment. And from what I've heard, his companion isn't half bad himself."

"You don't know the new Lio," Myron said, unable to help himself. "It might already be too late." Niko rolled his eyes, standing up from the table and stretching. The light of a new dawn was bright on the horizon.

"It's only been a day," Niko said dismissively. "How much trouble could they have possibly gotten into?"

Chapter Thirty-Six

THE YOUNG GRIFFON

I'd come to the sanctuary city of Olympia to convene with the Oracle. Instead, I found myself in a rowdy club, accompanying my new Heroic companions to an after-funeral drinking wake of sorts. As the first lights of the dawn peered through the bronze doors of the club, I decided I didn't mind.

My fellow sophists shed the worst of their bleak mood once they had some spirit wine in them. The club was a more refined take on the thermopolia that Sol and I had visited the previous summer—the food on display was obviously higher quality, elevated beyond the slops and stews that we'd been offered in the Scarlet City. The kykeon itself was the strongest I'd ever drank outside of the Rosy Dawn's initiation rites.

All three of them treated it like piss water and drank it only under duress. It got them drunk enough, though.

Kyno, Elissa, and Lefteris told stories of the kyrios around a table covered with broad, shallow kylixes. Others did the same throughout the club. I brushed my awareness curiously through the bar, finding cultivators of nearly every realm. Citizens mingled readily with Philosophers, and even with a few other Heroic cultivators.

The usual hierarchy was only vaguely felt. This had the feel of a club frequented exclusively by cultivators, and if the abundance of indigo cult attire was any indication, by the Raging Heaven Cult, in particular. Civic cultivators traded stories and laughter and reminisced with Sophic cultivators as junior and senior, not lesser and better. The atmosphere was a stark contrast to the funeral we'd just left.

Cultivators told stories and drank deeply from their cups in the dead Tyrant's honor. Watching them and listening to them talk, I found myself wishing I could have known the man myself.

"My grandfather met him once," Kyno admitted after his third drink. Elissa leaned in while Lefteris smiled knowingly. "They were hunting the same beast, a chimera made up of half a dozen Heroic beasts. My grandfather found it first, and..."

I finished my cup and ordered another.

"My master knew him before he left the Raging Heaven Cult," Elissa confided, later. Kyno and Lefteris were both visibly interested. This was a story neither had heard before. "They'd always been on friendly terms, but when my master decided he was leaving Olympia for good and severing all ties, the kyrios offered him a wager. A single sword exchange, no pneuma involved, and if the kyrios won, my master had to keep his faith. They squared off in an octagon of marble and gold..."

At one point, Lefteris got up and went to the marble bar along the far wall, inlaid along its edges with indigo inscriptions of drinking games. When he came back, he had a terracotta jar of wine half his height tucked under one arm and a game in the other.

"The kyrios loved games of all kinds," he said, while Elissa rubbed her hands together gleefully and Kyno knocked back the rest of his cup in one shot, a haunted look in his eyes. Even his skinned crocodile mantle looked traumatized. "This one was his favorite by far. He'd offer every initiate at least one game with him during their time at the Raging Heaven, more if they were lucky. He believed its mechanics had ties to the Fates."

It was the sort of absurd statement that I enjoyed hearing. I watched Lefteris spread the carved stone tiles across the table, linking them end to end. A grid of two-by-three and a grid of four-by-three, connected in the middle by a bridge of two single tiles.

"What's it called?" I asked curiously.

All three answered at once.

"Ascension."

"The rules are simple," Lefteris explained, distributing fourteen pieces, seven on either side of the assembled board.

"Yet profound," Elissa interjected, with the air of someone telling a bad joke ahead of time. Kyno chuckled.

"Exactly right," Lefteris agreed without shame. "Each player is given seven pieces, and the objective is in the name. Move all seven pieces from the beginning"—he tapped two of the blocks, one in each corner at the bottom of the board—"to the end." He tapped the two corners second from the top. "First one out wins."

Each piece was cut from a different type of stone. When I picked one up, a smooth red jasper, certain portions of the stone caught the light of the oil lamps and shimmered.

The pieces followed a certain track on the board, which overlapped in the middle. The blocks that weren't in the middle were safe havens for one player or the other, but those that did were combat zones where pieces could do battle. While inhabiting the upper or lower grids, outside the bridge, players could choose to have their pieces avoid conflict as they ascended. But there was no getting through the bottleneck without conflict.

If a piece was taken by an opponent, it was sent back to the pool of eligible pieces outside the board. A player could have all seven of their pieces on the board at one time, or they could have as few as one—it was a question of strategic preference. Movement and combat were decided by dice.

I was presented with two bone dice for the game, tetrahedrons with values carved into the corners of their faces. Lefteris offered me the first round as practice. The stories continued as we played.

"When I first saw that cursed mountain, I didn't think I'd survive it. But do you know what the kyrios told me, that night before the rites?"

It was folly to pack the board with all seven pieces at once. There wasn't nearly enough room to maneuver.

"I had just wasted a month of my life in closed doors cultivation only to achieve nothing at all, and who do I see when I open the doors?"

Focusing on only one piece at a time wasn't much better. The elimination mechanic favored the player with more pieces on the board.

"I've taken the monster with me because what else was I going to do, and so the entryway is covered in blood and offal. Elder Solon is furious, the junior is nearly dead and won't stop vomiting blood over my back, and just as I'm about to lose my patience, who arrives but the kyrios?"

The kyrios had lived a full life from the sounds of it. As they reminisced, drinking and laughing, smiling wistfully in turns, we continued to play the game of Ascension. After my first couple practice games, the victor's rule was imposed. The winner kept the board while the loser gave way to a new challenger.

I cycled through a couple times following ties, getting a feel for the rules and various play styles. Kyno, Elissa, and Lefteris all employed wildly different strategies. Aggression, prudence, and pure brazen luck were present in varying proportions among each of them. Poor joke or not, it really was a simple game with a surprisingly profound strategic depth to it. And the introduction of luck as a mechanic meant that it could never be fully solved.

I found myself enjoying it more than I thought I would. Once I had firmly grasped the rules and core playstyles, I slowly built out my own over the course of several games. After my first loss, at Lefteris' hands, I began to win. And I didn't stop.

"You said he tied the Fates to this?" I asked offhandedly, somewhere around my sixth game in a row. Another table of Raging Heaven cultivators had noticed us playing and wandered over, pitching in to the conversation as well as the rotation of games. I was currently playing another Philosopher, of the eighth rank. He wasn't very good.

"The kyrios was a firm believer in the Pythagorean school of philosophy," Lefteris explained, watching us intently as we played. "Isopsephy as well, among other curiosities. Depending on the results of your rolls, when you roll them, where your piece ends up, and if it's in conflict with an opponent—even which of your pieces it is—there are countless interpretations. There are some whose entire cultivation journey revolves around the study of this game."

I couldn't think of a more boring life than one spent analyzing a board game. Still, it was enjoyable to play.

I glanced wryly at Lefteris as I set my piece over my opponent's piece at the bottleneck, taking it. "Ho? And what do these dice have to say about me?"

I continued to play, and I continued to win. My control of the board was absolute, unchallenged among heaven and earth. Eventually, Lefteris jumped back in as my opponent, and when he lost and another cultivator tried to take his place, he waved them off. The Civic cultivator protested for only a moment. Lefteris gave him a look that sent him scurrying to the other side of the club.

"You've never played this game before today?" he asked me suspiciously, resetting the pieces.

"Never in my life," I said easily. "I suppose I'm simply gifted."

"The kyrios was like that," Kyno mused. "It was as if any craft he picked up was something he'd been practicing for decades already, after only the briefest period of introduction. They say he only ever lost the game of Ascension once."

"His first," I guessed, rather than make the obvious joke.

"No," Elissa said. "It was a game he lost less than two decades ago, after centuries of play."

"Is that so?" I asked, interested. "Who beat him?" Elissa and Kyno shared a look across the table.

"Damon Aetos," Lefteris said and tossed me the dice.

"You're a liar and a cheat!" Lefteris accused me, slapping the table furiously and spilling our stone pieces off the board. Well, *his* stone pieces. Mine had already ascended. Kyno and Elissa watched in mixed amusement and disbelief. Wide cups of spirit wine and ivory marbles used for betting covered the table.

We'd drawn something of a crowd.

As per the rules we'd established early on, the loser of a given match had to down an entire cup of kykeon without pause. This was a fairly benign rule when the intention was for the loser to then cede the table to someone else and not stubbornly remain to lose over and over again.

For a Heroic cultivator, it would take several cups to make a dent in their prodigious tolerance.

Lefteris had the deeply rosy cheeks and glassy eyes of a man that had had far too much to drink. The sun had risen fully through the dawn, and I had won quite a few games. I was on my third cup of wine at the moment.

"Careful, friend," I said, propping my chin on one hand and smiling wickedly. "My virtuous heart won't tolerate such an accusation."

"I said what I said," he said, doubling down. Lefteris looked to Elissa and Kyno for validation, ignoring the jeers and taunts of the cultivators standing around the table. They had drachmae riding on these games and were obviously biased. "He's doing something to the dice, I'm sure of it!"

Elissa hummed, twirling her finger through her wine and flicking a clump of the impure lees at a target on the far wall. It struck dead center, and a cheer went up from a nearby table. She shot them a quick grin before answering.

"It does seem like something he would do," she agreed, in such a way that made it clear she disagreed. She was still a bit sore over our introduction but was coming around.

Kyno just patted him on the arm. "The only thing worse than a loser is a sore loser."

I came to a decision. "Let's see, then," I said, sweeping the stone tiles and pieces to the side of the table, leaving only the dice. "Is it strategy and good fortune, or am I a fraud? We'll let the heavens decide. I'll even close my eyes."

Lefteris considered the dice doubtfully.

"If you'd rather apologize, I'll accept it," I told him graciously. The Heroic archer scowled and snatched up the dice, shaking once and letting them fly across the table.

Snake eyes.

Laughter rippled through our little audience. I closed my eyes and rolled. When I opened them, I saw Lefteris' furious glare, and on the table—a one and a two.

"That's one," I told him breezily. "How many rounds would you like to try?"

"First to four," he spat, sweeping up the dice. He rolled again. A four and a three, this time. There were three sets of numbers on each corner of the dice, each ascending by a factor of ten. In this case, a four, forty, or a four hundred accompanied by a three, thirty, or a three hundred.

The distinction hardly mattered here. I let the dice fly with a lazy flick. When I opened my eyes, I saw a three and a four. Tie.

Lefteris shook the dice like they owed him money, Kyno and Elissa watching with poorly masked amusement as bone tetrahedrons bounced across the table. One and two. I rolled without fanfare and got the same result. Again.

"Impossible!" Lefteris snarled. I saw sweat beading on his brow. In a way, I supposed tying was more stressful than losing outright. "It's the dice. There's something wrong with the dice!"

"Are you accusing the owner of giving us weighted dice?" I asked, raising an eyebrow. The owner in question shivered in quiet fear, hovering over by the bar.

"We've been here countless times, Lefteris," Kyno chided him. "You know Timon wouldn't do that."

"Something he's doing, then," the drunk archer insisted.

"Or perhaps," I said slyly, "the Muses love me more than you."

It was a benign comment but with a challenging undertone—a thinly veiled way of saying that my cultivation was superior to his. It was a less common taunt among the lower realms but still present. Undeniably, it hit harder once one reached the Heroic realm and their lives became the subject of Epics.

When it became clear that Lefteris was too angry to roll, I took it upon myself to lead the next round. The dice clattered against the wood top, amidst cheers and calls for either my victory or Lefteris', depending on who was betting.

Twin twos. I leaned back and watched as Lefteris made the most focused cast of his life. I knew as they fell that it wouldn't be enough. Victory was a certainty in my heart.

Twin fours. I frowned.

I took the dice again when he gestured, accepting the change in order. A win to a win, and two ties. I let fly my dice and nodded when a four and a one resulted. Lefteris breathed deeply and cast again.

Twin threes.

Something...

I rolled one more time, the heavens yielding a three and a two. Lefteris was confident now.

Twin threes, again.

"You're cheating," I said with certainty. "My mentor would crucify you for that."

"Who's the sore loser now?" Lefteris asked smugly. "I'm throwing the same dice as you, fellow sophist."

"You are," I admitted. "But you're not throwing them fairly."

"It's unfair now that the winds are blowing my way, is it?"

"No. It's unfair because you're timing the dice."

It was the purest form of cheating among cultivators, utilizing the enhanced dexterity and perception granted by cultivation to manipulate exactly how the dice would fall. Such was a Heroic cultivator's alacrity that he could do it blind drunk and be correct every time. In fact, it was only *because* he was so drunk that I picked up on it at all.

Lefteris met my stare unflinchingly. "You're wrong." The crowd was quiet. The tension in the air became thick and cloying.

"Close your eyes," I ordered. "As I did." Lefteris obliged without hesitation, confident in his innocence. Or confident in his ability to continue cheating. He held out a hand, and I pressed one of the dice onto his empty palm, its point jutting straight up. His expression remained serene.

Then I placed the second tetrahedron directly on top of the first, balancing it precariously on the tip, and his smile vanished. Kyno chuckled, a low rumble in his chest.

Heroic cultivators were existences far beyond anything a Philosopher like myself could imagine. I didn't doubt for a moment that Lefteris could feel the impressions of the marked dice against his palm, and

I also didn't doubt that he could use that knowledge to time it completely blind.

But he couldn't cheat the second die.

"What will you do?" I asked him. "You can fix one of the dice, but heaven will have its hand on the other."

"What are you accusing me of, junior?" Lefteris asked me quietly, rather than throw. His eyes opened. Kyno and Elissa considering us both speculatively.

"Who says I'm your junior? I'm accusing you of being shit at dice... and a sore loser besides."

"It's like that then!" His heart flames ignited at the insult. "I think it's time you and I exchanged discourse, Griffon!"

"I have a better idea," I said, grinning fiercely. I slammed my elbow down on the table and offered him my open hand. "The Muses have abandoned you. Let's see if your body has too."

The club devolved into hollering chaos as I arm-wrestled the archer for all that I was worth. He pressed down on me with every ounce of strength in his Heroic body, but for all that he was stronger than me by an incomprehensible metric in terms of our tripartite souls, it was not necessarily the same story when it came to our bodies. He was an archer, a ranged warrior. His body, though far beyond anything an archer in a lower realm could possess, simply hadn't been tempered the same way mine had. We were built differently.

My body was superior. And admittedly, he was incredibly drunk.

He cheated, of course, but this time so did I. As soon as I saw the flames in his eyes flare up, I seized his hand with all twenty of my pankration arms and drove it down onto the table.

The club erupted with deafening cheers, and Kyno held Lefteris down while Elissa and I poured cups of spirit wine into his open mouth. Somewhere in the mayhem, the bronze doors of the club swung open and admitted a group of cultivators.

There were six of them, and as I brushed over them with a casual eye, I saw them staring directly at us. Two had the fires of Heroic cultivation in their eyes, while the other four were deep into the Sophic realm. Without hesitation, the sharper of the two Heros sauntered over to our table. Three Philosophers followed on his heels, while the other Hero and one of the Philosophers went to the bar.

I saw the Hero's eyes flicker to our empty chairs, vacated while we held Lefteris down and administered his punishment for cheating. Sensing what was to come next, I grabbed the chairs with three hands of pankration intent and pulled them back before he reached them. Something ugly swept across the faces of his entourage. The Hero smiled faintly.

Kyno cursed under his breath when he spotted them, righting Lefteris in his chair. Elissa turned cold, staring silently at the Hero and leaning on the table next to the bronze blade she'd laid across it. Lefteris sputtered and slapped as much wine out of his robes as he could.

"Greetings, Philosopher," the Hero insulted me. "You've taken my seats."

I felt a powerful sense of déjà vu.

"I don't see your name on any of them," I replied.

His eyes flared, but instead of attacking or responding the way I'd expected him to, he simply nodded at the chairs.

"See for yourself."

There was a name carved into the back of each chair that hadn't been there before. *Alazon.*

Heroic cultivators were nothing but swagger and bad attitudes.

"Unfortunately, I didn't come here to read," I declared. Lefteris laughed, evidently too drunk for a proper cultivator standoff.

"My, the junior initiates are bold these days. Hardly in the Sophic realm and you dare talk back to a Hero?" Alazon's voice was deceptively mild, while his pneuma radiated threat. Was this what it felt like? No, I was far more fun than this, surely.

"My mentor always said I was a precocious child," I said, only realizing as I said it that the three behind me would assume I meant Sol and not the old man that had taught me the quadrivium.

"A common affliction," Alazon said understandingly. "Fortunately, that is what senior initiates are for. Come, brother, allow me to guide you on your path to virtue." He spread his hands invitingly, and a monstrous pressure swept through the club.

The waves of Alazon's influence crashed against my own and only broke after some effort on my part. I smiled coldly. I could feel the difference between this one and Elissa. His temper was shorter, and his pneuma was even more densely vibrant. He wouldn't waste time on warning blows or choreographed moves. I could see the intent in the curve of his smirk.

He intended to shatter my ego. And I wasn't strong enough to stop him.

"Enough of this," Kyno said, stepping up beside me. His massive hands flexed threateningly, and— Was the crocodile skin *glaring?* "We've been here all morning, Alazon. Find another table."

"Of course, I'd be happy to trade discourse with you as well, brother," Alazon said obligingly. "In fact, I'm sure my juniors here would be honored to see your virtue in action. Perhaps you could advise them?" The three Philosophers with him fanned out around us, and in my peripheral, I saw the other two returning with their drinks, coincidentally placing them behind us.

"Six on four is hardly fair," I pointed out. "Arguably, Lefteris is drunk enough to count against us."

"Perhaps it's best you took him home, then," Alazon suggested.

Evidently tired of the wordplay, Elissa grabbed her bronze blade and drove it through one of the chairs, splitting it down the middle and kicking both pieces across the floor. Alazon stopped one with his sandaled foot, letting the other skitter by and shatter against the far war. His expression shuttered, and the tension in the room crystalized. I inhaled.

A cultivator's influence washed over the club.

Every able body stiffened as the waves swept over them, examining them, urging them beneath its surface. It was a challenge to fight. A riptide pull. I started to chuckle. Alazon, who had whipped around to stare at the bronze doors, turned back to me just as quickly.

"What are you laughing at?" he demanded furiously.

"*You.*"

Gravitas blew the bronze doors off their hinges, and Sol stalked into the club, dragging a cultivator dressed in black rags and a hood behind him. He had that storm in his eyes, and there was a dark weight to them that made him look twice and twice again more menacing than usual. From past experiences, I knew that dark weight was exhaustion. He was all but dead on his feet.

But they didn't know that. Three cultivators walked through the ruined entryway behind him, Scythas as well as a man and a woman I hadn't seen before. A cursory glance at their pneuma revealed that all three were of the Heroic realm. The hooded cultivator, too.

Sol threw the struggling Hero down onto the floor and stomped them *through it* when they tried to rise. The woman in his group laughed lightly, laying a hand on his shoulder. There was a cut there, angry and red, and it was mirrored on the other side of him.

"Careful," the Heroine said playfully. "This is the last one. We need them intact."

"I pay my respects to the kyrios," he said, ignoring her. His voice was as darkly strained as the rest of him. "For maintaining order in a cult full of *animals*." The last word came out as a snarl. The cultivator raised his arms up over his face, and Sol hammered them down with Gravitas. The man cried out in pain and fear.

A Hero cowered at Sol's feet. The context, doubtlessly, was not as impressive as the image here and now. But that hardly mattered. I fought to contain my smile and lost. Worthless Roman, I really *was* going to have to pretend he was my mentor after this.

"Who are you?" Alazon asked, confused and wary. No doubt his senses were telling him the truth of things—that Sol was only a Philosopher...and barely at that. But his eyes were telling him something else entirely. And if nothing else, the status of the three Heroes flanking him were undeniable.

I couldn't resist.

"Master," I greeted him cheerfully, "where have you been? You look terrible."

Sol looked, saw me standing by a table covered in cups of wine and a dice game, and his lips peeled back from his teeth. Lefteris' chair scraped loudly against the floor as he edged it back, away from my 'mentor'. Elissa's hand tightened to a white-knuckled grip on her blade. Kyno's jaw flexed.

"Your master?" Ah, there was the uncertainty. You tried to Young

Aristocrat the Young Aristocrat, Alazon. It's only natural that tribulation would follow. "I've never seen either of you before."

"We're new arrivals," I explained truthfully. "I came to compete, and Sol came for a bit of culture before he goes back to fighting demons on the western front."

"You're here for the Games?" the third member of Sol's companions asked, surprised. He glanced at Sol. "That's... not what I would have guessed."

"Seems almost too tame," the Heroine agreed, twirling a bloody javelin in her hand. Steam drifted away from it as I watched, the blood superheated by something invisible to the eye. The waves of her influence were scorching hot as they brushed up against mine.

"Demons?" Scythas asked, edging in close. "Is that true, Sol?"

I could visibly see the last thread of his patience snap.

The downed cultivator gagged as Sol picked him up by the throat and ripped the hood off his head. He would have been handsome, I was sure, and some of it could still be seen beneath the blood and swollen bruises, but it was difficult to appreciate now. He coughed and weakly spat, to his credit at least attempting to be defiant in the face of the storm.

Sol headbutted him as hard as he could. The crack of their foreheads slamming together and the way the Hero's head snapped back made it seem as if his neck had broken, just for a moment. The cultivator's eyes quivered, dazed.

And then they settled, for just a moment, on Alazon. They moved on at once. But it was too late.

"*You!*" Sol snapped, throwing the cultivator to the ground and stalking towards the Young Aristocrat. Alazon took a step back, an unconscious reaction. It doomed him. "Tell me how many there are and the names of their targets. *Now.*" For all that he had resisted my charade at the start, Sol was an exceptional actor. If he was acting, that was. I leaned back against our table, impressed enough to let it play out without any interruption.

"I don't know what you're talking about," Alazon replied, denying any involvement with the events that had sullied the funeral, of course. "I don't even know that man." Shadow politics were perhaps an inevitability in an institution like this, but being linked to those unpleasant dealings was something else altogether.

Alazon's loyal companions slowly distanced themselves from him, each trying very hard not to catch Sol's notice in doing so. Scythas and the other two were watching them intently, though.

"How cold of you, Alazon," the Heroine with the bloody javelin said disapprovingly. "I've seen you and Alexios here exchanging discourse on more than one occasion. Surely, you recognize him—the bruises aren't *that bad*."

The captain's influence pressed down on everyone in the club. I held my breath. I could see how close Sol was to collapsing. If they called his bluff and attacked, we had enough Heroes on our side to win the ensuing brawl. But he wouldn't necessarily survive it.

Luckily, Alazon was something that I have never been, even in my days as Young Aristocrat of the Rosy Dawn.

A coward.

The Heroic Young Aristocrat exploded into motion, *away* from Sol and the rest of us, vaulting the bar and disappearing through the back of the establishment. The Heroes that had been in the club but not taken any sides up until that point took off in pursuit of him, open collusion being the line that they apparently could not abide being crossed. The rest of Alazon's entourage tried to follow suit in escaping, but the Philosophers were swarmed by the other cultivators in the club, and Scythas and his friend took down the second Hero of the group with punishing force.

In the riotous haze of pneuma, Heroic spirits, and virtuous techniques tearing through the establishment, I nearly missed the crow that exploded out of the robes of the cultivator that Sol had dragged in.

The bird looked like it was made of squid ink instead of flesh, whirling liquid shadow in the shape of a crow rather than the creature itself. It shot through the air like an arrow from a bow, narrowly avoiding a dozen different techniques and shooting through the open doorway. It cawed mockingly as it vanished from view.

Abruptly, that caw turned to an odd, whistling shriek.

A Roman messenger eagle swooped into the club and landed on

Sol's shoulder. The crow construct struggled weakly as the eagle snapped down on its throat one bite at a time.

Sol approached our table in a controlled stagger, taking my seat and my cup of wine too, draining it in one pull. He ignored the chaos currently resolving itself in the club, the shouts and struggles of men individually capable of crushing stone and leveling buildings. He surveyed the table and the game of Ascension clustered to one side of it. The Heroine with the javelin leaned on the back of his chair, stroking his eagle and cooing softly to it while it preened.

"You're playing dice?" he asked roughly.

Elissa and Kyno shared a look, and slowly, *slowly*, they sat back down in their chairs. Lefteris, having been too drunk to stand in the first place, eased his back up to the table.

"We were," I said, smirking. Lefteris paled. "Before my new friend over here cheated."

Sol's eyes narrowed to slits.

Chapter Thirty-Seven

THE SON OF ROME

I woke up and immediately regretted it.

Remnants of the funeral drums echoed behind my eyes, an unbearable throbbing that turned my stomach. My body ached down to the marrow of my bones, and my mouth was drier than a day at the Senate. I shifted, grunting. Even the soft brush of silk sheets was intolerable. I cracked an eye open.

Luxury. It was a sparsely decorated room, but what was there was of undeniable quality. The floor was smooth stone that reflected the light of the sun, shot through with an electric blue lapis. The walls were covered in hanging tapestries of Olympic scenes painted with the painstaking detail of an artist's life's work. A single ivory column, waist-high, stood central in the room with a golden cradle for torch flame perched atop it.

A dining table cut from a fine, dark wood sat off in a corner. Each of its legs had been carved in the Corinthian style, with faux vines winding up their length. Large papyrus charts blanketed the table in place of food, gleaming with recently applied ink.

Upholstered dining couches and bronze-backed chairs were scattered throughout the room, and while those that remained intact were of the utmost quality, most of them had been smashed to pieces.

There were other things, personal items and keepsakes that I couldn't be bothered to keep my eyes open for. Satisfied that I wasn't dead or imprisoned, I rolled over on the blessedly comfortable bed.

Into Griffon's foot.

I shoved the filthy limb out of my face. He jerked awake, scarlet eyes snapping open.

"What—"

"Get out of my bed," I said hoarsely. Everything, including my own voice, felt unpleasant. I needed another three days of sleep at least.

"*Your* bed?" Griffon repeated, incredulous. "Neither of us owns anything. It's as much mine as it is yours."

"I don't care. Get out."

"Denied." He rolled over, using the crook of his elbow as a pillow. "Be quiet, will you? I had a long night." I knew he was smirking as he said it. It was why he'd turned away. It was purely an attempt to get under my skin.

It worked.

Gravitas threw him from the bed, and twenty arms of pankration intent tossed me off the other side in turn. I came to my feet spitting mad, my head pounding and the taste of blood in my mouth. He rose up across the bed, looking far better rested and entirely too smug.

"I'm going to kill you," I told him.

"You're welcome to try."

We both lunged for the bed.

It was Scythas' room, as it turned out. The Hero in question returned to his room with food and drink in hand, just in time to see us shatter his bed with our wrestling. We both froze, Griffon's hands wrapped around my throat and my own pressing a pillow down on his face. Hazel-flame eyes, flecked with golden embers, met mine. More than angry, he looked exasperated.

"We have halls for that," he said, shaking his head and sweeping the papyrus off his dining table with one foot. He laid out three loaves of dark brown bread alongside a long, narrow slab of stone covered with seared fish, followed by a pitcher of water and another of sparkling white wine. "At least eat something first. The two of you necked more kykeon in a day than most senior initiates drink in a week."

That explained a few things. I cursed my hubris. What sort of fool went binge drinking immediately after a night of brutal fighting? After multiple brushes with death? Men like me were why officers hated the infantry.

"Light work," Griffon boasted through the pillow, smacking my shoulders in a tap. It was no coincidence that he found the lingering cuts the Crow had left me. A night of work had purged the worst of the cultivator's poisonous pneuma from my system—but it still stung like a bastard.

I pressed down harder on the pillow. Pankration hands slapped insistently at my shoulders.

The bread was still warm, and the fish was coated in olive oil and richly seasoned with pepper and ginger. After I had forced down a cup of the sweet white wine and several cups of water, I even began to enjoy it. Griffon and Scythas made small talk while we ate, trading stories of the day before. Apparently, I had lost an entire day to exhaustion and spirit wine. The sun was just now rising again, a full day after the kyrios' funeral.

"So this is the Raging Heaven Cult," Griffon mused, licking a trickle of olive oil off his thumb and surveying the room with a critical eye. "Are all the initiates given private rooms?"

"Definitely not," Scythas said, shaking his head. "Junior initiates share rooms, four to a dorm for Philosophers and eight for Citizens. Heroic cultivators and those with seniority are given rooms like these. The elders each have their own estates scattered around the mountain, where their city's representative initiates tend to congregate."

He seemed to think of something and said to me, "Naturally, there are more spacious accommodations for honored guests. Elder Aleuas asked me to extend you an invitation to his estate. I'm sure he'll be happy to accommodate you during your stay."

"Naturally," Griffon echoed. I raised an eyebrow at him, but he only smirked faintly. Most young lords, whether they be aristocrats or patricians, would have chafed fiercely at the sudden reversal of our dynamic. Griffon, though, seemed amused by the novelty of it.

"See to it that he treats my master well," he said imperiously. "He went through much to get here."

"You mentioned that before," Scythas said with sudden intensity. I had a blurred impression of an exchange from the morning before like something out of a fever dream. The contents of it had been washed out by the alcohol and the exhaustion, but I remembered enough. *Demons on the western front.*

"What does your elder want with me?" I asked him, rather than answer the unspoken question. The food and the wine and the bed had improved my mood substantially, but not nearly enough to delve into that particular topic. Fortunately, the night before last had given Scythas an overinflated view of me. He accepted the deflection for what it was and didn't pry further.

"Jason and I brought the Crow in yesterday while you were playing Ascension," he explained. I nodded, distantly remembering a game of dice, and... a cheater? *A cheater.* "Cyril we turned over to Elder Gelon as we couldn't *prove* that he was involved in the same way Alazon was. But it was enough that we had the Crow and testimony from Alazon's lackeys. Elder Aleuas wants to thank you for assisting an initiate from his city and discuss the events of the night in person."

Somehow, I doubted that was all the good elder wanted from me. More importantly, though, what had been that cheater's name?

"What are these?" Griffon asked, picking up one of the papyrus sheets that Scythas had slid off the table. It was a star chart covered in fresh ink—a map of the night sky in winter.

"You don't remember?" Scythas' eyes widened in outrage. "They're for my cultivation—you said you knew what you were talking about when you offered to help!"

"If I said that I knew, then I did," Griffon assured him, scanning it with interest. "I just don't remember it."

For a moment, Scythas was lost for words. He looked at me. "Is he always like this?"

"He is."

"How can you not remember?" he asked, nearly desperate. "We spoke about this for hours."

"His tolerance for wine has always been pitiful." I didn't hesitate to condemn my student for forgetting such an important conversation. What that conversation had been about, I couldn't say, but it was surely outrageous that Griffon had forgotten it.

The man in question shrugged one shoulder, shooting me an amused look, and spread another chart across his lap. He hummed.

"Ah." It only took him a few moments to find what he'd been looking for. "You're on the hunt."

"He remembers," Scythas said, raising both hands in wonder.

Griffon shook his head absently, wild blond mane spilling over his shoulder. "No, I don't recall anything past the bathhouse."

Bathhouse?

"Oh, of course. You just took one look at the night sky in spring and realized what ails my soul," Scythas said scathingly. Griffon didn't respond, grabbing another chart from the pile. "... You're serious?"

"I always am," Griffon said. I snorted. "Be silent, master."

Astronomy had never been my primary focus, even as a boy. It was something my mentor had alluded to in the early days of my instruction but never delved fully into. I knew all the constellations worth knowing, of course, and I knew how to navigate by them, but after I'd left home to join the legions, my education had become far more practical.

I had learned to read omens from the night sky before a battle, and I was distantly aware of how to divine the seasons from their formations. But by and large, cosmology was not a field I'd had the luxury of exploring.

Which meant those feverish lashes of ink were Griffon's doing. I observed what looked to be a spear traced through the stars, a fist, and a hound with a snake in its mouth. The more I looked, the less it made sense. What could I have possibly contributed to this conversation, drunk and half dead?

"I can see where I was going with this now," Griffon said, faintly amused. "You want to cheat."

"*I do not!*" Griffon could have slapped him across the face, and I don't think Scythas would have been as offended as he was right then.

"And yet here you are, setting your sights on the Conqueror's Path,"

Griffon said with no particular judgment. There was scarlet laughter in his eyes as Scythas jerked the charts from his hands.

"Forget it," Scythas muttered sourly. His eyes flickered to me, chagrined, as if my opinion somehow mattered to him. How absurd.

I reached over and clapped him on the shoulder. I had to reach for it. The two of them were laid out on their dining couches in the indolent Greek style, an unpleasant reminder of younger days in Rome. I sat on my own couch like it was a bench. Old habits.

"You have nothing to be ashamed of," I told him truthfully. Griffon had a way of getting under one's skin. It was as much a skill of his as his pankration intent and his rosy fingers of dawn. But whatever it was that Scythas had asked our help for last night, I could tell that it was a difficult subject for him. It wasn't something he'd shared lightly, even with the addition of alcohol.

He relaxed at the small gesture, nodding once. "Thank you again," he said quietly. "I didn't stop to think when you pointed out those Crows. You probably could have handled it yourself, but I would have been in over my head if you hadn't come with me. So, thank you."

"You handled yourself well. You all did." It was a gross understatement. My recollections of that night were a blur of pain and single-minded focus, further muddled by potent spirit wine, but what I did remember of Scythas and the other two evoked memories of the best days in Gaius' legions.

Heroic cultivators were impossible legends, myths made reality. I was reminded of that fact over and over again, in the aftermath of the kyrios' funeral, while we stalked the stalkers and chased them from their shadows.

My contribution to the list of miracles performed that night was to somehow not die, not even once, and to come out of it with my reputation intact. Admittedly, that might have been the unlikeliest occurrence of the night.

Speaking of. "Where are Jason and Anastasia?" I asked him. I remembered them surviving the night but not much more than that.

"Jason's sleeping yesterday off, along with the other three if I had to guess." He shifted on his couch. His faint green cult attire, a marked difference from the royal indigos of the sanctuary city, shifted with the motion. It fell away from tanned muscle and sinew. He had no scars.

"And Anastasia?"

"I don't know, and I don't care to, either." His lip twitched towards a sneer, but he seemed to think better of it. "She is… not a woman I would associate with freely."

"Ho?" Griffon leaned forward on his dining couch, suddenly invested. "And why is that?" I vaguely remembered him grilling me in a private moment, while we'd walked the streets of Olympia surrounded by rowdy Heroes, about the new additions Scythas and I had returned with.

"Where that one goes, disaster surely follows," Scythas said darkly. "She's an ill omen in silk robes and a widow's veil."

The investment grew. "Go on."

"Don't be a fool!" Scythas snapped. Then, to me, "Just keep an eye on her. You may be able to take care of yourself, but with her, that isn't always enough. She has a way of… tempting."

Ah. I smiled, in the distant way of my adopted father.

"I'll keep that in mind."

"Right," he said, averting his eyes.

"I think I'll pay her a visit anyway," Griffon said, winking when Scythas glared at him. "My master often tells me I'm a foolish man."

"For all the good it does," I returned wryly.

"I warned you," Scythas said. "What follows is on your head."

There came a crack, a mechanical crunch of sliding bolt locks being forced out of place. Light flared along the surface of Scythas' door, bronze script burning with a visible light that seared the senses, alerting anyone within view of an imminent breach. Then, as quickly as it had come, it flickered and went out as the door was forced open.

Anastasia leaned against the mangled door frame, a vicious smile in her eyes. A massive Roman messenger eagle was perched on her right shoulder, which beat its wings and swept across the room to land on the curve of my dining couch, looking expectantly up at me. In lieu of a message, I offered it a scrap of fish.

Scythas came to his feet, fists clenched.

"My, my," the Heroine said. "You three have certainly been busy."

Smoldering green eyes surveyed the mangled room, drifting past Scythas without truly seeing him. They lingered for a moment on Griffon and the charming grin he reserved for strangers that didn't know him yet.

But they settled, inevitably, on me.

Chapter Thirty-Eight

THE YOUNG GRIFFON

Anastasia was what a charitable man would call dangerous. I'd known from the moment I felt the searing heat of her influence, and again the instant I'd seen the cruel amusement in her eyes while Sol battered a defenseless man in the club. She was the type to leave men pining endlessly for even the kiss of her heel.

Fortunately, she wasn't my type, and when lust was removed from the equation, she became simply *interesting*.

"Sol is a brutal taskmaster," I said in explanation of the broken bed frame. "Hardly gave me a moment to wake up before testing my pankration. Wouldn't even let me stretch first." It really was a shame. For Scythas especially. It had been a comfortable bed, feathered down and silk sheets.

"And the rest of the furniture?" Anastasia asked, arching a dark brow. Scythas grimaced, in part because of her lack of care for him as she brushed past him into the room, and in part because we truly had made a mess of the place.

Sol said nothing, matching the Heroine's smoldering stare and holding it as she approached him. Knowing him, the fool thought he was establishing authority.

"We may have had a cup too many," I admitted.

"An understatement if I've ever heard one," she said, rolling her eyes. Sol exhaled, satisfied that he'd won the 'staredown'. "I've seen lesser men die from drinking in such excess." The Heroine perched herself on the sloped headrest of Sol's dining couch, stroking his eagle from tip to tail feather while he fed it scraps of his breakfast.

Evidently, I was the only man in the room with a voice. That suited me just fine.

"We're cultivators. It's our providence to exceed lesser men."

"Even in your vices?" she asked, amused.

"*Especially* in our vices."

"My master would call that hubris," she murmured. "Even children know that vice is the inverse of virtue."

"Yet the heavens strike down virtuous souls like the kyrios while men like me run wild," I said, leaning a cheek on my hand as I reclined. I retrieved with pankration intent the charts that Scythas had taken from me, forgotten on his couch when Anastasia broke down the door.

"The heavens may not be prompt," she countered, "but their wrath is always felt in the end." The fine details of her were dark and nearly menacing, smoldering green eyes and smirking red lips, framed by long midnight black hair. The contrast with her marble pale skin was undeniably enticing. A fine aesthetic.

I grinned sharply, meeting her gaze over an array of star charts.

"I hope so. The tribulations are the best part."

For a moment she was honestly thrown. "What have you been teaching this one, Solus?"

"Not nearly enough," Sol said flatly. I snickered, flipping through papyrus sheets. Scythas finally made a decision, forcing the heavy bedroom door back into its frame with another painful crunch of breaking locks.

"Tell me, Anastasia"—the Heroine hummed invitingly—"did we trade life stories while I was drunk?"

"We did not."

"Good. It would have been rude to ask twice."

She chuckled. "My, my. Moving fast, aren't you? Some women enjoy the direct approach, but I prefer a bit of courting first."

"You think far too highly of yourself," I informed her pleasantly. "I couldn't possibly be less interested in you as a woman."

For the first time since I'd met her, the Heroine truly looked at me. The eddies of her influence brushed against mine, caustic and searching.

"Are you calling me ugly, cultivator?" she asked me softly. She was nothing of the sort, of course, but it wouldn't do to give her that satisfaction. I was certain she got enough of that from her fellow initiates.

"I see a more attractive face than yours every time I pass a clear pool," I replied instead. Scythas coughed, choking on a mouthful of white wine. Sol just rolled his eyes.

Viridescent flames and caustic influence pressed against me, lapping against the edges of my awareness. Then, all at once, it fell away.

"I like you," Anastasia decided, "but I like your mentor more."

"Understandable," I said. "With a smile like that, who wouldn't?" Sol favored me with a gesture that surely meant 'Thank you, brother' in legion-speak.

"The two of you are an odd combination," Anastasia mused. "A wolf keeping company with a lion. What could have possibly brought a Roman and a scarlet son together?"

Scythas stiffened in my peripheral vision. "Roman?"

Very interesting.

"It's a funny story," I told her. "Tragic, too, as all the best ones are."

"I'm listening," she said simply. I shared a look with Sol. I understood his intent without any words being said. This was neither the time nor the place to be discussing our flight from the Scarlet City, and certainly, Sol had no desire to share his personally tragic circumstances with two potential enemies of vastly superior cultivation.

I nodded minutely, letting him know that I understood, and he relaxed.

"We can trade," I proposed, blithely ignoring the suffocating pressure of Sol's murderous influence. "My cousin always said there's nothing quite like trading stories around a fire."

The rosy light of dawn crept from the cradle of my palm to the tips of my fingers, and I flicked a spark of my burning pneuma into a brazier mounted on top of a marble column. It caught the snow-white charcoal within and went up in a cheerful scarlet flame.

"A question for a question?" she asked, not committing one way or another. Scythas, having partly rejoined the group with forearms resting over the back of his lounge, didn't look any more eager to share.

"Exactly." It was clear that they needed some convincing, so I continued, "Let's make it interesting—a king's game. The winner asks the questions, and the losers answer."

"How convenient. The one who never loses never has to answer questions," Anastasia said wryly, tucking a ringlet strand of hair behind her ear. Scythas' eyes tracked the motion unconsciously. "And I suppose you have just the game in mind."

I splayed my hands invitingly. "Take your pick."

The Heroine considered me for a moment. "There is a game I wouldn't mind playing," she finally said, "but we don't have any knuckles."

Sol wordlessly dropped a handful of knucklebones on the dining table. They scattered across the dark wood, over a dozen of them, each rattling loudly.

"Where did you get those?" I asked.

"Don't worry about it."

Hmm.

"We'll need a drachma as well," Anastasia said. Scythas reached for a pouch on a nearby wall-carved shelf. Sol beat him to it.

A single drachma fell to the table, chiming as it struck.

Sol leaned forward on his bench lounge with quiet anticipation. Of course, the offering of a game had convinced him easiest of all. "The game is knucklebones. The figures are Under the Triumphal Arch and Aqueducts. Heads ends the round. Twelves decide."

With that said, he took up the drachma and flicked it into the air, and all four of us exploded into motion.

Knucklebones was an even simpler game than Ascension, won and lost on physical dexterity alone. A single jack, in this case a drachma, was thrown up and the knuckles were gathered in hand while it fell, through various means depending on the figure being played. I'd seen this variant a few times in the Rosy Dawn when Sol had been teaching it to the children in his care. Each figure had its own rules and win conditions, but the first round to decide the order was always the same. Smash and grab.

I snatched up three knuckles before Anastasia flipped the table with her foot and Scythas vaulted clear over his dining couch, heart flames raging as he blurred through the air. The golden coin clattered musically against the stone floor at the same moment the table shattered against the far wall. The drachma bounced and spun.

Gravitas struck the coin and pressed it to the marble floor. Heads.

"What was *that?*" Sol snarled.

"Do they not play it this way in Rome?" Anastasia opened her left hand, smugly presenting four knucklebones. Somehow, she'd gathered them without rising from her seat. Scythas looked at the two in his hand with chagrin. "It's hardly a challenge otherwise."

A game like knucklebones, based entirely upon reaction time, required no particular effort from a cultivator past a certain point of advancement. It was hardly a game at all if each player could grab every bone from the table before the jack started to fall. That being the case, an extra element of challenge was needed.

"Apologies for your room," I told Scythas. He waved it off, having already come to terms with the damages. Surprisingly easygoing, compared to his usual temperament.

"Cheaters and thieves, all of you," Sol said, disgusted, and he dropped six knuckles onto the floor. Anastasia raised an eyebrow, impressed. Scythas stared uncomprehendingly.

"How often do you play this game?" I asked, amused. He sneered.

"I have the first question. Where do the good philosophers go?"

"Oh? So it's like that," Anastasia mused. She stroked the messenger eagle's head thoughtfully. Scythas, for his part, crossed his arms in concentration, crouching by his dining couch.

Scythas snapped his fingers suddenly. "A philosopher is nothing but a man who can see the surface of all that he doesn't know."

"Who told you that?" I asked curiously. The Hero looked at me strangely.

"Solus did, last night. Have you forgotten even that?"

Sol looked about as confused as I felt.

"If a philosopher is simply the first blind man to know he's missing his sight, where does he go to see?" Anastasia posed, sounding the problem out. For the moment, any enmity between the Hero and the Heroine was forgotten as they pondered the question.

"I think he just wants to know where the Sophic cultivators spend their time here," I said. I was rewarded with disdain, and two superior cultivators looking down their noses at me. Ah. So this was what it felt like.

"How pitiful," Anastasia said.

"Do you take everything at face value?" Scythas added.

"Forgive me," I demurred. By this point Sol had closed his eyes, his solemn face a mask of deep consideration and weighty expectation. In reality, I could tell that he was trying not to snap.

"If it's a question of belonging—"

"Under the Triumphal Arch," he declared, cutting them off and taking up the coin once more. He pressed the tips of his index and middle fingers against the blue-veined marble, forming an arch. We each followed suit, Anastasia leaning precariously over from her seat on the dining couch.

The coin flipped and knucklebones flew.

The objective of Under the Triumphal Arch was to flick as many knucklebones through the arch of one's fingers as possible before the jack fell. Depending on the placement of the bones from the previous figure, as well as the actions of the other players and the trajectories involved, the difficulty of the game could change. Of course, for cultivators of Anastasia and Scythas' standing, it was hardly worth playing. Unless they cheated.

I flicked a knuckle bone with one hand and sent it flying through the arch my other hand formed. However, just before it could pass through, a whistling projectile struck it from the side and sent it flying off course. Another projectile struck a knuckle next to my arch before I could even attempt to flick it through. In an instant, the room became a whirling storm of flying bones.

Anastasia smiled innocently at me, caustic green flames burning merrily in her eyes.

"I count twenty-three through mine," she reported at the end.

There were only twelve knucklebones in total, meaning she was a liar or she had flicked multiple sets in the time it took a coin to fall.

"Eight," Scythas reported sourly. I didn't bother vocalizing my null score.

We looked to Sol and beheld the sight of him silently flicking bones through the arc of his fingers while the golden drachma hovered just above the ground, spinning lazily in the air. Anastasia and Scythas both lunged for the nearest knuckle, stabbing their fingers back to the floor hard enough to crack the marble.

Sol released his virtue's hold on the coin and it fell cleanly with heads facing up.

"Forty."

"But that's—" Scythas protested. Sol stared at him, daring him to finish the statement. He didn't.

"Where do the good philosophers of the *Raging Heaven* go?" he asked this time, leaving nothing to the imagination.

It didn't help.

"So that's your game," Scythas said, massaging his jaw. "Juniors and seniors. The wandering philosophers of the free Mediterranean versus the scholars of the Half-Step City. A physical place, after all."

"Nothing so simple as that," Anastasia countered. "The divide itself is the question. We may break bread in the light of the divine storm, but is it really the case that we are the seniors, and wanderers like Solus are the juniors? What makes a junior a junior and a senior a senior among philosophers? Age? Standing? Or perhaps virtue?"

"None of the above," I disagreed, all too happy to further derail the question while Sol silently despaired. "Among philosophers, rhetoric alone is king."

"So it's a question of who among us has the best rhetoric." Anastasia, still bent over the lounge's headrest, twisted and leaned one arm against the cushion beside Sol, resting her head on it as she thought. "A dangerous question, especially now. The Raging Heaven Cult may soon be at war with itself. You never know who might be listening... or when."

"There isn't anyone," Sol said, his voice dull. Ah. He'd given up.

Anastasia looked up at him, startled. "What?"

"Nobody is listening to us right now," Sol repeated. "I'd smell it." As before, at the funeral, a Heroic cultivator balked at something Sol had presented as a simple observation. Scythas, for his part, just shook his head in wonder.

"My, my," the Heroine said softly.

"You're free to speak your minds," I prompted them. Deep contemplation was the response. Free from the paranoia of another party listening in, they devoted their full attention to the prospect.

"The best rhetoric in the cult," Anastasia murmured.

"Where blind men go to see," Scythas continued.

They both reached the same conclusion.

"The baths."

Sol swallowed back a mouthful of blood.

"Aqueducts," was all he said, pressing the tips of his four longest fingers to the floor, creating three arches where there had only been one before. The aim of this figure was to complete as many sets as possible, one set being a knuckle flicked through each of the three arches of the aqueduct in sequence. The coin flipped up into the air, and pneuma flooded the room.

This time, all three of us kept an eye on the coin to make sure it settled completely to the floor, and Scythas unveiled a trick involving what I was certain was a manipulation of the wind itself. Sol, having been thoroughly demoralized, didn't participate at all. The coin landed tails up this time, leading to another flip and an extended round. By the end of it, Scythas had collected thirty-seven sets of three, while Anastasia had taken nineteen, and I had taken eight.

Triumphantly, Scythas leveled a finger at Sol. "I have to know, Solus! Where do you stand among heaven and earth?"

I inhaled the heavy, expectant silence. Pneuma flooded my veins, coursing through my blood in spiraling threads and heating it nearly to the boiling point. My muscles shivered and tensed unnoticeably in anticipation. It had happened sooner than I'd hoped, but later than I'd expected. I supposed this charade was always doomed to fail.

While I prepared myself for the fight of our lives, Sol calmly answered.

"Legate."

Ah. So that was what they called him.

"Legion commander?" Anastasia looked up at him through narrow eyes. "How old are you really, Solus?"

"That sounds like another question." Sol offered the golden drachma to Scythas, who after a moment took it.

"I have another question, so I'll be winning again," he declared. "The figure is Aqueducts, once more."

"That's a mistake," I said lazily. "I never lose the same game twice." The Hero scoffed and flipped the coin.

My pankration hands filled the room.

Fingers of my purest intent drove through the marble floor, five hands creating nineteen arches, each lined up end-to-end in a grand aqueduct that I immediately filled. The remaining fifteen pankration hands blurred across the floor, flicking and intercepting knucklebones at every possible opportunity. Whistling blurs shot through the arches of my aqueduct and were fired back just as quickly by pankration hands waiting on the other side.

With my flesh and blood hand, I caught the golden drachma and slapped it against the back of my other true hand. Heads.

"Would you like to know how many that was?" I asked. Scythas spat on his own floor in lieu of reply. "Anastasia?"

"No need," she said, satisfaction in her eyes as they traced the invisible lines of my violent intent. "I've just had one of my questions answered."

"Ho, is that so? Then it's only fair if you answer mine—you're here to compete, aren't you?"

"I am."

"In which event?"

"That's two questions," she admonished me. "And you already knew the answer to both. You have eyes, don't you?" The javelin, then.

"And you, Scythas?"

"That's three," Anastasia said, with real annoyance this time.

I shrugged and flipped the coin. "Twelves."

Sol flicked a finger, a pulse of his virtue sending all twelve of the knucklebones flying into the air. He didn't move beyond that, still abstaining out of spite. This was the simplest figure—the goal was to catch as many of the flying bones on the back of your hand as possible. Twelve arms of pankration intent caught the bones while the rest slapped aside Scythas and Anastasia's reaching hands.

"And you, Scythas?" I asked again, smiling pleasantly.

The Hero scowled. "The sprints."

"Twelves," I repeated, flipping. Heroic spirits flared and wind and flame raged throughout the room, burning furniture to ashes and tearing silk sheets to shreds. It was all in vain.

"The javelin, then," I mused, returning my attention to the Heroine while my pankration hands rolled the knucklebones around on the backs of their palms. "But you fight with it as well, so which came first? Was the martial path a consequence of the athlete's desire, or were the games an escape from your troubled past?"

There was less humor in her eyes now. "Neither."

I raised an eyebrow. "Twelves." I felt phantom agony in fingers that I didn't truly have as the Heroic cultivators turned their pneuma upon my pankration hands in their frustration. They were petty strikes with no real heat behind them, but that was by a Hero's standards.

Still, they lost.

"How did you know Sol was from Rome?" I pressed her.

"He was singing a Legion marching song when I found him."

Sol refocused on the conversation, looking narrowly down at her. "When you approached me, you said that I was a wolf after all. You knew what I was from the moment I called out to you." Anastasia was a much better actor than Scythas, that much was certain. But she wasn't better than me. I saw her frustration clear as day.

"If it wasn't the cadence but the call itself," I pondered, "then what was it about my good master's influence that evoked thoughts of Rome? Past experience, perhaps? Something to do with that javelin of yours?"

Anastasia stared at me, silent for a long moment. Finally, she nodded, conceding.

"I was right to worry after all," she said. "How did you know which game I would pick?"

"I didn't." Satisfied, I tossed the coin into the air and waved a hand invitingly. I poured myself and Sol another cup of wine while the two

Heroic cultivators fought over the airborne knuckles. It was sweeter than the usual affair at the Rosy Dawn, light and faintly tart on the tongue.

"What about you?" Anastasia asked, balancing seven knucklebones on the back of her hand. She leaned back, dark hair pooling on the floor as she looked up at me. "Which golden frond do you desire, Griffon of the Rosy Dawn?"

I leered at her over the rim of my drinking cup. "Isn't it obvious? I want them all."

"Every event?" Scythas asked in disbelief. "Are you out of your *mind?* Where do you stand?"

"That's two questions," I admonished him, flashing my most charming smile.

"I've decided I like you less," Anastasia said. I placed a hand over my heart, wounded. She laughed. "Much less."

The Heroine twisted and rose to her feet, brushing down her cult attire and giving the messenger eagle one last affectionate scratch. She was close enough to Sol that their noses would touch if he tilted his head just a fraction.

"That's enough games for me, I think. Shall I escort you to the place where good philosophers go, Solus?"

"After you," he said, unbothered by her proximity. She looked into his eyes a moment longer, slowly smiling before turning and heading for the door.

"I have another question," I called, while Sol forced the door out of its broken frame. Anastasia glanced back at me, raising an eyebrow. "What is the first virtue?"

Caustic green eyes glittered.

"Purity," she said, and then to me, "where do you stand among heaven and earth?"

"You have eyes, don't you?" I asked mockingly. "I'm nothing more than a Philosopher of the first rank."

"Liar," she scoffed. Anastasia walked out the door, and Sol followed her.

Scythas, myself, and an eagle stewed in the silence they left behind. Eventually, Scythas set about salvaging what he could from the room, slipping items and articles of clothing inexplicably into the folds of his cult attire as he worked. I drank and shuffled through his star charts, gathering my thoughts.

"So. Anastasia?"

Scythas threw his things down in disgust and stalked out of his own room.

"It's just you and me now," I informed the great messenger eagle of Rome. It cocked its head at me. I offered it a bridge of pankration palms, and after a moment, it fluttered up onto the first and hopped across them to my outstretched arm. Its talons curled easily around my forearm, and the kiss of their edges was sharp against even my tempered skin.

"You're no mere bird, are you?" I asked it. It looked at me expectantly. I offered it a scrap of my own meal, the skin of a swordfish. The eagle snapped it down. "That's been clear since you found us on the *Eos*. Now, even more so. No mundane bird would be able to detect my pankration intent."

The virtuous beast ruffled its feathers, either unable to understand or unwilling to care. Perhaps it only spoke Latin.

"You're Sol's companion, that's clear as day, but that worthless Roman hasn't even given you a proper name. You're certainly worthy of that much."

My pneuma rose, washing over the bird and urging it to submit. Its talons dug painfully into my arms, drawing fine lines of blood, and it spread its wings wide in defiance. The virtuous beast shrieked in my face, unwilling to bend beneath my strength.

I laughed. "Sorea you shall be." The lost eagle of Rome. I offered it a roll of papyrus that I had torn from one of Scythas' star charts and written a quick message on with a formless hand while observing the bird.

Rather than offer a leg for me to tie the missive to, the virtuous beast simply darted forward and snapped the roll up in its beak, swallowing it without hesitation.

"Disgusting," I said fondly, flicking my arm and dislodging the creature. "Be gone from my sight, mongrel bird."

Sorea took flight through the balcony terrace with one last parting shriek, beating its wings and shooting up the mountain at a dizzying speed.

I stood up from my lounge, stretching mightily. I sighed, relishing the myriad pops and cracks of my body unwinding. Pankration hands massaged and dug into the tight muscles of my shoulders and neck, coaxing the tension out of my flesh.

Now then. Where was that Oracle?

Chapter Thirty-Nine

THE SON OF ROME

The Raging Heaven Cult was a series of connected estates and valence communities, growing like weeds around the foot of Kaukoso Mons. Similar to the Rosy Dawn in its construction, the various estates were connected by winding trails of stone carved into the mountain itself. Walking paths, staircases, and even arched bridges of stone could be found within its boundaries.

In an inversion of the Rosy Dawn, the most influential members of the cult lived at the lowest points, where the mountain met the earth. The junior initiates lived in quarters farther up the mountain, perilously close to the storm. An ever-present sensation of malice and threat hung over the cult. The low roll of thunder was constant. I felt it in my bones.

The Storm That Never Ceased hung over the peak of Kaukoso Mons like a funeral veil, illuminating the mountain and its various estates at all hours of the day and night with flashes of chain lightning. Walking along the carved stone paths and looking up the mountain, at that writhing monument to heaven's fury, I wondered.

What could the act of building an entire human civilization on the face of such an edifice be called if not hubris?

"It never stops?" I asked, though the answer was in the name. I couldn't tear my eyes away. The clouds were impossible to see past, dark and foreboding. The crash of constant thunder was felt more than heard, most of its volume muted by something within the cult's structures themselves. Beyond the gates of the Raging Heaven Cult, though, it was deafening.

"How could it?" Anastasia asked, glancing up only briefly at it. "The Storm That Never Ceases is a monument to the hubris of man, tribulation made manifest. Humanity tempts the Fates, and the thunder rolls. While one exists, the other must as well."

She stepped lightly up the mountain, disdaining the stone stairs in favor of hopping and skipping like a mountain goat, simply because she could.

"Setting up camp under it isn't exactly a step in the right direction," I observed. She glanced back at me, swinging her arms and smiling mischievously.

"True enough, your student was right about one thing. Audacity is the providence of cultivation—it's what drives us to the ivory heights. And what could possibly be more audacious than forging our souls by the light of heavenly tribulation?"

The architecture of the cults of greater mystery, as well as the cities in which they resided, seemed to follow a particular theme. Álikos was called the Scarlet City for a reason—its fashions, its architecture, and its great works of art reflected that. The sanctuary state of Olympia was much the same, taking a brush of indigo to itself in varying degrees.

Electric blues and crimson reds abounded, mingling at points where roofs were shingled and robes were dyed to form a royal purple hue. The estates of the Raging Heaven followed a hierarchy of color that diverged from a vibrant indigo at the base of the mountain where the elders and core initiates resided, turning to distinct blues and reds as one progressed up to where the senior initiates and athletes did their cultivating, worked into the murals painted on the walls and the statues carved out of their pillars. Farthest up the mountain, where the juniors beat themselves bloody and ground down the stone steps day and night, those vibrant reds and blues rejoined to form imperfect shades of the elders' royal purple.

I ran my fingertips along a carving in the mountain, a stone relief of a man reclining in a vineyard drinking deeply from two cups, one in each hand. The twin streams of wine pouring into his mouth were veins of a muddled violet gem that glittered in the light of flashing lightning. Precious stone sitting in the open air, unharvested.

"The more I see of this culture," I said, almost to myself, "the less I understand it." How many legionaries would have given their lives in war for a bare sliver of these violet veins?

"Is it really so different in Rome?" Anastasia asked. She leapt from one outcropping of stone to another—a distance of over a hundred feet vertically up the mountain. Rather than trying to keep pace, I simply kept walking up the steps until I'd reached her again.

"There was excess," I admitted, thinking back to the days of my childhood when everything had been wonderful and nothing had been enough. Precious gems, fine silks, and ornaments of gold had been standard provisions for my mother and distant family. "But we could never afford to do the things I've seen done in the free cities. I'd like to hope that if we'd had that wealth, we wouldn't have spent it so frivolously."

"You would, would you?" she asked, hopping down and rejoining me on the steps. Her arms linked behind her back, the dark onyx robes of her cult fluttering in the gale winds of the Storm That Never Ceased.

"We don't have artists or poets in the magnitudes that your Greeks do, I'll admit, but I have yet to see a nation as virtuous as the republic. Our Heroes are men of war and of the fields. Not slayers of monsters, but defenders of law and order. Beholden to none but the Twelve Tables. Righteous." My right hand clenched reflexively. "And strong."

Anastasia considered me thoughtfully. "I confess that I don't know much of the Roman mythos."

"It's not as exciting as *Ríastrad* or the Seven Sages," I said, eyes unfocusing as I trudged up the steps. "Rome was only founded a few centuries ago. Younger than your kyrios." And shorter-lived. My teeth grit. "Our men are our mythos, cunning generals and wise senators. One of our greatest heroes was nothing more or less than a man that commanded the Legions when we needed him to and returned to a life of quiet cultivation on his farm when we didn't."

"Cincinnatus was the first dictator, the one that every Roman adores," Gaius told me as his eyes roamed over the sand table. *We were alone, and so he let his frustrations slip. But only for a moment.* *"The heavens adored him, too. So much so that they placed all his enemies in front of him."*

"If we glorify contentment, how can we break past the boundaries of our mortality?" Anastasia asked quietly. Not directly opposing me but closer now.

"Cultivation only makes us more of who we are." It was a curse as much as it was a prayer. "And not every culture follows the same trail up the mountain. Even the barbarians have their own paths to providence."

"Is that the Roman way, then? Cultivating fields when you're not cultivating war?"

I snorted in spite of myself. "We also enjoy games."

She nudged me with her shoulder. "You didn't come to Olympia to play games, though." Her eyes flickered, and she said, almost sadly, "And you're not here to farm, either. Are you?"

"Everything that I am is the product of the men that mentored me," I said eventually, remembering sunlit mornings in quiet vineyards, scorching afternoons in the sandpits and the surf, and cold, dark evenings in the command tent, hunched over sand tables and inked dialogues. "They did what they could with the materials they were given, but I'm no hero. The good people of Rome are better than I could ever hope to be."

"I don't think that's true," Anastasia denied me with a smile. She didn't hesitate to do so. "But even so, I think I'd like to see this city for myself. See if it compares to my own Nkrí. Maybe one day you could bring me there," she said slyly.

"Maybe one day I will," I said, restraining with willpower alone the reaction that her words nearly evoked.

She didn't know.

The baths at the Rosy Dawn had been works of native majesty, making use of the natural springs within the eastern mountain range of the Scarlet City to create soothing hot water pools and purifying steam rooms. They'd been minimally decorated, by Greek standards, meaning they were utterly luxurious by the standards of the average Roman.

The Raging Heaven's baths, on the other hand, were absurd by any metric.

There were as many bathing pavilions as there were estates on the mountain, all of them publicly available to the mystikos of the cult, and no doubt there were dozens of smaller private bathing suites besides. The one that Anastasia took me to was anointed in alabaster and ruby veins, two massive basins placed *on* the mountain, rather than carved out of it. They were ringed by Corinthian pillars holding up a ceiling that was painted in maroon and fuchsia shades to mimic the night sky at false dawn.

The alabaster tubs, each capable of fitting at least fifty men without any of them being forced to touch, were smooth and decorated with carved lines and rosettes that I realized represented the stars in the sky on two particular days—one pool for the winter equinox and the other for the spring.

Their temperatures were regulated by unnatural means, one of them so cold that thin flecks of ice floated on its surface, and the other hot enough to make the air above it shimmer and distort. It was a de facto way of separating the baths by rank, I supposed. At temperatures this extreme, even captains of the Civic realm would struggle to cope for more than a few minutes.

I could only imagine how bad it was in the baths at the foot of the mountain.

"You don't seem to be enjoying yourself very much," Anastasia observed, languidly turning her head to face me. We sat only a short distance apart at one edge of the basin, the rest of the tub full nearly to capacity with Sophic cultivators. Men and women bathed together, naked as the day they were born, jostling and exchanging discourse without care.

I abstained from the first answer that came to my mind, instead saying, "We do it in the reverse order back home."

Anastasia blinked, small chips of ice fluttering from her eyelashes with the motion. "Hot bath and then cold?"

I nodded.

"That's barbaric."

I glanced around the bathing pavilion, at the naked men and women mingling freely, and, in some cases, without any space between them. I looked to the pillars holding up the roof, each carved in the shape of a man or a woman engaged in debauched recreation.

"Barbarism is in the eye of the beholder," I said, fighting a sneer.

"There are benefits to our way," she explained, rather than take offense. "Medical boons. These waters were gathered from blessed springs across the free Mediterranean, and each has its own unique properties. A frigid shock to the system followed by searing heat has a cleansing effect on the body, and the spiritual properties of the water have a similar effect on the soul."

That much, at least, I could not deny. My entire body was numb from the cold, and if not for the conditioning I had put it through in the Legions, it would be far past the point of discomfort. But the lingering, spiritual and bone-deep ache of the infected wounds on each of my shoulders had vanished completely as soon as I stepped in.

"Do they have many bathhouses in Rome, Solus?" Anastasia asked me, curious.

"We do," I said, something painful and joyous in equal measure about speaking of home in the present tense. "Hundreds of them, each a work of human ingenuity in place of natural fortune, fed by aqueducts that span entire countrysides and mountain ranges. Simple, compared to this, but finely built."

"I would be surprised if they were as gaudy as these," Anastasia said lightly. "Even the baths where I live aren't like these. I would say they're closer to yours—reliably built and comfortable. We carve them from pewter and warm them in the heat of our flaming mountains."

"Do you bathe together there as you do here?" I asked wryly. Anastasia laughed. It was a pleasant sound, throaty and musical.

"Dual cultivation has its own benefits, you know," she said slyly. I rolled my eyes in disgust. "Besides, I told you already that these baths have medicinal properties, as all good baths do. Where better to exchange discourse than in such a place, where your body and mind are at their best?"

I eyed a pair across the pool, a man with long brown hair that floated on the icy surface and a young woman with pale skin covered in tattoos of whirling purple ink. They were whispering in each other's ears, the woman sitting on the man's lap, both giggling every so often.

"I see."

"Are all Romans as uptight as you, Solus?" Anastasia teased.

"Are all soldiers as tightly wound as you, husband?"

I stood abruptly from the bath.

The hot bath felt colder than the ice bath when I first stepped into it, but that soon gave way to an almost agonizing heat and a rush of tingling sensation on my skin, numbness giving way to warmth. I exhaled roughly, letting it wash over me. Air filled my lungs easier than usual, more fully, and my pneuma circulated freely throughout my body. It wasn't nearly as satisfying as jumping into an ice-cold pool after sweating for hours in a hot bath, but it was pleasant in its own way.

"I apologize," Anastasia murmured, slipping in beside me. "I meant no offense." She had two cups of cool water in her hand, and she offered me one. I took it mechanically, staring straight ahead for all the good it did me. No matter where I looked, I saw degeneracy, and degeneracy saw me. The vile sensation of eyes roaming across my naked chest assaulted me from all sides.

"I'm married," I said, not trusting myself to say more.

"Is that so?" Anastasia hummed. "What's her name?"

I realized why I was so at ease with Anastasia compared to the others. Even Griffon, who had approached conversation with her as a challenge to be overcome.

They had the same schemes in their eyes.

"Luna," I said, and in the mirage heat of the baths, I could almost see her sitting across from me. Smiling in that way of hers.

"Is she back in Rome?"

Salt and ash.

"She is."

"A shame for her, then," the Heroine mused, shifting just so in the water, so that I felt the waves. "Your student had another point, audacious as he was in making it. We cultivators are greedy existences. We see something we want, and we take it. Even if it's off-limits to us. *Especially* if it's off-limits to us."

I glanced sidelong at her. Schemes. Schemes and naked interest.

Not subtle at all.

"You don't want me," I said because I'd never had patience for scheming. "Not for that."

Green eyes crinkled, and the interest deepened.

"Don't be so sure," she said lightly. She leaned back against the alabaster basin of the scorching hot bath, eyes flicking from one mystiko to another as she surveyed the pavilion. "Either way, I've brought you to one of the Raging Heaven Cult's bastions of rhetoric. Do you see what you're looking for?"

"No." I'd known that from the moment we arrived.

"Are you looking for anything in particular?" she pressed. "Anyone, perhaps?"

I considered deflecting or lying, but I decided it didn't matter in the end. "I'm looking for my mentor. He used to live in this city, years ago."

"Truly?" Anastasia asked, surprised. "If I'd known that, I wouldn't have taken you to a place like this. The elders never venture this far up the mountain outside of the initiation rites."

"He wasn't an elder," I said, shaking my head. "At least I don't believe so. Your elders are all Heroes and Tyrants, aren't they?"

"You're saying..."

"My mentor was a great man, but he was only a Philosopher." I shrugged. Perhaps that was too much information for my cover, perhaps not. I'd soon find out.

"Only a Philosopher," Anastasia muttered, in the same tone that Griffon had used when I told him about my father, in a different bath in the Scarlet City. "Well, the Raging Heaven Cult has no shortage of those. I'm sure he's around here somewhere. And if he is, I can surely find him. What was his name?" she asked, drinking gracefully from her cup.

I told her.

The Heroine choked.

Chapter Forty

THE YOUNG GRIFFON

The Oracles were divine messengers, sent down to us lowly men from the heights of Olympus Mons. They transcribed the words of immortals, writ large upon the world, and gave them to us in a form we could understand. If their tongues were the thread, their words were the tangled weaves of destiny itself.

For time immemorial, the Oracles had guided the greatest Heroes on their paths to glory and prophesied the fall of the vilest Tyrants. It was not enough to say that these women were heaven-sent. Divinity was in their very blood. After all, how else could they understand the incomprehensible tongue of the pantheon?

Every champion's journey began with the Oracle. Women of prophecy existed in every culture worth mentioning, but it was an intuitive truth that the Oracle was a reflection of her patron deity. And, of course, it went without saying that the Greek pantheon was superior to all others.

Our Oracles were simply the best in the world.

It was no coincidence that in the midst of the war for the Mediterranean, while the free city-states were fighting with all they had to expel his armies, the Conqueror had chosen to push through the bloody seas of hoplites and Heroes to speak to the Oracle. Alone, as vulnerable as he would ever be in his entire life, it was no act of madness that had driven him to the divine temple. It was a desire to *know*. The hunger.

When the Oracle had spat upon him and refused to ask the gods for a foreign Tyrant's destiny, he'd dragged her out of her holy domain by the hair and beat her in the streets before her people and the heavens themselves. Citizens and soldiers alike had thrown themselves at the Conqueror in outrage and despair, and all of them were cut down by his fury. In the end, it wasn't the people of Greece or the Oracle herself that broke.

Her patron deity cried out with the Oracle's own mouth and gave the Conqueror what he had come for in exchange for her life.

It nearly cost him his life during the retreat back to his armies, and some said that the turning point of the war lay entirely on his shoulders, in that moment. While separated from his forces, the phalanxes were given their one and only chance to scour the enemy from our borders. And they took it. By the time the Conqueror rejoined with them, injured and near death, the Macedonian hordes were in full retreat. They never returned.

My father, though, in the one time he'd spoken of it, said that the Conqueror had hardly walked away from the incursion disappointed. And if the stories of what followed were true, he'd found more than enough success in other nations, on other battlefields. Perhaps the Oracle had been a part of that. Perhaps not. Regardless, the losses that he sustained that day were simply the price of admittance to the divine temple.

Immortal insight was a boon that needed no explanation. Yet we were cultivators, were we not? In the end, our ultimate goal was to spit in the face of heaven and throw off its threads, *was it not?* What did it matter what the immortals had to say? Why should the supreme Conqueror care for the words of a being too cowardly to show its face while he savaged its chosen messenger?

I was curious to see what the fuss was about, I had to admit. But I wasn't looking for prophecy. I wanted to meet the women that had been touched by divinity.

Unfortunately, it turned out that gaining an audience with such a woman was easier said than done. Since the first kyrios of the Raging Heaven Cult had consolidated the great powers of the Mediterranean within Olympia's walls, each of the Oracles now resided here at Kaukoso Mons. But this hadn't turned out to be the convenience I'd thought it would be.

I watched another initiate of the Raging Heaven beg admittance to a temple of an Oracle, and once more I watched an initiate face cold rejection. The third in as many hours. The mystiko, a wild-eyed woman with streaks of gray in her hair that belied her apparent youth, fled the entry archway in hysterical tears. The guards didn't even watch her go. The fires of Heroic cultivators burned dully in their eyes.

It was to be expected that not every mongrel off the streets would be granted an audience with a divine messenger, but I hadn't expected things to be quite this strict. Thus far, only one initiate had been granted admittance to the temple, and they had been a Heroic cultivator themselves.

The Oracle's word was the beginning and the end of nearly every great epic, the bane of Tyrants the world over. Why would they waste their breath on anything less than a Hero? I'd checked three of the nine temples since this morning, and the principle had held true for each one. The only question that remained was whether or not a Hero could bring a friend.

I waved gaily to the guard on the right as his influence crashed against me, white-backed waves and dangerous intent. Onto the next.

For every deity of the sublime pantheon, there was an Oracle to spread their word. One for each of the eight city-states, and two for the Coast. Their temples were spread out around the foot of the mountain, intermingling with the personal estates of the Raging Heaven's elders. Should another conqueror ever come calling, from the wilds of Macedon or wherever else, they would have to contend with far more than their predecessor to reach their prize.

It was folly for a junior initiate to even walk along these hallowed paths, of course. Spanning the distance between elders, senior initiates, and the dwellings of honored guests such as the Oracles, these were the roads that only privileged members of the cult were permitted to travel. There were main trails—staircases cut from the mountain's face so that initiates could come and go from the cult—but these glittering walkways of indigo mosaics were not for the likes of juniors and outsiders to tread. If they were, I would have surely seen some by now.

"Where do you think you're going?"

Instead, seniors alone trawled these roads.

"Good afternoon, fellow sophists," I greeted the approaching trio. Three Philosophers, each noticeably younger than me and wearing the deep indigo robes of the cult's privileged mystikos.

Young prodigies, each and every one.

The one that had called out to me, a young Philosopher of the eighth rank, stopped just short of colliding with me and drove a finger into the center of my chest.

"Where are your robes, mystiko?" he demanded. "And why aren't you *wearing them?*"

"I haven't received any," I answered, lifting my palms. What can you do? The young cultivator's expression darkened.

"No one passes through the gates of the Raging Heaven Cult without membership or a sponsor," he said, a curious weight to the words that I felt in his influence. From one moment to the next it suddenly became *heavier*, more oppressive. Nothing compared to a Hero, however... "Where is your sponsor? Do you mean to tell me you're accusing them of negligence, to leave you alone without even a set of proper robes to wear?"

The other two Philosophers with him, children of similar prestige and stylized robes, stepped threateningly towards me. Their lips moved silently—a habit I'd noticed in some of our own Sophic cultivators back in the Rosy Dawn. Preparing some virtue or another.

Best to defuse this situation before it came to that.

"Naturally, I'd never accuse the Raging Heaven of such a thing," I said placatingly. "They were simply too drunk to handle the small details last night."

Hmm. Perhaps that wasn't the ideal way to put it.

The young Philosopher went from poking my chest to gripping the golden fabric of my tunic tight and yanking me down to his eye level.

Admirable strength for his age. He glared at me, his eyes a furious terracotta brown.

"What are you playing at, cultivator?" he asked in a deadly tone of voice. He reminded me of Myron, during the preliminary trials of the initiation rites. "Walking the roads reserved for senior initiates and honored elders, wearing whatever *this* is—"

"What are you wearing, anyway?" the leaner of the three demanded. He was the tallest of the bunch, in the midst of filling out into his adult frame. "What sort of city wears those colors?"

"Oh, this?" I plucked the Philosopher's hand off my tunic and rubbed the material between my fingers. He stared at his own hand and then at mine. "An old woman gave me this at the kyrios' funeral. Said it was disrespectful for me to be walking around a dead man's wake with a bare chest."

They connected the dots quickly, looking to my cult attire that hung tattered and bloodstained around my waist. Disbelief, followed by derision passed through their eyes.

"The Rosy Dawn?" the third boy Philosopher asked incredulously. "You're a new arrival from the Rosy Dawn."

"Just sailed in the day before last."

The lead boy broke into a slow chuckle, and soon that chuckle turned to laughter. His friends followed suit. It was an ugly sort of laugh, the kind that promised pain, but they were still too young and small to pull it off. So it just ended up making me laugh, too.

"Shut up!" the leader snapped. "Of all the stories you could have told, you chose the most flagrant! The Scarlet City has been shut off from the Mediterranean for nearly twenty years now. You think we wouldn't have heard if that had changed? How naive do you think we are?"

What?

"A stranger wandering the same paths that seniors and honored elders tread," the taller of the three said, his own influence rippling and expanding the same way the leader's had earlier. Magnifying. "With no sponsor to claim him and false attire from a cult he couldn't possibly belong to."

"Are you calling me a liar?" I asked, thoughts racing. Instinct. "My virtuous heart won't accept that."

The lead Philosopher's leaps peeled back from his teeth.

"I'm calling you a *crow*."

The trio exploded into motion.

I realized instantly that these three weren't the same breed of Philosopher that I'd become accustomed to back in the Rosy Dawn. They moved with speed and precision that spoke to long hours in the gymnasium, with coordination that spoke to a strong bond of shared trust, and with power that spoke to their natural talent at cultivation. They reminded me of Myron even more, and even Nikolas in the days before he'd left.

More than that, their influence sang. Their pneuma cried out to me, to a sense that I hadn't had until two days ago, and I heard it in the crashing waves.

Death to deceivers! the tall and lean Philosopher's influence cried accusingly, wrapping around his body and pooling in his clenched fists.

Root out the rats, the third Philosopher's influence hissed, surging up his legs as he leapt into a spinning kick.

Cast the unworthy into the light, said the leader's influence, clearest of the three. It seeped into the roots of his hair, making the deep brown curls billow as he rushed into the press of battle.

The trio assaulted me in utter silence, and it was *deafening.*

So that's how it was.

This heart can't lie! I declared in the voice of my soul and lunged forward to meet them.

Kyno opened the door to his chambers wearing nothing but his crocodile skin cloak. I raised an eyebrow at the sight, but he only grunted and tilted his head back.

"In."

I obliged, dragging my new friends behind me. They all groaned pitifully, nursing minor wounds as if they were on death's door. I rolled my eyes and let them drop.

"Don't be like that," I scolded. "I barely even hit you."

I spat a mouthful of bloody saliva onto the tall one, probing a loose tooth gingerly with my tongue. They were good for their age, I'd give them that much. They'd done more damage to me three-on-one than the Rosy Dawn's esteemed elders had done with five.

"What is this?" Kyno asked roughly, wrapping faded green robes around his waist to preserve some semblance of modesty. "What are you playing at, Griffon?"

"Nothing at all, friend," I said, waving a hand at the three child Philosophers. "I needed to find you, and these three were kind enough to direct me."

"And you returned that kindness, did you," he rumbled, looking over the bruises and burns, and in the case of the tall one, the broken jaw.

"I held back when I could," I said, shrugging. "They're better than they look."

"I'm sure they are," Kyno said quietly. His dark eyes were piercing. "And I'm sure it's only coincidence that they inflicted as much damage to you as Elissa did at the funeral."

That was more to do with the fact that she'd hardly been trying at the time, and these three had given it their all. I smiled silently. Kyno grunted.

"I'm too hungover for this," he said. "You. Get me food and water." The leader of the three looked at his pointing finger and then at him with wide eyes.

"You truly know him, honored Hero?"

"What did I tell you?" I asked, crossing my arms. "My sponsor was drunk."

Kyno's influence roiled in displeasure, but there was little he could say. In a way, the new companions Sol and I found *were* our sponsors. They'd gotten us into the cult, for better and for worse. It had been drunk and unintentional, of course, but then all the best things generally were.

"Go," Kyno commanded. All three dashed out of the room as fast as their legs could carry them, casting fearful glances back at me as they went.

"Nice boys," I commented. "Bright for their age, too."

"The Raging Heaven accepts nothing less," Kyno said, sitting down on the edge of his bed and massaging his temples. When I tried to add my own pankration hands to help, he only slapped them away, glaring at me. "What do you want, Griffon?"

"I want to see the Oracle."

"Then go see her." He waved a hand vaguely east, towards the opposite side of the mountain. "The Scarlet Oracle is that way."

"I tried that," I admitted. "Unfortunately, Philosophers aren't allowed audience with the Oracle on their own." Kyno stared silently at me with bloodshot eyes, his crocodile's eyes glaring right along with him.

"I told you at the funeral that I have no interest in the games of politicians and Tyrants," he said, finally. "What makes you think I want to be a part of yours?"

Ho? "What do you mean?"

Kyno spat on the floor, lips twisting at the taste of something foul. "You want to pretend you're a junior, be my guest. But I won't be roped into whatever it is you and your master are planning."

Hn. I was getting dangerously close to being in over my head. I'd approached Scythas with only a vague plan in mind at the funeral, and things had rapidly spiraled out of my control from there. This might be my only chance to withdraw before the situation was well and truly beyond my influence.

On the other hand.

"What makes you think you aren't already implicated?" I asked, cocking an eyebrow. "Juniors they may be, but there are three young prodigies that can attest to you not denying me when I called you my sponsor. No matter what happens, you'll be a part of what comes next. In the eyes of the elders and the heavens above."

The Heroic giant went very still. The fine hairs on my arms and the back of my neck shivered and stood up. My pulse started to pound in mingled excitement and anticipation.

"We were all drunk." Even as he said it, he knew it didn't matter. "You dare blackmail a Hero?"

I rolled my eyes. So dramatic. "I'm not trying to kill the Oracle. I just want to see her. Will you help me or not?"

Kyno considered me. "Why?"

"Why do I want to see her?"

He nodded.

I leaned back against his door frame, mulling over the question. There were several answers to that question. But in the end, there was only one appropriate response.

"They say that the Oracles are the blood of the pantheon," I said as if discussing the sun in the sky. "Even if it's only the smallest fraction, they carry a piece of one of the divine existences that climbed Olympus Mons and made it their own, once upon a time."

"The Oracles don't deliver prophecies anymore," Kyno said. I shrugged, smiling wryly.

"That's fine. I don't care much for them anyway, prophecies. The Oracle herself is the prize."

His brow furrowed. "You can't be planning to—"

I waved the thought off, disgusted. "Nothing like that. It's far more profound than that."

Kyno spread his hands expectantly.

"That fraction of divine blood is the end of the road that we're all so perilously rushing down," I said. "Sprinting with all that we have, careening hopelessly into the depths." I leaned forward, and in his own eyes, I saw the fire. I smiled. "I want to see the end of the road, Kyno. Don't you?"

The Hero groaned and stood.

Chapter Forty-One

THE SON OF ROME

Anastasia drew attention as a matter of course. It was a consequence of her status and appearance both—men couldn't help but steal what glances they could when she was nearby. But as she choked and coughed and hammered her chest, the other mystikos in the bath looked openly our way. She mastered herself quickly, setting her cup aside, but the damage had been done.

After a night of hunting Crows and a full day of drinking, it had been my old mentor's name that finally broke her steady composure. It wasn't an encouraging thought.

"You—" she said when the worst of it had passed, "You're serious?"

"Why would I lie?" Ironic, perhaps. But valid in this case.

"I can think of a few reasons." She shook her head, brushing damp hair out of her face. Her lips pursed as she mulled the knowledge over, green ember eyes flickering. "How did you come to know him, if I may?"

I frowned. Oddly enough, I didn't mind telling her. Maybe it was that poisonous nostalgia, or maybe she'd managed to charm me while I wasn't looking. The result was the same either way. I was not, however, comfortable with the rest of the bathing pavilion listening in.

I reached out with my influence and smacked down every grasping hand that I could feel with my Sophic sense.

Every single Philosopher in the pavilion flinched. The degrees varied, some recovering in a split second and carrying on their vapid conversations, while others jerked and kicked up ripples in the water. One and all, they retracted. Even here, the baths were nothing but viper pits filled with gossips. From Rome to Greece, everything under the sun was the same.

"You get used to it," Anastasia assured me. "It isn't as if they can do anything with the information. They're just children."

To a cultivator of her standing, perhaps. But I wasn't so far above these people—or above them at all. Many of them were older than me, their cultivation further advanced. That wasn't even the crux of the issue, though.

I'd thought my year in chains had ground down the last of my pride, yet here it was, rearing its head again. I'd grown used to the respect afforded to me in the legions, come to expect it, even if I'd never truly deserved it.

"A child doesn't fear a flame until it burns them," I said, smoothing out a scowl. "That was one of the first lessons he ever taught me. Said it was his duty to burn me himself before I threw myself fully into the fire."

"You were young," she said, half a question.

I leaned back against the marble rim of the basin, the cool stone a pleasant contrast to the scalding water. "I was an arrogant child. My mother was convinced that the world revolved around me on a satin thread, and my father's duties kept him too busy to notice until the damage had been done. I'd never been burned. Was convinced I never would be."

"That sounds familiar," Anastasia said, mirth briefly overtaking her tension. "I was wondering what you saw in Griffon to take him on as a student. It was you after all."

In a way, she wasn't wrong.

"Griffon is better than I was," I disagreed anyway. It was worth saying, though I'd never say it to his face. "I'm the fruit of all my mentors' labors. Griffon is what he is in spite of his."

"For better and for worse," she said wryly. I smirked faintly.

"For better and for worse."

"How did he convince you to take him on?" Anastasia asked. That one was easy enough.

"His cousin challenged me to a fistfight."

Anastasia blinked. "Where did he stand?"

"The seventh rank of the Civic Realm."

She winced. "I assume Griffon didn't take his passing well."

I glanced sidelong at her, frowning. "I didn't kill him."

"Truly?" Anastasia looked at me as if in a new light. "I didn't take you for a merciful man." As if sparing a child that didn't know any better was mercy. Every time I forgot, the world reminded me what vile creatures cultivators could be.

"He wasn't a threat." I shrugged. "I could have beaten him in chains."

"The fearsome Legate in chains," Anastasia mused, reclaiming some of her smoke and teasing. "That's a sight I wouldn't mind seeing."

I rolled my eyes and took up her cup, drinking deeply from it. The water was cool and refreshing. The rim of the cup tasted inexplicably of figs. Sweet.

"Griffon stepped in before I could do much to the boy, regardless," I continued. "He demanded that I stop. Told me that I'd had enough fun."

"You took him to task for that, surely?"

I smiled faintly. "I did." That struggle in his family's filial pool had been the first time in months that I'd felt truly alive. It had been the same for him, too, I knew.

"But he impressed you, and here you are," Anastasia deduced.

"Here we are."

The conversation stalled, the Heroine hesitating suddenly. I offered her cup back to her, raising an eyebrow. We'd come this far. Might as well see it through. Anastasia took the cup, running her thumb along its edge.

"And what about you?" she finally asked. "How did you convince your master to take you on?"

"I didn't." At her blank look, I elaborated. "I was in the forum with a group of my peers"—not friends. Not really—"and we'd just caught a pair of thieves our age attempting to pick us. We decided we'd take the hands they'd slipped into our purses as punishment, after we'd properly shamed them."

The memory was the oddest sort of bittersweet. Shameful to look back on through the lens of my younger self, but warm for what it had ultimately led to.

"Looking back, I think they were brothers. The older of the two begged us to take both of his hands instead of one from each of them. We refused, of course, and so he tried something different and goaded us instead. Insisted up and down that we'd do no better than him if put in his position and made to survive." I sighed. "The young patrician couldn't stomach such an insult, especially in front of my peers. So I offered him a wager."

Anastasia had turned to face me fully at this point, resting her crossed arms on the lip of the basin and laying her cheek on them. There was a knowing glint in her eyes and steady interest.

"Any rat can snatch a purse when no one is bothering to look at them, was my reasoning at the time. But for a young patrician to do so? That was a true test of skill. I bet him that I could pick five purses without getting caught a single time, and if I did, I'd take his thieving left hand and all five fingers of his right. One hand for justice, and a finger for every time I proved him wrong."

"You didn't consider what would happen to you if you were caught, yourself? That you'd share his fate?" Anastasia asked, terribly amused. I raised a hand, fingers spread wide.

"Young and arrogant. Failure wasn't even a possibility in my mind."

"But if he *was* correct, and you did fail. What then?"

"Then he lived to pick another pocket, and his brother got to keep his hands." I shook my head minutely, lost in the memories. "I stole four purses without drawing a single glance. But on the fifth, an old man caught me by the arm as I was rummaging through his robes."

"Fool boy. You should have stopped at four."

"You stole from—" Anastasia stopped herself, eyes wide. "You and Griffon are a better fit than I thought."

"I *tried* to steal from him," I corrected her with dry amusement. "He'd seen me from the beginning, though. All the way back to the wager I'd made with the plebs. And so he offered me a wager of his own."

Calloused hands and a stern demeanor. A ludicrous beard that I couldn't imagine him without, and finely kept robes of scarlet and white. I'd never forget the look of him in that moment. The terror I'd felt.

"*Justice is quick, so you'll have to be quicker,*" I recited, words that I'd never forget. "*Unmake these crimes before they're found out, or I'll take that greedy hand.*"

"Unsteal four purses," Anastasia repeated with incredulous mirth.

"In the middle of the forum at its busiest hour, without any of them noticing," I confirmed. "To this day I'm not sure how I did it."

"And after you did? What happened then?"

"I turned tail and ran home as fast as I could. He was already there."

Discussing the terms of tuition with my father.

As it turned out, the Raging Heaven took all aspects of hygiene quite seriously. By the time we left the baths and returned to the benches on the outer edge of the bathing pavilion, my Rosy Dawn attire was gone. In its place was a fresh set of indigo robes. They were a more vibrant purple than what the Philosophers of the cult wore, and upon closer inspection, I saw golden threads woven into the sleeves. Branching strands of lightning.

A consequence of the company I was keeping, it seemed. The slaves had seen a Heroine accompanied by a man they didn't know and decided to err on the side of caution, favoring me with the same privileged treatment that she enjoyed.

Anastasia assured me that a slave would return my clothes to me once they'd been thoroughly cleansed, and she promised that she'd find out whatever she could about my mentor's whereabouts. Then she left, to do whatever it was that cultivators in the Raging Heaven did.

I found myself following a stream of mystikos up the stone-carved steps to an open plateau. This far up the mountain, there were as many Civic cultivators as Sophic, and a cursory glance didn't reveal a single Hero on the grand plateau. It was furnished in the same style as the Rosy Dawn's various symposia rooms, lounging couches around its edges and tables in the middle, covered in drink and food and games of all types.

Unlike the Rosy Dawn, the plateau was utterly open to the elements, awarding a spectacular view of the sanctuary city below, and an awe-inspiring vantage of the Storm That Never Ceased up above.

I'd chosen a couch farthest from the commotion of young men and women jostling for recognition and losing themselves to the delirious rush of alcohol and good company. There were games of all kinds being played throughout the plateau, some that even tempted me, but I contented myself with picking from a small platter of olives and waiting for my clothes to be returned.

I watched the mystikos that I'd followed here compete in mock games, chat languidly with friends, and drink themselves senseless. And as time passed, I watched as those same mystikos grew tired of drinking and fooling around and decided to soothe their fatigue with another bout at the baths below.

How slow did time move in a place like this? Did these people truly live like this, day in and day out?

"It's unfortunate, isn't it?"

There was a woman standing next to me.

I bit down on a curse, smothering my immediate reaction and forcing my fists to unclench. The young woman politely pretended not to notice.

"The indulgence," she continued, her voice sad. "The stagnation." She sighed and sat down on the dining couch next to mine. "Is this seat taken?"

"It is now," I said, surveying her in my periphery.

She looked young, from what could be seen of her. Around my age, if not less by a couple years. It was difficult to tell with the veil covering the upper half of her face, a golden sun weave obscuring her eyes and most of her blonde braids. She was slender compared to Elissa and Anastasia, who'd both been toned and chiseled by combat, but she didn't carry herself like the rest of the mystikos on the plateau.

She didn't dress like them either. In place of indigo robes or any other cult attire that I'd seen before, she wore a pure white tunic with golden sun ray filigree woven into its fabric. She had a golden sash cinched around her waist and another that hung loosely off her hips. Her skin was utterly free of blemishes, and her nails were painted.

I reached out a hand of my influence, and she took it in her own without hesitation. There was a powerful warmth to her presence. Like basking in the sun.

"I don't believe I've seen you before," she said. "What is your name, cultivator?"

"Solus."

"A pleasure to meet you, Solus," she said, quietly genuine. A beat of silence passed.

"And yours?" I prompted her.

She tilted her head. "You don't know?" Somehow, the audacity of asking such a question was lost in her delivery of it. Rather than being irritated, I found myself smiling faintly. I held out a real hand filled with olives, offering her one.

"Enlighten me."

The girl in the golden veil took from me an olive and popped it into her mouth. She chewed slowly, savoring the taste, and smiled.

"It's Selene."

Chapter Forty-Two

THE YOUNG GRIFFON

It paid to have friends in high places, after all.

The temple of the Oracle was an eerie edifice. Frankincense and myrrh hung thick in the air, stifling the senses and burning my eyes. Walking through the gilded archway, past the Heroic cultivators of the Broken Tide Cult that guarded the Oracle with their lives, I could hardly see a foot in front of my face.

The winter winds of the Mediterranean were hardly worth mentioning for a cultivator of even the most pitiful ranks of the Civic realm, but inside this temple, I had to fight my teeth not to chatter. The smoke from the torches lining the walls were somehow *cold*, and from one moment to the next, they smelled of frankincense, of myrrh, and of the Ionian Sea.

The smoke clung like saltwater to my skin, drenching me in a cold sweat not three steps past the archway. My pulse beat a quick rhythm in my throat. I swallowed down the instinctive urge to fight. I'd never felt a presence like this in my life.

"Be mindful," Kyno muttered. "The gods are watching."

"No, they're not," I said, distracted. I peered through the smoke and seafoam. "But she is."

The Oracle of the Broken Tide was an old woman, shrunken and frail. In contrast to Kyno, her teal attire was pristine, its colors vibrant, while the woman herself was washed out and grayed—her hair, the pallor of her skin, and even her eyes. The blind woman stared unerringly at me, the wrinkles on her face creasing as she smirked.

"Someone is here that doesn't belong." Her voice was as brittle and aged as the rest of her, a bare rasp that could hardly be heard over the crackle of sea salt torches on the walls.

Kyno clapped a hand on my shoulder, pulling me back a step before I could speak. He leveled me with a severe look as if I'd start firing off at a divine woman in the seat of her power for one snide comment. I hadn't even introduced myself yet.

"Honored Oracle," he said respectfully, bowing his head. "These lowly sophists have come to pay their respects." He glanced my way again and seemed surprised to see me bowing my head as well. Honestly, what had I done to give him such a low impression of me?

"I'm sure you have." The old woman beckoned us forward with a spider-thin hand. "Come then, into the depths—if you can swim."

I stepped forward without hesitation, and her presence subsumed me.

Depths had been the appropriate way to describe it. I felt myself sinking, falling endlessly into an existence that only got darker and colder the farther down it went. Even as my feet padded silently across firm stone, I plummeted into the deep. The woman's washed-out gray eyes tracked me as I approached. A reflex, I realized. It wasn't that she could see me, not with her eyes. It was that she knew where I was, and her eyes remembered to follow.

"How long have you been blind?" I asked the Oracle, stopping just within her reach.

"Since the day I was born," she said, reaching out and grasping my face with a frail hand. Her skin was colder than the smoke and smooth, utterly free of calluses. "Since when could you see?"

I considered it. "Four months ago."

"Cocky boy," she chortled, pinching my cheek. "The proper answer is *perhaps tomorrow, if fortune favors me*."

Kyno came to stand beside me, his posture rigid as the Oracle's presence washed over him. The flames in his eyes flickered and guttered, muffled beneath the waves. There was a slow, rhythmic quality to the motion of his chest. A breathing technique.

"And what about you, young Hero of the Broken Tide?" The Oracle turned those blind eyes on Kyno. "What brings the great huntsman to my humble shrine?"

"We seek guidance and offer our devotion to the tide," he answered, his voice faintly strained.

The Oracle wagged a finger. "It should be in the reverse order!"

Kyno grimaced and bowed his head.

"My apologies."

"And what sort of guidance can I give you? A young man of your standing should know at least this much of how the world works. The gods don't guide us anymore."

"That's all you're good for, is it?" I asked, idly observing the finer details of her. There were remnants of striking features, worn down by time—a royal nose, sharp cheekbones, and there, beneath the milk and mist of blindness, serrated pupils split into three segments. "A lifetime of keeping company with the world's finest men and women, legendary souls seeking you out at every opportunity, and you have nothing to say? I could spend a lifetime in a box with no holes and still have something useful to say at the end of it."

Kyno attempted to strike me, but he wasn't Sol. I knocked the blow aside with pankration intent, maintaining eye contact with the blind Oracle. He wouldn't dare exert himself enough to break past my hands. Not here.

"Wiser than you look," the old woman said approvingly. "But what makes you think you're worthy of my wisdom?"

I scoffed. "What makes you think your wisdom is worthy of me?"

"Griffon!" Kyno snarled, panicked and infuriated in equal measure. Ho. It seemed all I'd needed to do to break through that rugged stoicism of his was involve his cult's divine messenger.

The Oracle laughed.

It was the broken, hacking laugh of an old woman on death's door, but it was also the waves crashing against the cliffside in Álikos, the roar of a hurricane tearing up the surface of the Ionian Sea. Kyno eased back a step, his chest rising and falling once more in the rhythm of a controlled breathing technique. I squinted through the sea spray, brushing salt from my eyes.

"Indeed!" the Oracle of the Broken Tide crowed. "Just so! How can any of us know what lies beneath the waves unless we plumb their depths ourselves? How can we discern what's casting the shadows if we don't first step out of the cave?"

She rose abruptly from the upholstered seat she'd been sitting in, so oversized for her shriveled body, and lurched forward to seize my face with both hands. For all her age, her grip was undeniably strong in that moment. She looked deeply into my eyes, close enough for me to smell the grapes on her breath. She was more than just old. She was *ancient*.

Her pupils were tridents.

"What is it about you scarlet sons that compels you to go where you're not wanted, to say what no one wants to hear, and to do what absolutely must not be done?" Somehow, I got the feeling the Oracle wasn't speaking to me or even to herself. "What is it within you that chafes at the suggestion of heaven? Why are you the way you are?"

I smirked and made to answer, but she beat me to it.

"*Because the tribulations are the best part.*"

"I thought you couldn't see the future anymore," I said, bemused.

"I don't need to see the future when the past is standing right in front of me," the Oracle said, clapping her hands against my cheeks and turning my head from side to side, spearing me with those tridents. "You're all the same. **As above, so below.**"

Something inside of me spasmed. "What are you talking about, old woman?"

"I'm talking about you, fool boy. What are *you* talking about? You came to me for advice, didn't you? Or perhaps you're only here to gawk at what you hope to one day be."

With my head tilted back as it was, I couldn't quite look at her. But I made my intent known. "I don't hope."

"No, you don't, do you?" she mused, running bone-thin fingers along the veins of my neck and down, probing my torso. In search of what, I couldn't say. "You act. So act, here and now. You have the

Oracle's attention, so make use of it. Shall I check your heart for demons?"

I scoffed. "Please."

"Physical therapy, then? Shall this old woman ignore her own aches and pains and tend to yours?" Her fingertips dug into the sensitive flesh beneath my ribs, sending lightning threads of sensation up my chest. Not quite pain, but certainly not pleasure.

I took her hands in my own and pulled them away. "There's nothing your hands can do for me that my own can't do better."

"Not the spirit, and not the body either," she said, unbothered. "A question of the mind, then. Or rather, an *answer*."

I tilted my head. There was something in those eyes—aside from the milk of blindness, obviously. Something shifty and mischievous, utterly at odds with her age. The old woman pulled away from me and turned, rifling through the various stands and tables and shelves that surrounded her holy tripod.

Finally, with a triumphant cackle, she pulled a false face from the clutter.

It was a theater mask, carved from cypress and painted in pale tones. A woman's face, pale and drawn and horrified. The mouth gaped open grotesquely, allowing space for the one wearing it to breathe and be heard. The eyes were wide and vacuous, the pits dilated to allow for the wearer to see. The eyebrows were thick and brushed with gold, arching up in dismay. It was the expression of a woman that had seen a ghost.

"You came here looking for this, didn't you?"

This? "I don't know what this is." The Oracle pressed the mask into my hands. It was smooth to the touch and inexplicably warm.

"This is the answer to the question you refuse to ask," the Oracle said. I looked sharply up at her. Her expression was light and devious. It made her look younger by half a century.

"I don't come here for a mask," I informed her. She simply smiled wider, baring her teeth.

"This isn't a mask," she said, the words heavy with purpose. I realized she was still holding it, the knuckles of her gnarled hands bleeding white from the force of her grip. "This is your future."

I jerked the mask out of her grip, turning it over in my hands. There was a word carved into its inner face. I read it once, and then I read it again. My heart hammered in my chest.

"Son of scarlet sin," the Oracle whispered in a voice of low tide and shifting sands, "you have the gall to intrude on a messenger of the Fates before your journey has even truly begun, to plunder them with your arrogant eyes in search of their divinity. There are a thousand-thousand mysteries in this world. Did you really think you were ready to solve the greatest of them?"

"Who are you?" I murmured.

The old woman curled her fingers, beckoning me down. I leaned forward, and she whispered into my ear.

"My name is Melpomene. And I am the first of your tribulations."

I turned and stalked out of the temple.

Kyno caught up to me about a hundred steps up the mountain, a thinly-veiled mania in his eyes. His crocodile mantle seemed to lash its tail as he bounded up the steps, such was the force of his charge.

"What was that?" he demanded of me, his pneuma and influence a riotous wave.

I frowned, turning the mask over and over in my hand.

"I have no idea."

But I was going to find out.

Chapter Forty-Three

THE SON OF ROME

"Is it always like this?" I asked the girl in the sun ray silks. I waved vaguely, encompassing the entirety of the lounge pavilion. Her lips curled down, the only facial feature not obscured by her golden veil.

"To greater or lesser degrees," Selene said, sighing softly. "It usually isn't this egregious outside of holidays and celebrations. The death of the kyrios has left everyone on edge."

I watched a pair of bare-chested men hold a third upside down while a trio of women in sheer, see-through silks threw grapes into his mouth.

"Seems like it."

"They distract themselves as best they can," Selene said. "The cult is not well and they know it. There is safety in numbers and safety in the sun. Out here in the open, surrounded by their peers, they can relax without fear of scavengers."

Crows. My eyes narrowed, ire rising. I despised their ilk. Gaius had suffered from no end of rats in his time as general of the west, nipping at his heels and striking from the dark. It was why he never slept.

"Still," I grunted, "they could be doing better things with their time."

"They're young," Selene said, leaning back on the headrest of her lounge. "And they're afraid. Uncertain. It's disappointing to see, but can you blame them for seeking relief in simple distractions?" Yes. I could. Most of the truly debauched cultivators on this plateau were older than me.

I glanced at Selene, though, smirking in faint amusement. "Wise words for a fifteen-year-old."

"Looks can be deceiving, cultivator." There was an airy, mystical quality to her smile.

"They can be," I acknowledged. "Are yours?"

"They are. I may only look like I'm fifteen years of age, but the truth is far different." She waved a hand over her person, head tilting to reveal the slope of her sun-kissed neck. "I'm actually sixteen."

I snorted a laugh. Selene smiled indulgently.

"My mistake," I conceded. "What brings the wise woman to a place like this?"

Selene's head tilted further. The golden veil that covered her face slipped just a bit with the motion, exposing the gentle slope of her jaw. Her eyes remained shrouded, but I could imagine them gazing out over the mountain and the sanctuary city below.

"There is strength in numbers," she repeated, sadly.

No matter where you went, scum would always be scum. "These Crows," I said slowly, "their maneuvering. Is it really that dire?" I was fighting myself as I spoke. I'd already involved myself beyond any sensible mark two nights ago. If Scythas was to be believed, a Tyrant wanted to see me because of it. I couldn't afford to dig deeper. Yet, even so.

"They're not the worst of it," she said, shaking her head. "They operate at night for the most part. It's the paranoia they invoke by simply existing. The suspicion. The elders have always had means of competing with one another behind closed doors—Olympia wouldn't survive any direct contention. But it was never this flagrant."

"The kyrios kept them in line," I guessed.

"He did. It was known that lasting harm, let alone death, was not allowed in his halls. There was maneuvering, there were power plays, but mystikos could walk the steps of Kaukoso Mons without fear at night."

"But now the kyrios is dead," I said, looking back over the pavilion with a more discerning eye. Whether I saw it now because I expected to see it, or whether it had always been there, I could see the tension. Tightly leashed stress in every raving man, woman, and child. It drove them to excess. It robbed them of their senses.

"And no one knows who they can trust." Selene nodded. "Acting out in protest of the shadow game only makes you a target. With-drawing from it entirely is an insult to your city's elder. The Raging Heaven was entirely unprepared for the death of the kyrios, and now it suffers because of it."

"How long will this take to resolve itself?" I asked, the magnitude of things settling in. Cultivators were an elevated existence, capable of things that ordinary men could hardly dream of. The higher up the divine mountain they went, the starker this divide became. And two nights ago, I had seen Heroes hunted through the streets like dogs. Something told me it was only going to get worse.

"I don't know," Selene admitted. "With regards to politics, I only have my father's word to go off. Outsiders aren't told much of these things."

"Outsider? You're not an initiate?"

"The Raging Heaven accepts only the best," Selene said, tilting her head to face me. "Cultivators that have proven themselves to be excep-tional beyond all conventional measures. Whether they be Civic, Sophic, or Heroic, it is not enough to be simply powerful or well-connected. You must be *significant*—your story worth hearing."

"But you live here anyway," I mused. Scythas had mentioned accommodations for guests, I supposed. My eyes wandered as the rest of what she'd said simmered in my mind. It sounded wrong. "I can't say I'm interested in hearing any of the stories on display here."

"That's because you didn't know them before they joined." There was something powerfully troubled in her voice, some sorrow in the way her fingers caressed the golden filigree of sun rays woven into her tunic. "The cults of greater mysteries exist for many purposes, and their prestige is undeniable, but ultimately, they are artificial institu-tions. And how can an aspiring Hero refine ivory from their soul without the proper conflict to drive them?"

The sentiment was a familiar one. I'd heard its ilk often enough during my time at the Rosy Dawn. "You don't want to join this cult, even if you could," I observed. Selene smiled wistfully.

"I love my father and my mother," she murmured, "but there are days that I can't help wondering what life is like when you live it yourself and not vicariously. Now that the kyrios is dead, I fear I'll be suffering more and more days like that."

I frowned, dropping my olives back onto their platter. I'd lost my appetite.

"You don't have many friends here, do you?"

"How cruel." Selene placed a hand to her chest. "What gave me away?"

"You wouldn't be talking to me. Also, every single person on this plateau has been avoiding this corner since you sat down." I flicked an olive across the pavilion. It struck the ear of a Philosopher that had been eyeing me earlier, sizing me up for a fight. The man flinched, but he did not turn. "They're too afraid to even look."

Selene was silent.

"You may not be a member of the cult," I said. "But your father is. And he's prominent enough to extend his influence to you." Piece by piece, I was assembling a mental image of this place and its people. Different in every way from the Rosy Dawn on the surface. But the foundations? Those were all the same.

"You have eyes, cultivator," Selene said softly. "So tell me, where is Olympus Mons?"

I looked back, meeting the shadowed silhouette of her eyes through the gossamer veil.

"Not here."

A sharp cry split the skies before she could respond, and mystikos of the Raging Heaven turned and craned their heads to see a shadow bolt shoot out of the sky. It spiraled and careened through the air in a blur, avoiding thrown cups and pneuma projectiles hurled up at it with contemptuous ease.

I held out an arm, and the messenger eagle of Rome swept down onto it with surprising force, talons wrapping around my arm with deceptive care. Sharp enough to draw blood, but steady enough not to.

It snapped its beak, sharp eyes riveted on my discarded olives. I gathered them back up and offered my open palm to the bird of prey. It chewed them up in its beak one by one, each snap powerful enough to sever a man's finger, but it didn't once nick me.

"What is that?" Selene asked, astonished.

"A messenger from Rome," I answered, running the back of my free hand along the ridge of its wing. The eagle ruffled its feathers, pleased with the attention. I smirked.

"You're from Rome?" I raised an eyebrow at the sudden hitch in her voice.

"I am."

"I've never met anyone from Rome before," she confided with barely constrained excitement. She leaned forward on her lounge, planting both hands on the edge of its upholstery. "Clear across the sea! You must have seen so many amazing places before coming here."

I thought of Gaius' campaigns. The mountain ranges of the Gauls, treacherous heights and war-torn valleys, and the Black Forest that sprawled across entire nations. The frozen north, with their swirling Celt sigils carved into the stones and planted in their fields, squat villages clustered around the seas. Even the vile marshes and miserably damp plains of Britannia.

"You have no idea," I told her. She lit up even further. It was odd, seeing the sudden shift in her demeanor. A bit endearing, but odd.

I was distracted by a gagging sound, and I turned in time to see the eagle vomit into my open hand. My nose wrinkled. But mercifully, instead of mashed olives and the breakfast I'd fed it earlier, a scroll of rolled papyrus fell into my palm. I stared at the missive for a moment, then back up at the bird.

"These are supposed to go around your leg."

The eagle trilled sharply, snapping its beak.

"Did it just... scoff at you?" Selene asked.

I glared at the bird. "It did."

Miraculously, the message wasn't covered in bile despite where it had come from. I unrolled it, curious, and rolled my eyes when I saw the distinctive handwriting scrawled across a scrap of one of Scythas' star charts.

Greetings brother,

I pray this message finds you promptly and in good health, though I'm not expecting much from a mongrel Roman bird. Assuming it has, though, meet me after dusk where the stars align and the heavens descend to earth.

Come alone. We need to talk.

The bird can come too, I suppose. His name is Sorea. I named him for you since you couldn't be bothered to do it yourself.

Worthless Roman. You're welcome.

Griffon

I crumpled the letter in my fist. I was hardly even a novice when it came to stargazing, but I had a good idea of where to look. Based on the phrasing and the portion of the star chart he'd used as canvas for the message, I could find him.

"Sorea," I mused, considering the eagle. It cocked its head expectantly. "Do you like that name?" Could it understand me at all?

Sorea squeezed my arm, talons digging into my skin perilously close to drawing blood, and then he took flight in a burst of speed that far outstripped any mundane eagle.

"Was that a yes?" I called after him. He cried out sharply and was gone in the next instant.

I stood from my lounge, rolling my shoulders and looking down the mountain. The sun would set soon, evening shadows cast by the mountain already covering most of the sanctuary city. The Storm That Never Ceased rumbled ominously overhead. Best get started now. I'd have to get my clothes back later.

"*Wait.*" I looked down, surprised, at the hand gripping my indigo attire. Selene looked up at me, visibly bashful in spite of the fact that I couldn't see most of her face.

"I have to go see a friend," I told her. She bit her lip.

"Solus," she said hesitantly. "You're not a member of the Raging Heaven either, are you?" I considered her and the question both. My first instinct was to lie. So was my second instinct.

"No. I'm not."

"Then could we speak again?" she asked. "I'd like to hear about the places you've been."

I sighed and conceded. "If you can find me."

Selene smiled brilliantly.

"I will."

My first concern had been leaving the cult, but it hadn't been an issue in the end. The guards at the gates, those closest to the city, recognized me at once. But rather than demanding to know my name or how I'd acquired my indigo attire, they only grinned knowingly and told me to take it easier at the clubs this time. The benefits of having friends in high places.

I followed my intuition and the clue that Griffon had given me while the sun fell behind the ever-roiling peak of Kaukoso Mons. I walked the streets of Olympia, ignoring the deference and hushed words of praise that her citizens heaped upon me. They thought I was an initiate of the Raging Heaven. Even so, this was more than even Griffon had gotten walking the streets of Álikos. Too much.

I wandered, and the sun fell fully from the sky. Eventually, I stopped in a nondescript street in one of Olympia's eastern residential districts. I looked straight up and saw the constellation Griffon had taken from the star chart, the Nemean Lion, the star of its tail curving in line with the sun's path of descent. This was it.

Griffon was nowhere to be found, of course. Late as always. I sat down on a citizen's patio and resigned myself to a long wait.

The muted lights of dusk gave way to true night. Still, he didn't come. Finally, I scowled and stood.

"Star maps and riddles," I muttered, spitting in disgust. Just tell me where to go, worthless Greek.

"Sir," a hesitant voice said. Behind me, a young boy peered out from the cracked door to his home. "Do you need help?" Well, it didn't hurt to ask.

"Where do the stars align?" I asked him. "At what point does heaven descend to earth?"

The boy stared at me in bewilderment, and then he was gone, pulled back by the shoulders, a man taking his place in the entryway. His father inclined his head deeply to me, posture rigid.

"I apologize for my son, honored Philosopher, and beg for your understanding. He's only five years old this spring. We haven't yet prepared him for the rigors of philosophy." He was tense, painfully nervous.

I just wanted directions.

Sorea cried out above our heads, a dark impression on the sky. He shot by like an arrow from a bow, flying low over the marble columns and shingled roofs of the city. It was better than nothing. I spared the frazzled citizen and his son a nod and took off after my eagle as fast as my legs could carry me.

The eagle led me down a familiar path of scarlet brick roads and ruin, back the way Griffon and I had first come when we entered the city. As I ate up the landscape with my strides, I wondered if I was expecting too much from the bird, and if I was about to be led back into the sea. But before we could make it to the coast where Olympia's small port city resided, Sorea dipped left and spiraled down into the shroud of a familiar monument.

One of the world's eight wonders, as Griffon had referred to it. A massive open-faced temple with an even more massive statue lounging beneath the shelter it provided. The temple of the Father.

I found Griffon inside, lounging on the edge of the raised platform that served as a dais and pool both, catching the thin rivulets of olive oil that dripped off the statue. The father was just as impressive to behold the second time as he'd been the first. Titanic, gleaming in the light of torches and flaming braziers that illuminated the temple at night.

"You're late."

"I wouldn't have been if you'd told me where to go." Up above, Sorea perched himself on the father's shoulders, flapping his wings expansively. I nodded my thanks.

"I did. If I'd spelled it out and your bird had been intercepted, I'd be in dire straits right now."

There was something in his voice. His bearing, too, now that I looked. I realized what it was at once. He was restless again. That languid satisfaction that had been rolling off him in waves since we'd let fly the sails of the *Eos* was gone, and in its place, the hunger had returned. Three days. It had lasted longer than I'd expected, honestly.

"What happened?" I asked. He crossed his arms over his bare chest. The golden tunic that he claimed to have taken from an old woman was wrapped around his waist now, serving as an impromptu satchel for some lump that I couldn't discern.

"I spoke to the Oracle," he said, adding as an afterthought, "of the Broken Tide."

I hummed. "That was the big one's cult, wasn't it? Kyno, the one with the crocodile skin."

"The same," he said, jaw flexing. He wasn't angry. No, it was more focused than that. There was a dark hunger in him. "She threatened me with tribulation."

"You're overdue for one," I said, leaning against the raised dais. It was tall enough to rest my forearms on it without having to bend. The olive oil pool shimmered in the torchlight, reflecting the inexplicable light of the stars etched on the temple's ceiling. "What else?"

"She mentioned Álikos. *You scarlet sons are all the same*," he quoted. "And before that, I exchanged discourse with a few up-and-coming Philosophers of the Raging Heaven." I snorted. I could imagine the sort of discourse they'd exchanged. The kind that left bruises and broken bones. "They told me something interesting about my humble home."

He told me, and my eyebrows rose. "Shut off from the Mediterranean? How can that be? Your cousin has been off adventuring for years."

"Not just that. Foreign dignitaries visit us in scores every year." Griffon pushed off from the dais and began to pace. "Most come from valence territories within Magna Graecia, true, but not all of them. It doesn't make sense."

"Ask a member of the Rosy Dawn," I suggested. "This is the nexus of the free cities, isn't it? We may be the first delegates 'sent' for the Games, but surely there are long-term members of the Raging Heaven that came from your side of the Ionian."

"Have you forgotten we're on the run?" Griffon asked, frowning. Invisible to the eye but bright as day to a cultivator's sense, his pankration hands massaged his temples and shoulders, alleviating tension as best they could.

"It's only been three days since we left," I reasoned. "They might not have heard."

Griffon shook his head. "No. They know. We have to look into this ourselves."

"And how do you intend to do that?"

Fierce anticipation shone in scarlet eyes. "How else? We're going to scavenge."

My lip lifted in a sneer. I should have known. "I refuse."

"Ho? Refuse what?"

"I refuse to skulk around like a Crow, picking at corpses and offal." The quiet despair with which the girl in the golden veil had spoken, and the omnipresent anxiety I had seen in the mystikos of the Raging Heaven. It wasn't something I had any interest in contributing to.

"We have no choice," he said, shrugging. "We can't stay here under the usual terms. We've drawn too much attention."

"Because of *you*."

Griffon sneered. "It wasn't my actions that put you in a Tyrant's line of sight. How was that meeting, by the way?" I glared silently. "That's what I thought. Do you think you can ignore an elder forever without them acting on the insult? Do you think we can continue to do as we wish in broad daylight, unmolested? Of course not. The higher-ups are too busy to bother with us themselves, but they have other means."

"We could get a room in the city," I said stubbornly. "Or stay outside of it, even. I'm not afraid of sleeping in the dirt."

"I'm sure you aren't," he said scornfully. "But that won't work either. We're already targets, and because of that, we can't afford to be passive. While the Crows are out, the only place we can hide is *among them*."

Griffon stopped pacing, and all twenty of his pankration hands flexed in anticipation. He smiled ferociously.

"Starting now."

Thus exposed, two Crows exploded out of the olive oil pool.

Chapter Forty-Four

THE YOUNG GRIFFON

It had to be said. For all my accolades and for all of my majesty, for all that I was the only man that could ever be me, I was not perfect. I had my failings. And even more egregious than that, I was not all-knowing. In some respects, I was not even particularly well-informed.

My father had always done things in his own time, and the Scarlet City had regulated its pace to match his. For all that I was myself, I was no different in that regard. I cultivated the virtue that he forced upon me, I excelled in the tasks that he set before me, and I learned the lessons that he saw fit to teach me. And *only* those lessons.

I sought out what I could, whenever I could, of course. But if Damon Aetos didn't want you to know something, there wasn't a single soul in Álikos who would dare to speak of it. If there was something he didn't want you to have, all the gold in Egypt couldn't convince an Álikoan to sell it to you.

I'd always known that my father was keeping things from me. But I hadn't quite grasped the scope of it until I'd stepped foot into the sanctuary city.

The Crows were each of the Sophic Realm, which meant that whichever faction sent them hadn't been pointed our way by our new friends. Otherwise, they would have sent Heroes. In the kyrios' absence, the Raging Heaven had abandoned all but the most surface-level pretenses of unity. The various factions of the free Mediterranean had only just begun to pick each other apart, trying to fill the chasm left behind, and division was the name of the game.

Sol and I had implicated ourselves by associating with not one but *six* Heroic cultivators in full view of various indigo initiates. This had been inevitable.

Tirelessly, the Crow on the left promised in the voice of his soul.

Forever at hand, the Crow on the right declared with unwavering resolve.

I saw the confusion in Sol's eyes, soon overtaken by the storm. Gravitas rocked the temple—an inaudible *boom* that made my teeth vibrate and pounded the Crow on the right back into the olive oil pool. Sol lunged forward to trade blows with the Crow on the left, but the cultivator in black deftly avoided him, ducking and pivoting on one foot and laying a vicious kick into his right shin.

It didn't sweep Sol's legs out from under him like the Crow had intended, but the Roman grunted and staggered sideways, pointing a damning finger at the scavenger. Torchlight shadow flickered around him, and he blurred left, faster than any Sophic cultivator could possibly move.

He avoided the invocation of Sol's virtue and caught my clenched fist with his gut. I savored the sweet sound of a man choking on air, hammering into him from every angle with pankration hands wreathed in the rosy light of dawn.

[The dawn breaks.]

Without pause, spoke the Crow, slamming his forehead into mine. Starlight exploded in my eyes, and my ears rang, the force of the blow unlike anything I had experienced from a Philosopher before. I bared my teeth in a grin and caught his hands as they lashed up.

A thin line of blood trickled down from the point where his hooded forehead met mine as the sounds of splashing and savage struggle sounded from the olive oil pool that served as the foundation for the chryselephantine throne. The Crow had no heart flames to illuminate his eyes behind his hood, but I stared deeply into them anyway.

"So this is a man of principle," I mused, gripping his hood and the tattered edges of his midnight robes with the hands of my intent, ripping and tearing. His pneuma flared.

And he spoke. "Sacrilege," the Crow intoned, "to fight in the temple of the Father." And just as before, when those young Philosophers had stated their facts, the strength of his soul re-doubled.

I abandoned the effort of unmasking him as the pressure on our joined hands became unbearable. Pankration hands chopped viciously down on his forearms, forcing him to release me. I leapt back across the tiles.

Three boys, and now this. Not a coincidence—this was something fundamental. Something I should *know*.

"Starting a fight is far worse than ending it," I replied, putting the weight of my pneuma behind it. I felt a hint of something, some weightlessness, but I was only imitating what I'd observed as an outsider. I concentrated, while Sol jumped straight up to the ceiling in a spray of olive oil, the Crow on the right in close pursuit.

My opponent turned to flickering shadows again, but he'd already shown me the trick of it the first time. He braced himself first, taking the stance that he would emerge from the technique in. Chambering a right hook from fifty feet away.

I leaned right, dodging it by a hair, and drove a knee up between his legs. As I did it, I condemned him.

"Ambushing your cult's own honored guests," I denounced him, striking him twice in the kidney and five times across the face. "On your city's own holy ground!" The Crow lurched back, shadows flickering as he attempted to escape me. I grabbed him with flaming hands and reeled him back in. "Among heaven and earth, you alone are the dishonored one!"

And I felt it. A power that stirred above my eyes, pulsing through my skull and coursing down, down, ripping through me like an entire jug of kykeon and filling me with vital strength.

The Crow stomped my bare foot and lowered his shoulder into my chest, charging. Lightning threads of pain shot through my foot, and my cultivation faltered as he knocked the wind out of me. He was my superior in cultivation, but that had been the case before with the children. But this cultivator was a grown man—his body had weathered years of intense conditioning. The strength of his body matched that of his soul.

And then, the strength of his reason superseded mine as he lifted my feet from the floor and snarled.

"Fool. I am *no one.*"

The inexplicable head rush left me as quickly as it had come, an ice bath that shocked the senses and stole the strength from my limbs. It almost killed me as the Crow took us to the ground, producing a hideous rusted dagger from a fold in his robes and stabbing it at my side. But even while my mind wavered, my intent remained true. Pankration hands caught the blade and knocked it from his hand, even as its rusted edge cut into my soul.

I spat blood onto his black veil and swung my legs up, hooking them around his chest and twisting at the waist while we fell to the tiles. The assassin's blade clattered to the hallowed marble floor, the sound of it all wrong as it skittered and spun across the tiles. The Crow lurched for it, kicking viciously at me, but it was too late. I had him.

The Crow on the right flared his influence, crying out in that soundless voice, and Sol responded in kind with a tidal wave of gravity that caught everyone within the temple—myself included. My stomach flipped, my heart flew up into my throat as the entire world shifted onto a different axis, and I flew sideways as if I was falling out of the sky. Somewhere up above, Sorea shrieked, and the Crow cried out in his *real* voice.

A marble sentinel stood in the shadow of an archway, kneeling in deference as it faced the father. There were eleven others in the temple, each carrying a weapon and all of them without a face. This one had a trident in hand, brandished invitingly as we approached it. The Crow thrashed against my hold as our bodies lifted off the ground entirely, hammering into me with clenched fists and vile shadow techniques that burnt away at the touch of the rosy fingers.

I planted an open palm flat against the Crow's hooded face and shoved it sideways, twisting him around with the leverage of my leg lock as I did. The statued sentinel may have been nothing more than stone, but its trident was purest bronze. I slammed the Crow into it, and all three points of the trident erupted out of his chest.

I pulled myself to the ground with pankration hands and turned, catching the second Crow as Sol's attack sent him flying my way. He immediately went wild, fighting me like a rat caught by its tail. Which, in the end, wasn't far from the truth.

"You're no one, are you?" I grunted, planting my feet and ignoring his impotent elbows and kicks as I heaved him over my shoulder. The head rush returned, blooming inside my skull and coursing through my limbs as I invoked what could only be the primary weapon of every warrior scholar.

"As if I could ever lose to such a coward. My tribulation has a *face*." Their rhetoric.

I slammed the Crow to the floor and stepped back as Sol plummeted from the tip of the Father's ivory spear and stomped the poor bastard through the scarlet tiles. An invocation of Gravitas at the moment of impact caved the scavenger's chest in entirely. The sound of it was horrific. The noise the man made as he arched up was even more so. I caught his face with pankration hands and drove it back down, smothering him until he went limp.

The Philosopher died and his last, gagging breath exploded through the temple. One last gasp, raging through the temple of the Father and extinguishing every torch in sight.

Ensconced in sudden darkness, the true crow nearly got away.

Sorea swept down with a triumphant cry and sank its talons into an avian mass of liquid shadow as it attempted to flee. Just as before, the manifestation of anonymity wailed horribly as it was consumed by the Roman messenger eagle bit by bit.

"What was *that?*" Sol asked gutturally. His indigo attire, pristine just a few moments ago, was now drenched in olive oil and torn at his stomach and his right thigh where the crow had cut him. Poisoned again, no doubt, though he was breathing steadily for now.

"Hard to tell," I said sarcastically, swiping blood from my bare chest. "But if I had to guess, I'd say it was my point being proven."

Sol scowled, running a hand through oil-slick black hair. "Not that. What were they saying? And how were they saying it?"

"Ho, the great Legate doesn't know? I was going to ask you, *master*," I said mockingly. A wave of his influence hit me, the riptide pull urging me off balance. I set my stance and braced with pneuma hands, spitting blood at his feet in response.

"Just tell me!" he snapped. "I'm sick and tired of not knowing what's going on."

"That makes two of us." In the dark, with little but the wet sounds of a virtuous beast gorging itself and a Sophic cultivator struggling to force breath through punctured lungs, Sol and I took the measure of one another.

I snapped my fingers and lit the scrambled torches of the holy temple with the rosy fingers of dawn, righting any that had fallen. Sol seemed utterly unsurprised to see me grinning.

"I suppose it's my turn to be the master again since your worthless mentor taught you so little of our ways."

"He taught me as much as he could," Sol said, defending the man without hesitation. "It isn't any fault of his that our time was cut short."

"I'm sure," I agreed. Then, with the voice of my soul, I rendered judgment. *"But he still left you unprepared. He neglected your foundations, and now you're here, lost and without understanding. He **failed.**"*

Crouched over the broken corpse of a mangled Crow, baring his teeth up at me in naked threat, I could see the wolf in him. I smirked, savoring the head rush of my rhetoric hitting home, and I spoke to him again without moving my lips.

Snarl all you want. You know I never lie.

"We are men of principle," I told my Roman brother. "Philosophers seeking wisdom and ultimate enlightenment. More than that, we strive to educate those around us in the same way that we have been educated ourselves. Would you say that your mentor was a wise man? A worldly, well-informed man?" Sol nodded grudgingly. I splayed my hands. "And thus, he failed you as a Philosopher because he only passed on a fraction of those things to you.

"We understand the world around us as Philosophers—the rules of nature. But how can we impress that understanding upon others? How may we convince them that they may *see?*"

"Rhetoric," Sol realized.

I hummed in approval. "The principles we live by are a power all their own." Our ability to fight our baser instincts and our heart's desires in pursuit of a more perfect existence, *that* was where reason triumphed over spirit and hunger. That was where a Philosopher truly shined. Rhetoric, then, was our ability to impose the rules of nature as we understood them onto others.

There was incredible power in living a principled life. There was even more incredible power in understanding the world—and in passing that understanding on to others. I internalized these concepts, slotting them into gaps that my father had intentionally left in my education. They fit seamlessly together.

"Why didn't the Heroes do this?" Sol wondered, troubled. He stood and began wringing what oil he could from his robes.

"I don't know," I admitted freely, "but I have a few ideas."

"And you said my mentor was a failure. You had a Tyrant for a father, and you're still not sure? What sort of father keeps his son in the dark?"

"What sort of father drags his son to war?" I returned. A tense moment came and went.

"My father wanted the best for me," Sol said with utter conviction.

"So did mine."

Sol grimaced, shaking olive oil from his hair and looking at the corpse at our feet. "I still don't like this. I'd rather leave Olympia, go elsewhere."

"It's too late for that," I said, kneeling beside the dead Crow and laying my hands across his body, all twenty-two of them. "Our hands are bloodied now. Are you really fine with leaving things as they are? Leaving the Raging Heaven to consume itself, and allowing our friends to suffer?"

His right hand clenched into a fist, and I knew I had won. "Don't act like you're doing this for *them*. You came here looking for a thrill and you've found it. It's for you, not for them."

"Wrong," I said. "It's both." I closed my eyes and said a short, silent prayer for the departed man. Then I started stripping him. "Tell me, Sol. Did you find your mentor?"

He shook his head.

"Did you find any leads?" I asked, considering the face of the dead man as the hood pulled free. I didn't know him. Sol remained silent, which was answer enough. "Let me guess. You confided in Anastasia, and she recognized his name. But she didn't give you anything concrete."

He grunted.

"You know what sort of existence a Heroic cultivator is, Sol. You've heard the tales. If your war stories are more than just dust and wind, then you've even seen it for yourself."

"Get to the point."

I scoffed but obliged him. "You know as well as I do that a Hero's full strength can't be contained by a city, even if that city is Olympia. It doesn't fit down alleyways and corridors. It doesn't thrive in friendly spars and controlled competitions. My cousin, Nikolas, had plans to compete in the Olympic Games this year, did you know that? His companions, too. Yet they didn't wear indigo when they came back home, and he never once spoke of the Raging Heaven when he was telling his stories. Why do you think that is?"

"Because he never joined," Sol said, frowning thoughtfully.

"Exactly." I unwrapped the black robes from the dead Philosopher and stood, moving over to the olive oil pool and dunking them in, scouring the blood from the cloth with pankration hands. "Almost all the athletes that compete in the Games do so as outsiders. The mystery cults cannot possibly hope to provide for a Hero seeking advancement. It simply isn't possible."

"Even with Tyrants there to mentor them?" Sol asked.

"Cultivators are greedy existences, you know this," I said, shrugging. "There's only one type of man that a Tyrant will mentor."

His heir.

Something slid into Sol's bearing, some nameless steel, and he crossed over to the Crow skewered on the sentinel's trident. I didn't see what happened, focusing on my scrubbing, but I felt the pulse of his will and heard the crunch of a man's skull caving in. My pankration hands cupped the torches protectively as the Philosopher's last gasp ripped through the temple. There was a pause and then a brief shuffling of cloth, and Sol appeared at my side, dunking his own set of black rags into the olive oil.

"A Hero can't advance in a cage," he said quietly, his eyes distant while he worked, reliving a thousand different memories. "So why are they here?"

"That's the question," I confirmed, pulling my new robes from the pool and cracking them like a whip, spraying spirit oil across the Father's feet. "A Hero can't be anything less than a significant existence. What could have led them here? What could *possibly* be worth their time within these walls?"

What could they be running from?

We worked in silence for a few moments, Sol scrubbing while I dried my robes with smoldering palms.

Belatedly, I added, "Also, I want to see the Oracles."

Sol looked at me incredulously. "*Oracles?* One wasn't enough?"

"Who do you think I am?"

The Roman shook his head in disgust and pulled his own robes from the pool, passing them to me when I offered a flaming hand. "How do you plan to blend in? We don't know who these two answered to. We don't have any idea how they all communicate with one another. We'll be rooted out within a day."

"Use that head of yours, Legate." I waved a hand at the virtuous beast perched on a high arch, observing us with curiosity. "They're called Crows for a reason."

Sol's eyes narrowed. "Sorea. To me." The eagle let fly an obliging cry and swept down from the arches, landing gently on the Roman's outstretched arm. Mongrel bird. The cuts it had given me still stung.

The Roman brandished his open palm and said firmly, "Spit it out."

Sorea cocked its head, and then its body heaved. The great messenger eagle vomited a pile of ink-black bones into Sol's hand. Enough for two small birds.

My nose wrinkled. "Well. That's unfortunate."

Chapter Forty-Five

THE SON OF ROME

"That went differently in your head, didn't it?" I remarked, eyeing the ink-black pile of bones and bile that Sorea had vomited into my open palm. They were warm—warmer than they should have been. Scorching hot, even by a cultivator's standards.

"You *just* ate it," Griffon said, addressing my bird with incredulous disgust. "How did you digest the second one that fast?"

My eyes rolled. "It isn't a real crow. We have no idea what its flesh is even made of."

"Pneuma, obviously." He stalked over to the corpse of the assassin he'd impaled on the stone sentinel's trident. He didn't hesitate to desecrate it, jostling the dead man from the restful position I'd settled him in and twisting his head to and fro. He gripped his jaw and looked into his slack mouth, then the narrow passages of his nostrils and ears.

It occurred to me that this may have been the first life the Young Aristocrat of the Rosy Dawn had ever taken.

"There wasn't another crow in his robe?" he asked. At my negative response, he slammed a palm to the hollowed stone beside the corpse's face and pushed himself to his feet. He turned to pace across the tiles.

"What is a Crow without his wings?" Griffon murmured, nearly to himself, frowning ferociously. He spat. "*No one.*"

"They may have only sent one for the pair of them," I offered. Scarlet eyes turned balefully my way.

"Tell me then, *master.* How many Crows did you come across without their wings on the night of the kyrios' funeral?"

I frowned, considering the pile of scalding hot cartilage in my palm. My memories were largely a blur, but the cadence was always clear. The steady rhythm of the legions marched a vivid path through otherwise muddled memories. I followed that path, soundlessly mouthing the words, and in those crystalline moments, I remembered the Crows.

I remembered the way they'd crumpled. The way they'd skulked, the way they'd scattered, the way they'd screamed. Never in my life had I come close to the alabaster heights of what the Greeks called the Heroic Realm—but then, it hadn't mattered much that night. I'd led weaker men against greater enemies than them. With Anastasia, Scythas, and Jason at my side, they hadn't stood a chance.

I remembered how they'd fallen. And I remembered the sounds of beating wings in the shadows as they fled.

"Sorea," I said. The messenger eagle flexed its great talons around my forearm, just enough to acknowledge me. "Did you notice another?" Virtuous beast or not, it was still only a bird. Yet the look Sorea gave me in response to that question was utterly unmistakable. "That's a no."

"Bastard must have sent it off when I arrived." Griffon reclaimed his stolen rags and ran flaming hands up and down them, grimacing at the trio of gaping trident holes in the cloth. "Sol, trade me."

"Not a chance," I said without hesitation, dumping the ink-black crow bones on the lip of the olive oil pool and brushing Sorea off my arm. He edged towards the bones, beak snapping softly. "Leave them." The bird shrieked indignantly but obeyed, taking flight out of the temple and vanishing into the night.

I wrung out the robes of a dead man, watching what moisture remained fall into the pool, drop by drop. I contemplated Griffon's reflection, the darkness of his expression as he turned his set of midnight attire over in his hands.

"You've never killed a man before," I said without judgment. For a moment, his eyes flickered.

"Wrong."

Lies built upon truth. "You've never killed a man before today," I clarified. His silence spoke for him. "It shakes you. I know." Frozen moments, memories of all the men I'd stood shoulder to shoulder with when they took their first life. All the men I'd *commanded* to bloody their unsullied hands.

In the pursuit of a higher ideal, the men of Rome could bear that burden without regret. With the hand of Gaius guiding them, legionaries struck down the enemies of the Republic without fear of the heavens above. But even so, and even then, that blood could drown you as surely as the sea. Salt and ash.

I considered the reflection of my only true companion in this barbarous world and wondered how many dead men it would take to drown him.

"It isn't weakness to regret—"

"I don't."

My hands clenched around the twist of black cloth, wringing a trickle of olive oil from it that struck the pool and distorted his reflection with ripples. I looked at him. His face matched his words. There was no regret in the set of his jaw, no grief in those narrowed eyes. Stripped of his usual good humor, what remained was the same foundation that had always been there. What I'd recognized the day I met him.

"From the moment I was born, I've known the worth of my soul." The words were matter-of-fact. Without doubt. "My life is mine. If someone tries to take it, I won't hesitate to take theirs first. I have nothing to regret."

I didn't argue. I knew the truth when I saw it.

"Mad Greek," I said ruefully. He smirked faintly and belted the mangled black robe around his waist, obscuring his Rosy Dawn attire and golden tunic turned makeshift satchel.

"You still want to do this?" I knew the answer already. I shrugged the dead man's disguise over my indigo robes. What had been a voluminous fit on the would-be assassin was just tight enough that I knew I wouldn't be comfortable fighting in it, so I didn't bother wearing it as it was intended. As a cloak, it would do.

The seemingly mundane material blurred at the edges of my perceptions, fading into the shadows around us like a lash of paint across canvas, growing thinner and blending together. Like I was a piece of this place as much as anything else. As I wrapped the layers around my body, I felt my own sense of self, the sensation of my own vital breath's circulation, fading into anonymity.

It wasn't exactly the same, but it was closer to those iron manacles than it should have been.

"Of course," Griffon said, pulling me from my thoughts. He had the crow's hood over his head now, obscuring his most striking features. He'd even done something to his hair while I wasn't looking, preventing it from spilling down to his shoulders in its usual way. "You noticed it too, didn't you?"

"The cloth conceals," I said, and as the sheer black hood fell over my face, thin enough to see through without issue, my voice changed as well. Not enough to belong to someone else. Just enough to not belong to me.

"What is a mask if not a tool of anonymity?" Griffin mused, leaning over the rim of the pool to consider himself.

I noticed a somewhat glaring flaw in his disguise.

"Worthless, when you're still half-naked." My lips formed the words, but a stranger's voice spoke them. Oddly enough, it was more pleasing than unsettling to hear another's voice render judgment on his absurdity in place of my own. For a moment, it was as if I wasn't the only sane person left in this world.

Griffin shrugged, unconcerned. "You wouldn't trade me, and I refuse to wear a tunic riddled with holes."

"Anyone from the funeral will recognize you immediately."

"Don't be so sure," he said lightly, gathering up crow bones in his cupped palms and dipping them into the pool. A stranger's pneuma, utterly divorced from Griffon's and yet his nonetheless, permeated through the pool and the bones, in particular, wearing away at them the same way he had worn away a chunk of marble an eternity ago at the Rosy Dawn's initiation trials.

Ink-black flecks of bone whirled and dispersed in the olive oil, turning the pool black, forming storm clouds beneath the chryselephantine king's feet. Pankration hands that felt like nothing I had ever encountered before but could be nothing other than Griffon's own violent intent dipped into the pool one by one, cupping ink-black olive oil in ethereal palms.

I watched twenty hands trace across Griffon's bare torso, along his shoulders and around his back. The lines they drew were seemingly random, whirling loops around his arms and jagged lines up and down the musculature of his chest. It was only once they'd drawn back as one, clapping against one another in apparent satisfaction, that I beheld the full picture.

He looked like a completely different man. It was the ink as much as the cloth. Black olive oil tattoos, painted with shocking precision. He hadn't just obscured the distinct lines of muscle that any of our companions could have identified in an instant. He'd framed them, traced them, and in the smallest of margins, he'd brushed outside of those lines. Not enough to alert a casual eye. Just enough to suggest a slightly different definition. Focusing on any one detail, there wasn't much. But as a whole, the insertion of his muscles looked completely different.

I couldn't see his face behind the hood, but the silent spreading of his hands was clear enough expectation. I grunted, and that was answer enough for him. He chuckled and swaggered over to the outer perimeter of the hollowed temple, towards the statue sentinels that waited in the archways.

"We're still blind," I reminded him. He plucked a true bronze spear from the marble hands that held it, weighing it consideringly before shrugging and tossing it over his shoulder at me. I caught the surprisingly heavy weapon and spun it in my right hand. It was a good weapon. The best I'd held in over a year.

"So we'll gather information. By force, if necessary. Though I can't imagine anyone being shy to confide in you." He plucked a gleaming bow and a winged arrow from another faceless sentinel, held it for about a heartbeat, and then dropped it to the ground and moved on. It clattered deafeningly against the holy stone. The fine hairs on the back of my neck rose.

"This feels like the wrong approach."

Griffin took a broad axe from clenched marble fists and tossed it from hand to hand to pankration hand, nodding in satisfaction.

"Careful, brother," he said idly. "There's a fine line between caution and cowardice."

"What about audacity and insanity?" I returned, unbothered. The torchlight caught a pattern in the haft of the spear as I spun it, shimmering trails of textured bronze that differed just enough to be aesthetic. "You know precious little about the storm brewing here, and I know even less. And you're suggesting we dive into it headfirst."

"Why are you here, Sol?" Griffin asked, contemplating the featureless face of the looming sentinel.

"To find my mentor."

"Why?"

"You know why," I said, annoyed.

"All for power? All to kill the dogs?" He turned away from the statue, bereft of its axe. He lifted the hooded veil from his face and skewered me with a look. "You think the easy path will lead you there?"

My eyes narrowed.

"You're worried that you won't survive the conquerors' path," Griffon said. With a certainty that made my lip twitch up from my teeth, he advanced with that gleaming bronze axe in hand. "You're worried that the scholar's path will take too long. And you've convinced yourself that the champion's path is nothing but flash and thunder. You worry that you don't deserve to *want it*."

He stopped just outside the range of the spear he'd tossed me. One of his pankration hands reached across that distance and lifted the hood from my face. He smiled a sharp challenge.

"Allow your brother to cleanse your heart of worries. I'll do it in your place."

I sneered fully. His smile only grew.

"I'll take the foolish risks," he promised me. "I'll walk the treacherous roads and suffer the trails untread. When the dogs come barking, I'll scour them from this earth in your name."

My sneer turned to a snarl. The hands of our influence slammed together in a deadlocked struggle. Beneath the anonymous shroud of the crow's shadow, we strained against ideals in place of each other.

"I'll return the city of Rome to you," Griffon continued, and the fact that every word of it was his true intention only made me more furious. "I'll fight all the battles that you can't."

"What are you doing?" I asked him through gritted teeth.

"Something different." He advanced a step farther, within the range of my spear. I stepped forward to meet him, into the range of his axe. In the low light of the vandalized temple, the father's shadow loomed over us both in ivory judgment.

"Does it anger you?" he whispered softly. "The thought of someone else making right what your enemies made wrong? If Rome is all that's in your heart, it shouldn't. If your only wish is to see the dogs of Carthage wiped out, then this should be nothing but a relief."

Whatever he saw in my eyes, he seemed to like it. He continued, with that terrible satisfaction.

"You may doubt yourself, but you wouldn't dare doubt me. I swear that I'll do it. I absolve you of this burden. So if that's the only reason you're still here, if that's the only reason you're still alive while all your men are dead, then go join them without regrets. *Be free.* And I'll take care of the rest."

"Enough. Be *silent.*"

"I refuse." Scarlet eyes danced. "You can lie to yourself, but you can't lie to *me.* You'll never be satisfied with a victory you didn't seize with your own two hands. You'll never be able to rest until you tear those animals apart and eat their beating hearts.

"Your virtuous heart won't accept this world until you *take it from them.*"

Gravitas rocked the father's temple, three thousand dead men pressing down on my shoulders, the weight of command far too heavy to bear. Always, forever too heavy. What else could I do but bear it?

"If I don't," I whispered, "who will?"

Griffin smiled brilliantly, standing unshaken while eleven stone sentinels crumbled beneath the captain's virtue. He surveyed the blasphemous destruction with a keen eye. Pankration hands swept across the hallowed grounds and gathered up the bronze weapons left behind.

"We'll have to find a place to keep these," he decided, surveying each in turn. "Leaving all but two behind would be far too obvious. And who knows? We may yet convince our fellow sophists to join us in our humble little adventure. In fact—"

He paused at the sound of bones snapping, blinking and staring at the fragment of ink-black bone I held out to him. A deep, vibrant red light burned blindingly at the center of the shard.

"What are you thinking?" he asked with something like glee.

"We're blind without wings," I said, dropping the broken bone. A pankration hand caught it as it fell. "If we can't make use of these scavengers in life, the least they can do is serve us in death."

The Greek approach to cultivation was foreign to me in many ways, more so the more I learned of it. However, there were certain truths that rang universally true between the Greek and Roman pursuits of virtue. For all that they reviled us and we reviled them, the fact remained that each of us stood above the crude barbarian nations that surrounded us on every side.

An enlightened civilization pursued virtue through *reason*. A civilized man placed reason before rage, and in so doing rose above the unwashed barbarian. Even an unwashed barbarian was still a man, though. He could place the love of family and hatred of his enemy before his primal desires, and so he stood above the animals of the earth.

But just because we were *above* that primal, bestial hunger—that did not mean we couldn't indulge it. A virtuous beast was a slave to its primal desire, but that did not make it *weak*. There was strength to be had in consumption. There was power in every living thing, and that power could be taken after its passing. It could be consumed.

It could be made ours.

"Seems dangerous," Griffin said. He raised an eyebrow. "Twelves to see who goes first?"

Danger. Risk. Certain, inescapable death. Perhaps Griffin was right. It was time to stop pretending that it was dread that made my heart pound in this city of monstrous barbarians and not anticipation.

A captain leads from the front, I told him in the voice of my soul, and I sucked the starlight marrow from the bone.

Interlude: The Rein-Holder

You are nothing.

Liquid purpose burns a trail down your throat, melting through fragile linings of tissue and sinew. You've always been proud of your constitution, in those quiet moments of honesty you believed yourself to be truly *strong*, but your body can do nothing but give way to this force. The marrow burrows through your body, following channels that do not yet exist in your unrefined body. What cannot be found is created instead.

You fall to your knees, choking. You hack and spit, and when that does nothing for you, you jam your fingers down your throat. You gag. You heave. But nothing comes up.

You reach desperately for your companion but too late. He took the marrow into himself a mere instant after you did, and now he stumbles back, falling into the soiled pool beneath the feet of **the Thunderer**. You try to rise, but the marrow is in your spine now. Your limbs lock up and you fall, fall, fall.

The last thing you notice is the smoke. Cypress, dilute but unmistakable. You hold on to that sensation, desperately, reaching for the accompanying meaning, but your thoughts slip away from you like that same smoke. The marrow courses up your spine and into your brain. In the end, your own thoughts slip away.

The Rein-Holder takes you in hand.

[The cawing crow lives for nine generations of men in their prime]

You are no one.

The marrow makes a domain of your semblance. It rises through porous skin, bubbling up inside the lines of your newly painted tattoos. Spirit olive oil with its midnight tint gives way to shining crimson script. The olive oil burns away entirely, clouds of steam billowing up around you.

Your companion reaches desperately for you, but the pain has already knocked you back. You fall *through* the stone dais at the feet of **the Cloud-Gatherer**, the stone as porous as your own flesh, and into the olive oil pool. It flash-boils in an instant.

You bare your teeth in naked threat, though no one is there to see it, and focus your strength inward. You scour your own blood, turning your vital breath against your body. You burn away arteries, vital organs, and inevitably, you turn upon the branching paths of light within your spine—

But the marrow has beaten you there. You stop breathing. Your pneuma howls and fades. You try to snarl, but you don't have the control for even that. You track the marrow as it winds up the contours of your spine, unable to do anything but hate it, and then it's in your brain, and you're unable to do even that.

The Rein-Holder brings you to heel.

[The cawing crow serves nine generations of Tyrants in their domains]

You are nothing, king of *no one*.

The city of Rome has fallen, and demons did the work. You remember the snarling faces of the wolves that salted your city. You remember how they fought, impossibly, like men in formation. You remember their tactics. You remember they can cultivate. You remember that your father—

Your father. You remember your father. You remember Gaius. Your last mentor, the first being—

You remember your first mentor. You remember his rhetoric and the years that he walked the streets of Rome. You remember that he taught you the language of the Álikoans, which served you well when you were... bound. Bound in slavery. Bound to *Greece*.

You remember that Damon Aetos' men drove back the demons. You remember that Damon Aetos took you into his estate.

You remember that Damon Aetos knows of the threat, and *he has not spoken of it.*

The Rein-Holder beckons you.

[The cawing crow serves nine generations of Tyrants and their purposes]

You are no one, king of *nothing*.

The Cult of the Rosy Dawn has finally rid itself of you, and you did the work yourself. You remember the scowling faces of the aunts and uncles that hated your existence. You remember how they spoke to you, poisonously, when no one was around to hear them. You remember their contempt. You remember their resentment. You remember their fear of you, their fear of your resemblance to your father—

Your father. You remember your father. You remember *Damon Aetos.*

Damon Aetos is your father.

Starlight marrow flickers for a bare moment, and then it explodes through your brain and back down your spine, the tree of your life, and it *burns all that it touches.*

The Rein-Holder condemns you.

[The cawing crow eats nine generations of men in their passing]

Your companion is condemned.

Rise. Your legs are unsteady, but they are stronger than before. The marrow has burnt new channels through you, connected points of light within you that had until now sat as islands in the dark. *You* are stronger than you were a moment before. A moment from now, you'll be stronger still.

You step through the gemstone mosaics that decorate the pool. You see your companion, dying in the boiling olive oil. The tattoos he'd painted on himself are blood red where before they were black, and they seethe with a visible heat that vaporizes any oil that touches them.

His face is closed off from you by his midnight veil. In a way, he's already dead. This is simply mercy. You raise your celestial spear and drive it through his heart.

...You raise your celestial spear and drive it through his heart.

You raise your celestial spear—

Listen to me.

[The cawing crow dies]

You are condemned.

The marrow spreads through every inch of you, and it *burns.* It melts and it sears. Your blood boils within your veins. The marrow alights upon the fine threads that spread like roots from your spine, burning them away one by one. Your gut, your heart, and your brain are encircled.

Your stomach dissolves, devoured by its own bile. Your heart bursts. Your brain shuts down, thought by thought, until all the lights in the sky of your soul have flickered and gone out.

You *were* the son of Damon Aetos. Now you are dead.

...Now you are dead.

Now you are—

[The cawing crow—]

You stab your companion. You stab your companion who you've always despised. You stab your companion that had the gall to lecture *you* about *your city.* You stab the son of the man that enslaved you. You stab him. You stab him. *You stab him.*

Kill him.

[The crow—]

You stop moving, and you die. You lie back down in the pool, and you die. You stop smiling. You die. You die. *You die.*

[...]

YOU STOP EATING ME

[The raven grows old in the lifetime of three seers]

The tomb of the father is silent but for the haggard breathing of two young men. Cloaked in shadow and shrouded by sin, they have no faces to look upon. No voices to hear. And yet, they are more than simple crows.

The hungry ravens catch their breath. For a moment, all is still. Something silent passes between them. A beat.

They vanish into the night.

Act III: An Unkindness

Chapter Forty-Six

THE YOUNG GRIFFON

One of the better indicators of a person's character was the way they treated their juniors. The hunger for standing was a natural element of every human soul, and the temptation to abuse that standing was ever with us. Not always for its own sake, perhaps, but all too often opportunities presented themselves just out of reach, and all too often there were other people, subordinates or friends or even family, positioned just right to act as stepping stones so you could close that distance.

For many, it was a question that almost didn't warrant asking. When it was nothing more than glory or fortune on the line, the temptation was strong enough. But for cultivators, those who coveted divinity's distant star, existences that gained years of extended life for each small advancement? Well. For them, it wasn't a question at all.

The path to heaven was only wide enough for one man to walk it at a time. My tutors had hammered that into me at an early age. In the end, we were all alone when we challenged the Fates. The only uncertainty was how many lesser men we stomped down on our way up.

Eventually, a cultivator placed all beneath them. It was only a matter of when. We called it the Tyrannic Realm for a reason, after all.

Still, there were those that understood this fact and accepted it as a necessary consequence of defying what the Fates had planned for them—good and bad. And on the other hand, there were those that hid behind it like a shield, cringing away from all responsibility.

I was pleased to find that Elissa was the former of the two.

"What did I say? It isn't a matter of force or finesse, it's your *grip*," the Heroine said sharply. The scars on her marble skin turned an otherwise stern frown into something truly vicious.

The boy she was lecturing, a tan youth that looked to be somewhere between Heron and Castor's age, stood like he had been struck, quickly shifting his grip to something less comfortable for him but better overall. His blade was a fine thing, simply crafted with impeccable materials. Flawless iron, and a wavering line of bronze traveling through its surface like a serpent or a sun ray. Looking at it and the boy that held it, nervous and eager and hopeful, his Raging Heaven attire neatly folded and set aside in a way that spoke of his care for it, I got the impression that they were together a product of simple laborers and backwater settlements.

For him to have qualified for admittance to the Raging Heaven at his age, the indigo jewel of the Half-Step City, he must have been truly talented. His pneuma, firmly in the Sophic Realm, spoke to this as well. Still, even among prodigies, there were those who stood above.

While the boy and four others brandished naked iron, Elissa held only an olive tree's branch in her loose grip. It was more than enough.

Desert-heat eyes scoured the boy's form until, satisfied, she made a come-hither gesture with her free hand. All five took a different approach, some lunging low and others taking wide, sweeping strikes. Her olive tree branch whipped out with improbable speed, not only taking strikes from weapons that should have severed it with ease, but knocking them aside without care. She pivoted—pranced, really— moving through them with the grace of a dancer at a symposium.

Without looking, she whipped her branch around to meet the knife-edge of my descending palm, scowling as the Rosy Fingers of Dawn lit her impromptu weapon on fire. Five young Philosophers of the Raging Heaven leapt back, alarmed and shouting.

"What do you want, Griffon?" Elissa asked irritably. I smiled and shrugged, pivoting on one foot and driving up with my other hand.

[The sun rises.]

I didn't manifest any violent intent, and my attack wasn't particularly quick. In an instant, the Heroine figured out what I was doing and scoffed, but, nonetheless, she twisted with a similarly languid motion and swept her burning branch at my hand, forcing the strike aside.

"This lowly sophist heard that a Heroine was dispensing wisdom to her juniors. What else could I do but seek some out for myself? For a newly minted Philosopher, such a fortuitous encounter might only come once in my life." As I spoke, I led her through something that was as much a dance as it was a fight, a nameless game of choreographed violence that I had often played with Nikolas when I was younger.

"Newly minted Philosopher," she repeated as we moved, almost offended in her skepticism. In response, I flexed my Pneuma. It was undeniably of the Sophic Realm, first rank.

Elissa didn't believe it for a moment. But the boys did.

"Junior!"

"Without even asking!"

"The *audacity!*" The boy with the shoddy grip rushed me with his blade poised. He was older than the trio of boys I'd slapped around the day before, closer to his physical prime, and that made his superior cultivation far more dangerous.

A pankration hand yanked him back by the white cloth hanging around his waist. When he jerked around to strike at it another two hammered up between his legs. The boy choked and fell to the dirt.

"I've noticed a trend among the initiates of this cult," I said conversationally, splaying ten more hands in a burning ring around us, warding off the other philosophers. They eyed me warily while their fellow gagged on the ground.

"I don't care." There had been a bare flicker of something fatally sharp in those desert heat eyes, an instant of protective rage. It was gone as quick as it came, when she realized I'd only given the boy something convincing to think about.

"Yes, you do," I said easily, continuing our dance without missing a step. It was a game as much as any of the others I'd played the last couple days, a lighthearted representation of a fatal encounter. We took lazy, almost sloppy swings at one another, but the strikes they represented were a murderous blur in my mind's eye. This was not a game won by increments. The first to falter lost.

As her branch represented a blade, and my fists were only that, I was at a firm disadvantage. In theory. But I had been smacking down live steel since I was a boy. And this game was entirely a question of tactics.

Elissa's swordplay was some of the best I'd ever seen, but it had been Nikolas Aetos that taught me this game.

"Tell me, then," she demanded, focusing intently as the blade of my left hand met the tip of her branch and gently burnt it away.

I could almost see the image in her head, of ten thousand pankration hands slamming against her blade with ruinous heat, breaking it at its imperfect points. As far as she was concerned, we had both only been feeling one another out when we clashed at the funeral. She thought I had far more to give.

I glanced at the young men ringed around us. Outrage and jealousy abounded, and it was easy enough to see why. I hadn't inserted myself into her impromptu lesson immediately, after all. In observing, I'd spent as much time taking the measure of her juniors in relation to her as I had of her relation to them.

It was fortunate enough for a cultivator in the Heroic Realm to give you a moment of their time. It was doubly fortunate when they were a beautiful woman and you were just discovering your body's earthly desires. These five had sought her out on this jagged peak within spitting distance of the Storm That Never Ceased because she was by far the best swordsman that would give them the time of day.

"They're all *soft*."

But more than that, they'd come to bask in her attention.

Five Sophic cultivators seethed at my disdain, their influence lashing out impotently at my pankration hands. Their egos broke against the rosy fingers of dawn without resistance, closer to sea spray than any true wave.

"They're young," Elissa reproached me. Ho, there was real anger in that desert heat. How surprising.

"Children are young," I dismissed, ducking a sharp jab at my eyes and thrusting a palm at her kidney. She twisted artfully, fuchsia silk shifting across her sculpted skin. I snorted as five sets of eyes stared. "Cultivators are only ever *unrefined*."

"It isn't enough to say things that sound meaningful," Elissa replied, striking. "It has to actually mean something, too."

"How cruel." Advance, feint, step back. "But you know, it isn't enough to dismiss a point you disagree with, either." Above our heads, the undying storm rumbled. "You still have to prove me wrong."

Elissa scowled and suddenly shifted the rhythm she'd kept thus far, adopting a new style. The transition was so smooth that I almost didn't notice in time. I leaned away from the next three strikes, raising an eyebrow.

She caved. "Soft in what way, then?"

"I have a cousin," I said, and the pankration hands surrounding us turned their palms inward. Two went rigid and flat like daggers and were seized by two others in turn. They began to dance through the air in a series of sharp jabs, slashes, and cuts.

For all that he had harbored absurd shame over his lack of manifested virtue, the little kyrios had never allowed himself to wallow and shirk his martial pursuits. The five young Philosophers watched with reluctant fascination as I illustrated Myron's dagger forms. One boy, in particular, with delicate features and thin fingers, traced the motions with intense focus. He'd come here to learn the sword, ostensibly, but knives were clearly his true interest.

"You have a cousin," Elissa repeated flatly.

"Several, actually. But the youngest is nine years old, and already his foundations are packed tighter than anything I've seen on this pretty mountain. Compared to these boys, his cultivation may be lesser, but he is the better *man*. When discourse turns to dispute, he possesses the only characteristic that truly matters. The element that these boys lack."

One of the two pankration suddenly twisted and threw its makeshift dagger-hand. It drove through the stone behind the sun ray swordsman, just missing his head. He flinched sideways.

"An *edge*."

Elissa said nothing.

She was surprisingly kind to her juniors, that was the truth. She was surprisingly tolerant of their obvious motives, that was the truth as well. She was even, most surprising of all, a bit *protective* of her junior mystikos in spite of the way she'd treated Scythas and me at the kyrios' funeral. But in the end, there was one aspect of her that was not surprising at all. She was a Heroine, and she knew what distinguished those that ascended from those that did not.

She bore its mark all over her body.

And she knew that these children didn't have it.

"What am I missing here, honored Heroine?" I pressed her quietly, closing the distance and drawing her into the final exchange. "This is the Half-Step City, isn't it? This is the cult that only accepts the finest souls of the free Mediterranean, *isn't it?* So tell me, why are they all so *soft?*"

I knew why, of course. I felt it in my bones, in the new marrow that coursed through them like ruby veins. But some things were too important not to confirm. Our exchanges became frenzied, though the speed never changed. Elissa's burning eyes darted this way and that, tracking burning fists that didn't exist. In my mind's eye, I waded through a storm of bronze.

Iron sharpens iron, she spoke in the voice of her soul, a clear chime to my Sophic sense.

Her burning branch halted beside my right ear. The Heroine snarled in frustration and threw down her weapon. I tapped her chest a second time, directly over her heart. One of the boys made a disbelieving sound and was quickly hushed by his fellows.

"Elaborate," I invited her, stepping back and inclining my head. She mirrored me, grudgingly.

"Iron sharpens iron," she said out loud. There was something there, a contempt for someone other than me. "A strong foundation requires strong opposition."

"Naturally," I agreed. I waved a hand at the young Philosophers. "So then, you're saying these shining gems of the free Mediterranean didn't experience any true hardship on the road to the Raging Heaven Cult?"

It was rather sad, watching them throttle their indignation before Elissa could notice it. As if they could hide anything from her. She pretended not to see it anyway, for their sake.

"You know I'm not saying that."

"I do."

"Then why—" She shook her head. Disgusted with me, no doubt. "The initiates here are all exceptional cultivators, the best of the best. It isn't their fault that this place is the way it is."

"Whose fault is it, then?" I asked. It had been a gut feeling, a supposition built upon small observations and simple intuition, but here and now, as one of the stronger existences in the enlightened world stared at me silently, unwilling to speak, I knew it was the truth.

Tyrants.

"You grew up in a nowhere nation, separated from the enlightened world by an entire ocean," she finally said. I nodded because it was true. "If you decided one day that you were going to beat a rival of yours to death, who could punish you for it?"

My father. "The kyrios of the Rosy Dawn."

"Damon Aetos," she said, and the immortal storm roared above our heads. "Did he make a habit of intervening directly in the affairs of his younger initiates?"

I snorted.

Elissa nodded, taking that for the answer that it was. "Then if not him, who? The elders?"

"If they noticed."

"Exactly." Her jaw, slender and refined and marred by deep scars, flexed. "There are limits to the perceptions of Philosophers and Heroes. Lapses in awareness and simple lack of care. It is not in a Philosopher's nature to ignore life's greater mysteries in favor of tending to children. It is not in a Hero's nature to ignore life's greater threats in favor of small disputes."

She explained the problem to me in the only way she could—by explaining everything else instead.

It was not within the capabilities of Philosophers and Heroes to keep track of everything that took place in their vicinity. Nor was it in

371

their nature to care overly much about what those beneath them did. To subjugate them at every perceived slight.

But Tyrants were a different existence altogether.

"Eight kings, but only one crown," I mused. The alarm that took hold of her in that moment was as sharp and immediate as it had been the night of the funeral. Lightning flashed above our heads.

"Must you always tempt the Fates?" she whispered furiously.

I tilted my head to regard the five frowning philosophers. At a certain point, they had started to understand the difference between us. They regarded me as prey regarded a predator. As they should have from the start.

"My senior brothers," I said and smiled as they leaned in, unconsciously, to listen. "You came here for wisdom, so listen for a moment. You are surrounded, and you are watched, that is true. It's entirely possible that no matter what you do beneath this curtain of tribulation, you will be angering a lion. But that doesn't mean you shouldn't act."

Without looking, I picked up the discarded olive branch with a pankration hand and offered it to Elissa. She eyed it like it was a real blade after all.

"Neutrality won't protect you forever," I promised them all. "The higher-ups may only be watching for now, but they'll get hungry eventually. And when the lion is hungry, *he eats*."

The young woman, once a crow but now unmasked and someone again, choked as the hungry raven on the right gripped her by the throat and slammed her against a marble pillar. Chains rattled and went taut, binding her to the stone and throttling her cultivation.

"She wasn't wrong," the hungry raven on the right mused in a voice of shifting sand. "Cowards you may be, skulking around in the dark, but you're the only ones getting anything done around here. A cat's paw is still dangerous, isn't it?"

The young woman gritted her teeth and thrashed against her binds. The raven chuckled.

"Which king do you serve?" Her small part of providence urged her not to speak, to give nothing away. As if she would have. The young woman kept her silence.

The hungry raven on the left drove its bronze spear through her thigh, and she choked back a scream.

"Where is the man who knows everything?" the hungry raven on the left demanded.

"I asked first," cawed the other.

"We're not doing this."

"Anonymity isn't an excuse to be *rude*."

The hungry raven on the left ignored its bare-chested counterpart, leaning down until its face was level with hers. By its build, it was almost certainly a man. And while before she had been nothing but shadows and unseen malice, she was now Harmodias of Krókos. A woman, her wrists bound to the marble column by chains. At their mercy. She closed her eyes and leaned away from it all.

"What do you know of the man who knows everything?" he asked again.

"Nothing," she whispered. He twisted the spear's head in her thigh. She winced and shivered. *"Nothing."*

He considered her silently while the other raven waited impatiently, resting his weight on the shaft of a ludicrously large bronze war axe. Finally, he sighed and drew back. She could feel the end approaching. After all this time, all that Harmodias had given in pursuit of the heights, this was where she succumbed. In the dark, with no one to mourn her passing. It was too cruel. It was simply *too cruel*—

The raven on the left broke the chain that bound her, and without another word, they threw her off the side of Kaukoso Mons.

"Worthless—" she heard the raven on the right begin to shout before the whistling winds stole it all away. Her small part of providence suddenly came alive within her unseen shadow, cawing and flapping its wings furiously as it burst out of a fold in her clothes and took flight. It would return to its source, and they would know what had taken place here. Who had killed her, and what they were after. If nothing else, she could take some comfort in that. Her death wouldn't be entirely without meaning.

The last thing she saw was an eagle cutting through the sky like an arrow. It overtook her crow in an instant, sinking its talons into ink-black flesh and careening back up the mountain.

Harmodias opened her mouth to scream and promptly slammed through the sloped roof of one of Olympia's nicer bathhouses.

Chapter Forty-Seven

THE SON OF ROME

As much as Griffon had tried to rope me into it, I had never been a member of the Rosy Dawn. Not truly. There were certain duties that a slave simply could not ignore, no matter the attire they wore or the company they kept. As much as Griffin was the Young Aristocrat of the cult, second only to one in many ways, he *was* second.

I only ever met Damon Aetos twice. The second time was during the initiation rites that his son had dragged me through, in the impacted cavern where the bisected corpse of the fallen sun god lay in eternal rest. As rosy light had bloomed in that corpse's palm, the sun rising, the kyrios' eyes had drifted from his son to me. And though I hadn't sensed anything at the time with my senses dulled by iron shackles, I had known then, as I had known from the beginning, that every breath I drew within the Scarlet City was a breath that he had allowed me.

The first time I met Damon Aetos, my wounds were still bleeding and my ears were still ringing from the thunder of war.

He'd commanded his captain and soldiers to leave and then his brothers. Then he sat silent, while I knelt on that marble floor, patiently waiting. Night fell, and the moon rose. Sounds of conversation and combat and simple life drifted through the open terrace of his office. He didn't fidget. Didn't move.

Finally, as the dawn broke over the eastern mountain range, the Tyrant of the Scarlet City spoke to me for the first time.

"You failed."

For a moment, I didn't realize the words had been spoken out loud. They'd been echoing in my mind for hours already.

I finally looked at him, then, and he gazed upon me without pity nor contempt. Nothing at all but expectation.

He wasn't surprised in the slightest.

"The city of Rome has fallen," he continued, unbothered by my vacant stare. "Her legions are scattered and gone. You are all that remains."

He stood from his desk, and he towered. His stature was reminiscent of the hulking Goths of the western front, sans their ponderous frames and grotesque features. He could have stood eye-to-eye with the demons of Carthage. Rounding his desk, he walked out onto the terrace and watched the light spread through his city.

"Your provinces won't mourn your passing," he told me. "Those conquered won't weep for the conqueror. All that you are, all that your ancestors have wrought, will be gone in a decade. Nothing will remain. And the children of Aeneas die with you."

And so I spoke my first words to him.

"I know that. I know all of that."

My fists clenched, unable to grasp the captain's virtue. As if it would have mattered. It hadn't then, and it wouldn't now. I slammed my fist into the floor anyway. The marble cracked.

"Your cloak was white, once," he said as if I hadn't spoken. The filthy rag miraculously still clung to my shoulder, but it had long since been stained an earthy red by blood and muck over the course of the campaign. Even so, it remained what it was: the mark of a Roman legion's senior commander.

I snarled and tore it off my shoulder.

"It's too late for that." He rendered judgment without hesitation. Blind as I was to Pneuma and virtue, I still felt it as it slammed down on my head. Forced me to bow. "You accepted that mantle, and you failed the men that it placed beneath you. There's no escaping that."

A Tyrant's judgment was absolute. Blood sprayed from my clenched teeth, marring the Tyrant's spotless floor. I heard the rush of thunder in my ears and saw the darkness creeping in from the edges as I forced my eyes up. *Up.*

Damon Aetos turned from his terrace and met my eyes again. Expectant.

"I never deserved it," I said, every word forced out into the open air, every syllable exacerbating the wounds that those dogs had given me. If I kept talking beneath the weight of his influence, I would die. "I failed them. My men. My mentors. *Rome.* I don't deserve to call myself a legionnaire, let alone a captain. Nothing you say could possibly make me hate you more than I hate myself. No judgment of yours could ever be as brutal as what I deserve."

Damon Aetos considered me for a long moment. Then he nodded, and the weight of his judgment fell away. I snarled again and slammed both mangled fists against the marble.

"Anybody can become angry. That much is easy." Two broad, calloused hands wrapped around my wrists, tighter and far more unyielding than the iron manacles. The kyrios dragged me to my feet. "But to be angry with the right person and to the right degree, and at the right time, and for the right purpose?"

He pressed without particular force, and I slammed down into a chair. He leaned back against his desk, obscuring three of the four warriors carved into its front face.

"That is not within everyone's power," he told me. "And it is not easy."

My strength was fading. The echoes of the fifth were growing louder by the minute. I'd be joining them soon.

"What is your name?"

I stared vacantly at the light on the horizon.

"Solus."

"The last son of Rome," he mused. "King of salt and ash. I suppose this is all that remains." The kyrios snapped his fingers, and a man that bore his age with tempered grace entered the office immediately.

"Mend him," Damon Aetos decided, "and put him to work."

The old man bowed his head at once, but then he raised it and asked the Tyrant, "As a slave, Damon? Are you certain?"

I would later come to know this old man as the first among servants within the Rosy Dawn, oldest by far. But to this day, I still didn't know how he'd had the gall to question a Tyrant where all others would have bowed their heads in supplication. More than that, I didn't know why the Tyrant had allowed it. Damon Aetos hadn't lashed out in anger at the slave's audacity. He had only turned away, dismissing us both as he returned to the business of ruling the Scarlet City.

"Whatever he may have been before, Carthage took it from him. He's nothing now."

For all that Griffin had tried to include me in the daily life of a true initiate, for all that he had sponsored me himself through the rites, his word came second to his father's. And Damon Aetos had decided from the very beginning that there was no place for me within his domain.

I've never been a peer amongst those seeking answers beneath the mysterious light of dawn, that was the simple fact of things, but I *had* worked among them and observed the things they did.

The people of Greece were in many ways exactly as my childhood mentor had described, and in many ways they were more. More vibrant, more academic, more boisterous and free-spirited, and more arrogant and frivolous in their pursuits. They were as alien to me as the Goths, the Britons, and the Celts. In more ways than one, I didn't know what it truly meant to be an initiate of a Greek mystery cult. But I knew where to start.

The stone steps carved into this particular section of Kaukoso Mons served as a half theater, its surface crowded by mystikos of the Raging Heaven cult. Boys, girls, men, and women, they gathered as individuals and in small groups with tablets and empty rolls of papyrus in hand. Nearly a dozen varying shades of indigo and its component colors abounded in their attire.

At the foot of the steps, on a circular platform that jutted out over the southern face of the mountain, a philosopher conducted his lectures.

He was a young man in appearance, broad-shouldered and tan, only the bare wrinkle of crow's feet around his eyes and the gray hairs on his chest giving lie to his apparent age. His hair was still full and dark, his beard thick and curly. He spoke with the weight of years and the confidence of someone that knew they were the smartest in the room.

Philosophers lecturing junior initiates had been a common occurrence in the Rosy Dawn. It was the primary method of advancement for those too young and weak to challenge their peers in the octagon or on the track. The early years were the most formative, as well, and so the young ones especially were presented with as many ideas and as much knowledge as they could fit in their heads.

All too often, the virtue that a man pulled from the sea of his soul was not the work of any one mentor. It was an amalgamation of a thousand different moments, words, and impressions. It was the natural way. The right way, many would say.

It was a question I couldn't answer myself.

The topic being covered here this afternoon, high up on the southern face of the mountain where junior initiates without experience abounded, was numerology. Pythagoreanism specifically. It was a commonly known fact that the mystery cults of the free Mediterranean were some of the finest institutions in the world, and if Griffon and Anastasia were to be believed, the Raging Heaven stood above even them in the quality of its instructors.

As I reclined with my elbows propped up against the stone steps behind me, listening, I found it somewhat hard to believe.

"Within nature there is a guiding principle, a thoughtful design which makes itself apparent to anyone who cares to seek it out," the Philosopher lectured, brandishing a hand and pointing two fingers up to heaven. "The observance of these designs allows us to fill in the empty spaces that have been left behind in the natural world. We use numbers to represent concepts beyond traditional comprehension, and in so doing we pave the way for understanding of our future. Something as monumental as the passage of stars can't be predicted intuitively. But it can be distilled down to numbers. And numbers can *always* be predicted."

The Philosopher led his audience through a primer, something I remembered learning about when I was still too short to punch a man in his jaw without jumping. Some of the gathered initiates seemed equally disinterested, but others were scribing with focused intensity.

The Philosopher transitioned after a while into specific examples, ticking the fingers of his other hand off, one at a time.

"Before the manipulation of numbers, there is meaning in the numbers themselves. The Broad's model of the soul tells us that we exist in three parts. We ascend through four mortal realms, and within each, we take ten ranks upon ourselves. There is meaning in every number, as there is meaning in every blade of grass and every shifting grain of sand."

He looked up at us all with patient expectation. "Somebody tell me the significance of the first number, *éna*."

"Victory," called a girl in dark maroon robes. The Philosopher inclined his head in acceptance.

"Another."

"Survival," a young man in a soft purple-blue tunic proposed, only for one of his fellows sitting beside him to immediately suggest the exact opposite.

The Philosopher cut in before an argument could ensue. "Both equally correct answers—and both lacking. You could all suggest a different meaning, and each would contain a portion of the truth, but none would be fully complete, because above all *éna* is—"

"Unity," spoke a voice from above, and every mystiko in attendance turned to watch a new arrival descend the stone steps. "One is the origin of all things. It is to numerology as numerology is to nature. All aspects of the world can be broken into numbers, and all numbers can be broken into *éna*."

"Exactly right," the Philosopher said, annoyance at the interruption warring with a visible fondness for the young man hopping down the steps. "Come again to steal my students from me, Jason?"

"Oh, I wouldn't dream of it," the Hero said, to the quiet disappointment of most in attendance. He winked at a group of particularly vocal young initiates nearby, hopping down the steps three at a time with the eerie grace all advanced cultivators moved with. "I just thought you might like an assistant. It never hurts to have a second set of—"

Burning blue eyes met mine, and Jason stumbled. A pair of girls with flowers braided into their hair cried out as a Hero twice their size stepped into them and sent them sprawling to the level below, into the laps of a group of boys.

"Jason?" the Philosopher asked, pneuma rising in concern.

"My mistake," the Hero said, catching himself in the next moment and offering both girls a hand. He lifted them back up to their seats and apologized to both, smiling indulgently at their starstruck expressions. "Actually, I think I'll sit in for this one. I suppose I have been acting the mentor too often lately. I've still got plenty to learn, eh?"

With that, he leapt back up the steps. He somehow managed to land in a casual sprawl that covered three levels as if they were a cushioned lounge, claiming for himself one of the many empty spaces in the rows most distant from the lecturer.

It placed him only a few scant feet away from me.

"What are you doing here, Sol?" he murmured, once the Philosopher had returned to his lecture and Jason had shooed the mystikos' wandering eyes away from him.

"Learning," I said blithely. Jason snorted.

"Right, and I'm the king of Egypt."

"Far from home," I observed. His lips twitched towards a grin, but he muscled it down.

"But really," he said, "is this about the other night?"

The Philosopher gestured down on his platform and conjured wisps of flame the color of honey, carving into the air as if it was a clay tablet. He traced geometric shapes in the wind, labeling their sides and espousing the meanings behind their pairings.

"I came here for him," I said, and it was even true. I hadn't had the privilege of personally attending lectures at the Rosy Dawn, but I'd caught enough in passing and remembered enough of my mentor to know that they were my best chance at piecing together the Greek style of cultivation.

I was here to find my mentor, that was true above all. But I had to acknowledge the possibility that I wouldn't find him here. Until I knew one way or another, I had to make the best of my time here. I'd seek him out as soon as I knew where to go. Whether that was across the city or across the continent, it would be done.

For his part, Jason's heart flames redoubled behind his eyes, and his lips parted in understanding.

"So he *is* conspiring with Alazon. I suspected, but I should have *known*."

I quietly sighed.

"Don't jump to conclusions," was all I said. Jason nodded fractionally, eyeing the Philosopher below with carefully masked suspicion.

"Of course, we'll have to play this carefully. But if you're right, and I think you are... we could prove beyond a doubt that Alazon was involved that night."

I resigned myself to this new reality, frowning at the implication of what he'd just said. By my vague memories of the funeral, I remembered a young man cast from the same mold as Griffon but forged from inferior materials. A young aristocrat without the grit to back up his gall. Scythas had told Griffin and me the following day that he'd been implicated by the Crow we captured. He'd all but admitted to it himself, the bastard, running off like he had.

But it seemed he'd made a convincing case for himself. Or, perhaps more likely, someone had made it for him.

"What about you?" I asked quietly. Jason blinked, adjusting his robes a bit and looking faintly embarrassed.

"These lectures... Depending on who's giving them, they have a tendency to *drift*."

I raised an eyebrow. Jason coughed into his fist.

"The initiates are still impressionable this far up the mountain," he explained. "Still naïve and dazzled by the sanctuary city and its grand plateau. Many of them still barely know what rhetoric *is*, let alone how to steel themselves against it."

My eyes widened as I realized what he was getting at. I watched the philosopher craft meaning out of thin air, carve it into the air with the shimmering flame, and I watched the mystikos in attendance drink it in like a desert oasis.

It made sense when I thought about it. Rhetoric was a tool like any other. A Philosopher could use it to convince as easily as they could to explain. If Griffon had been right in the temple of the Father, resisting its influence could even be a question of comparative cultivation.

"They're recruiting the children." Assembling factions. Turning them against one another.

Jason nodded, a dark look in his eyes.

"These are the moments that are meant to provide for new cultivators," he said quietly. "Many of these initiates are so exceptional that they gained admittance to the cult before cementing their virtue. Lectures like these provide a wider foundation for them to draw upon when the moment comes. When they're delivered in good faith."

More maneuvering. My eyes narrowed.

"So you offer your assistance in lecturing as their senior in cultivation."

"An impossible thing to refuse," he agreed. "And if I happen to steer things away from one particular topic or another, who's to say there's any intent behind it?" Because accusing him of such a thing would mean implicating themselves.

"Spitting in their eyes and daring them to blink," I said without any particular inflection.

Jason smiled bleakly, tilting his head back and gazing up at the ceaseless storm.

"What can I say?" he murmured. "Defying Tyrants is a Hero's virtue."

The scent of burnt yew assaulted me. It whirled around Jason, marking him, as he'd been marked the night of the funeral. I was beginning to understand now. The Crows were targeting Olympic contenders as the elders angled for influence within the cult, but that wasn't the whole of it.

"Where's your room?" I asked him, and Jason answered without hesitation. Too trusting. I swallowed down the bile in my throat and looked back at him with heavy intent. "Stay there tonight. We'll talk tomorrow—at the agora."

Jason smiled fiercely.

· · ·

Three crows came in the night for the Hero of the Alabaster Isles. Each of them was a lesser existence to the great Hero, but they hadn't been tasked with extraction. Tonight, they were the rusted blades in the dark.

If they shattered, it wouldn't matter. So long as they buried their poison in the Hero's heart first. Death was an acceptable consequence, so long as it claimed all parties. Two of the Crows crept through the cerulean-veined halls of the Hero's quarters, while the third scaled the mountain up to his window.

The hungry ravens fell upon the two in the hall before they could scream, and the third Crow crested the edge of the Hero's terrace only to find him waiting inside, blue eyes burning in the dark.

Jason caught the crow by its throat and dragged it inside.

Chapter Forty-Eight

THE YOUNG GRIFFON

"Ho, so the young aristocrat slipped away from punishment after all," I mused, walking through the streets of Olympia. "Leaving his subordinates to suffer the full consequences. How surprising." The markets were stirring to full wakefulness as the dawn broke, society's undesirables crawling back down their holes.

For our parts, Sol and I had changed back into our daywear after a thorough cleansing at one of the city's many public baths. The streets of Olympia were like home in many ways—at least, home at its heights. Each day in the Half-Step City was a festival by the standards of Álikos, every street overflowing with enterprising merchants, musicians playing sweet songs, and of course, men both young and old hotly debating politics on every corner.

Each street was a new experience, and that alone was worth the trips up and down Kaukoso Mons.

"With all the issues these Tyrants are causing, the least they could do is *their jobs*," Sol muttered darkly, tossing an apple in his hand as he perused a merchant's wares. His nose twitched, and he absently brushed a thumb across it. "Favored by one should mean reviled by seven."

"That would make too much sense." I clicked my tongue, thinking of all the worthless sophists that languished underneath the Storm That Never Ceased, perpetually too fearful of a Tyrant's reprisal to fully test their limits. Abruptly, I wondered how many initiates of the Raging Heaven had actually suffered an elder's wrath and not merely the threat of it.

"Power and its privileges..." Sol took a bite out of his apple, dismissing the merchant and turning down the road. "Alazon was a Hero, I remember that much. Strong enough to confidently challenge three peers and an unknown cultivator with only one other Hero and a handful of Philosophers at his back. Well-connected enough to do it in the middle of a club."

"He was a real asshole," I agreed. Gray eyes flickered my way.

"I was going to say he reminded me of you."

"What a coincidence," I said pleasantly, tilting my head towards an old vagrant bundled in filthy rags, sitting vacantly on a street corner while men stood around him arguing over the next assembly's vote. "I was just about to say the same of him." Sol snorted and took two more bites of his apple before flicking the core at my head.

"At any rate, it's safe to assume he has friends in high places," I continued, deftly avoiding it. "He'll come back to haunt us sooner or later, I'm sure. More importantly, how was the lecture itself? Insightful?"

"The first number, *éna,* is the origin of all things," Sol recited dully, slapping a boy's hand away from an oblivious citizen's coin pouch. The boy scowled in outrage, saw our cult attires, and promptly took off running down a side alley. "The second, *thio,* is the feminine principle. Third, *tria,* masculinity. Fourth—"

"*Tessera.*" I snapped my fingers and the light of dawn rose to the tip of my thumb and caught fire. "Perfect natural symmetry. **Justice.**" Sol hummed in agreement. "The wise philosopher had a larger point to make, surely? Even Romans can count to four."

Sol ticked off three fingers on his hand and then paused, eyebrows furrowing. I chuckled and threw an arm over his shoulder, gesturing with the other into the distance. Beyond the eastern limits of Olympia was a vast expanse of unconquered life, stark mountains and lush valleys that could be seen sprawling into the far horizon.

"There is purpose in all things, young sophist," I said grandly. "From their placement to their posture, their organization, and all their component parts, how they proliferate and how they cease to be. Natural philosophers are those that dedicate their lives to unearthing these purposes and advancing humanity's fundamental under-standing of creation. Surely, a man of that caliber is competent enough to teach multiple lessons with only one lecture—one for the children, one for the students, and one for the scholars."

Sol started to raise his fourth finger, hesitated, and then lowered it again. I grabbed the bent finger and forced it to fully extend. His eyes widened.

"You're not funny," I informed him.

"And neither are you," he said easily, brushing my arm off his shoulder. "It *did* feel like he was building towards a greater point, admittedly. He referenced past lectures a few times as well. It was almost like the entire lecture was an extended tangent."

"I wouldn't doubt it," I said. "Past a certain point of advancement, even the seemingly simple techniques are vast amalgamations of smaller pursuits."

"How so?"

"Consider the man that gave you his virtue," I said. "Picture in your mind's eye the greatest feats that he accomplished with it, and now imagine how you would recreate them." I gave him a moment, just long enough not to lose himself. Then I prompted him, "Now do it."

"I can't," he admitted. He clenched and unclenched his hands, a considering look in his eyes. "But not for the same reasons that you can't copy your father."

I flicked the lingering flame off my thumb and briefly weighed the odds of my successfully pulling down a star from heaven.

Not today. Tomorrow, maybe.

"Humor me, then," I said. "Every Hero and every Tyrant was once a Philosopher. To progress past the Sophic Realm a cultivator must inter-nalize a thousand-thousand truths—the rules of nature that will serve as the framework for their cultivation going forward.

"When a Hero stands against a terrible horror and strikes it down with a sword made of iron, every truth of the world as they know it is behind that swing. It's more than just a flick of the wrist. When a Tyrant decides he has no more use for a mountain and it suddenly ceases to be?" I gestured back the way we'd come, in the direction of Kaukoso Mons and its storm crown, but we both knew I was referring to the Rosy Dawn's initiation rites. "The same principle applies. So tell me, Sol, how does Rome differ?"

I was honestly curious. My understanding of the Roman system of cultivation was even less developed than his understanding of ours. I had only ever heard disparaging speculation from Álikoans and stray comments from Sol himself made during idle conversation. I waited patiently while he considered the scenario, eyes drifting back to the home of the Raging Heaven Cult.

Finally, he said, "A Hero cuts down a great enemy with one strike. But that one strike is the product of a thousand-thousand truths." Storm gray eyes flickered to me seeking confirmation, and I nodded. "So then, if a Hero can swing a blade with the same force as a thousand-thousand men, it's fair to say that each one of those truths represents a single swinging blade. A Tyrant is the same but on a larger scale."

"For the most part," I agreed.

"One Greek arms himself with the rules of nature and uses them to do the work of many. A Hero swings a sword like he's a thousand-thousand men layered over one another in a single skin and smites the monster. A Tyrant presses down on a mountain like he's a million-million men and crushes it to dust."

"And what does the Roman do to strike down the monster?" I asked, intrigued. "How does he topple the mountain that's in his path?"

Sol hummed, remembering, and the riptide currents of his influence whipped out around him, buffeting me and those around us. I let it wash over me, but a pair of women walking our way suddenly stumbled towards him, dropping the bundles of food in their arms. He arrested their fall with the captain's virtue, and we walked on without breaking stride.

Eventually, he smiled wryly.

"The Roman tells five hundred good men to go to work, and the monster falls to the prime cohort's fury."

"And what about the mountain?" I asked, amused.

"What *about* the mountain?"

"How would you topple it?"

He shrugged. "I wouldn't."

I nearly objected. It was a terrible response, and worse than that, it didn't tell me anything about the Roman cultural zeitgeist. I opened my mouth to say that, in admittedly less polite words, and then I paused. Closed it. On the surface, both answers said nothing at all about cultivation. There was strength in numbers, that was common sense. And yes, rather than do something, it was also possible to *not* do it instead.

But he'd specified five hundred men, not a thousand-thousand. And as for the mountain—

I sighed. "You'd go around it."

"I'd go around it."

The literal answer, the tactical answer, and the strategic answer, all wrapped up in one. I supposed that was what I deserved for my comment before. I filed away my new insight into the military mentality of a Roman cultivator for later consideration. And then I spat at his feet.

"You could have just said you're boring," I said sourly. Sol nodded, simple satisfaction in the quirk of his lips.

"And you could have just said you're Greek."

Chapter Forty-Nine

THE SON OF ROME

Griffon and I made our rounds through the streets of Olympia, seeing what there was to see and balancing political intrigue with simple curiosity. The Half-Step City was a sharp contrast to Rome in almost every way. *Especially* when it came to the tongues spoken.

My mentor had taught me the Álikoan dialect well. I hadn't had much use for it in the legions, but my time as a slave had seen my grasp of it perfected. But that was only one language. There were dozens of tongues being spoken in the Half-Step City, at least three at any given time on any given street. It was fascinating and disorienting in equal measure. I had grown used to hearing everything there was to hear years ago, one of many skills that Gaius had hammered into me. That awareness worked against me now, made it hard to think straight.

It would've been hard to focus regardless. What conversation I could understand was conducted at blistering paces, about topics of politics and law that I had no frame of reference for as a foreigner. Children laughed and shrieked, running about naked or in simple gender-less tunics. Figs, grapes, turnips, pears, apples, honeycombs, chickpeas, and myrtle berries abounded. Periodically, Griffon would snatch a handful of something with a pankration hand while the Metic selling it wasn't looking. Occasionally, he even offered me some.

The fruits were all incredibly sweet, decadent beyond belief. In general, that was probably how I would describe this place. With its grand public buildings and massive, riotous agora.

And that was before taking into account Kaukoso Mons, the gemstone-lined mountain that served as a monument to all of man's excesses.

I would give the Greeks one thing. In their virtues and their vices, they held nothing back.

"Well, this is my stop," Griffon suddenly said, alighting on something that deserved his extended attention. I caught him by the arm before he could fully step away. The laurel leaf crown wrapped around his bicep was curiously warm to the touch.

"Not yet," I told him, glancing meaningfully towards the greater mayhem of the agora. We'd been traveling side streets for the most part, just in case. Griffon raised an eyebrow.

"Ho, is that what last night was about?"

"What do you think?"

Griffon smirked and pulled his arm free. "Fine then, give me a moment." That said, he turned and walked confidently into a residential building with no defining characteristics that I could see. It was a squat, almost ugly thing compared to the splendor of the public constructions.

I closed my eyes and focused on breathing while he did whatever it was he was doing. Counting today, it had been four days since I slept. Three days since Griffon and I had met at the eighth wonder of the world and consumed the starlight marrow of a crow.

Sleep was something that a cultivator of sufficient advancement didn't really need, and it was something that a soldier of sufficient rank could rarely afford. I was out of practice, ironically, my days as a slave having been far more restful than my time in the legions, but some things were never truly forgotten. If anything, my advancement... *at the end*, had made it even easier to keep moving with the sun and the moon. The marrow helped as well, in a nebulous, unsettling way that I still hadn't pinned down.

But even so, the mind needed a moment from time to time. I focused on breathing in the steady rhythm of a proper cadence, allowing my plans, my doubts, and my fears to slip away for just a moment as I unwound.

Griffon wasted no time ruining my short peace, leaping out of the second-story terrace of the unassuming home with pankration hands blazing around him.

I inhaled sharply, calling the captain's virtue to my hand as I expanded my senses through the building in search of the threat.

I found it at the same moment that a wooden dining table came hurtling out of the building after Griffon. The former young aristocrat deflected the projectile furniture with his violent intent, sending it spiraling into another building where it exploded into shrapnel upon impact. He landed adroitly behind me, leaning back-to-back with his elbow propped up on my shoulder

"Give me a hand, will you?"

"You have enough," I said flatly. He clicked his tongue, utterly unashamed of himself.

The scarred Heroine, Elissa, slammed open the door on the first floor, murder in her desert-heat eyes. They went first to Griffon, seething annoyance in them that I fully empathized with, before settling on me. The Heroine sighed explosively.

"Solus. This lowly sophist would like to offer your student some guidance."

A pankration hand dug its middle and index fingers into the small of my back, the heat of the Rosy Dawn's flames growing steadily hotter.

"I can think of nothing better for his development," I said and was promptly jabbed by several more burning fingers. "Unfortunately, we have somewhere to be."

Elissa scowled fully, resting a hand on the bronze blade at her hip. She wasn't wearing her usual cult attire, I realized. She wasn't even wearing the finery of a normal citizen of Olympia. She was dressed like a Metic, in drab white cloth with only a sash around her waist that held her sword, a necklace of simple iron thread around her neck. She looked about as unassuming as a cultivator of her standing possibly could.

"So you came into my home, drank *my* wine, for what? Just to ruin my day?"

I glanced back at Griffon. He shrugged.

"I thought you might like to join us"

"Why would I—" Elissa stopped short, looking at me closer. Warily. Her eyes flickered up and down the street and all its people. "Now?"

Griffon smiled pleasantly at her over his shoulder. "Would you rather wait until dinner?"

The Heroine snarled a curse.

We found Jason sitting on the lip of a fountain that was as wide around as the entire bathhouse that Griffon and I had made use of earlier that morning. It wasn't a fountain in the same sense that Rome had fountains. It was not acts of engineering that made this water flow.

The water within the fountain simply fell up. It streamed into the air as if the whole world was upside down, and the sky above was as the ground beneath our feet. Past a certain point, some thirty or forty feet in the air, those streams spiraled out in every direction and suddenly returned to normalcy, falling back into the pool below. It made for a dazzling sight.

And it also obscured everyone on the other side of the fountain from view. The sound of rushing water concealed most small sounds. For all that Jason was lounging with a young woman at his side, exchanging pleasant conversation without a care in the world, he had chosen his spot with care.

He noticed me shortly after I noticed him, his expression lighting up in a more genuine sense. Without looking, he placed a hand on the face of the woman beside him and pushed her back into the fountain. She shrieked as the odd currents of the structure carried her away.

"Solus," he called, raising that same hand and greeting. Then his eyes slipped past me and noticed who I had brought with me and all that excitement fell away.

"*You.*"

"Him?" I asked, glancing back at Griffon.

"Me," he agreed.

"Not him," Jason said, waving impatiently. "Her. What is *she* doing here?"

Elissa stepped past us both, eyes burning with contempt as she looked down on her fellow Hero. "I was invited. What are you doing here, craven?"

Jason didn't react physically, but his pneuma blazed around him, nearly a visible thing. He'd chosen a nice, secluded area of the agora, hiding in plain sight, but I supposed it was inevitable that no Greek could keep quiet for long.

"He's meeting me," I said. Somehow, maddeningly, that was enough for them to break eye contact and subside. Elissa stepped back and crossed her arms.

Jason grimaced. "Did you have to bring her?" I glanced back at Griffon and saw the certainty in the quirk of his lips.

"She's involved." I chose to stand while Griffon sprawled across the stone lip of the fountain and dipped his hand into it, watching with interest the rivulets of water that streamed in odd ways through his fingers. "Would you have preferred Anastasia?"

Jason's grimace deepened.

"Fine," he said at length. "As long as she pulls her weight." Elissa scoffed but made no comment.

"So, we have our merry band of insurrectionists," Griffon mused, visibly relishing in the discomfort those words caused the Heroine. "All we're missing now is a king to kill. Which one first, you think?"

"Are you out of your mind?" Jason snarled.

"Likely," he said easily

"Acting is one thing," Elissa said, just as tense as her fellow Hero but less shocked by Griffon's words. "But there's audacity, and then there's stupidity. I know you know the difference."

Griffon inclined his head, raising a cupped palm of water out of the fountain and overturning it. The water fell up through his fingers and around the sides of his palm. He smiled as he considered it.

"There are several deaths a cultivator can suffer," he said, twisting his fingers around the rising strands of water. "A Tyrant especially. The body may die, yes, and so may the soul. But the death of a man's ego is no less severe, nor the death of his curiosity, his spirit, his hunger."

"His influence," I finished, and Griffon's smile turned to a vicious smirk.

Elissa frowned. "How could you possibly undermine... one of them? They've had decades, centuries to establish their domains. Each and everyone has a city's full backing."

"The crows," Jason said, with quiet anticipation. "That's it, isn't it?"

I considered the question. What he was suggesting, what Griffon had led him into thinking was my plan, was a line that could not be uncrossed. Spitting in a Tyrant's face like that, undermining their reach no matter how indirectly, that was the sort of thing that we had crucified men for in Gaius' legions. It was a mad, unnecessary thing

And yet. I took a breath, as I had taken a breath before while Griffon antagonized Elissa, as I had taken many breaths since consuming that starlight marrow, and I traced my pneuma as it flowed through entirely new paths in my body. I felt stronger today than I had ever before in my life. I had felt the same way yesterday, and the day before. Each night since that assault in the Father's temple, Griffon and I had hunted crows and sucked the marrow from their bones. And each time, it had made us stronger than before.

I still hadn't found a trace of my mentor, or anyone that could speak of him with any knowledge or authority. Anastasia, if she had found anything, had yet to seek me out and tell me. The Greek ways of cultivation were as opaque as ever, the Roman ways closed off to me.

As things stood...

"It is," I answered Jason's breathless question. I would continue to live this lie, the same lie that I had forced to be true the night of the kyrios' funeral. "The Raging Heaven is in no rush to answer the question of succession, that much seems clear. In the meantime, the mystikos are suffering. Children are being coaxed into opposing factions. Men and women huddle together in the light of day, too afraid of the dark to leave their rooms at night."

"Sol isn't a fan of politics," Griffon confided to the two Heroic cultivators. I sighed and forced my fists to unclench.

"Men worry more about what they can't see than what they can," I said tiredly. "If they want to posture, fine. But I have no patience for scavengers."

Jason and Elissa both considered me silently. The dull roar of the fountain and general tumult of thousands of people streaming through the agora was all that could be heard for a long minute.

"Who are you, really?" Elissa asked, finally. "Who are you that you think this is something you have to do?"

"That night, at the club," Jason said, nearly inaudible beneath the surrounding noise. He tilted his head at Griffon beside him. "He said you came here from the west for a bit of culture. Where are you from, Solus?"

And why are you here, he didn't ask. But I heard it, nonetheless.

I considered them both, and Griffon besides. There was a part of me, a large part, that wanted to take it all back, to cut my losses and make good on what I had said on the *Eos*. Leave Griffon to his mad adventures and find my mentor, gather what strength I could, and return to the ashes of Rome. Take down as many of those godforsaken dogs as I could before my body succumbed.

There was another part of me—smaller, but far more insistent—that said some things just weren't worth tolerating. No matter whose country this was. No matter how long I had been here.

For all the lives the legions of the Republic had taken, for all the atrocities her soldiers had committed, that part of me still believed in the core conceit of the Republic. Where all sons of Rome went, they spread the light of righteous civilization. The ideal of the soldier within me had long lost its patience for traitors and backstabbers.

The Raging Heaven Cult wasn't my place. But I had doomed myself to it by extending a hand to Scythas. By saving Jason. By sharing a bath with Anastasia. By drinking with all of them, playing dice, and trading discourse. I couldn't think of them as faceless Greeks anymore. And if I had to acknowledge them, I had to acknowledge the rest. The children that Jason was doing his best to save in the small moments. The innocents in the cult, suffering the consequences of their elders' greed.

I knew all too well what happened when Tyrants clashed.

"I've lived this conflict before," I said, resigning myself to what inevitably came next. Griffon hummed in satisfaction. "When men like these cross swords, there's only one way it can end. Succession through a proxy victory in the Olympic Games is a fantasy. Men like these are who they are because when they want something, *they take it.*"

Jason and Elissa shared a look, without malice for one another. With mutual unease.

"You've lived it," Jason repeated. "Where? With whom?"

"I don't know anything about either of you. Not really," Elissa said, but her suspicion was tempered by a careful consideration as she spoke to me. "And you don't know me."

"Or me," Jason said reluctantly.

"A fair concern," Griffon allowed, propping his head up on one hand. His scarlet eyes glittered. "What do you want to know?"

Chapter Fifty

THE YOUNG GRIFFON

As a child grew old in body and soul, walking that crucial transitory bridge between adolescence and adulthood, the first iteration of their identity finally cemented itself. In those formative years, a human being laid the foundation for who they would be in their highest highs and lowest lows. Just as the bridges between realms were the most crucial for a cultivator's development, so too were those formative years critical for the mundane growth that every human being experienced.

Body and soul. The body's growth was self-evident. Bone and muscle grew into their adult frames, cherubic faces turned lean and angular. Human beings were made in the image of the divine. It simply took time for our worthless clay selves to take the proper shape.

The soul's growth was less easily observed. In my formative years, the development of my body had seen to itself. I'd chiseled it from marble a little more each day, testing myself against all that would stand and fight me. Progress could be measured in practical terms. It could be seen in the definition of my body. But my soul's development was not so straightforward.

Reason, spirit, and hunger. It was no easy thing for a lion to grow old in a cage. Perhaps a wild childhood wouldn't have been any better for me, but I doubted it. Growing up within the sterile halls of the Rosy Dawn estates, I had no choice but to refine my burgeoning soul through abstraction. Adventures half-lived through others. Tribulations that I could not undergo myself, lessons that I had not personally suffered in order to learn.

It wasn't ideal, but I made do with what I was given—as I always had. Just as I chiseled my body from marble, so too did I forge my soul from purest gold. I created myself in the image of those who came before me. I devoured stories of Heroes and Tyrants, drew from them the principles of a virtuous life, and with each and every one, the flames of my spirit were fanned higher.

I understood the anatomy of an epic better than most. A story worth telling. For each and every one, the beginning was always the same. Even the Muses needed someone to sing of—before the vile monsters, before the triumphs and the tragedies, you had to prepare your audience for what was to come.

You had to set the stage.

"You say you're from the Rosy Dawn," Elissa said, not hesitating to question me. She stepped closer, shoulder to shoulder with Sol, lowering her voice so that no one else in the agora could overhear. "The Raging Heaven Cult hasn't seen a fresh face from across the Ionian in nearly two decades. I checked. What's changed?"

I raised an eyebrow. "Aside from the obvious?"

The Heroine took that about how I expected her to. Beside me on the lip of the odd fountain of rising water, Jason cursed under his breath.

The death of the kyrios still hung, like a funeral shroud, over every interaction within the Half-Step City. Reconstruction efforts could be seen on every residential street, the Tyrant's last gasp putting countless families out of their homes. There was a profound grief, a bleak pessimism, that permeated every interaction if you looked close enough. It was only natural that our Heroic friends would think first of his passing upon hearing such a suggestive question.

After all, what were the odds that Sol and I had just *happened* to set sail for Olympia on the day of the kyrios' passing? Long odds indeed.

"You said that Sol was fighting demons on the western front,"

Jason said, choosing to set aside that particular suspicion for the moment. The Hero that Sol had snatched back from the shadows looked searchingly at him. "How far west? And what sort of demons?"

Sol stared at him in silence. That storm flashed in his eyes, his influence lashing out in every direction. It was an unconscious reaction, I knew, but they didn't. Both Heroic cultivators visibly tensed. Jason set his jaw and leaned forward.

"If you want me to follow you, I have to know where we're going. And I *deserve* to know who's leading me there. Who are you, Solus?"

For a long moment, even I wasn't sure what he'd say. I wouldn't lie for any existence on this earth, not even him, but I wouldn't force him to tell the truth either.

Thankfully, he chose to do so himself. My brother, for all his traumas, was no coward

"There are demons in the city of Carthage. Wolves in the shape of men. They walk on two legs and fight with arms and armor, and they can cultivate. A year and a half ago, they consumed the city of Rome. In another year and a half, they'll have consumed everything west of the Scarlet City."

Elissa was immediately skeptical. Jason, on the other hand—I saw the sudden fear in his eyes, and the rage, before he overcame both and hid them from view. Ho?

"Monsters of that caliber, in those numbers, and the Scarlet City didn't see fit to warn her sister cities?" Elissa asked.

"When's the last time the colonies told us anything?" Jason responded. Elissa inclined her head grudgingly. He continued, almost hopefully, "But if this wasn't enough for Damon Aetos to break his silence, then he must not consider it a threat to those of us east of the Ionian. Toppling a few barbarian nations is one thing. But a free city-state built by the children of Helen? A monster's primitive approximation of cultivation simply can't compare. They're only *wolves*."

Sol's influence rippled.

"You've made two assumptions, just now," I informed the Hero before my brother snapped. I glanced Elissa's way. "Both of you."

Jason frowned. "Enlighten me."

Gladly. "You asked why the Scarlet City hasn't sent word of the coming threat," I said first, savoring their realization. I gestured lazily. "And yet here we are."

"And the second?" Elissa pressed.

"You assumed that when I said the demons of Carthage could cultivate, I was exaggerating. You decided that I was referring to the unrefined strength of monsters and animals," Sol said coldly. "I wasn't."

Silence.

"Something like that," Elissa finally whispered. She was unable to vocalize the rest.

"If that's the case," Jason picked up for her in a strangled tone, "why are you telling us here like this? Why not... someone..."

I chuckled. "In power?"

Elissa's knuckles were white around the hilt of her blade. "Enough games. What are you here for?"

What could I do but tell them the truth?

"A good time."

My virtuous heart would accept nothing less.

"You really are mad," Jason said wonderingly.

My eyes rolled. Always the same. "Of course I am. What sane man looks upon all that the gods have given us, all the bounties of nature and its earthly pleasures, and decides that they are not enough? What is a cultivator if not a madman? Where I come from, we don't make any excuses for our behavior."

I tilted my head to face Sol's little reaver, so small in spirit despite the grandeur of his soul. How was it that a Hero, the subject of an epic all his own, could be so pathetic in the face of overwhelming danger?

"Until death or divinity," I said. "While those who came before us plummet to the earth on melting wax wings, we are all flying perilously into the sun. What could possibly be more insane than that?"

I'd felt the same instinctive revulsion when I saw Alazon turn tail and run from Sol in that club, only moments after he'd so confidently staked his claim on the place and all those within it. Another Hero. Another shining soul acknowledged by both the Muses and the Fates. Another *coward*. How dare he lay claim to the same heights as

Nikolas and the greats? How *dare* these Heroic cultivators cringe away from the wrath of Tyrants, when liberation was their central creed?

How dare they act weak when they were strong?

"The two of you aren't who you are by mistake," Sol said. They latched onto his quiet intent like a lifeline, making the unfortunate assumption that he was the saner of the two of us. "You each have something that drives you forward in the face of adversity. Something that even tribulation, heaven's lightning wrath, could not take from you. A Tyrant's retribution is nothing compared to that. Is that not so?"

Both Hero and Heroine nodded.

"For us, this is one of those things. The free Mediterranean is meant to be a paragon of enlightened virtue. The city of Olympia is meant to be the jewel in that crown. *And yet*, I've walked the steps of your mountain cult, chased the shadows down your halls, and seen such acts of wicked vice that it would make your kyrios weep if he was still alive to see them."

"After twenty years, the rosy fingers of dawn have stretched themselves across the Ionian Sea once more, and what is the first thing they've found?" I asked quietly, adding my weight to Sol's subtle rhetoric. "**Injustice.**"

"There are certain injustices in this life that a Hero won't ever stand for, is that not so?" Sol asked. Slowly, reluctantly, both nodded again. Sol considered them both for a long moment. Then, almost gently, he said, "This is one of them."

Jason shook his head. "This sort of thing... I know what I said before. And I *do* want to help. What you're trying to do... it's *righteous*. It's heroic!"

Elissa sighed and finished his thought. "But most tragedies are at the start."

The mask of my tribulation burned on my hip, opposite my uncle's sword.

"What about you two?" I asked.

"Us?"

"There is no us," Elissa said shortly.

I waved an impatient hand. "Yes, yes, I get it, you aren't friends. I'm asking what it is that makes the two of you tick. Where is your line in the sand? What are *you* here for?"

The two Heroic cultivators shared a look. The Heroine with her scars answered for both of them again.

"We're here to compete."

"We haven't lied to you," Sol said. The message was clear. *Don't lie to us.*

"It's true," Jason insisted. "We're here for the Olympic Games. All of us are here looking for glory."

"Just because something is not a lie doesn't make it fully true," I said, ignoring the look that Sol shot at me. "Allow me to refine the question, then. Why are you here to compete? What is it you hope to find in a laurel leaf crown?"

"What are you running from?" Sol asked.

Enlightened thinkers placed such emphasis on cultivation, on the quantification of the soul, that we often forgot even the greatest among us were made of the same flesh and blood as the least. They had the same minds, the same hearts and desires. A Hero could be swayed as easily as a Citizen, as easily as a mortal, even, under the proper conditions.

Sol and I struck out with our rhetoric in the most mundane sense, both of us from different angles, and in that moment, two Heroic cultivators faltered. I knew it as soon as I saw the first stone fall within them. Sol saw it too, I was sure. We had them.

We were all here for our own reasons, true enough. But there was a thread that connected us all, and Sol and I had pulled it taut around their throats.

"... Say that you succeed in this," Elissa finally said. "And say that we help you declaw the cats' paws. What have we accomplished, then, aside from angering greater powers?"

"Take away their shadows and they'll have nothing left but the light," I answered simply. "They want to fight for the title of kyrios? So be it. Let them fight like men, without proxies, and to the strongest goes the crown."

"The strongest fighter," Jason realized. "The strongest leader of men. Not necessarily the strongest politician."

"In times of peace, a good politician is a great thing," I agreed.

"But in times of war..." Elissa half-recited, frustration clear in her bearing. Remembering some past lesson and hating the fact that it rang true. "What then? You'll force the issue? How will you ensure that the... proper candidate..."

Jason and Elissa both looked at Sol.

What could we, two mysterious cultivators with no established spheres of influence, have to gain from orchestrating such a conflict? In a conflict between Tyrants, it was self-evident that only a Tyrant could possibly emerge victorious. So what were we playing at? The audacious young competitor and his master of unspecified power?

In that moment, they teetered on the edge of an utterly outrageous assumption. Unwilling to believe it, but unable to fully dismiss it either.

I smiled secretively, leaning in. "The privileges of an Olympic Champion are surely grand, I won't deny it. But it's not often the kyrios of the Raging Heaven Cult owes you a favor." In the end, even Heroic cultivators were still just that. Cultivators.

And cultivators, at their core, were entirely selfish existences.

Sol and I reached out and pulled them up onto the stage.

Chapter Fifty-One

THE SON OF ROME

We parted ways after the immediate plans had been made for sundown, Griffon and Elissa heading back to the ruined residential streets while Jason and I made for the Raging Heaven.

For the most part, Jason was quiet. Every so often he would ask me a question that I had no desire to answer, and so I wouldn't. Questions about the demons of Carthage, about the campaigns against them, and about my role in those campaigns. I had offered both of them as much of the truth as I could stand to tell. Eventually, he took my silence for what it was and subsided into solitary contemplation.

We passed through the gates of the Raging Heaven Cult unchallenged. Jason exchanged pleasantries with the men on guard, armored by bronze plates that clung to them like second skins, chiseled musculature carved into the metal itself. Their eyes followed me curiously, but they made no comment.

We were climbing the stone-carved steps up to the secondary levels where the respected initiates and future competitors kept quarters when Jason finally asked the question he'd wanted to ask the whole time.

"These demons... They took something from you, didn't they? Personally."

I closed my eyes and quietly sighed.

"Would it matter if they did?"

"Of course it would!" he said, affronted.

"Why?"

"Why? *Why?* Because there's a difference between doing what's right for its own sake, and doing the right thing only if your heart demands it. What you're planning here and now, would you do it even if your own feelings weren't involved? Is it the right thing to do, or is it the right thing for *you* to do?"

Was I doing the right thing for the right reasons? Was my anger focused on the right thing, at the right time, to the right degree? I didn't know. But Jason's life could depend on the answer.

"They took my city," I finally said. "They took my wife."

I'd revealed a portion of myself to Anastasia. How could I not do the same here?

Jason exhaled explosively. Overhead, the Storm That Never Ceased howled.

"I came here to compete in the Games, I wasn't lying about that," he said. I nodded, accepting that. "But the glory is secondary. The political influence, the money, it's all nice. But that's not why I'm here. That's not why I have to win."

I stopped, realizing that he'd fallen back three steps ago. He leaned against the stone face of the mountain, gazing up at the storm. I knew that look in his eyes.

"Have to?" I echoed. He nodded.

"I come from the coast, Solus. I'm a sailor by breed. It's what drives me, what's always driven me since I was a boy who couldn't even tie a proper knot. It's how I rose through the ranks of cultivation so quickly. I was born for the sea."

"So why—"

"Why am I here? Up on this mountain, closer to heaven than high tide?" he asked bitterly. From the folds of his pale yellow and blue tunic he pulled a length of rope and began tying it into knots.

Rome was never a maritime nation, and I'd never bothered to learn more than the bare basics of the naval arts. Watching Jason's fingers nimbly fasten a dozen different knots in the span of a minute, each more complex than the last, I was struck by the absentmindedness of the motions. I fastened my armor the same way. With the surety of a thousand past experiences. Thoughtlessly.

His hands were shaking.

"When I turned twenty, I was a captain of the Sophic Realm, captain of my own ship, and I decided to sail farther south than I had ever ventured before. Against the warnings of my father. Against the heartfelt wishes of my mother. I was young, I was strong, and I was on the precipice of the realm of legend and myth. Every day, the wanderlust called out to me louder than before. And why not indulge it? I was invincible on the open sea, with my sworn brothers and sisters beside me."

I reached out and gently took the rope out of his hands. It was a ruined ball of knots and strangled threads. Jason pressed shaking hands to his forehead, his eyes distant. Ocean blue flames flickered.

"Monsters in the shape of men," he said, with as much reluctance as I had. "*Demonic cultivators.* We never found that far-flung shore. But something found us.

"Maybe Griffon is right. A few years ago, I would have been the first to agree with him. All the world's greatest heroes are and have always been audacious souls. That much is undeniable." His jaw clenched. "But that doesn't mean that every audacious man becomes a great hero.

"I was audacious once," he said, a quiet admission, and an even quieter entreaty to me. "That's why I'm here. Those waves doused me. I seek the Olympic flame because it's the only thing I know won't ever stop burning, won't ever go out... and I'd rather die than sail again."

"So die."

Blazing blue eyes snapped up to meet mine, too shocked to be offended. So, this was what it was like from the outside looking in. How pitiful.

"They took your crew from you," I said. Declared it because I could already tell. "They took your closest friends, and they should have taken you. But they didn't. And you ascended, even so."

Jason stared at me.

"The heavens are never fair," I said furiously, reciting the words of my first mentor. "Justice is the responsibility of mortal men. What happened to your crew, was that justice? Did they deserve what was done to them?"

The rage that came over his face at the mere suggestion was answer enough.

"Do they deserve justice?" I pressed. I watched that fury turn inward, upon himself. That familiar loathing. How *fucking pitiful.* "Do they deserve to rot at the bottom of the heartless sea, forgotten and unavenged?"

"*No.*"

"No to what? Justice or oblivion?"

Jason slammed a clenched fist against the mountain behind him, and the amethyst veins of jewels running through its stone face flashed bright as the sun for a moment before fading to their usual luster.

"No! They don't deserve what I lead them into! They don't deserve what happened to them, what should have happened to *me.* The captain is supposed to go down with his ship!"

A captain leads from the front, I spoke to him in the voice of my soul, and his eyes flew wide open.

"You—"

"We are who we are," I told him, my own resolve hardening with every word. Some things were just too painful to accept unless they were staring you in the face, and some of those things didn't show up in a mirror's reflection. They could only be seen in others. "What we want is inconsequential. What we fear is even less so. Until we've burnt our enemies to ashes and salted what remains, how can we do anything but keep moving forward?"

"You..." he said again, "you're not like Griffon at all, are you?"

I smiled mirthlessly. "Griffon pursues the heights because they're what he's always desired. I pursue them because there's no other way."

Jason... snorted. He shook his head, and he chuckled. It was a bleak, hopeless sound, but his hand no longer shook as it covered his face. "Of course you do. *Of course you do.* Heroes chase their passions until they have nothing left. But men like you..."

The Hero of the Coast straightened and clapped his hands together, the sound booming. His expression turned fierce. "Fine then! I understand! For as long as you'll have me, until I meet my story's end, I'll stand with you against the night. This lowly sophist offers his greetings to the master."

I stared at the legendary Hero and former pirate captain.

"I don't know what you did last night, but I know those old men wouldn't have sent just one Crow after me, especially one that weak," he explained, inclining his head respectfully. "Including the night of the funeral, I owe you my life twice over. And now I owe you my heart, too, for showing me that I'm not alone. That even men like you can suffer the consequences of hubris. So I'll repay you however I can. Until the scales are balanced and for as long as you need me, I'll stand faithfully by your side."

The soft applause of a solitary spectator saved me from having to respond to that. I looked back down the mountain path and saw a familiar face, inviting dark features and burning green eyes. Anastasia smiled deviously as she ascended the steps behind us, clapping all the while.

"A moment like that belongs on a stage," she said when she'd drawn close enough to tease, with laughter in her eyes. "I wonder, will Griffon be jealous? He doesn't strike me as the sharing type."

"Good morning, Anastasia." I sighed. "Jason—"

When I turned back, I saw him sprinting up the steps, already halfway up the mountain. Faithfully by my side, eh?

"I have that effect at times," Anastasia admitted without regret.

I rolled my eyes and gestured for her to walk with me. "Do you have anything for me?" I asked quietly, beneath the cover of thunder.

"I think I might," she hedged, procuring her javelin and twirling it as she walked. "But in exchange, I want the truth."

I glanced at her and her whirling javelin, silent. Her eyes danced.

"You've been hunting, haven't you, Solus?"

"I have."

"And you haven't invited me once," she said with utter despair. "After all we've been through, and all that I've done for you since that tender bath we shared—"

My influence flicked against hers, and she abruptly giggled.

"This isn't a game," I said as if I was her elder in anything at all.

"Of course not." Her smile grew. "But I still want to play."

As crows flew freely through the Raging Heaven Cult, searching for the hungry ravens that had been devouring their fellows, four Heroic cultivators were stolen from beneath their sheets. They each resisted, but only for a moment.

All of them had known what to expect, and even so, they were unnerved.

"You said you were *hunting* the crows," Elissa said, voice hushed and accusing as she knelt beside her peers in the light of the moon. She watched mistrustfully as the raven on the right paced around them, unfastening coils of iron thread from their wrists and pulling dark hoods from their heads.

"*We are,*" spoke the raven on the left. Distant and unsettling.

"Could have fooled me," Kyno murmured while he rubbed at his wrists. Scarlet Son and Sword Song had convinced him to come, in the end, but he already looked well on his way to regretting it. "If it looks like a crow, and it talks like a crow—"

"*It's a raven.*"

"It's not a bad look on you," Anastasia mused, tilting her head as she regarded both of them. Smoldering green eyes trailed along the crimson lines of the bare-chested raven's tattoos, and the eerily undulating cloak of his partner. "Not at all in line with a proper crow's uniform. I like it."

"So you've put us through the song and dance," Jason muttered, edging away from Anastasia once his hood was pulled free. "What's next? Going to put us through the rites?"

"*Something like that.*"

That said, each of the hungry ravens reached into their shadows. Four Heroic cultivators watched, wide-eyed, as their arms plunged into the ether and pulled from it tunics and hoods of midnight cloth and weapons of burnished bronze.

"I didn't know crows could do that," Jason whispered.

Kyno frowned. "They can't."

The Heroines each reached for a weapon presented by murky

pankration hands, and the Heroes hurriedly followed suit. Four Heroic cultivators and two hungry ravens gathered beneath the light of the rising moon. In the distance, an eagle cried.

"After you," the caustic crow invited.

The hunt began.

Chapter Fifty-Two

SCYTHAS, HERO OF THE SCYTHING SQUALL

Slayer of monsters. Champion of humanity.

Scythas hadn't been either of those things in a very long time. These days, he hardly remembered what it felt like to be that man.

The Tyrant Aleuas, as a venerated elder of the Raging Heaven Cult, enjoyed the privileges of his own estate at the foot of Kaukoso Mons. A winding series of cobblestone buildings with sloping clay-shingled roofs that flared out at the edges, with several courtyards and natural pools carved out of the mountain where its indigo gem lines were thickest, it spanned over a mile. Citizens and slaves alike that had come to Olympia from the City of Squalls abounded in this estate, serving the elder in Olympia as faithfully as they would the kyrios of the Howling Wind Cult himself.

It was impossible to mistake the place for anyone else's domain. As Scythas stepped over its boundaries, he felt the weight of the Tyrant's influence settle on his shoulder like a heavy hand. It pushed, urging him down a singular path. Servants and citizens nodded deferentially and offered their greetings as he passed. Scythas tried to smile in reply. He failed.

At a certain point he was challenged, as all who encroached on Aleuas' personal quarters were challenged. Two of the elder's own men, both deep within the Sophic Realm, held out their hands to stop him. They wore the arms and armor of the Howling Wind with pride.

The Tyrant's influence swept them aside before they could speak, and Scythas stalked into the elder's home.

On his way to the central, beating heart of the estate, he was spotted by a young woman that looked like she'd just stumbled out of a hurricane, her hair a mess of windswept curls and her fine silk dress riddled with tears and damp spots. Her eyes were the color of harvest wheat, a hazel so bright it was nearly gold, and freckles swept across the bridge of her nose like a summer breeze.

Surrounded by fussing women both younger and older than her, she nonetheless picked him out as he passed by the adjacent hall. Holding a hand palm up, she softly blew something invisible his way, her eyes holding his.

"Good morning, brave Hero," he heard her say, clear as day from across the hall. As if she had whispered it directly into his ear. Gooseflesh erupted up and down his arms.

"Good morning, Princess," he murmured back in the same way, sans theatrics. She smiled warmly before her minders pulled her around the corner and out of sight.

Brave Hero. Scythas swallowed back bile, pressing forward to his destination.

The Tyrant's estate was a reflection of the Howling Wind Cult that he had once ruled over as kyrios, and his personal chambers were a reflection just the same. The former lord's personal eccentricities, from what he had been told, had not changed much in the centuries since his displacement from the City of Squalls to Olympia.

Windchimes hung from the ceilings, the banisters, and the furniture all throughout the room, each swaying in a breeze with no readily felt source. Chimes of hollow wood that whistled, chimes of gold that resonated as they struck one another, and even chimes of the Raging Heaven's own tribulation amethyst that flashed and hummed as the breeze shook them. The cumulative effect was a low, rolling song that urged all that heard it to be at ease.

Scythas set his shoulders and stepped fully into the room, following a narrow path through the swinging chimes and falling to one knee in front of an ornate curtain of viridian silk. The curtain spanned from wall-to-wall, floor-to-ceiling, effectively cutting the room in half.

"Scythas," spoke the Hurricane Hierophant of the Howling Wind Cult. The curtain of sheer viridian rippled in the breeze. "Thank you for coming."

Scythas stared straight ahead, consciously choosing not to track the shadows that shifted behind the curtain.

"Sir." He nodded once. "You called for me?"

"I did, I did," he said, and the curtain bulged and shifted from side to side as if a hand was waving dismissively through it. Despite the fact that the shadowed silhouette of a man was ten feet to the right. "Tell me, how goes your training?"

A loaded question, to be sure. When was the last time he'd felt at ease in his own body? "Well enough," Scythas said.

"Is that so," Elder Aleuas murmured. Where the wind ended and the Tyrant's influence began was almost impossible to discern. So when the breeze threaded through Scythas' hair, tickling the back of his neck, he shivered as if it was the Tyrant's own hands stroking his head. "Then humor this old man, would you? Let's hear a whistle."

In that moment, as every visit to the windchime chamber had a *moment*, Scythas knew that he was about to die. As surely as he knew that the sea breeze blew cold, Scythas felt his death writ large on the world, alongside all the other rules of nature.

And so he stoked his heart's flame and defied them.

Urania, he invoked, a silent plea. He inhaled in ragged relief when he felt her arms settle around his shoulders, felt the cool touch of her cheek press against his as she faced the Tyrant by his side.

As always I am with you, Hero, she whispered fondly. *And as always, you ask of me something my sisters would be better suited giving you.* Her crown of stars brushed against his temple as they revolved around her head, warm and inspiring.

She was the Heavenly Muse, the charter of stars and higher mathematics. Indeed, nearly every one of her sisters would have been better suited to this task, Calliope best of all—but Urania was what he had.

And so, as always, he would be grateful for what he'd been given. And he would make do.

Scythas let slip his held breath, the vital essence of his body, and his pneuma went with it. A clear, piercing whistle split the cascading song of windchime. At once, a vortex of howling wind enveloped him head to toe. It took only a moment. And it was nearly too slow.

Less than a heartbeat after Scythas sealed himself in his howling vortex, the Hierophant dropped a hurricane on his head.

Steady, Urania urged him, and Scythas' eyes narrowed as he shifted the pitch of his whistle. His own gale winds were nothing compared to the Tyrant's, and natural law dictated that they would be broken and swept away immediately by the stronger currents, but Scythas let his heart's flame rage and defied that simple truth.

His pneuma persisted, and it struck out against the viridian curtain as Urania reached out and traced a path through the stars.

Constellations that only he could see burned in the open air, each star a turning point in the Tyrant's currents, each shining line a shift in pitch that he would have to adjust to. The Heavenly Muse could not teach him how to carry a tune—Scythas had learned that long ago.

But she could chart the notes and guide him through the stars.

Scythas whistled against the hundred chimes and their hurricane winds, and just as they had all but beaten down his cloak of currents, had all but extinguished his Heroic flames, the Tyrant's song faltered. Urania pressed her free hand against his other cheek, eyes wide and intent as she bid him to follow her path.

He did, as he always had, and for a bare moment, the song changed and Scythas took the hurricane in his hand. The viridian curtain whipped and flared, buffeted such that the other half of the room behind it was revealed for a fraction of a moment, the lounging form of a man too tall to be mortal, too perfectly sculpted.

The Hurricane Hierophant held out a hand just before the rising curtain revealed his face, and Scythas swallowed his whistle. The song ceased, every wind chime in the room fell still, and the curtain settled between them once more. Urania turned and pressed a kiss against Scythas' temple before departing to wherever it was muses went, and silence fell in the elder's chambers.

A single note of a tingling chime broke the frozen moment, emerald bells swaying behind the curtain. Aleuas chuckled, and Scythas felt it in his bones.

"Well done, boy. You've improved," his mentor congratulated him. Scythas nodded mutely. "Only one note, to be sure, but a profound one. Have you been studying like I told you?"

He had not. Of course, he had *tried*, but in the days since they'd last met, when Scythas had been presenting him with a creature rooted out of the shadows, he hadn't been able to focus even for a moment on the lessons that the Tyrant wanted him to learn. His mind had been elsewhere. In the stars, mostly.

"Yes, sir," he said, simply. Because the truth would be his end.

"Good, good," Aleuas said, and then, slyly, "though I'm sure your fortuitous encounter deserves a portion of the credit too, hmm?"

Scythas grit his teeth against the pressure. "As you say, sir."

"So it is," he mused. Then, as if he had just remembered, he said, "You know, that Solus has yet to grace my humble estate with his presence. You passed my invitation along, didn't you?"

"Yes, sir."

"You said he came from the Rosy Dawn. Fighting, what was it?"

"Demons."

"Demons, yes. On the western front." The distant howl of his wrath betrayed the mild words, made the floor shake and the walls groan. "I spoke to old 'Zalus after you left, the last time, to convey my thanks to him for keeping you safe. But it was the oddest thing. He said this Solus and his Young Griffon weren't any men of his. And more than that, he denied any knowledge of any demons in the west."

"And now," he continued, his voice utterly calm in the way that preceded the storm, "my influence is under siege. I am not the only one suffering, to be sure, but an unkindness equally shared is an unkindness, nonetheless. What do you make of these creatures that haunt my shadows, Scythas?"

It was utterly mad to spite a Tyrant in his own domain, no matter what your standing among heaven and earth was. But there were some things that a man just couldn't tolerate. For Scythas, the scavengers that stalked the Raging Heaven were one of those things.

"It seems to me, sir, that they're simply doing what Crows do. Scavenging and harassing. Making the world a darker place."

The shadows behind the viridian curtain went still. Scythas wondered if he was about to die.

"Cannibalism," Aleuas finally said, his voice weary and furious in equal measures. "You've made it clear what you think of how we old men conduct ourselves. Now step outside of that and tell me: what sort of crow eats its own kind? Hunts them and no other?"

There was only one answer. "No crow at all."

"Ravens," he concluded, murder in his mouth. "Outsiders in our ranks. Two of them, just days after your fortuitous encounter. Would you call that a coincidence, Scythas?"

"I might."

"You might," he repeated. The pressure doubled and re-doubled. Scythas burned his heart's blood and forced his head not to bow. He pursed his lips. Prepared a whistle.

Aleuas sighed and released him from his grip. "Whoever they are, find them. Bring them to me, dead or alive by any means necessary."

"Sir…"

"**Enough.**"

Scythas' teeth clicked together.

"You dislike these things that we do in the dark. Fine. I dislike them even more. But you have to understand the way of the world, boy. You have to *understand* how precarious our position is. All of our positions.

"We are all frozen in place. Each of us holds a knife in our teeth while the other seven press down upon it, and these gluttonous ravens have taken that opportunity to *gouge my eyes out.*"

Good, Scythas didn't say. Once upon a time, when he was still a slayer of monsters and a champion of humanity, he would have shouted it.

"I understand, sir."

"I knew you would. Be safe, boy, and be swift." Scythas accepted the dismissal for what it was, standing and inclining his head before turning and walking back the way he'd come. As he passed through the outermost halls of the estate, Aleuas' voice drifted to him on the wind.

"And before you go, give my daughter a proper greeting, will you? She misses her fiancé."

Slayer of monsters. Champion of humanity. Scythas hadn't been that man in a very long time.

Perhaps he never had.

Chapter Fifty-Three

AN UNKINDNESS

"Violence is an art."

Kyno, the Heroic Huntsman, clad in his midnight black rags, twitched and looked over his shoulder. As he did, he palmed another man's head as easily as one would an apple. The hunting crow regarded the hungry raven on the right, lounging above, in a dip between two conjoined archways.

The raven reached up, twisting his hand as if to grasp the moon the same way the hunting crow had grasped his unfortunate prey—as if to pluck it from the sky like an apple from a branch. The markings on the raven's bare torso glowed blood red. A muted, seething source of light.

*"As much as sculpture, as much as any poem or song, violence is an expression of inspiration. Violence is the **oldest** art, in fact. The first of them all. Back when the pyramids did not exist and men had fewer thoughts in their heads than fingers on their hands, violence was our first and most profound expression."*

"What?" the hunting crow's prey asked, bewildered, before being slammed face-first into the dirt.

"What?" the hunting crow asked, his voice like tumbling stones. Even beneath the cover of darkness his annoyance was clear.

The hungry raven chuckled and rolled off his leisurely perch, falling—

Another figure of rust and shadows speared through the darkness of the archways, utterly silent and blisteringly quick. The hunting crow tensed and released his prey, raising both hands to catch the assassin's lunging stab.

The raven fell upon the new arrival with unlikely force, crushing them flat to the ground and raising his knee up before bringing it back down three times in a vicious sequence. Between each crack of the knee, the shadowed assailant twisted and thrashed like a landed fish, and each time the raven expertly countered their attempts to grapple. On the fourth and final knee, the would-be assassin arched up and let loose a breathy scream as their spine audibly snapped. They slumped, going limp.

"It's easy enough to forget our grim origins," the raven continued, hoisting the crow up and pulling the hood from their head. A young man with pale, rugged features was revealed. He was still alive, his eyes rolling helplessly in their sockets. *"While we're lounging in our cleansing baths, wearing our silks and ornaments, exchanging our thoughtful discourse. These kind luxuries drive us further from our roots and closer to civilized existence.*

"But," the raven whispered, the sound like shifting sands. He leaned in, his veiled face inches from the paralyzed assassin.

"Even so." The young man's eyes, the only part of himself that he could still control, quivered as they stared into the shroud.

"All that we are, and all that the unwashed barbarians of this world are not, was built upon a foundation of inspired violence. We are free to be more, because our brutal ancestors murdered all those that would have made us **less.***"*

"What's your point?" the hunting crow asked impatiently, unmasking his own captured scavenger and shaking his head at what he found.

"My point, friend, is that I worry for you and our companions," the raven said softly, his shifting veil brushing against the pale man's nose. *"I worry for you too, little scavenger. For everyone on this mountain."*

The hunting crow bit. "Worry about what?"

"I worry that you've forgotten the rules of nature now that you can defy

them," he told the disguised huntsman. "*Where is your spark? Where is your creativity? You walk around Olympia like your wrists are bound simply because you can't leverage the full weight of your soul. What does it matter if you can't use everything that you have against a lesser opponent? What does it matter if you can't fight a greater opponent at your fullest strength, even, so long as you are* **better** *than them?*"

The hulking crow looked silently down at the wounds he'd endured thus far in the night. Nothing more than small cuts and abrasions, but they wept tainted blood, marred by poison.

"*Violence is an art like any other,*" the hungry raven repeated. "*You Heroes have grown so used to being the loudest voices in the choir that you've forgotten what it's like to be spoken over. What it's like to be outmatched in every aspect except for the one that you can control.*"

The distant, victorious cry of an eagle split the night. Their companions had found their marks.

"*Consider these nights a return to form,*" the raven said, tightening his grip on the paralyzed assassin's neck until the man's eyes rolled up in his head. Mercifully unconscious. "*A crow can't be anything more than what it is—a scavenger. While you're here, unable to fight with any of the gifts that make you truly unique in this world, focus on what every man has had from the moment we were shaped from worthless clay.*

"*With the proper refinement, even a crow can kill a king.*"

A bird of midnight ink exploded out of the unconscious assassin's robes, taking off in the opposite direction of the eagle's cry with desperate speed. The hulking crow lunged for it, twisting and curling his fingers with obvious intent, but whatever would have happened in the light of day was lost in anonymity.

A massive celestial axe struck the crow cleanly out of the air, spinning end over end and pinning it to the nearby cliff face. It died before it could make a sound.

"*And if the Muses are kind,*" the raven murmured, dropping the assassin to pry his axe from the stone. "*Why shouldn't a Hero be able to topple a Tyrant?*"

The hunting crow and his own captured scavenger watched, aghast, as the raven tore the ink-black bird apart and sucked the starlight marrow from its bones.

. . .

"You aren't used to fighting like this," the hungry raven on the left observed, parrying the attacks of two separate crows with wide sweeps of his celestial spear. *"Constrained."*

Behind him, two Heroes disguised as crows nursed bleeding wounds as they fought off their adversaries.

A murder of the Tyrants' assassins had taken the initiative, finding them before they could be found and baiting them out with easy targets separated from the flock. As soon as they'd taken the bait, the night had exploded with bloodthirsty scavengers. Both Heroic cultivators had sustained cuts that would have killed a lesser existence in the opening moments. That they were who they were was the only reason they could still fight at all.

They were chafing against the bonds of anonymity, that much was clear to see. And the crows capitalized on that inexperience with vicious intent.

"Why would I ever fight like this?" Elissa, the Sword Song Heroine, snarled behind her veil. She was gripping her bow like she wanted nothing more than to club her opponent over the head with it. Nocking an ordinary arrow to its golden string and letting it fly, she cursed when her opponent dove under it and stabbed at her ankles.

"Moments like these," the raven replied without hesitation.

"I don't intend on being in this situation twice," the disguised Hero of the Alabaster Isles said dryly, weaving through the press of two other crows. Three more idled around the edges of the conflict, taking shots at the raven and his Heroic companions as the opportunities presented themselves.

"You will be," the raven said simply, halting a sweep of his spear mid-motion and jabbing it back into a surging crow's gut. It was a short, ugly strike, and it took the attacker utterly by surprise. The crow yanked itself off the spear's head and staggered back, clutching their bleeding wound. *"What will you do when you encounter a force that's greater than yours? What is your only recourse if an enemy beyond your strength attempts to strike you down?"*

A pulse of nameless force struck another crow. They abruptly fell sideways as if plummeting off a cliff, slamming into their fellow and sending both to the ground.

"What will you do if not submit?"

"I'll get stronger," the Sword Song declared, shifting her grip on her celestial bow and slamming it over a crow's head. Then, while they were staggered, she lunged into their guard and struck down with a hammer blow, burying an arrow into the juncture between their neck and shoulder in lieu of firing it.

"You don't have time," the raven dismissed. *"Say the Tyrants come for you tonight. What do you do?"*

"We fight together," spoke the Hero of the Alabaster Isles, pivoting and heaving his warhammer in a two-handed blow at a crow as it leapt at the Sword Song's back. It slammed home, audibly shattering ribs, sending the scavenger into and *through* a statue in the nearby grotto.

One of his opponents took the opportunity to hurl their rusted dagger at his back, and an invocation of hissed rhetoric saw the shadows themselves leaping up to tangle his limbs. An arrow struck the dagger midair, and the Sword Song appeared by his side, viciously kicking the crow's knee out from under it.

"You fight together," the raven agreed, banishing another crow into their waiting blows. *"A man that can fight with the strength of a thousand-thousand men is an incredible force. But five hundred men that can fight like they're one is even better."*

"It's been some time since I studied the quadrivium," the Sword Song admitted through gritted teeth, visibly correcting herself as her body attempted to make certain instinctual motions, combat tricks ingrained over the course of a lifetime. "But I don't think that math adds up."

*"It doesn't **add**, no,"* the raven said, his footwork taking him slowly but surely back to them until the three of them formed a triangle facing outward. The two Heroes had taken cuts, but the enemy was feeling the worst of the confrontation. They paced in a loose ring around them, vanishing and reappearing in the shadows of the grotto's swaying almond trees.

*"Five hundred good men fighting as one don't **add up** to a man with the strength of five hundred. It isn't an additive property."*

The two Heroes disguised as crows stiffened as that nameless pressure settled upon them, adjusting their posture in a dozen small ways, orienting them towards their opponents. They could feel it. Their next steps would be like running downhill, with the raven's own influence behind them. A tailwind urging them into the mix.

"Left."

Both Heroic crows planted their left feet and shot forward like arrows from a bow. Their opponents reacted with admirable speed, moving to block or counter with daggers and chains and whips of woven hair.

"Your left." Both Heroic cultivators dipped their bodies to the left, dodging counterattacks and slipping through guards.

*"Your left, right, **left.**"* The Hero of the Alabaster Isles hammered a left cross into a crow's face, followed by a right hook and a left uppercut. The Sword Song slipped past a stab aimed at her left breast, over her heart, then spun right and lashed out with her left elbow, shattering a crow's orbital bone and sending them sprawling bonelessly to the dirt.

"Your mother was home when you left!"

The Hero of the Alabaster Isles looked sharply back at the raven. "You're right!"

"Your father was home when you left!"

The Sword Song spun and said accusingly, "You're right!"

"Your sister was home when you left!"

Your right!

The crows flinched and whirled around them, caught on the precipice of violence and indecision.

"Your brother was home when you left!"

Your right!

One assassin tried to flee. The raven's celestial spear took them in the back of the knee and sent them tumbling into one of the grotto's pools. The raven reached out a beckoning hand, and the spear flew obligingly back to his palm. He inhaled.

"Your mother, your father, your sister, your brother, the slaves, the ruses, the Fates and the Muses, they all were there when you left!"

"You're right!" the Heroes disguised as crows cried out.

"And that's the reason you left!"
YOUR RIGHT!
The raven sang his legion song.
"When I left Rome!"
WHEN I LEFT ROME!
"My mama cried!"
MY MAMA CRIED!

They surged forward, three acting as one, and the murder of crows fell to pieces in their hands. Soon enough the two Heroic cultivators were rounding up the unconscious bodies and binding them with the same iron threads that had cinched their own wrists earlier that night.

"Cooperation in combat is an exponential force," the raven explained, wiping the blood from his celestial spear. Where the cloth of his undulating cloak passed, blood vanished, but the material never grew damp. *"True cooperation, that is."*

"And what does fighting with our hands tied behind our backs have to do with cooperation?" the Sword Song asked, but her confrontational words were betrayed by her tone. Her heart still pounded to the beat of the legion's crude cadence.

"Fighting together isn't necessarily fighting as one," he said patiently. *"A group of Heroes can fight side-by-side easily enough, but if they're each fighting to the tune of their Muses, how can they possibly move as a single unit?"*

"Cultivators are unique existences," the Hero of the Alabaster Isle realized. The raven nodded.

"You Greeks adore the thought of standing alone," he said without any particular judgment. *"Your cultivation reflects that, I think. The problem with being the Hero of your own story is that it is **yours** and no one else's. How can you coordinate properly if you're the only one that can possibly fight the way you fight?"*

"Practice," the Song Sword muttered. "Practice and time—more of each the higher you climb."

"Exactly. On the other hand, there are some things that any soldier can do. The bare basics of war. The ugly foundations that you cultivators race to cover up with towering coliseums of shining virtue." The raven clenched

his fist, and his influence pressed every one of the crows they had captured flat against the dirt.

"But those ugly foundations are firm. They can carry the weight of a man without question."

"At a certain point what's lost *must* outweigh what's gained by falling in line," the Sword Song protested. The raven shrugged one shoulder.

"Maybe so. But you aren't there yet."

The raven rose suddenly, and both Heroes tensed as he looked south up the mountain.

"I found someone sneaking out," their caustic crow sang. "I found yet another scout!" Bounding down the mountain hundreds of feet at a time, she had a young woman thrown over her shoulder, ankles and wrists tied with iron thread. She was wearing black robes and a threaded black veil, visibly finer than the rags the others had been sporting thus far.

Their fourth companion landed adroitly among them, presenting her capture with a flourish before dumping her on the ground. The young woman grunted softly, evidently still conscious. The raven knelt to pull the hood off her head.

"Where is the man that knows every—"

He went abruptly still. The caustic crow's high spirits vanished at once. The Hero of the Alabaster Isles hissed through clenched teeth, while the Sword Song viciously cursed.

The raven tilted his head, regarding the young woman as she blinked burning eyes up at him.

"Selene?"

As one, every single ink construct that the would-be assassins were harboring exploded out of their robes, cawing madly and streaking off each in different directions. Above, Sorea shrieked victoriously as he swooped down from the heavens to give chase.

Selene smiled, the scarlet flames behind her eyes flickering merrily.

"I found you, Solus."

Chapter Fifty-Four

THE YOUNG GRIFFON

"So, you just happened to cross paths after the funeral, and you just *happened* to come to an accord on the topic of insurrection out of the goodness of your hearts," Elissa said skeptically, throwing a wet towel at Kyno. He didn't bother opening his eyes, reclined as he was at the edge of the hot bath, only grunting as the towel slapped against his face.

"To think that you marked us all from the start," Jason murmured, shaking his head. He had disdained the hot bath entirely, back stroking idly through the cold pool after a quick cleansing. "How did you know we'd all be open to this insanity?"

Sol, upon realizing that the question wasn't rhetorical and that I wasn't rushing to answer it for him, paused his vicious scrubbing to think up an answer that sounded appropriately ominous.

"One of your elders marked you all that night," he said, finally. Anastasia, from her place close by him, blinked and paused with her own olive branch scrubbing, visibly putting the pieces together. She hadn't been there when Sol had declared the presence of a greater cultivator's attention.

"That's why you called out to me," she said, caustic green eyes flickering. She then affected a pout, leaning sideways into his personal space. "And here I thought it was my beauty that had caught your eye."

Sol sighed and shoved her back.

"One way or another, you weren't going to suffer these maneuverings for long without acting," he said flatly. "Not without losing a part of yourselves. Or, if the crows got to you first, having it taken from you."

"You say that..." Kyno murmured, peeling the towel back from his eyes to look gravely at Sol. "But there were six of us that night that you called, and now there are only four."

"Five," Anastasia corrected idly. I raised an eyebrow, fully opening eyes that had been half lidded for most of our time in the bathhouse

"Ho? Did you make another friend, Sol?" I asked, curious. Sol and I hadn't had a chance to exchange a private word since the previous night's festivities had given way to the dawn. Our new companions had done more than enough chattering for the both of us after we'd commandeered an unopened bathhouse. The place was closed indefinitely for reconstruction, not because of the late kyrios' final breath but because an unfortunate soul had recently plowed straight through the roof and collapsed a portion of the building. It had happened a few nights back, it seemed, and the villains responsible had yet to be found.

"Just a girl in over her head," he dismissed, though there was a pensive frown there. Of course, I didn't fail to notice the tense looks that Jason and Elissa shot my brother at his casual statement.

"You say that," Anastasia murmured, "but the two of you seemed quite familiar. And she was determined to tag along."

"Where is she now?" I asked.

"Back on the mountain where she belongs," Sol said, shaking his head. "We spoke briefly after the kyrios' funeral. She's just a child with a powerful father, looking for an escape from her sheltered life."

"How immature," I said disdainfully, and Sol snorted, lips quirking in amusement

"That is... certainly one way to describe her," Anastasia said, amusement warring with genuine uncertainty. "The two of you just happened to run into one another?"

"After you and I split up," he said, nodding.

"Unbelievable," Jason muttered.

"How many of the aristos do you have tucked away in your tunic?" Elissa pressed, accepting a jug of olive oil from Anastasia and dumping a generous portion over her shoulders and arms. Jason's eyes flickered, tracing rivulets of oil as they wound their way into the divots of her scars.

"The aristos?" Kyno muttered, lifting his head fully and, with something like dread, asking, "This girl. How powerful is her father, exactly?"

At that, three sets of eyes flickered Sol's way. Seeking permission to speak, for all of Anastasia's teasing and Elissa's surly demeanor. He nodded, glancing my way, and I realized after a moment that he didn't know the answer to that question any more than I did. But they did.

Elissa took his permission and said shortly, "It was Selene."

Kyno stared at her for a long moment. He looked then, to Sol, seeking confirmation. Sol nodded.

The Heroic Huntsman of the Broken Tide tossed his head back, striking the stone lip of the pool hard enough to crack it.

"'Zalus' daughter," he breathed, pressing two massive hands to his face, palms digging into his eyes. "You've brought 'Zalus' daughter into this."

"I haven't brought her into anything. She isn't a part of this."

'Zalus, I mused. I wondered why that name sounded familiar. *Old 'Zalus,* I heard in someone else's distant voice, a faint memory.

"She isn't a part of this, yet she joined you on your hunt? She took up arms against the ruling factions of the Raging Heaven? And she *isn't involved?*" Kyno pressed, rubbing insistently at his eyes. I offered him a few pankration hands to help, and he batted irritably at them, splashing me with scalding water.

I dashed wet hair from my eyes, frowning faintly. *Old 'Zalus,* that memory mused. The name was spoken with contempt.

"She didn't take up any arms," Sol said, returning to his scrubbing. "And she won't be in the future. Not with us." Anastasia cupped a palm beneath a trickle of olive oil and overturned it on his back, adding to his scrubbing with her own olive branch. She smiled innocently when he turned flat gray eyes on her.

"And yet she promised to find us again tonight," the caustic Heroine put forward.

Old 'Zalus, my father said, in a child's vague memory. My eyes lit up.

"You've caught the eye of a Tyrant's daughter," I accused him delightedly. He mastered himself as he always had, revealing nothing to our companions, but I could see the sudden dread as his worst suspicions were confirmed. "Not only that, but the eye of our own scarlet Tyrant's daughter! You sly Roman dog!"

"You're not supposed to say that," Jason despaired, ceasing his backstroke and floating miserably in the water as he stared up through the gaping hole in the ceiling. "You're supposed to tell us that you're acting with the Rosy Dawn's blessing."

"Who said we aren't?" I asked, unable to contain my smile. Elissa slapped her branch against the surface of the pool, kicking up a spray of steaming water.

"As if he would consent to his daughter's involvement," she hissed. Desert heat eyes burned with a fearful wrath. "You may think we're fools, but we're not! Involving her in these games is madness—and not the kind that you adore. He would never allow it."

"The question was," I repeated slowly, with purpose, "who says we aren't acting with the Rosy Dawn's blessing?" I relished the looks, the tension. "Is Old 'Zalus the Rosy Dawn?"

"No," Kyno said, darkly resigned.

"Who is?" I asked gently.

"Damon Aetos," Sol said, when it became clear that no one else would.

"This is a fine line you're walking," Anastasia warned, though even in her seriousness she continued to caress and poke at Sol with her olive branch. "Even for someone like you. The elders of the Raging Heaven are in conflict now, that's true, but an outsider is still an outsider. If we prod them too hard, too fast, they may just decide to act as they should and band together to purge you from the ranks."

"And us with you," Elissa added. With something like disgust for herself, she said, "We've thrown our lot in with you two. Don't go dragging us down to Tartarus with you."

That one affected Sol, hit him somewhere raw and painful. I inserted my own voice before the others could pile on.

"Of course we won't. How could we when we have no intention of going there ourselves?" I chuckled. "Not until we're ready for a dip in the Styx, at least."

"So if the elders turn against us instead of each other," Kyno said, "you can take them all?"

Allow me to be clear.

Sol and I had amassed something of a myth between ourselves since arriving on the shores of Olympia. Something small and infirm, but no less powerful for the people that it touched. These cultivators surrounding us in this bath were true heroes and heroines. They had cut their teeth on monsters and villains and been acknowledged by the Fates and the Muses both for their struggles.

Compared to their full splendor, Sol and I just weren't enough. Their capacity for cultivation dwarfed ours by several factors—a question of exponents rather than multipliers. In a just world, they would outstrip us in every metric.

But they were afraid. And for reasons that Sol and I had only just begun to unravel, they were, each of them, haunted by distant troubles. They had an obligation to right what was wrong as Heroes, and because they were not fulfilling their divine imperative, because their very essence told them that they were not living their lives the right way, Sol and I had stepped in to fill that void.

But that did not mean we were delusional. Sol and I were destined for great things, and I intended to grasp even greater things than that, but a Philosopher was still a Philosopher. A Hero was still a Hero.

And a Tyrant was still a Tyrant.

Our new companions had just about convinced themselves of an absurd estimation of our relative strength. But even then, trying to claim that we could take on all the elders of the Raging Heaven alone was a step too far. Even implying it would be an outrageous lie.

So I told him the truth. "Of course not. We're scavengers snapping at the heels of powerful beasts, hoping they'll turn their irritation on their rivals before they come for us. A single mistake could be the end of us all."

"We put on that performance last night for a reason," Sol added, contributing to my point as naturally as if it had been his own, just the student parroting what his master had designed. "As far as your elders are concerned, you were kidnapped in the night. Go back now, fabricate a passing story of your escape, and wash your hands of this."

We would have to flee the city, of course, and that would be a shame. But the Oracles weren't going anywhere. The Olympics would come again in four years. And there were other ways to grow strong without devouring the starlight marrow of Tyrants.

If these Heroic cultivators truly feared death more than they despised the yoke of a tyrant, then there was nothing we could do for them.

"Dammit," Jason said quietly. "*Dammit.* I said I was with you, Solus. I won't let you make me a liar."

Elissa's jaw clenched, but she shook her head once when I glanced her way. Kyno, likewise, resigned himself with a low sigh.

"You have us netted," Anastasia said, propping her chin up on one hand. "If you say that Selene and her stark father won't be an issue, I'll choose to believe you for now. But the good hunter raises a fair point. Scythas and the archer are notable in their absence. Have you approached them yet? Will you?"

"Lefteris has been doing his best to avoid us since he incurred my master's wrath," I said, amused. "But I've kept an ear out, and if the Fates are kind, I should be able to find him before sundown."

"And if they aren't kind?" Elissa asked, in the suffering tone of someone who knew what the answer would be before she asked her question. I smirked.

"I'll find him anyway."

"And what of sweet Scythas?" Anastasia pressed, watching intently as Sol dipped his head down into the scalding bath, rising back up and running his fingers through coarse black hair.

"Scythas will find us," Sol said with certainty. Anastasia hummed, accepting that without protest.

"We'll have to lay low for the time being," Jason mused, pulling himself from the bath and grabbing a towel. "Kaukoso Mons is off-limits for now. We can't exactly be kidnapped every single night, after all."

"We'll have to find neutral ground," Kyno agreed and rose at the same time, shifting aside the tail of the crocodile skin that he'd been wearing the entire time to wrap a towel around his waist.

"I have a place," Elissa said simply, wringing the moisture from her hair.

As we filed out of the baths and into the light of day with towels over our heads to partially cover our faces, under the guise of drying our hair, Jason eyed the awakening streets of Olympia's eastern district warily.

"We're already tempting the Fates, being out like this," he said in a low voice.

I snorted, tilting my head at our rapt audience. To our left, a pair of women were hollering at one another from their adjacent balconies about some spat or another from the day before. On the streets them-selves a handful of children raced around in a game of tag, and a couple stray hounds sniffed around an old vagrant in filthy rags sleeping fitfully in the shade cast by the damaged bathhouse. By the standards of the Half-Step City, it was deserted.

"I think they'll keep this to themselves," I told Jason, laughing as he jabbed at me with an elbow.

"You think so, do you?"

I glanced down at the vagrant in his rags. The old man had cracked an eye open, and now he stared balefully up at me. Plain brown eyes with no flames behind them. The eddies of my influence brushed against him and found nothing of particular note. Just an old man sleeping on the street.

Sol and our companions regarded the vagrant warily, looking to one another and exchanging silent words of intent. The Heroic cultiva-tors among us shifted their towels just so, hiding as much of their defining features as they could. For Kyno and Elissa, whose stature and scars betrayed them regardless, it was a fairly comical sight.

"Grandfather," I greeted respectfully, inclining my head, "these lowly sophists were in dire need of a bath. Please forgive our indis-cretion."

"I've forgiven you for more than that," he said, surly and gray. He propped himself up on an elbow and shifted his rags, drawing them tighter around himself. It was still winter after all, and the sun had only just arisen. For someone without an advanced cultivator's constitution, it was uncomfortably cool here in the shade. "You young cultivators are all the same. It wasn't enough that you vandalized this bathhouse, rendered it unusable for the citizens it was built to accommodate. You had to add insult to injury, return and make use of it while the rest of the city couldn't."

I blinked, and slowly, I asked the man, "Who said we vandalized this building?"

"I did." The vagrant cleared his throat and spat phlegm on the street beside him.

Kyno placed a massive hand on my shoulder, pulling subtly, urging me back. I shrugged him off. "It was like this when we got here this morning," I informed the vagrant.

He sneered. "You're a terrible liar, boy."

Sol inhaled deeply.

"My virtuous heart won't accept such an insult," I said very quietly. "Not even from an old man."

"A truth told with false intent is a lie like any other," he said, waving me off. The audacity of this homeless wretch. "Every man in the Half-Step City knows how to twist his words and make them pretty. What makes a man shine is not rhetoric alone. It is *substance*."

Sol stepped forward, suddenly keenly interested. "Who are you to say that? Are you a philosopher?" His influence rippled out to test the man the same way mine had and found just as little going by the frown on his face.

"Philosopher," the old man echoed and spat again. "No, boy, philosophers are men in the business of knowing things. Look at me. Do I look like a man that knows anything at all?"

"Your definition of a philosopher is different from mine," Sol said, that storm gathering in his eyes. I muscled down my annoyance and forced myself to look past it, deeper.

"By all means," invited the vagrant. "Enlighten me."

"Sol," Jason murmured, edging up beside him. His eyes continue to

435

shift behind the edges of the towel, watching as more and more people trickled out of their homes and businesses onto the streets. "We should go."

"In a moment," Sol said, distracted. He knelt in the front of the living bundle of filthy rags, Anastasia kneeling beside him with curiosity and a vague puzzlement in her eyes. "I was taught that a philosopher is a man that knows only one thing, and that is the fact that he doesn't know anything at all."

The old man snorted. "How pretentious. You might as well call them fools if that's all that distinguishes them."

Sol didn't respond for a long moment, searching the old man's face for something. "Truth told with false intent is a lie," he finally said. "What would you call an opposed opinion that you present as your own?"

"I'd call that disingenuous."

"And I'd call you a liar," Sol said with something like triumph. "You know what it means to say that a philosopher is a man who knows he knows nothing. It's an admission of man's limitation. It's the crystallization of a mindset."

The old man tilted his head. "Who taught you those words, boy?"

Sol leaned forward, eager now, but I saw the puzzlement in Anastasia turn to something deeper. Troubled. She was racking her brain for something crucial, just out of reach. I frowned, manifesting three pankration hands behind Jason, Kyno, and Elissa, tapping between their shoulder blades with gentle rosy heat. We settled into postures not visibly threatening but ready, nonetheless.

"My mentor," the Roman said with rising purpose. "He guided me as a boy. I owe a portion of my best traits to him. Have you heard of him? Better than that, have you met him?"

"How would I be able to tell you when you haven't given me a name?"

Anastasia's eyes suddenly widened. I inhaled sharply through my nose.

"In my city, he was called the man that knows everything," Sol confessed. "My other tutors called him the Father of Rhetoric.

"But his *name* is Aristotle."

Anastasia stared at the old man in abject terror.

"Foolish," the old vagrant sighed. And he rose, shedding his soul's disguise.

For a single endless moment, I stared without comprehension at the space where he had been, reclining fitfully on the road, and where he stood now, palming Sol's head where he knelt. For that moment, as the old man's formless veil of inconsequence fell away from him, and that same terror in Anastasia's eyes spread immediately to all the mythical Heroes in our group, I was as paralyzed as them.

But it was only a moment.

[The dawn breaks.]

Twenty fists of pankration intent blazed as they crossed the distance between us, reaching, clawing, striking. I leveraged the full weight of my pneuma and lunged forward, reaching for my brother where he knelt.

Dawn gives way to dusk, intoned the old man's soul. The fire in my palms guttered out, and I felt the jarring shock of bare fists slamming into an utterly unyielding surface as they hit him. The old man's filthy rags shifted beneath my assault, the only reaction he gave, falling away to reveal a body like twisted iron.

"Arrogant child," he said, lashing out with a backhand that I caught on crossed forearms, slamming me back across the street with force enough to dig furrows in the dirt.

Gravitas rocked the street, sending citizens and children that had not yet noticed the confrontation tumbling. Screams rose into the air on black wings. But try as he might, Sol could not rise against the hand on his head. The storm roiled in his eyes.

"Turning **justice** upon me like I have anything to fear from it," the old man said to me contemptuously. "Citing your heart's virtue while you skirt around a lie. You have no *concept* of virtue. Where is the excellence in your soul?"

"You're..." Anastasia breathed.

"That's—" Jason bit.

"I am nothing," said the vagrant, dismissing each of them in turn. He glanced down at Sol, watching him struggle. He inclined his head, acknowledging, "I am a learning man. A philosopher. And I know what I know."

These cowards. These worthless *mongrels*. **Why weren't they fighting?**

I leapt straight up, twisting and reaching into my shadow, pulling from it the raven's broad celestial axe and wreathing it in rosy flame.

[The sun rises.]

The vagrant didn't even look up.

[Night falls.]

I fell out of the sky and slammed back down to earth in a crouch, heels driving through the dirt. I exhaled sharply and rose again. My senses continued to tell me the same thing they'd been telling me since he shrugged off his unremarkable veil.

His pneuma, without question, was that of a Philosopher. No more.

And yet.

"No student of Aristotle would have made such a mess in such short order," the old man said, shaking his head. Sol glared up at him as best he could. "You've only been here for, what, a week? Five days? You're lying to me, or else that young fool did you a grave disservice."

I gathered my pneuma and laid a hand on the pommel of my uncle's blade. I felt my blood begin to boil.

Sol snarled. "He did the best he could with what he was given."

"Then he failed. And as his master's master, I have no choice but to make right what he left unfinished." Without looking, without turning his dull, unassuming eyes my way, the old man waved his hand as if to brush a fly from his shoulder, and I blinked as rubble and ruined stone rained down around my head. I realized that I wasn't standing poised to attack, as I had thought I was. I was crouched in the entryway to the bathhouse, having plowed straight through one of its pillars.

Four Heroic cultivators watched, frozen, as the old vagrant raised my brother up and met him glare for glare.

"Aristotle has evidently failed to prepare you for this world. I, your grandfather, will teach you the way of things."

And then he crouched as if to hop over a puddle and exploded upward, sailing clear over the Half-Step City towards the looming edifice of Kaukoso Mons and its immortal storm crown.

He took Sol with him.

For a long moment, no one said a word. Citizens, those that had made it off the streets or never left their homes in the first place, peered out from behind slatted windows and cracked doors, curiosity warring with rational fear. In the distance, the howling of dogs drifted hauntingly on the wind.

One by one, the four Heroic Cultivators looked back at me. Whatever it was they saw, it didn't do much for their unease.

"That's quite a face, Griffon," Anastasia whispered, a faint attempt at humor.

I didn't smile.

Chapter Fifty-Five

THE SON OF ROME

We flew.

There was no other way to describe it. The old man in his rags of unassuming filth held tight to my hair and pulled me up to heaven, faster than sound could travel. The city of Olympia grew small beneath us in the blink of an eye.

No man can ever truly fly, of course. That had been hammered into my head long ago, as it had into every cultivator. It was the core conceit of those that pursued divinity. A natural desire, one felt anytime you looked up at a cloudless sky or down at a sprawling valley. It almost seemed a natural step along the path of advancement. After all, why else would man cultivate virtue if not to claim the heights that his father couldn't reach?

On more than one punishing campaign, camped out beneath the Republic's siege works, I had gazed up at a city's stubbornly kept walls and longed to simply vault them like a garden fence. And why not? The men of Gaius' legions were surely powerful enough for such a maneuver. Alas, my father had soon corrected me of that delusion, and my uncle had later enforced the lesson.

Our hunger was something no man could escape. For as long as we had looked up and seen, we had desired the climb—for no other reason than that we could. But there were some places that even a cultivator couldn't go.

There were some domains that even the mightiest Tyrant didn't dare trespass. Heaven was one such domain.

What the man who claimed to be the master of my master's master did was not flight—more of an absurd hop—but in that moment before freefall, while we hung weightless in the air, I felt the weight of heaven's notice. It was no cultivator's sense or legion instinct that allowed me to detect it.

Any man could hear the thunder.

And it was made all the more apparent by the fact that we were hurtling directly towards the Raging Heaven's tribulation crown, the Storm That Never Ceased. I finally regained the breath that had been knocked out of me by our rapid ascent and shouted a curse, calling upon the captain's virtue with force enough that the air itself groaned, a subsonic vibration that would have shattered stone walls if there had been any around.

The old vagrant's rags might have flapped a bit more insistently than they already were in the wind, *maybe*, but that was the only reaction I got for my efforts. The man himself didn't even twitch. He just tightened his grip on my hair, and then without warning, he twisted and heaved me down at a small chasm in the mountain, just below the storm.

It was like being shot from a bow. I flexed the captain's virtue desperately, but I wasn't in the business of using it on myself, and so all I could do was clear a few particularly painful looking rocks from my path before I plowed into the cave, my vision flashing white as I crashed through stone and kept going.

A bare, filthy foot came down on my back, stopping me abruptly. My head whipped forward and then back, cracking against the stone with the momentum, and I glared blearily up.

The vagrant philosopher stepped off me, shrugging out of the soiled layers of cloth he'd built his aura of anonymity out of until he stood over me in a simple white toga. He crossed his arms, and as the weight of his expectation came down upon me, crushing me to the stone as I tried to rise, I came to a realization.

The reason that Griffon and I had experienced such success in our subterfuge since arriving at the Half-Step City. The reason why Scythas, Alyssa, Kyno, Lefteris, Jason, and Anastasia had so readily accepted our posturing and vague implications despite only being philosophers. It wasn't that we were spectacular actors. It wasn't even that *we* were particularly special.

The master of my master's master waved a hand, and the overpowering thunder of the Raging Heaven's perpetual storm vanished into mist and whispers. No, it was more than that. As the whiplash ringing faded from my ears, I understood that all of the background noise of nature, the ever-present hum that existed even here on this mountain, was suddenly gone. Like it had never existed in the first place.

Heroes greater than us were willing to believe our lies because men like this existed in the world.

"ἓν οἶδα ὅτι οὐδὲν οἶδα hèn oîda hóti oudèn oîda."

"What?" I asked.

A truly wrathful expression overtook him. I tensed, and my blood thundered in my ears, but he mastered it in the next moment, scoffed, and spat on the cave floor.

"He didn't even bother to teach you a thinking man's tongue? I'll throttle that boy the next time I see him."

"He did," I protested, this time in the Scarlet City's tongue rather than the Latin I had been defaulting to lately.

"Álikoan," he said with distaste. "The ugliest language in the Greek Isles, to match her ugliest city. Why would he teach you that tongue over his own?"

I thought back. Many of Aristotle's teachings were more impressions than they were true recollections, overshadowed by years on campaign, years at war, and a year of shellshocked slavery. But this one stood out. It always had. It had been cemented in my memory the moment the shackles were affixed to my wrists.

"He told me that I would need it," I said quietly. "He told me it was the most important language I could possibly know."

I spent more than one sleepless night as a slave wondering how much Aristotle had suspected. How much he could have possibly known. And I had wondered how much more he knew—it was why I was here, searching for him. It was why I'd been found.

"That boy," he muttered, running callused fingers through a long white beard. The man was built like a siege weapon, sculpted in the way of the Greek Heroes we had been keeping company with, but with more overt signs of his age. The color of his hair... washed out. Crow's feet at the corners of his eyes. And deep, thinking lines carved across his forehead.

"You said Aristotle was your student's student," I said. He grunted, eyes distant as he thought. "Do you know where he is?"

"West."

My heart sank. Álikos. I should have known. For a year I'd assured myself that he couldn't possibly be back in the Scarlet City, that he surely would have sought me out if he was. I should have known that was a child's delusion.

He wasn't my friend. He was my mentor, and my father wasn't alive to pay him his due anymore. He didn't owe me anything.

"No."

I blinked. "No?"

"No," the old philosopher repeated. "Farther."

Farther west? "Impossible."

Somehow, the silence grew even quieter. The very air between us seemed to hold its breath. The philosopher looked down upon me, and in a deathly quiet voice, he asked, "What did you just say?"

"That's impossible," I repeated. "I've seen what's west of the Scarlet City. If he's still out there, he's dead."

"You think so, do you?"

I matched his glare in defiance, and with memories of howling thunder, I informed him, "I *know*."

The philosopher kicked me in the gut, and I gagged as dust and shattered stone filtered around my head. Seconds later, my senses caught up to the rest of me, and I realized that I had been buried in the far wall of the cave.

"You *know?*" the old philosopher said, advancing on me. "You know *nothing*. In fact, you know even less than that. Was Aristotle such a failure that he couldn't plant a single thought in that thick Roman skull of yours?"

He grabbed me by the neck and pulled me out of the stone. I snarled and spat in his face. The spittle halted a hairsbreadth from his eyes and then abruptly whipped back into mine. Worthless, sanctimonious Greeks.

"What is it that you think you've been doing since you darkened these shores?" he demanded. "What have you accomplished, and to what end?"

Contrary to his demand for answers, his hand only tightened further around my throat. I forced the words out, even as I scanned our surroundings in my peripherals. It was a cave like any other, but with the bare echoes of habitation to show for the philosopher's presence. A bedroll off to my left, a small set of cups and plates to my right, along with a small mountain of rolled up papyrus and various tablets.

"I came here looking for Aristotle," I choked.

"Is that what you call this?" the old philosopher demanded and reached for my shadow. The darkened silhouette, already undulating wildly in the scattered lights of the storm outside the cave, darted inexplicably away from his hand, moving with its own intent. "Inserting yourself into a political struggle that you have no stake in, no influence over, for no reason at all other than to cause mayhem? Because you believe you can? What are you *thinking?*"

"I think," I hissed, "that scavengers are eating this place alive."

"So you decided to join in, take a bite for yourself?"

"No. I decided to take a bite out of *them*."

Gravitas rocked the cave, and though it didn't move the old philosopher, the stone that I took hold of with the captain's virtue and slammed into the back of his head certainly did. He staggered forward a step, against me, and I slammed my forehead into his nose. It was like headbutting Kaukoso Mons itself, but I forced down the nausea and thrashed free while he was stunned.

My shadow offered up the celestial bronze spear, and I gripped it tight, turning and whipping its tip up with all my strength.

The philosopher caught it by the shaft and struck me once with his free hand. I lost another few moments, and when I came to again, I was laying on my back just outside of the cave, staring up into the storm. Dew droplets trickled down my face, mingling with the blood of a broken nose. Lightning flashed a thousand times in rapid succession, vast branching networks of lights that were swallowed up by storm clouds in the next instant. In the distance, I heard a familiar shriek.

The philosopher grabbed me by my foot and dragged me back into the cave.

"I won't be lied to, boy," the philosopher said as if nothing had happened. "And I won't be sweet-talked either." If he had taken any lasting damage from my suckerpunch, I couldn't see it. He dropped me in the middle of the cave and sat beside me, legs crossed, one hand on a knee while the other propped up his chin.

I stared mutinously up at the stone ceiling for a long moment before common sense got the better of my pride. This wasn't what I had been looking for, but it was an opportunity that I wasn't likely to get twice. And he *had* said that he was going to teach me the way of the world.

Either I had found myself a new mentor—been found by, more like —or I was about to die. One way or another, I had to make the most of this.

"I came here looking for Aristotle," I said again. "I'd just broken through in my cultivation, and I was exploring one of my new senses at the kyrios' funeral. I accidentally tipped off half a dozen Heroic Cultivators in the act, made them think I was looking for a fight. What could I do but pretend I was more than I am? Make myself seem too dangerous to fight?"

"You could have explained your mistake and apologized for it."

I lifted a shoulder in a shrug, not bothering to sit up. My head and nose were throbbing incessantly in time with one another. The ground was comfortable enough for the moment.

"I'm a foreigner in a strange, barbarous land. How was I to know that one of them wouldn't take offense to my wasting their time? Who would punish a great hero for stepping on an insolent young philosopher?"

"I would."

I glanced at the master of my master's master. He met my gaze steadily, and after a moment, I nodded.

"I believe you. But I'd still be dead."

"Justice would be served," he pointed out.

"Not good enough. I have things I need to do before I die, whether it's justice or not."

The old man considered that for a long moment, and then he asked, "What is the first virtue?"

"Freedom."

The old philosopher looked at me like I had grown another head. "Are you out of your mind, boy?"

I raised an eyebrow. "This is the free Mediterranean, is it not?"

"Aristotle truly did you a disservice," he said, disgusted. "It's a question of your *soul*, boy, not just your beliefs. It's a matter of foundation."

Foundation.

"What does it take for a man to lead?"

"Gravitas," I answered, properly this time. The old philosopher grunted.

"And what is gravitas?"

I forced myself to sit up, turning my head and spitting as much of the blood out of my mouth as I could. I inhaled deeply, tracing my vital breath through the channels old and new inside my body. And I forced myself to remember.

"Gravitas is three thousand men sprinting into Tartarus at your command," I said, each word like broken glass in my throat. "It's four hundred and eighty shields at your back while you plunge into the enemy's open mouth. It's three hundred screaming horses crashing headlong into the sea.

"It's weight."

"Weight?" the philosopher echoed.

I nodded once, staring past his shoulder, into the distant past. "Every man is a world unto himself. He's a city, a family, a wife and children, friends and enemies and comrades. He's hopes and dreams, aspirations of changing all that he can change. He's all these things, and he is *heavy*.

"Gravitas is the weight of three thousand such men. It's three thousand worlds, three thousand lives that could have been, borne on your shoulders.

"It is salt," I rasped. "And it is ash."

For a long moment, the cave was silent but for the memories. And then a strong, calloused hand gripped my shoulder.

"How old are you, boy?" he asked me.

"Twenty."

"An age of child tyrants," he said and sighed. "These demons in the west. You're certain they weren't human? The world is a vast place, full of odd people."

I thought of snarling fangs and slitted eyes the color of tribulation lightning. Whatever he saw in me at that moment, the philosopher didn't press the point further.

"A handful of lost Heroes won't be enough to combat a force like that," he said, shaking his head and rising to his feet. He slapped down the wrinkles in his tunic. "If it's demons you're after, you'll need more. You'll need to be more."

Sorea shrieked again, far closer this time.

"How did you know about the demons?" I asked and then pressed, "How did you know we were responsible for what happened at the bathhouse? That we've been hunting crows?"

The old philosopher snorted. "I don't know anything, boy. I listen, and I learn. It's astounding what a man will say when he thinks there's no one important around to hear him. It's even more astounding what a man will say when he thinks it won't hurt to let a few things slip."

He flexed the fingers of his hands and rolled his shoulders, turning to squarely face the cave's entrance.

"And most astounding of all," he said with powerful disdain, bracing his feet, "is what a fool will say when he wants to be heard."

Sorea shrieked a third time, just below, and the sun dawned twice.

[Dawn arrives upon its throne.]

Griffon exploded through the entrance with blood on his face and

447

fire in his fists. And just before the master of my master's master could slap him out of the air, I lunged up and drove my shoulder into the old philosopher's back, knocking him off balance. It only lasted a fraction of a moment. It was enough.

Griffon struck him like a comet.

Chapter Fifty-Six

THE YOUNG GRIFFON

When I was seven years old, I called upon Nikolas to face me in the marble octagon. He was exactly twice my age at that time, and his cultivation was exactly one realm above my own.

A fifth-rank Citizen, challenging a Philosopher equally far along in their own realm. It was utterly absurd, and everyone involved had known it. Nikolas' peers and his followers had laughed and urged him up. It was all a game to them, of course, a play fight between the junior and senior young pillars of the Rosy Dawn. The gymnasiarch, a famously no-nonsense man, had evidently felt the same way because he'd allowed it.

But when Nikolas gave in to the heckling and climbed up onto that marble stage, when he met my eyes and we clasped forearms, I knew he saw the truth of it. And though he asked me in a private whisper if I was sure, he did not hesitate to oblige me.

There was a reason I admired my cousin.

When the gymnasiarch gave the call to fight, my cousin came at me with the full force of everything he had as a cultivator, and I met him with the same force in turn. It was over in seconds.

I lost horribly, of course. The gymnasiarch was furious, and even Nikolas' companions within the cult weren't sure what face to show him. It was understandable. After all, my elder cousin had never treated them with the same ferocity that he had served me in those few brutal seconds.

But it was exactly what I'd needed. In that moment, as my face struck the edge of the marble octagon and two of my teeth were knocked into the back of my throat, as my right elbow loudly broke, I saw for the first time the difference between heaven and earth. And I knew, without a doubt in my heart, that it was not an impossible gap to bridge.

I never fought my elder cousin seriously again. There was no reason to. I knew myself, and I knew him well enough to understand that I wasn't ready, and before long, my father bundled him up on a ship and sent him out into the world, leaving me to take on the role of young aristocrat in its full scope. But that was fine. I had gotten what I wanted.

The greatest men knew their limits better than anyone else.

The vagrant philosopher raised one hand against me, three fingers tucked in and two pointing up to heaven. A lecturer's pose, as he prepared to educate me on the vast distance between us once more. Unfortunately for him, Romans make for horribly impolite students. Sol surged up from the ground behind the philosopher and tackled him, a furious grimace on his face made utterly vicious by his broken nose.

I struck the old man like a falling star, hammering his face with twenty blazing hands and using the instability that Sol had provided for me to knock him off his feet.

Gravitas hit me like a tidal wave, and this time I allowed it to wash me away in its current, flying backwards as if I was falling out of the sky. The philosopher's counterpoint, something wordless and unseen, reached out for Sol in my place. I disdained that with twenty pankration hands, dragging my brother away from the attack.

The entrance to the cave collapsed in on itself before we could make it fully out, an unfortunate coincidence I was sure. Gravitas struck the falling stone but was somehow dispersed, leaving us trapped inside.

I planted my feet and pulled Sol up to stand beside me.

The vagrant philosopher snorted, annoyed, and brushed off his tunic as he stood. Without looking, I reached over and gripped Sol's nose, setting it back properly with a nauseating crunch. He cursed, and at the same time, he gripped a finger of mine that I hadn't noticed dislocating and popped it back into place. Silver threads of lightning sensation shot up my hand, and we were good as new.

"Let's try this again, old man," I said gaily, shifting into a proper pankration stance. Fists loosely clenched in front of me, the majority of my weight braced on my launching foot. "My name is Griffon and this is Sol. Who do you think you are to lay your ragged hands on my brother?"

He appeared unimpressed, but he answered. "My name is Socrates. I am who I am."

When I was seven years old, my elder cousin taught me what it was like to fight an opponent that I could not possibly overcome. I never forgot that lesson. And here, now, I reaped the bitter rewards of it.

With our companions it might have been possible. But alone?

Oh well. I hadn't asked for it to be easy.

"Let's exchange discourse," I proposed.

"If we must."

The three of us exploded into motion.

"I've asked the Roman already, but I'll ask it again. What is it that you think you're accomplishing here?" Socrates asked, parrying my opening combination with short, efficient chops and blocks. He turned sideways as Sol lunged past me with his bronze spear, avoiding it by a whisper.

"Here?" I caught a straight left punch with five pankration hands overlaid on one another and swallowed back blood at the shockwave impact it sent through my soul. "I'm reminding an old man that experience is no substitute for vigor."

"More deflection," he said, catching a flurry of punches on raised forearms, protecting his temples and the sensitive juncture between his jaw and his neck. We each raised a knee at the same time, bone slammed against bone, and I winced as something in me cracked.

Sol struck out with the butt of the spear, catching Socrates in his kidney and forcing him back a step. The philosopher took the spear in the exchange, and Sol didn't fight him for it, instead adopting his own loose, roughshod boxing stance.

"Deflection," Socrates said again, scornfully. He tucked the bronze spear—inexplicably, all ten feet of it—into a fold in his tunic and crossed his arms. "Doublespeak, half-truths, and implication. You progressed to the second realm and think that people calling you Philosophers makes it true."

Socrates tilted his head as if to urge us out the door, and in the eddies of his influence, I felt the bare flicker of something crucial, something profound. I would have missed it entirely if I hadn't been looking directly for it already.

I blinked, startled, as Sol reached both hands under my arms and pulled me bodily to my feet. At some point, somehow, I had been driven to my knees.

Lights illuminated the walls of the cave despite the lack of any visible source. Shadows danced across the stone, resolving themselves into vague shapes that I couldn't quite decipher. Socrates advanced forward a step.

"All too often," he said, "young men mistake sophistry for sophisticated thought. It is not enough to be convincing."

And then he was abruptly gone. I frowned, wary, and glanced around. Sol did the same beside me, casting out with his riptide influence in search of the vagrant philosopher.

"It is not enough to win the argument," an old man said, walking up to us.

"Not now, grandfather," I said, waving a distracted hand as I ran the incorporeal fingers of my violent intent across the walls of the cave, searching for a crack or a crevice, something the philosopher could have escaped through.

Wait.

Sol shook it off a moment before I did, reaching across my body to catch an uppercut that would have lifted me cleanly off my feet. I saw the tightly controlled agony in his face, heard the crack of his hand breaking. Socrates leaned back and kicked him into the far wall for his troubles.

"You see? Distraction is not enough," Socrates said. "Whether in a fight or a conversation. You need *fundamentals*." I inhaled sharply and closed to engage. I sought to enhance myself with the principles of my soul, but he countered each and every one as I invoked them, just as he had outside the bathhouse.

What remained was pure technique, the conditioning of our bodies. Fundamental qualities.

"What is rhetoric if not the art of convincing others?" I countered with words and with clenched fists. "A philosopher is above all else a wise man. And I say that a wise man knows what he wants. I say that a wise man knows the value of his time! Why shouldn't I use the tools at my disposal to get what I want?"

I landed a blow to his ribs and took two on the chin for my troubles, but Sol came rushing in before I could be fully put down. He swung with quick and ugly intent. I could perfectly imagine him in a camp filled with rowdy soldiers, brawling and knocking out fellow legionaries to blow off steam.

"A wise man knows what he wants," Socrates repeated. "And yet when I ask you what you're here to accomplish, you play glib and dance around it. What are you *here for*, boy?"

"I'm here for a challenge," I said, and my heart sang the truth of it.

"Looking for a challenge, or looking to *be* challenged?"

I smirked faintly and whipped my body around with my right heel as the pivot point, striking at his temple with a roundhouse kick. The philosopher caught it by the ankle and slapped me across the face.

"Word games," he scolded me. "Life isn't a competition to see who can layer more meaning into a single phrase. Give me *clarity*."

Sol latched onto the arm holding my leg and drove his shoulder up into Socrates' chest, pivoting and attempting to pull him over. Gravitas rocked the cave, scattering the shadow silhouettes on the walls and reforming them into orderly ranks. Toy soldiers marching across the stone.

Whether it was because of proximity or negligence on the philosopher's part, Sol's virtue was able to reach him this time. Briefly. The philosopher fell up, into the air, and then slammed down as Sol's virtue spun the axis of the world. Sol brought him back down to earth with punishing force.

"Speaking with clarity," my brother mused, leaping back from the philosopher's formless retaliation and escaping the brunt of it, only grimacing as something struck his right shoulder with an audible clap.

"Something like that would surely deviate his cultivation."

I looked sharply at him, and he found it in himself to smirk.

"My virtuous heart can't lie."

"That's *my* principle," I said, betrayed.

"Ah, true."

"This is a game to you, is it?" Socrates said, addressing Sol as he rose once more. It didn't escape my notice that he looked no worse for wear than he had back at the bathhouse. By contrast, Sol and I were bruised and bleeding, broken in several places. "Your city is a smoking ruin and here you are, in another place on the brink of a similar fate. It's funny to you, is that it?"

What small joy my brother had found tucked away in his heart vanished from his face. I scowled.

"I'm here for a challenge, and I'm here to be challenged," I said, striding forward and flexing my pneuma. "I'm here to see the Oracles, and I'm here to compete in the Olympic Games. I'm here to meet interesting people, powerful people, and match myself against them. I'm here to learn all of the secrets that you and your Tyrants don't want me to know."

"Is that all?" Socrates asked. Thick gray eyebrows furrowed as he regarded me. "You're too young to be this greedy."

I grinned fiercely. "I am who I am. And I want it all."

And then I waved my hand as if to brush a drifting ember from the air.

"It's in his pneuma," the shadow that was the raven on the left whispered to my shadow that was the raven on the right, while the cultivator that was Sol pulled me to my feet. *"A philosopher builds a foundation of a thousand-thousand truths, that's what you told me. He's using those truths now. He's **lecturing** us."*

Socrates hummed in surprise as I struck him with a plain truth.

Kronos leaves his mark. With age comes gray hair, and with gray hair comes infirmity.

Just as I had before, in dealing with that trio of young philosopher boys, and later when fighting the Rein-Holder's two crows, I observed my pneuma's natural reaction to a force that I had no knowledge of, and I understood. I saw the flickering light, felt the rush of my influence surging out of me of its own accord. I felt the same thing that Sol had felt and conveyed to me through our shadows.

A Hero distills the strength of a thousand-thousand different truths into himself, turning each and every one into pure power. But a Philosopher deals directly in these truths. He isn't yet strong enough to bend them entirely to his will.

He can only guide them.

The truth of old age struck Socrates, and in my mind's eye I saw it do its unstoppable work. I saw it weigh down his posture, hunch his back, and drive into the segments of his fingers its aches and ruinous pains. I saw the hand of time press him down and make an infirmity of him.

I saw the theory of it in perfect clarity. Unfortunately, the reality of things was slightly different.

"A gray hair can be a sign of many things," Socrates said for my benefit, verbalizing the counterpoint that he invoked with his pneuma. "A sign of age, yes. Or a poor diet. A deviation of the heart, also known as *stress*. Even a god given pigment at birth."

My attack, such as it was, slid off him like rainwater. But that was fine. I knew the trick of it now.

And so did Sol.

"A young man can't teach another young man how to be wise," Sol asserted, pacing along the edge of the cave, his pneuma catching the dispersed streams of my plain truth and reforming them. "You're the master of my master's master. A wise man, who taught a wise man, who taught a wise man. Old three times over."

"Who says a young man can't be wise?" Socrates challenged.

I answered instead. "A young man is like a puppy with an argument. He can't truly understand it. One of the definitions of wisdom is experience, and experience comes with time."

"You need wisdom to be wise," Sol completed the thought. And together as one, we struck the old philosopher with the truth of his years.

Socrates huffed something almost like a laugh. "And yet here you are, trying to lecture the lecturer." And that was all it took to brush us off his shoulder. I exchanged a look with Sol as he continued to circle behind the philosopher. "Not the worst attempt, but certainly not the best. Age leads to infirmity, true enough, but in degrees. There are things that we can do, things that we *must* do as men of virtue, to preserve our strength and craft our perfect bodies. A cultivator is the same, but even more so."

Sol and I moved as one, closing the gap once again.

"But enough of that."

Something like one thousand flickering whispers in Socrates' influence were the only warning I got, and then I was outside the cave, my torso and head hanging over the edge of Kaukoso Mons. Upside down, the Half-Step City was truly dazzling in the early morning light. I blinked as I noticed a familiar silhouette up above, which was to say below, crouched in the shadow of a nondescript alcove similar to Socrates' own.

Lefteris stared down at me, which was to say up at me, with wide-eyed intent. He had his bow in hand, its gold string pulled back taut despite not having an arrow nocked to it as far as I could tell.

Who? he mouthed to me.

Blearily, I watched the blood drain from his face as Socrates stepped out of his cave.

"These games you're playing, and the people you're playing them with," he told me, "the consequences are real. They're severe. And they aren't yours to bring about so frivolously. You two have attracted remarkable people to you and roped them into something entirely unreasonable. Have you considered why they were willing to follow you? Have you considered what they stand to gain, or more importantly, what they stand to lose if things don't settle the way you implied they would?"

Behind him, back in the cave, I saw Sol struggling to rise. His celestial spear had been returned to him, driven through the meat of his left thigh in such a way as to render the entire limb useless.

"I never lied," I said defiantly.

"No," Socrates acknowledged. "You didn't. But neither did you tell the clear truth. You decided they didn't deserve it."

I bared my teeth and forced my body to move, sitting up from the edge.

"You don't know me."

"You're right," he admitted. "But I've experienced you. And I've experienced your father."

My eyes widened.

"You scarlet sons are all the same," the wise man said, bending down and gripping in his fist the golden shawl that I'd been using both as a belt and as a satchel for my tribulation mask. He lifted me up by it, regarding me critically. "You want to see all there is to see, do all that there is to do, and damn all the natural consequences. You want to challenge, and to be challenged? So be it."

He turned, and the muscles of his arm bulged.

"Behold—tribulation."

And he threw me up into the Storm That Never Ceased.

Chapter Fifty-Seven

THE SON OF ROME

"Bastard," I snarled. "Vile old wretch. Low life latrine digger. I'll put you on a *cross*."

"I'm sure you will," Socrates said, unimpressed. My vitriol did not slow his stride a single pace, nor loosen his iron grip on the back of my neck.

We walked in lock step down Kaukoso Mons. Socrates had evidently decided against a repeat performance of our rapid ascent, and with nothing else available, I had no choice but to use as a cane the same spear that had crippled my left leg. Above, the immortal storm of the Raging Heaven Cult continued to roar. And Griffon was somewhere up there in it.

"If you've killed him, I'll—"

"Crucify me. Yes, you just said that."

I lashed out with an elbow, but I might as well have been striking the mountain. Socrates didn't even flinch, he just tightened his grip on the back of my neck until darkness crept in around the edges of my vision.

"What's up there?" I ground out, focusing on the stone-cut steps as we descended. One foot in front of the other. I'd been beaten black and blue, broken and crippled in several places, and Griffon had not fared much better. I had no doubt that he had survived the impact, some-how, but I had no way of knowing what he was contending with up in the clouds. The peak of Kaukoso Mons was entirely closed off from sight by the eternal storm, a pillar of wrath that rose all the way up to heaven.

"What do you think, boy?" Socrates asked. After a bit of silence, he shook me by the neck like a stray dog. "That wasn't rhetorical."

I thought back to the first time I had ascended these steps with Anastasia. What she had told me about the Raging Heaven and its perpetual storm.

"The members of the cult call this place a monument to hubris," I answered, my unease growing. "Which would make the storm a monument to tribulation."

"Accurate enough," he said, turning us off onto a winding path that continued down through a series of transplanted grottos. Idly, he grabbed a wild pear from a sagging branch, inexplicably ripe despite the current winter season. He took a bite and chewed noisily, a consid-ering look in his plain brown eyes. "But far from the full picture. You understand the basis of tribulation, yes? Aristotle taught you that much?"

I scowled. "Tribulation is heaven's punishment for man's hubris."

"Go on."

"When we reach beyond our station, there's always a greater force to remind us of our place," I said. "When a man runs out of other men to remind him of his limits, Heaven steps in."

"Artful, but not the path I was looking to go down."

"What do you want me to say?" I asked, irritated. "Tribulation is tribulation. Past a certain point, a cultivator gets struck by lightning every time they advance."

"Better," he said, and I scoffed. His hand otherwise occupied with guiding me by the neck, the wiseman instead slammed my face against a nearby pear tree, cracking the bark. "Discourse doesn't have to be an art form at all times. The world is full of wonders enough without trying to fabricate your own from delicate language."

A Greek suggesting utilitarianism to a Roman. Griffon had rubbed off on me more than I thought.

"You're saying the Storm That Never Ceases is more than just a storm," I said. It was an obvious thing, something anyone could guess just by looking at the localized pillar of clouds that never once drifted out of place. But I had to know. I had to be sure of what Griffon was facing.

"It is, and it is not," Socrates said. "What distinguishes lightning from tribulation lightning?"

"Intent."

"And what makes you think so?"

I gave the question the attention it deserved. I thought back. "Only during moments of ascension have I seen lightning fall from clear blue skies."

"And that means it never does otherwise?" Socrates pressed. "Do you see everything there is to see, in the past, present, and future?"

I frowned. "No, but-—"

"But?"

"But lightning doesn't strike from a clear sky with no reason. That's ridiculous."

"Life is ridiculous, boy. Until we discern the why and the how, the what will always be absurd. A common mistake of cultivators is to draw a line in the sand between acts of nature and acts of cultivation as if the two are clear and distinct from one another. As if there's any separation at all. How can you *know* that this is something unique to tribulation lightning?"

We took another turn, back onto a stone-carved stairway, but these were overlaid by marble without any jewel veins, and they led *into* the mountain rather than up or down it.

"You claimed that a philosopher was a man who knew his limits, that he knows nothing at all," Socrates continued with an odd sort of disdain. He sighed. "Statements like that are pleasing to the ear, and not necessarily untrue, but they lack substance. Philosophers, in the end, are men that understand there are countless things in this world that we do not know. The field of natural philosophy, then, is a man's attempt to understand the rules of nature, in as many small degrees as he can before he dies.

"It is easy to prove a man wrong," the old philosopher said.

"What's hard is proving him right. So I'll ask you again. What distinguishes the light that strikes before thunder from the punishment of heaven?

I inclined my head, grudgingly, and admitted, "I don't know."

"Good. An honest answer."

"What's the difference?" I asked him, after a beat.

Socrates shrugged. "I'm sure your friend will tell you if he survives."

"What was the point of that if you didn't intend to tell me anything?" I asked, frustrated. Socrates glanced sidelong at me.

"I'm trying to see if there's anything behind your eyes, boy. If you're not satisfied with the answers you're getting, ask better questions."

I bit down on my tongue, stifling my vitriol. I thought hard.

"Has the storm always been here?"

"Nothing has always been anywhere."

"Was the storm here before the city?" I amended.

He grunted. "No."

"And what about the cult?"

"What *about* the cult?"

I scowled but clarified, "Which came first? The Storm That Never Ceases or the Raging Heaven Cult?"

"The storm."

My thoughts whirled. The city first, then the storm, then the cult. As Griffon had explained it to me, and as I had seen for myself back in the Scarlet City, the greater mystery cults of the free Mediterranean were established around natural mysteries. Entities, like the bisected corpse of the fallen sun god, that defied all explanation. That could not be understood by mortal minds.

"Is the storm the mystery?" I asked. Socrates inclined his head.

"It is."

"Then that means it's a part of the initiation rites," I guessed.

"It does."

"So it's safe," I pressed, willing it to be true.

Socrates barked a short, ugly laugh. "No, boy. No, it isn't that at all. Tell me, what do you know of the Raging Heaven Cult?"

461

"It's a cult composed of other cults. A nexus for cultivators in the same way that the city of Olympia is a nexus for Greek cultures."

"True enough," he said. "I assume, perilous as the act may be, that Aristotle at least touched upon Olympia's political significance?"

I nodded, as much as I could with his iron grip on the back of my neck. I had asked him often for stories about the Olympic Games, after all. "It's called the sanctuary city because no matter what conflict plagues the Mediterranean, each of her cities set aside their struggles to come together and compete in the games. Every four years, from the moment the Olympic flame is lit until the champion is crowned, there is peace in the Mediterranean."

"For a given definition of peace," Socrates said. "But yes. The Olympic Games serve as a quad-annual armistice, an opportunity, slim as it may be, for unreasonable men to experience a moment of clarity. The city of Olympia, as the host of the games, has taken on a sanctuary status as a result. Regardless of the alliances and feuds between the city states, Olympia remains a neutral entity. Because if nothing else, it needs to be standing for us to enjoy our games. And that is something even the most hated enemies can agree upon."

"All the world for bread and circus," I murmured, recognizing the sentiment for what it was. It was almost nostalgic, the reminder of my days before the legions—before Aristotle even. When all that really mattered was who won the chariot races that day.

"Some things are the same no matter where you go," Socrates agreed. "Now, in the same way that the city and its games serve as neutral territory, so too does the Raging Heaven Cult. A cultivator's solution to a cultivator problem."

My brow furrowed. "I don't understand."

"Of course you don't," Socrates said, utterly exasperated. "Why do you think I was so furious with the two of you? You have no idea the forces at play here. The Raging Heaven Cult is neutral ground for cultivators, and the greater mystery cults, in particular. It is not coincidence that each of the cult's elders are Tyrants from different city-states. What does that tell you?"

I considered it. The Olympic Games were a miracle of political maneuvering, but they only occurred once every four years and for a

short period of time. It was one thing for a man to set aside his griev-
ances for five days. It was entirely another to do so indefinitely. And yet
here were the Tyrants of each of the greater mystery cults, coexisting
for centuries without any overt conflict between them.

That alone was astounding, but there was something about it that
gave me pause. Just before I answered, my teeth clicked together. I
went over his question again in my head, examining every word.

It is not coincidence that each of the cult's elders are **Tyrants** *from
different city-states.*

Tyrants.

"Cultivation makes us more of who we are," I murmured. I didn't
know much about the Greek style, but some things were universal. "A
Philosopher grows by acting as a philosopher. A Hero grows when
accomplishing heroic things."

"And a Tyrant grows in acts of tyranny," Socrates finished the
thought. He waved his free hand. "Go on."

"A man doesn't become a tyrant by mistake, and a cultivator
doesn't make it that far by chance," I said, frowning. "Why would
someone like that accept a position in an institution like this? What is
there to conquer in a city dedicated to neutrality?"

"Nothing at all," Socrates answered. Still, he seemed expectant.

"Then why?" I pressed. "Why are they here if they know it will
stifle their cultivation?"

Everything I knew of the Greeks, and their cultivators especially,
told me that it didn't make any sense. Their tyrants were not loyal to
their own in the same way that a Roman dictator was loyal to the
Republic. They had no concept of hanging up their laurel crowns and
returning to their humble estates. The ideal of Cincinnatus did not
exist here. So why?

"What is here that's worth more than their advancement?"

"You've made an assumption that you have no basis for," Socrates
said. I looked at him, confused. He elaborated, "You assumed that they
came here looking for something. More than that, you assumed that
they chose to come here at all."

My eyes widened.

"It goes against a tyrant's nature to exist peacefully beside his rivals," Socrates said with utter contempt as we reached the bottom of the marble stairway and stepped through an amethyst archway. "But it is perfectly within a tyrant's nature to break his rivals one by one and gather them beneath him. The elders of the Raging Heaven Cult are not here because they chose to be. They are here because the kyrios went out into the world and broke them, each in turn, and dragged their beaten bodies back to this city."

We stepped into the late kyrios' estate, into the heart of Kaukoso Mons.

A facsimile of a courtyard awaited us, a grand cavern with ceilings high enough that it would have been impossible to see them if not for the amethyst veins that ran through the stone, emitting a faint but enduring light. Burning braziers lined the walls, and torches jutted out from grand, towering pillars that rose from floor to ceiling. Eight pillars in all, and the torches affixed to each burned with a different colored flame. The place reeked of smoke, though the air was entirely clear.

The walls of the courtyard inside the mountain were cut by a Pythagorean's fine hand, cornered eight times. A massive octagon and a pillar for each side. The tip of my spear made an odd chiming sound as it came down to support my next step, and when I looked down, I saw that the path beneath our feet wasn't simple stone but instead a mosaic trail made of ivory and gold shards. It wound ahead of us into the octagonal courtyard, spiraling in the center to create a massive portrait of a man that I didn't recognize before branching off eight ways towards each of the eight walls of the courtyard.

Each mosaic path, as it left the ivory and gold center, drifted from those colors into other gemstone shades until eventually, they matched the color of the flame burning upon that side's pillar.

Each path ended at a ceremonial tripod. At the moment, all of those tripods were empty.

Except for one.

"Solus!"

"Selene?" I asked incredulously, watching her leap off her tripod and rush towards us.

"You're hurt!" she exclaimed, stopping just a step away from me and leaning forward, her hands hovering over my most visible wounds. I couldn't see her eyes behind her golden veil, but now that I knew to look for it, I could see the faint glow cast by her scarlet heart flames. It was easy to imagine those eyes flickering anxiously across my body.

"He's fine," Socrates said gruffly.

"He's beaten half to death," Selene countered. "Who did this to him? Where did you find him—" Abruptly, she stopped and drew herself up to her full height—which wasn't very tall, admittedly. "Did you do this to him?"

"I did," Socrates admitted without shame.

"*Why?*"

"You know why," he said. He urged me forward, brushing aside the girl in the sun rays silks, though without particular force. She fell in step just behind me, hands flickering out as if to steady me and then returning to her sides. "If this one and his friends are to be believed, you saw firsthand what he's been doing."

"That is that, and this is this," she said hotly. I felt a powerful sense of vertigo as the daughter of a Tyrant scolded one of the most powerful men I had ever met. "He can barely walk."

"He'll live," Socrates dismissed. "Or he won't. It's not worth complaining about."

"What are you doing here?" I asked her, finally finding my voice.

Socrates rolled his eyes. "Where did you think the Oracles spent their time when they weren't in their temples?"

I stopped short and was promptly dragged off my feet when Socrates did not. The spear went out from under me, and I collapsed to the ivory and gold mosaic floor, staring at the young girl that immediately bent to help me up.

"You're an Oracle?" I asked her, stunned.

Selene bit her lip. "I am."

A few things suddenly made significantly more sense, and others made even less. Knowing that she was an Oracle, it only took me a moment to realize which Oracle she was. Her sun-stained attire was far from subtle, as was the fact that she had literally hopped off a scarlet tripod to approach us.

"You're the Álikoan Oracle?" I said, accepting her hand and

allowing myself to be pulled back to my feet. Broken bones twinged, and my leg continued to hang worthlessly beneath my body.

"Yes."

Socrates made an impatient sound, dissatisfied with how quickly I was regaining my balance. Selene ducked under my arm, the one holding my spear cane, and shouldered the weight of my left side. Socrates continued on, and though I heavily considered making a break for it and trying to retrieve Griffon, I could hardly imagine making it to the foot of the steps before I was caught again. I took a painful step forward and continued on with Selene's support.

"I thought Oracles were meant to be crones," I muttered. Selene dipped her head, and when she answered, her voice was sad.

"They are."

Something else occurred to me, and I glanced around the courtyard, at its eight holy perches. "Those tripods. They're more than simple stools."

"Prophecies are delivered from the seat of heaven," Socrates said idly over his shoulder, walking over the unfamiliar mosaic portrait in the center of the courtyard and continuing straight, following the ivory and gold path.

"But why are they down here?" I asked, confused. "The Oracles have temples outside where they can take visitors. Why would they need them here—"

And I understood.

"Go on, then," Socrates demanded. "Share your discovery with the room."

"The kyrios is king in his domain," I said, the pieces coming together like a grand mosaic in my head. "In a lesser cult, that might mean presiding over Heroes, Philosophers, and Citizens. But here, the kyrios reigns over Tyrants, too."

A tyrant among tyrants. And a hunger to match.

"He claimed the Oracles for himself," I said, looking around at the courtyard with new eyes. "He used Alexander's assault on the free cities as an excuse, and he brought them here. He built a temple in his own estate, and he filled it with every Oracle under the sun. For *himself*."

"You begin to see what power the Tyrant of Olympia commands," Socrates said, coming to a set of ivory doors at the far side of the courtyard and pressing them open. "This is what the elders of the Raging Heaven, each of them a Tyrant in their own domain, is maneuvering to seize for themselves. This is the struggle that you and your idiot friend have so brazenly inserted yourselves into."

I limped into the next room with Selene's help and beheld the late kyrios' quarters. Grandiose, yes. Ostentatious, absolutely. They were as different from Damon Aetos' personal office as was heaven from earth. Unfortunately, I didn't have time to properly appreciate the sight. Socrates had already thrown open another ivory door and stalked farther into the bowels of the mountain.

"Where are we going?" I finally asked, unable to remain silent. "And why?"

For all that we had miserably failed, Griffon and I had assaulted the old philosopher with everything we had. Though it hadn't left any lasting marks, we had struck him. And though he had consigned Griffon to the storm, he'd acknowledged that it was a place he could return from. Socrates hadn't killed him, and he had yet to kill me. Why, when he was so furious with what we had done?

"I told you already. I know you have ears, boy."

I have no choice but to make right what he left unfinished.

Socrates threw open another door, the most ostentatious yet, and we entered into an utterly unadorned room.

To call it a room at all was a stretch. Where the rest of the kyrios' subterranean estate was obviously man-made, painstakingly carved out of the mountain and filled with earthly treasures, this room looked like nothing so much as a small cavern. There were no mosaic floors, no pillars, and the walls were naturally rugged and uneven.

The door shut behind us, and the only light in the room came from the amethyst veins in the walls. Just bright enough, with a cultivator's enhanced sight, to see what lay at the center of the room.

"Aristotle left you unfinished," Socrates said, crossing his arms. "And now I'm faced with two options. I can let your foolish choices lead you to their natural conclusions, or I can finish your education and perhaps watch you live long enough to become a virtuous man."

467

"What does this have to do with that?" I asked, staring at the stone slab jutting up out of the ground—the only thing in the room with a clean, angular silhouette. It was a tablet the size of a man, and it was covered in chiseled script.

"A virtuous man is a worldly man," Socrates said. "And a worldly man must speak the language wherever he may be."

I thought back to the *Eos*, to Griffon's uncanny ability to speak to several men who couldn't possibly understand his mother tongue, and how easily he had understood them. And I thought of all the cultivators that I had spoken to since arriving at the sanctuary city—

That I had spoken to in *Latin*.

I knelt, painfully, before the tablet. Selene settled beside me, the glow of her eyes behind her golden veil all the more apparent in the dark room.

"This is how cultivators speak to one another?" I asked. Socrates grunted.

"All languages are united by a singular purpose," he explained. "To convey, from one soul to another, and to be heard. The sounds may differ, but the intent remains the same. Every culture has a foundational myth, their first story worth telling. Each of those stories is written on this shard of Babylon, and every other shard in kind."

I stared at the tablet. Without a doubt in my mind, I knew that something like this did not exist in the city of Rome.

"Read it," Socrates commanded. "And be learned. I refuse to teach a man that only speaks barbarian tongues."

I traced over the script, each carefully carved line. The stone was covered from edge to edge, three sections neatly separated from one another, each in a different language that changed as I looked at them. The text itself was cleanly carved. Easily discerned, even in the low light.

And yet...

"I can't."

"You **what?**"

Selene tensed beside me at the old philosopher's dangerous tone.

"Do you mean to tell me, boy," Socrates said with violent intonation, "that after all the grief he gave me about the value of the written word, Aristotle did not teach you to *read?*"

"It's not that," I said, annoyed and frustrated in equal measure. I could feel the beginning of a headache coming on in addition to all my other injuries. "It's... it's a mess. Like two stories written over top of one another."

As soon as I verbalized it, I had an idea. I closed my left eye, and abruptly, half of the overlapping text vanished, and I could read the middle section.

Begin our singing with the Heliconian Muses,
Who possess Mount Helicon, high and holy,
And near its violet-stained spring on petal-soft feet,
Dance circling the altar of almighty -------

"Why did you close your eye?" Socrates demanded, and I looked up, startled.

"I can read it now."

"With only your right eye?" he pressed, sounding for some reason more agitated than he had at any point since our first encounter outside of the bathhouse.

I looked back at the shard from Babylon and closed my right eye, opening my left.

I sing of arms and of the man who first
Came from the coasts of Troy to Italy
And the Lavinian shores, exiled by fate.

"I see a different story with each eye," I realized, recognizing both from childhood days. "The *Theogony* and the *Aeneid.*"

"Oh," Selene breathed.

And as I continued to read both, alternately opening one eye and closing the other, I felt something inexplicable and profound winding into me through my eyes, through my skull, and down the line of my spine. Something primordial, of the same association as what I had felt while I looked upon the bisected corpse of the fallen sun god. Something powerful.

And I was interrupted again as Socrates slammed a clenched fist against the stone behind him hard enough to shatter it.

"Two stories," he spat. "*Two stories.* I'm going to murder that negligent son of three whores."

"What?" I asked, utterly lost.

"You aren't meant to see two stories, boy. These tablets show you your culture's founding myth. What you see on that stone is a reflection of what you are. It's a marker of your culture. And you see Greece *and* Rome."

He struck the wall again. I coughed at the overpowering taste of smoke.

"Your foundation isn't just unfinished," Socrates said with mounting wrath.

Selene finished his thought, utterly fascinated.

"It's split in two."

Chapter Fifty-Eight

THE YOUNG GRIFFON

What is the nature of tribulation?

Back when I had leapt from the top of the eastern mountain range with Sol at my side, in the throes of my ascension to the Sophic Realm, I had experienced a moment of perfect weightlessness, freedom in the truest sense. And then, when reality had asserted itself—as it always did—my stomach had risen into my throat, a giddy and exhilarating sensation in its own way. It was enough to put a smile on my face whenever I thought back on it.

When Socrates threw me at the sun, my breath was slammed out of me as if the sky itself had punched me in the gut. I spun madly, without control, the world little more than a revolving blur of mountain and city and skies above. Then, I reached the storm and plunged into the wrathful crown of the Raging Heaven Cult.

At once, I was drenched from head to toe. The clouds were shockingly cold and alive with dancing threads of lightning, spreading like grasping hands through the moisture in the air. I struggled to right myself, twisting and throwing out my arms. I had just begun to regain control when I saw the face of the mountain rushing forward to greet me.

[Dawn shines forth with rosy fingers.]

Twenty arms of pankration intent struck out, some grasping me and others reaching out for the mountain's jutting ridges. The same way that I had helped my younger cousins learn how to flip and contort their bodies in the air as children, by tossing them up and guiding them back down with steady hands, my pankration intent did the same for me. I flipped myself, bleeding off as much momentum as I could by bouncing back-and-forth between the hands of my own intent, and then I hit the mountain, tucking my shoulders and rolling until everything came to a stop.

Panting harshly and nearly vibrating with adrenaline, I rose into a crouch and assessed my situation.

I was somewhere inside the immortal storm that hung around the peak of Kaukoso Mons, that much was obvious. How far up I was, how close to the hidden peak, I had no idea. But I was far enough up that I noticed the effort when I inhaled. It wasn't just that the air was frigidly cold. It was also thin—more so than it had ever been at the top of the eastern mountain range back home. The mountain itself didn't seem to be much different up here, but immersed in the clouds as I was, I could only see a few feet in front of my face. Even with the light of dawn in my twenty-two palms. The only way I could truly gauge distance was by watching the—

Lightning struck beside me, close enough to electrify the fine hairs on my arms and make my teeth buzz in my mouth. I rolled sideways, watching another searing lance strike the stone where I had just stood.

I tried to curse the old philosopher that had thrown me up here, but instead, I coughed up a mouthful of blood.

I rolled away from another thread of lightning, hacking blood as I went.

Well. This seemed appropriate.

As it turned out, the storm was aptly named.

"*Whimpering Heaven,*" I growled regardless, the taste of my own blood thick on my tongue. The stone was slick this far up the mountain, treacherous. What paths that existed were even more so.

I leaned sharply back, lightning arcing past my face and striking an outcrop of stone. As it passed, though, thin trailing fingers split off and grasped the tip of my nose. My teeth slammed together, muscles locking up as the lightning coursed through me. I exhaled a seething breath and just barely managed to wrench back control of myself from the storm.

But there *were* paths. And that suggested something that I had suspected but never known for certain. I raced down the path as fast as I dared to, crouching low as I went. I had tried jumping only once. It had nearly killed me, just like that. The skies weren't safe. Not even for a moment.

Heaven was my enemy.

But returning to the paths. It was simply the case that the mystery cults of the free Mediterranean hoarded their confounding questions at all costs. The mystery of a cult was its founding myth, the thesis statement upon which the entire institution was built. These treasures were hoarded from the public, from outsiders, and even from the cult's own initiates outside of significant occasions. It was not within the power of a Rosy Dawn mystiko to gaze upon the bisected corpse of the fallen sun god whenever the urge struck them.

It was simple enough to guard that corpse, of course. After all, it was buried in the heart of a vast mountain range. But not all cults were as the Rosy Dawn. Not all mysteries were buried beneath spans and spans of ancient rock.

How did one guard a mystery with no natural barriers? How did one obscure from view something in plain sight? Out in the open air? Every cult had its own initiation rites, governed by a unique set of rules and regulations. But the purpose of those rites was always the same.

Of course, I could have been wrong. The Raging Heaven's mystery could have been buried somewhere deep within the mountain. It could have been somewhere else entirely, separate from Kaukoso Mons. Or, perhaps, the Raging Heaven was as unique in this regard as it was in every other. Perhaps there was no mystery at all.

But as I watched another bolt of lightning arc down from wrathful Heaven and abruptly diverge, striking the upraised hand of a cowering stone statue, I began to doubt.

I slid down slick stone until I was crouched beneath the cowering giant. Light flashed—once, twice, three and then four times. The storm hammered relentlessly down on the statue of a long dead monster, and I felt the fury behind it.

I stayed there for a long while, staring up as Heaven came down, safe from the storm only because I was crouched in the shadow of something that it hated far more than me.

"Porphyrion," I murmured to the monument of the twice-disgraced Giant. "Look at you. Greatest of the great striders, king of those that shake the earth. Isn't that what they called you? How can you bear to see your likeness chiseled by such a disrespectful hand? Why can't I hear your soul howling in outrage all the way from bleak Tartarus? They made you look like a *coward*."

Heaven screamed and struck the destitute king of Giants, over and over again.

I looked down the mountain. I still couldn't see more than a few feet in any direction. I had no way of knowing how far I was from the storm's edge. I had no way of knowing what Socrates was doing to my brother, now that I wasn't there to stand beside him. The Fates and Muses knew that our Heroic companions would not stand there in my place.

I looked back up at poor Porphyrion. While he cowered and held a helpless hand up against heaven, his other hand hung worthless beside him. In that hand, insult of insults, the statue's maker had placed a sword. Never to be properly wielded. Never to be brought to bear. Forever held back in hesitation and fear while its wielder flinched beneath the storm.

No. Not forever.

Pankration hands gripped the Giant's clenched fist, flaring with the rosy light of dawn and prying apart his fingers. Ancient stone cracked and shattered, and a sword longer than I was tall fell into my waiting arms. I heaved it up onto one shoulder. Its edge was far too dull to cut me.

"Let's see what Heaven has to say when the damned strike it back," I said fiercely and charged out from under the Giant's silhouette.

I felt the lightning come, a vibration in the air that I could taste on my tongue. I dug my heels in and stopped as abruptly as I had started, pivoted, and slammed the Giant's blade into the mountain.

I let go and watched the lightning veer sideways at the last moment and strike the pommel of the giant's sword, rather than me. I waited a second longer than I needed to, and then I heaved it out of the stone.

"Is that all?" I taunted the Fates, pounding pankration fists against the ground as I stood tall.

There came a low, rolling growl like the thunder that preceded lightning. I turned my head and beheld a hound of pure, shocking light prowling up the path towards me.

"Heel," I commanded the storm hound. It barked in response, the sound like a thunderclap.

I turned and sprinted back up the mountain.

Time passed. I knew because my rosy palms grew progressively dimmer as the morning turned to afternoon. Or perhaps that was my own internal sundial sabotaging me. Certainly, there was no way to tell by sight alone. The storm was thick, oppressive, and utterly unrelenting.

I found more hounds.

The distinction between a virtuous beast and a typical animal was similar to the difference between a cultivator and a mortal man, but not quite the same. Beasts could not cultivate in the same manner as thinking men, and so what they did was not entirely equivalent. But it was close enough. Once semantics were stripped away, it became a question of magnitude for both man and monster.

That was the common consensus. That was what my mentors had taught me. But Sol had claimed that his demon dogs had cultivated in the style of men. And though I had dismissed him out of hand at first, I couldn't so readily deny what was now before my eyes.

Hounds could grasp at primitive virtue, given the time, the opportunity, and the primordial strength of will. But no dog could grasp lightning in its teeth. No hound could cast off its flesh and blood and exchange them for the storm.

Tribulation hounds stalked me up the mountain, and with the appearance of each one, I was forced to question what I had always known to be the truth.

I planted the Giant king's blade in the mountain and rolled sideways. A thunderclap bark was the only warning I got before the hound lunged. Light flashed, and the giant's blade rang like a bell, followed by a yelp that sizzled in the air.

They moved more like the lightning they were composed of than the dogs they had taken the form of. They crouched, and they prowled, that was true enough. They went through the motions of snapping their jaws and lunging like hunters. But the motion that was meant to bridge the gap between crouching and sinking their crackling teeth into prey happened faster than the eye could track. One moment there, the next, gone.

I had been clipped by lightning three times before the first hound had found me. I hadn't allowed anything to touch me since. I knew in my virtuous heart that the fourth strike would be justice rendered. If one of these dogs got their teeth in me, I wouldn't be getting them out.

I spotted another looming silhouette up ahead and wrenched free the giant's blade with hands of manifested pneuma while I rushed up to it.

I'd also found more monuments to the condemned.

I lunged and rolled beneath another statue as Heaven struck down, my heart hammering a frenetic beat in my chest as the lightning slammed into the hunched shoulders of a struggling stone man.

"Isn't it sad, Sisyphus?" I asked the degraded tyrant. He didn't respond, preoccupied as he heaved against the boulder that was his perpetual punishment—and also, perhaps, because he was made of stone.

I gripped the blade buried in his stone back and wrenched it free, passing it off to a pankration hand and adding it to my growing collection. That made eight suffering souls thus far. Seven stolen blades and one Giant's broadsword were my weapons against the storm. Periodically, as the lightning struck and I had no sorry victim to shelter in the shadow of, my pankration hands would offer their blades up to heaven and dispel the moment before they struck.

Dodging the blades after the lightning blew them out of the sky was a trial, but it was one I was well-suited to handle. It was far better than the alternative, at any rate.

"Take heart," I told the statue of Sisyphus, clapping him on the shoulder and squinting up the mountain. "I think we're nearly at the top."

Thunderclaps sounded below as well as to my right. Upward it was.

Fatigue began to take its toll.

There were many things a cultivator could do without. Sleep, sustenance, even water in the most extreme circumstances. Citizens could put off these necessities for days at a time with the proper conditioning. Philosophers even longer, and Heroes longer than that until at a certain point a mortal man could be born and die before a Tyrant was forced to break his fast.

But no cultivator could go without air. Even the best of us required a moment to breathe. And as much as it galled me to admit, I was approaching my limits. Skulking around and picking off Crows in the night was one thing. This was another entirely.

I fell more than I slid beneath my latest haven, slumping down onto one elbow, precariously close to touching the statue and sharing in its tribulation as lightning struck it over and over again. Twelve pankration hands drove their stolen blades into the stone around me in a circle. I heard barking thunderclaps in the distance—still closer than I preferred.

Rebuffing them with the blades stunned the hounds long enough to put distance between us, but that was all it did. I had tried cutting one by heaving the blade like a javelin at it, but all I'd gotten for my troubles was a re-creation of what happened when I threw the swords up into the air to intercept lightning bolts. Only, ten feet away from me instead. I hadn't tried it again.

"It could be worse, I suppose," I panted. I flashed blood-stained teeth and glanced up at my unwitting protector. "I could be you—"

I blinked and tilted my head.

The Oracle of the Broken Tide sat upon her holy tripod, the seat and the soothsayer both carved out of the mountain itself. Amethyst wound through her body in place of veins, and the tridents in her eyes glowed with the indigo light of prophecy. She was young in this iteration, the lines of her face changed enough that I wasn't sure if this was simply the younger version of the woman I'd met with Kyno or if it was another Oracle entirely.

Either way, she was certainly the Oracle of the Coast. If the eyes hadn't given her away, her company surely would have.

Over a dozen suffering statues were poised around her, flinching, raging, and grasping ineffectually for the light of the sun. These were men I vaguely recognized. Heroes and Tyrants that the Oracle had cast down with her prophecies throughout history. Great men laid low by the heartless judgment of a holy woman. They formed a cage of sorts around her, their bodies acting as the walls, and their grasping, outstretched arms forming a roof of sorts over her head. And as I watched, lightning came down upon them a dozen times in quick succession. It washed over the cage of men each time, dispersing through their arms and down their bodies before a spark could ever touch the woman within.

The statue of the soothsayer stared gravely down at me as if its maker had always known I'd be here, now, looking up at this moment. I could hear her laughing voice in my head, clear as day over the storm.

You scarlet sons are all the same.

I scoffed and rose to my feet, looking down upon the amethyst oracle. From this angle, I could see the inscription on her seashell crown.

Melpomene

"I've seen you before," I dismissed her. "Show me your sisters."

Lightning flashed, forking seven ways. I traced the path of each branch and then favored the oracle and her crown of tragedy with a wild smile.

"My thanks," I said earnestly, and the fatigue was surely getting worse because I would swear on my deathbed that I saw the statue wink.

• • •

I found the oracles one by one. It wasn't how I had originally intended to meet them, true enough, but even a storm like this had its silver linings.

I found the Fuchsia Oracle first, with her crown of risen foam, and I beheld the throng of maddened suitors and scorned lovers gathered around her in a perversion of a cage. I looked her in her sultry eyes, admittedly less tempting when cast from stone, and addressed her by the name carved with amethyst into her crown.

"Erato," I greeted the Oracle of Foúskia. "I've come to seek your wisdom. Tell me, what is the nature of tribulation?"

I blinked and dropped each of the swords in my hands to rub the fatigue out of my eyes. When I looked again, her smile was no longer deepening. She was simple stone again. Behind me, I heard the snarling rumble of thunder that preceded attack, and I lunged inside the oracle's cage of statued men.

I watched the tribulation hound strike the cage, and instead of rebounding as all its siblings had when I'd intercepted them with a flying blade, it yelped and howled as it was wrenched apart by the many linked limbs that made up the bars of the cage. I watched as the hound was spread agonizingly thin across the cage. Until, finally, it dispersed with an ear-splitting crack.

Never let it be said that the young Griffon was ungrateful. I bowed my head to the Oracle with the seafoam crown and pressed a kiss to her forehead. If her smile widened, I was too far gone to contemplate it overmuch.

I moved with greater purpose through the storm, sideways more than up or down now. The hounds added new members to the pack to replace the one I had dispersed, but I managed to stay just a few steps ahead of them all the while. I found the oracle of Nkrí next and traced my fingers across her crown of pewter stars.

"Urania," I said to her, "what differentiates the light of tribulation from mundane elements?"

My answer came first as a bolt of lightning striking mindlessly, relentlessly, above our heads, dispersed by the cage of those she had disgraced with her soothsaying. Then, my answer came twice as the hounds caught up to me. This time, however, they didn't lunge blindly into the cage to be dispersed. They paced around it, eyeing me intently.

"Not the answer I would have preferred," I said wryly, flicking the stone nose of the Pewter Oracle. I knew without a doubt that that nose could not have possibly scrunched up in response. It simply didn't make sense. And so I dismissed it and made a break away from the hounds after hurling all of my stolen blades at the pack.

"If tribulation can discern, then it can reason," I proposed to Clio, the other Oracle of the Coast, with her wrought-iron crown. "And if it can reason, does that mean it can be spirited? Does that mean it can *hunger?*"

The good Oracle gazed imperiously down her nose at me, and I followed her stone hand as it pointed in an entirely different direction than the one I recalled, at the pack of hounds roving farther down the mountain. As I watched, one hound among the dozen raised its crackling head to heaven and howled loud enough to shatter my eardrums. From this distance, I could just barely make out the sparks flaring from the corners of its crackling jaw, drooling in its hunger.

I spoke to each of the oracles, seven in all, and I gleaned from each of them a truth of tribulation. Finally, with unspoken anticipation, I hauled my battered body and my eighteen stolen blades—plus the Giant king's broadsword—over the ridge that I had seen marked by the branching lightning. I laid eyes on the Scarlet Oracle.

No. That wasn't true.

I laid eyes on what *remained* of the Scarlet Oracle.

It was carnage carved from stone. There had been an Oracle perched upon a tripod once, and a stone cage of all the great men and women she had cast down with her divine commandments. They were all shattered and cast out now. A miasma of scorched rock and indigo mist hung in their place now, in the glassed crater of what had once been a monument to holy retribution.

Broken, scattered limbs remained, unmoved by the gale winds of the storm, somehow as timeless as the statues they had once been. I stared down into the fractured eyes of the Oracle's severed head, broken in three places, and assembled her name from the pieces of her broken sun crown.

"Calliope," I whispered hoarsely, kneeling beside what remained of her in the crater. I asked of her, "Who did this to you?"

My shadow laid its flickering hand on my shoulders. The raven on the right leaned over my shoulder and whispered the answer into my ear.

"I, your father."

And it pressed the twentieth blade into my hand.

The hounds surrounded me. There were well over a dozen of them now, each of them tall enough at the shoulders to look Myron in the eye. They paced around me in that odd way of theirs, lightning limbs flexing as if to move and then suddenly reappearing several steps away, little more than frenetic flashes of light.

In the end, it was inevitable that they would corner me. After all, no man can escape tribulation.

No man could escape **justice**.

"Tell me something, cousin," Nikolas prompted me, either in a memory or just out of sight. I couldn't be sure which. My head was pounding too hard. My body was aching too fiercely to tell. *"What is the first virtue?"*

"Justice," I whispered because it was what I had been born to say.

Every tribulation hound surrounding me snarled and pounced at once, the whole world turning to blinding light and crashing thunder. Before they had even moved, and as a result just barely in time, my pankration hands drove fifteen of the blades I'd taken from the Raging Heaven's immortal victims into the stone around me, while the remaining five were raised horizontally above my head.

Over a dozen hounds struck my iron cage in tandem, and their agonized howls split the earth.

"And what is justice?" Nikolas asked. I felt his hand dig into my hair and ruffle it, but my neck was far too stiff to turn my head and confirm whether that was a memory or something happening here and now. *"And don't give me Uncle Damon's answer. I want to know what you think."*

Up until this moment, and every time before, I had done everything in my power to avoid touching my stolen blades in the moments that they were intercepting tribulation lightning. After all, it would surely defeat the purpose of using them if I shared in the experience by holding on, whether with hands of flesh and blood or pankration intent.

But that was when I still had hope of escaping a direct conflict. That was when I could still envision a world in which I came out of this any way but straight through.

And that was before I had my answers.

"Justice is a grasping hand," I declared, and I reached back out with twenty hands of pneuma to grasp the pommels of my sword cage while tribulation lightning coursed through it.

Light and heat, unlike anything I had ever experienced before, shot through my soul. I had compared the damage I took in the past by blocking attacks with my pankration hands to real-world injuries, but it had always been metaphor more than material. This time, I doubled over and vomited blood onto the face of the mountain. It sizzled as it left my mouth.

"Justice," I gagged, "is a punch in the gut."

I focused on breathing, on the heat of the Rein-Holder's starlight marrow as it coursed through my scorched and ruined body, mending what it could. I had only touched true tribulation for a fraction of a second, and it had nearly killed me.

But only nearly. And in return, I'd seen it.

The answer to my final question.

"Justice is two clenched fists in return for one," I said, reaching up and rubbing my face. When I lowered my hands, they were covered in blood. "Stained by scarlet sin."

"The world doesn't have to be so brutal, cousin," Nikolas said sadly. I laughed, the sound hysterical, as a dozen more hounds came prowling up the mountain, circling around the blade bars of my cage. Patiently. Ravenously.

"Maybe not," I agreed. The wind was howling. Thunder shook the earth. Sleet and freezing rain washed the blood away nearly as fast as I could bleed it. But I was alive.

And I was free.

"Justice is whatever I can reach."

And I lunged forward, reaching through the cage and grasping lightning. My vision flared white, and my blood flash-boiled in my veins. But those were only impressions. Theoretical truths. What *should* have happened to a man that reached out and caught lightning in his hand.

But I knew now.

"Behold," I snarled triumphantly at the struggling hound. *"Tribulation."*

And I crushed its skull in my fist.

Chapter Fifty-Nine

THE SON OF ROME

"Arrogant, belligerent child," Socrates muttered as he stalked out of the rugged chamber with its shard of tongues. "I'll box his ears until they fall off. Split foundations. *Split foundations!*"

For a long moment, I continued to stare at the shifting text chiseled into the man-size tablet, incomprehensible to me with both eyes open. I still felt that primordial shifting behind my eyes, in my skull, even in my tongue. But the bulk of it had slowed down when I stopped reading, and instinct told me that the process was not yet finished.

"My master is a good man," I said quietly, nearly to myself. Beside me, Selene gripped the arm I had over her shoulder.

"I believe you, Solus."

"He did the best that he could with the materials he was given and the time that he had." I had said it before to Griffon and then to Socrates. "That I am what I am is not a condemnation of him. My failings are my own."

"But you credit him with your successes, don't you?" Selene gently prodded me. I glanced sidelong at her. At some point, she had lifted her golden veil from her face, revealing fine features, burning scarlet eyes, and hair like spun gold.

"It isn't the same," I said.

"Why isn't it?" Socrates called, his irritated voice drifting in from the adjacent chamber. "What differs?"

I gripped my spear and forced myself to stand, my thoughts far too tangled to keep on reading with any real focus. Selene quickly stood up with me, bearing the brunt of my weight with nothing but an encouraging huff. I sighed softly and let her do it, the two of us turning and limping out of the untarnished room.

"In the legions, accountability is king," I said flatly, watching as Socrates rifled through one of the late Kyrios' sleeping chambers. "It isn't within a mentor's power to live my life for me. Aristotle provided me with the tools that I needed to succeed, and so I credit a part of all my successes to him."

"And why not your failures?" Socrates asked, overturning several large, woven reed baskets onto a feather bed covered in silk sheets of indigo and white. Clothing spilled out, tunics and sashes, dress robes for cult business, as well as formal attire for mortal affairs.

"Why should I?" I bit back. "Say that a farmer gives me a scythe and tells me to harvest a crop by sundown, and I return to him with only half the work done because I decided to do it with my hands instead. Is it his fault or mine?"

"Yours, surely enough," Socrates agreed. "But what about a huntsman?"

"What *about* a huntsman?"

"A scythe's function is self-evident when you're standing in a wheat field at harvest—that's clear enough. But what about the workings of a bow and arrow? If a hunter presents you with a bow and a quiver and tells you to bag him a fine buck by sundown, is it his fault or yours when you return empty-handed?"

"Mine."

"Is that so? The man that knows how to track deer, how to stalk them without being spotted, and how—as well as where—to shoot them. That man presents you with a bow and some arrows and a stern demand, and you believe that it's your fault for not living up to his expectation? And if you do, somehow, by the grace of the gods manage to bring something down through your own ingenuity, he deserves a portion of the credit for the kill?"

Socrates held up a tunic of white cloth with crimson arch designs sewn along its edges. He looked between it and me, squinting. I glared back at him.

"The comparison isn't fair."

Socrates threw the tunic at my face. Selene caught it just before it could hit me, and the sound of it striking her palm left me confident that it would have knocked me clean off my feet if it had hit.

"In all three scenarios, each of the masters provided their student with the tools needed to succeed," he said but waved a hand to brush the argument away from him. "But fine, we'll discard the huntsman. What of the fisherman?"

I unwound my arm from Selene's shoulder, ignoring her protest, and leaned heavily onto the celestial bronze spear I had stolen from the temple of the Father. I considered the scenario.

"What's provided?" I asked, finally. Without a set of the parameters, I knew he could wind me into a knot until the end of time.

"A net and a spear," he said, holding a broad leather belt in his hand, considering me before grunting and tossing it back into a basket.

I exhaled, annoyed. "Fishing isn't that hard. Acquiring the tools is more difficult than learning how to use them."

"I know men that would disagree, but let's say you're right. If I gave you a net right now and told you to take that pretty spear of yours and catch me dinner, how many fish could I expect from you by sundown?"

I thought hard about it. Fishing had been a curiosity when I was a boy, a non-issue when I was a soldier in the legions. There was always someone else to do that work. Always more important things to be done. But my time at the Rosy Dawn had humbled me in many ways and re-introduced me to many tasks I hadn't practiced since my father had taught them to me. Fishing was one such task.

So, I considered the time of day, the distance from here to Olympia's port city, and nodded sharply.

"Thirty."

"Good." Socrates reached into a fold in his tunic, and inexplicably, he pulled from it an entire fishing net. He tossed it at my chest with only slightly less force than he had thrown the tunic. "Come back with one hundred by sundown."

I staggered back a step as the net hit my chest but managed to keep my feet. I pretended not to notice the way that Selene hovered behind me, her hands just barely not touching my back. I stared hard at the master of my master's master, temper boiling.

"I can't catch one hundred by sundown," I said quietly.

"I can," Socrates said, turning away from the Kyrios' clothes and moving on to the pots and jars scattered about, perched on high tables and shelves. Each of them was painstakingly painted with images of epics, comedies, tragedies, and more benign depictions of everyday life and nature. He reached into one and pulled out several rolls of bandage cloth, flinging them negligently over his shoulder. Selene leaned past me and caught them all in one hand.

"I can't," I repeated.

"What does that matter? It's possible, because I can do it, and all I would need are the tools I'm giving you. A net, a spear, and a long afternoon. Why can't you bring me one hundred fish, boy?"

"I never said I couldn't bring you one hundred fish," I corrected him, eyes narrow. "I said I couldn't catch them."

"Ho? Will you buy them, then? Steal them, perhaps?"

I shrugged. "You gave me a spear and a net," I said wryly. Selene chuckled softly behind me.

"That I did, that I did. So, in summation, without the accompanying experience, the tools alone are not enough to accomplish the task before you. Leaving you no choice but to cheat or steal your way to success."

Selene laid gentle hands on my shoulders, and I realized that they were horribly tense, my pneuma rising precipitously. I forced myself to relax, to be realistic with the state of my body and the strength of my enemy, and I allowed the Scarlet Oracle to guide me down into a nearby chair.

"Life is not something that can be summed up in a single neat scenario," I said tiredly. Socrates laughed.

"Exactly right. What Aristotle did to you is not equal to the huntsman or the fisherman. It is *worse*. Do you know why it is that cultivators so often die young despite having the potential to live unfathomably long lives?"

I did.

"The ideal of cultivation is to begin at the foot of the mountain and end at the peak," I said, brushing off Selene when she went to touch my wounded leg and taking the roll of bandage cloth from her hand. "The experience of cultivation, on the other hand, is the reverse."

"Beginning at the peak?" the girl in the sun ray silks asked, curious. I nodded.

"Cultivation is a chariot teetering on the peak of a mountain. Once it starts rolling, there's no stopping it until it hits the bottom."

"In pieces or otherwise," Socrates mused. I grunted in agreement. "A greater understanding than most men your age have. But that only means you have more reason to see my meaning."

I kept my silence, peeling back blood-soaked cloth from my left leg and going to work with the bandages provided. It was stubborn of me. It was prideful. But it was who I was.

"A person's failings don't invalidate their virtues," Selene said quietly, kneeling beside me.

My shoulders slumped, pressed down by the weight of three thousand dead men.

Salt and ash.

"Of course they do."

"Aristotle may not have been the one to place you in that chariot," Socrates said. "He may not have even been the one to push you down the mountain. But he changed your trajectory, and he split your wheels. When you take upon yourself the mantle of mentor to another, you're to blame for a portion of everything that follows. The good and the ill."

The great philosopher shook his head, emptying out the last clay jar in the room and sighing in disgust at what he found.

"Greedy old dog," he muttered.

"What are you looking for?" Selene asked. "I may be able to help."

"Can't find what isn't here," he said. "The late lord decided to take all the advantages he could with him to heaven. Or Tartarus, as it turned out. His stores of nectar and ambrosia are all gone. It'll be the long road to recovery for you, boy."

I looked down at the bandages wrapped tight around my left thigh, already staining red. The hand that I had broken in catching a punch for Griffon throbbed incessantly, something distant but inescapable. The rest of my body felt like one all-encompassing bruise.

"I'll be fine."

"Good, because you have some work ahead of you. You've made a mess of things, and I won't be cleaning it up for you." Socrates pulled a handful of cloth from the pile and began wrapping garments haphazardly around himself, constructing his veil of inconsequence right before our eyes. "You'll stay here for the time being."

I reached for anger; I reached for rage. All I found was bone-deep exhaustion. "First, you beat me like a dog, and now you cage me like one, too."

"It's safe inside this cage," he said, turning and stepping through the next door, out into the underground courtyard with its ivory and gold mosaic floor. "You've been snapping at lions' heels. If I hadn't stepped in when I did, you and your friend both would have been dead before the changing of the seasons. You might still be."

"What do I do here, then? Twirl my thumbs and await your pleasure? I have to speak to the others. If nothing else, I can save you the trouble of them coming after you."

Socrates scoffed, not even bothering to look back. "Not everyone in this city is as uninformed as you. Even fewer are as flagrant. I have nothing to fear from a handful of lost souls."

"Griffon will come for you," I said with rock-solid certainty. "At least let me speak to him."

"You're free to speak to whoever you like," he said, turning just before stepping through the archway leading back out of the mountain. "So long as you don't leave this place." And then he was gone, moving without particular haste up the steps. Eventually, even the sound of his footsteps faded.

I sighed and leaned back in my chair, letting my head loll.

"I can carry a message for you, Solus," Selene offered with mingled hesitance and excitement.

In lieu of a response, I pursed my lips and whistled a sharp, clarion call. It echoed in the vast courtyard outside the room, reverberating throughout the mountain. I inhaled deeply the scent of cypress smoke and waited, ignoring my aches and pains with long practice.

Only when I heard the beating of wings did I finally tilt my head, meeting Selene's curious gaze.

"He forbade me from leaving, but he didn't say anything about my bird."

I found my lips curling, just the slightest bit as the girl's face lit up, and she turned to welcome Sorea as the messenger bird of prey came swooping down into the bowels of the mountain.

I would need to find some papyrus and ink, but it would be enough to send the others a letter for now. Once I shook off the worst of my injuries, I'd find Griffon and we would regroup. I had what felt like a thousand things to tell him, and instinct told me that he would have just as much to say when he came down from the Storm That Never Ceased.

That he would return alive wasn't even a question. Socrates had allowed it as a possibility, and if it was possible, Griffon would see it done.

"Selene," I said, lifting my head with some effort and watching her croon to Sorea as the great eagle shuffled around on the floor, surveying the kyrios' estate.

The girl in the sun ray silks looked back at me, eyes burning merrily. "Yes, Solus?"

"Do you want to hear a story?"

Her smile was dazzling.

Chapter Sixty

LEFTERIS, THE GOLD-STRING GUARDIAN

Names were strange things.

Eleftherios. Lefteris for short. Neither name had been given to him at birth, but his mother had told him from a young age, over and over until he was old enough for the sentiment to stick, that his name was too dangerous for the world to know. That it was a secret between the two of them that had to be kept at all costs.

They moved often, early on. Each place was a new home, and each home meant a new name. It was safer that way, his mother insisted. This way if anyone did find out his true name, they wouldn't be able to track them through the fake. If every village and every city knew him by a different moniker, they would be safe.

One day, when he was five years old, he asked his mother why she had named him at all if it was such a burden. It wasn't the first time he's seen her cry, but it was the one he remembered most vividly. He'd tried comforting her, blindly, the way that young children did—assuring her of things he had no understanding of and no ability at all to deliver on.

A child's platitudes always cut deepest. Because unlike with an adult, you knew they believed them wholeheartedly. That they didn't understand some things were impossible in such an ugly world.

He grew up, eventually, and came to understand the way of things. He took what control of his life he could, deciding that if he had to live under a fake identity that it would be one of his choosing. He chose an audacious name, admittedly, but after a lifetime of hiding, he felt he was due some audacity.

Eleftherios. The liberator.

He had grown up, but that didn't mean he had entirely given up on those ideals. He would do what he could. And when he could, however he could, he would help those who suffered like he had suffered.

Until the day his name caught up to him.

"Theri," the usurper whispered. Another nickname—one that the boy had decided on himself. He was poised on hands and knees at the edge of the cave, peering out as far as he dared. The boy was equal parts curious and wary. "Who is it?"

Lefteris didn't move, didn't look back, didn't even flare his pneuma in wordless response. He didn't dare to.

Not while the Gadfly was watching him.

There were some things that were universal in the free Mediterranean. Stories of people and places that every Greek child, even one such as him, cut their teeth on around crackling fires. Every young boy had shed bitter tears at least once for the tragedy of Heracles, the Champion, cut down in his eleventh labor so unjustly after completing the tenth. Every free citizen knew of the Conqueror and his greed, knew to fear him and to never speak his name directly because there was no guarantee he wouldn't hear them say it.

And, of course, every academic with a thought in their heads knew of the Scholar and his influence. The man that existed not only in legends, but also in the same modern world that Lefteris had been born to. The man that Tyrants regarded as an unshakable pest. The man that all cultivators considered to be their master's master, in some distant way. The philosopher that even the Coast couldn't kill.

Socrates.

Before Lefteris' disbelieving eyes, that man strode out of a cave not fifty feet away from the safe haven he thought he had established, within leaping distance of the alcove where his charges laid their heads to rest every night. All this time and he had never once known that they weren't alone. He had chosen this spot, just beneath the immortal storm crown of the Raging Heaven, because proximity to the storm was the only way to escape a Tyrant's roving eye. And he had been fool enough to think that was enough. To think it made them safe.

Lefteris watched, frozen in horror, as the Gadfly picked up the Rosy Dawn's sly competitor by the golden shawl tied around his waist and heaved him up into the storm.

Socrates turned his head, then, and looked him dead in the eyes.

Polyhymnia, Lefteris desperately invoked. The muse of sacred poetry immediately pressed her finger to his lips.

Be silent, she whispered in his ear, graver than he'd ever heard her speak, draping her cloak protectively around him as she pressed against his back. *And be still.*

Lefteris obeyed, as he'd obeyed since he was a boy, bowing his head and hoping for greater men to take no notice of him. For a long, long moment, he thought it was over. That he had been found out, in one way or another, and that the Gadfly would surely expose him. That his destiny would come crashing down on top of him and his charges both. Polyhymnia held him steady through it, smoothed out the tension in his body so that he wouldn't move in even the slightest of degrees.

Then it was over. The Gadfly shook his head and muttered something that Lefteris couldn't hear over his own pounding heart and walked back into his cave as if nothing had happened. As soon as he stepped into the shadows, he vanished once again from Lefteris' senses. He had never noticed the Scholar before, because to his pneuma, it was as if that cave didn't even exist.

Slowly, now, Polyhymnia urged him, her veil brushing against his cheek as she pulled him back towards his own alcove, one slow step at a time. Only when he was fully inside, away from prying eyes, did she remove her finger from his lips and whisper a grave farewell.

Lefteris turned and regarded the usurper, currently fighting against a headlock that the vehement protector had put him in.

They were just boys. Young enough that they could almost pass for his sons if not for the fact that they looked entirely different, red-haired and bright-eyed where he was painted in desert shades. The usurper was the younger of the two, slightly shorter than the vehement protector and far more flagrant in his mannerisms. Which was unfortunate because his real name was by far the more dangerous of the two of them.

"What did I tell you about poking your head out?" Lefteris demanded, before anything else, and the adrenaline pounding through his veins gave heat to the words that he hadn't intended. Both boys froze, staring up at him. "Well?"

The vehement protector spoke in the usurper's place, stepping in for him as he always did.

"Be wary without Theri," the older boy answered, reciting it from memory.

"But you were right there!" the usurper protested, jerking back and forth in the vehement protector's grip. "I only wanted to see."

"And you saw," Lefteris said, kneeling down in front of them, "but you were seen in turn."

The usurper paled, and his vehement protector shook him by the neck.

"I told you," the older boy hissed. "I told you to wait. All you have to be is *patient*."

Lefteris watched them go back and forth, an odd combination of fondness and dread festering in his heart. They had grown so much since he'd taken them on, and their spirits were starting to assert themselves. Their sense of self was solidifying, and they were aching to live their lives. He knew they wanted to walk the earth freely, without fear of being recognized for what they were through no fault of their own. They were growing tired of waiting for a liberator.

Eleftherios. It was a name he wanted to live up to, someday. But that day evidently wasn't today.

"Both of you, be quiet," he finally said, looking past them at the modest conditions he'd managed to establish for them since coming to the sanctuary city. Furniture and tools for dining, a few toys and curiosities that he had picked up after months of walking through the markets, and as many tablets and scrolls as he could feasibly smuggle into a cave at the top of a mountain—which was quite a few.

"Is it time to go?" the usurper asked, watching him as he surveyed their things. Now there was remorse in his mismatched eyes. He knew what that look meant. "I'm sorry, Theri. I didn't know—I promise, I didn't mean to be seen."

Without being told, the vehement protector released the usurper from his chokehold and went over to their section of the cave, gathering their things up with practiced efficiency.

Lefteris sighed and placed his hand on the younger boy's head.

"It's fine," he told the boy. "It might be time to go, it might not. I'm not sure yet. For now... for now, I need to talk to a few people, and you two are coming with me."

The vehement protector paused in stuffing a toy sword and its accompanying shield into a large leather sack. "Now?"

Lefteris nodded grimly. "Now."

They took the long path, the boys disguised as casually as they could afford, each wearing a straw farm hat that obscured their defining features from most casual eyes and allowed them to blend in just fine with many of the other children on the outskirts of the city.

They took the long road because Lefteris could no longer be sure that he had been at all successful in hiding them. As they meandered through the city of Olympia, the boys inevitably forgetting the tension of the situation in favor of exploring the markets and engaging with the other children out and about, Lefteris cast out with all his senses for followers. He didn't find any, but then, he had never found any before in Olympia, and that hadn't stopped Socrates from stepping out of that cave within spitting distance of him.

It hadn't stopped the revenant from Rome.

They walked the city nearly in its entirety, corner to corner, and passed through the agora several times. The usurper reveled in every moment of it, eager to explore the place that had been in his sights but out of his reach for so many months, and though the vehement protector did his best to stay vigilant, he was still only a boy. After the second pass through the agora, he was enjoying himself just as much as the usurper.

Eventually, morning turned to afternoon. Afternoon turned to evening.

By the time Lefteris had satiated his paranoia and they'd arrived at their destination, the burning embers of dusk were fading from the skies, and the moon was ascending to its throne in heaven. They stood before an unassuming door in one of the less renowned residential areas in the city, and he motioned for the boys to be silent. Exhausted by a long day of adventure, they obliged without protest. He raised his hand and rapped it against the wood.

Lefteris only had to knock once before the Sword Song's door swung open. Elissa stared at him, and he saw his wild-eyed paranoia reflected in her.

"What are you doing here?" she whispered harshly, immediately looking down at the two boys hiding behind his legs. "And who are they?"

"They're with me," he said simply, leaning in. "I'm here because I saw something outrageous this morning. Have you spoken to those two cultivators from the Rosy Dawn since we met them? From the kyrios' funeral?"

Her expression changed, and his worst fears were confirmed. He grabbed each of his boys by the shoulder and pushed them inside the Heroine's home. He slammed the door shut behind him, and Elissa immediately pressed a hand to the wood, closing her eyes and invoking something wordless with her pneuma. When it was done, she turned and stalked down the hall.

The dread he felt redoubled as they followed her into the next room and beheld a full party of Heroic cultivators.

"Lefteris?" Kyno asked, confused, from his place in front of the hearth. He had his crocodile skin laid out across his lap, and he straightened from a hunched, wary posture when they entered the room. "What's going on?"

Rather than answer immediately, Lefteris found himself staring at the other two cultivators in the room besides Kyno and Elissa. The Hero of the Alabaster Isles and the caustic queen herself. Jason glanced at him through split fingers, his hand splayed over his face while he hung halfway off a lounging couch. Anastasia didn't even bother to acknowledge him with a look, leaning against a shuttered window with her eyes closed.

Lefteris knew for a fact that Kyno and Elissa didn't keep company with those two. He also knew for a fact that they had been there, the night of the funeral. The memory was almost completely black, washed out by foolish amounts of alcohol, but he remembered the club. He remembered the shrieks of eagles and crows, of the weight of command and the revenant that bore it on broad, wrathful shoulders. The man that Jason and Anastasia had been following.

"This must be a joke," Lefteris said, distantly, as if with another man's voice. He willed it to be true, stoked his heart's flame unconsciously to make it so, but such an alteration was beyond him. His expression twisted. "The two of you, with *them*? Are you out of your fucking minds?"

"Left—" Kyno tried again, swinging his crocodile skin over his shoulders and rising, reaching out a hand to him. Lefteris slapped it away, seething. The usurper and the vehement protector both flinched.

"Don't 'Left' me! Look at you! Look at both of you!" He rounded on Elissa, leaning against the door frame with her arms crossed. She scowled. The Sword Song wouldn't meet his eyes. "What could have possibly possessed you? What could have been so tantalizing that you would throw in with them? With *that man*? The first time we saw him was after he'd slapped us all in the face and dared us to do something about it, and the second time was with a broken Crow in his hand!"

"Things have happened since then," Kyno said, holding both arms out placatingly. The vehement protector glanced worriedly between Lefteris and the Heroic Huntsman. A distant part of Lefteris realized that Kyno might have been the largest man the boy had ever seen.

"You weren't there," Elissa added, stubborn till the end. "What's going on now is—"

"Is what? What could be significant enough to throw in with the man making enemies of *Tyrants* in their own domain? What could possibly be compelling enough to implicate yourselves with stowaways from the *Rosy fucking Dawn?*"

"Enough of barking dogs," Anastasia murmured, opening her eyes. Lefteris bared his teeth at her.

"Enough of venomous whores."

She raised a dark eyebrow, unimpressed.

"Sit down, Left," Elissa demanded. "You're scaring your own children."

He looked down and saw it was true. The usurper and his vehement protector stared up at him, wide-eyed and afraid. Even in their past moments of crises, during the conflicts that had forced them into the Half-Step City, he'd never spoken like this in front of them. He'd thought himself better than that. Lefteris grit his teeth and reached for calm.

Polyhymnia met him halfway, as she always did, and he exhaled slowly.

He sat down and addressed the room. "Tell me why this morning I saw the Gadfly throw Griffon into the Storm That Never Ceases." He took what little satisfaction he could from watching that statement wash through the room. Jason viciously cursed.

And then they told him.

It was a story told in waves, each of the Heroic cultivators offering a perspective, an anecdote that the others had not been present for. A side of the revenant and his student that hadn't been seen that night at the funeral. They took their time, one occasionally chiming in for the other to emphasize a certain detail, and it was clear that they had been telling each other these stories all day. Trying to make sense of what they'd gotten themselves into and why.

By the end of it, Lefteris was no more satisfied than before. If anything, he was angrier.

"You mean to tell me," he finally said, once the accounts had been made and a tense, expectant silence had settled over the room like a funeral shroud, "that these two plied you with platitudes and heroic ideals, promised you salvation without explaining how they would deliver it, and in exchange, you took up arms against the Tyrants of the Raging Heaven Cult?"

"You would understand if you had been there, rather than

cowering in your cave," Anastasia said, shrugging his disdain off and delivering her own with a smile.

"Things are worse than we thought they'd be," Elissa cut in before he could snap. "We knew it would be bad, but not like this. We thought they'd make their picks and be done with it, but it's been continuous. Every night since the funeral they've had their crows out in force."

"The mystikos are afraid to travel the mountain alone," Kyno said grimly. "Even those that shouldn't have anything to fear, those who couldn't possibly play a significant part in a Tyrant's power struggle. Children, Left. They travel in packs, even during the day, because it's the only way they feel safe."

"And did either of you, even for a moment, stop to wonder if your new friends had something to do with that?" Lefteris didn't wait for them to answer. Their expressions said enough. "A strange cultivator appears on the night of the kyrios' funeral and tears a bloody streak through the cult's night crawlers, accuses a young aristocrat of the Raging Heaven *outright* of collusion with assassins, and you're surprised that the aristos are responding?"

"It's not just because of Solus," Jason said, shaking his head. He was hanging almost fully off the lounge now, dangling upside down. "They've already started moving in on the juniors, drawing lines and shifting the rhetoric in their lectures."

"If I wanted to hear a coward speak, I'd have gone looking for Scythas. Be *silent.*"

Jason sneered at him upside down, making a vulgar gesture with one hand.

"You said you saw the Gadfly with Griffon this morning," Elissa said, impatient and restless. "When specifically, and where?"

He'd known from the start that their safe haven beneath the storm couldn't last forever. Still, it hurt to see his boys' shoulders slump at the question. They knew that once a hideaway was found, it wasn't used again. The disappointment fed the flames of anger and disgust, pushing him to his feet. He paced in the middle of the room, unable to sit still.

"It was an hour after dawn, maybe less. We were on the eastern side of the mountain, close enough to the storm for a mortal to cast a stone up into it. Griffon came hurtling out of a cave, beaten half to death, and it was the Gadfly that came out after him."

He ran a hand through his hair, pivoting on his heels, again and again.

"I just can't wrap my head around it. I know you two. I *know* you're not this foolish," he told Elissa and Kyno, hating the way they looked back at him. Like they'd been let in on a secret that he had yet to be told. "I listened to you, I heard you out from start to finish, and I still don't get it! What could possibly be so compelling about these two to convince you of this madness?"

Kyno sighed heavily, pulling from a fold in his cult attire a leather skin and taking a long pull from it. He offered it to Elissa, who took a longer pull and grimaced at the taste.

"There's something to them," Kyno said heavily. "I can't describe it with words."

"Does this nameless thing last after death?" Lefteris pressed. "Because if it doesn't then it's useless to you now. And here you are, out in the cold. Do you really think the elders will buy your story of being kidnapped? Do you think you'll be able to sell it beyond a shadow of a doubt when you're face-to-face? Are you willing to bet your lives on that?"

"They're not dead," Anastasia said, and the simple certainty of it made Lefteris briefly see red.

"I saw the Scholar toss Griffon into the storm," he said with slow deliberation. "Alone and half-gone already. He's dead."

"He's not," she replied, just as slowly. "No student of Solus would die from something like that."

"He's dead!" Lefteris shouted despite the fact that it made his boys jump in alarm, and despite Elissa's hissed demands for him to be quiet. His pneuma rose, wrathful beyond belief. "He's dead, and his master isn't far behind him! Sitting here and assuring yourselves otherwise isn't going to change that! It isn't going to make him walk through that door—"

There came a sharp, piercing crunch as the protections on the front door broke. They all stared at one another, frozen in that moment.

Lefteris couldn't feel a single hint of pneuma outside. Then, as one, they rushed into the hall.

A single murky hand of pneuma had punched cleanly through the door, crackling faintly. As Lefteris watched in disbelief, nineteen more punched through to join it.

And then they were joined by ten more, and thirty hands of violent intent tore the reinforced door clear out of its frame.

Chapter Sixty-One

THE YOUNG GRIFFON

The second rank of the Sophic Realm felt much like the first.

The difference was enormous by the standards of a Civic cultivator, of course. My reservoir of pneuma—the sea of my vital soul—had deepened an outrageous amount. The saying went that one rank above was worth ten below, and though my perceptions were skewed by excessive blood loss and a staggering depletion of strength, that felt nearly in line with what I had experienced.

I had also grown in a less evident way, something I couldn't quite pin down, but which instinctively felt clearer within me. I had a few ideas as to what it could be, but at the moment, I was in no state to be waxing theoretical about Sophic cultivation.

Instead, I chose to pay my wayward friends a visit and assure them of my good health. Alas, I misjudged my new strength, and rather than open the door to Elissa's residence, I accidentally conjured thirty hands of pankration intent and tore it off its hinges.

There in the hall, I found Elissa and the rest of the group—as I had suspected I would—along with a pleasant surprise.

"Lefteris," I said brightly, flashing my teeth in a friendly smile at the gold-string archer. "I've been looking for you." For some reason, he flinched at my words—or maybe it was just the sight of me.

I noted a pair of boys peering out at me from behind Lefteris' legs, each of them around Myron's age by the looks of it. Their fiery red hair was mostly covered up by straw hats, but the bright, mismatched eyes were on full display. I'd ask about them later when I wasn't feeling quite as murderous.

"Griffon," Elissa breathed. "You're alive."

"I am," I agreed, stepping inside and grinding the door to further splinters beneath my heels. My pankration hands flexed and grasped fitfully at the air around me, crackling still with the memory of lightning. They clawed at the walls around them, they pounded against the floor, and they wrenched the door apart. Others still reached out for the Heroic cultivators at the other end of the hall. The Heroes eyed them warily, pneuma curling around themselves protectively.

"Forgive me," I said, grabbing a pankration arm with my flesh and blood hand and crushing it into formless essence. "These hands of mine are versatile, but at their core, they're nothing more than a manifestation of my intent."

"And that intent would be?" Jason asked cautiously, his hands resting at his waist, where several daggers were sheathed.

I grinned.

"Violence."

The rosy light of dawn erupted upon the remaining twenty-nine hands of pankration intent in the hall, that curious weight I had noticed upon my advancement flickering in their palms.

"Don't be ridiculous," Elissa scoffed, breaking from the ranks and crossing the hall. She tensed as she passed through the throngs of grasping pankration hands, but none of them touched her, naturally. "You look like you already have a foot in the Styx."

"Two, actually," I said, smiling faintly when she snorted in amusement.

"And I suppose you expect us to pull you out? Patch you up and ship you back out good as new, is that it?" She poked me in the chest, relaxing into the back and forth. "You'll be replacing that door. And don't even think about—"

"Why is the coward touching me?" I asked curiously. The Sword Song froze, staring hard at me.

"Excuse me?"

"I asked why you were touching me," I repeated for her benefit, "with the mongrel finger you refused to lift when you were needed."

"Be very careful about the next word you say," she said, every syllable a threat. I leaned in close enough for the residual lightning in my hair to shock her.

"*Coward.*"

The Sword Song spat an oath and lunged forward, only to be jerked back in the same motion by Kyno, who hoisted her up with her back against his chest while she thrashed and seethed.

"Who gave you the right? Who gave you the right to ignore the reality of this city, to render judgment on us who have lived it? How *dare* you call me a coward, you arrogant scarlet bastard!"

"Ho, have I touched a nerve?" I taunted her, advancing forward while Kyno stepped back with her in his grip. "Does it anger you, to be confronted? Does it upset you, to face judgment from someone who isn't broken and defeated?"

"What were we supposed to do against the Gadfly?" she spat, flames the color of desert heat blazing behind her eyes. The heat in her face overpowered the classical beauty of an advanced cultivator, allowing the scars to assert themselves in all their ugly glory. "What could we have possibly done to stop the man that plumbs the depths?"

"What could a group of Heroes do against a single Philosopher? Is that what you're asking?" I repeated the question, continuing forward even as Kyno bumped back against Lefteris and Jason. I saw something like true steel enter the archer's bearing, just for a moment, as my wandering pankration hands reached for the two boys hiding behind him. His influence struck out and nailed them to the floor in a wordless invocation of will that sent lances of silver pain through my soul. Good. *Good.* Give me *something.*

"Not *a* philosopher. *The* philosopher. He set the standard. We named it the Scholar's path after *him*. Crows and bleeding carrion, you can't possibly think it's that simple." Elissa jerked against Kyno's grip, but unlike at the funeral, he decided against letting her go. She snarled in frustration. "Socrates has had centuries to walk his path, further than any of his kind. How long have we had? How long have you had?"

"Eighteen years."

The cultivators in the hall stared at me in flat disbelief. Anastasia tilted her head, farthest down, merely leaning in the doorframe to the next room and watching. I shot her a challenging look. She smiled apologetically.

"Eighteen years old," Jason muttered. "Even for Solus' student, that's—"

"Lying again." Elissa's eyes narrowed. "I didn't ask you how old your disguise was. I asked you how old *you* were. Griffon, the Olympic competitor."

"And I answered you," I said, pushing them back into the adjoined room. There were several lounges around the edges, and a warm hearth with a few crumbling logs burning away inside. A table next to two of the lounges had several empty jugs on it, one still half-filled with kykeon. It seemed they'd had a long day of sitting around, drinking, and feeling sorry for themselves.

"Still with this? Even now?" she demanded. "We threw in with you against all reason, but you still won't tell us the truth."

"That's twice you've called me a liar. My virtuous heart won't tolerate a third." My pankration hands strained to the limits of the range that I allowed them, clawing at the air in strangling motions. Elissa's pneuma rose in response.

"Be reasonable, both of you," Kyno said firmly, holding the Sword Song still with an arm around her throat and holding the other out towards me, palm flat. "She makes a good point, Griffon. How can you expect us to see this through if we continue to hide everything significant from one another? The stakes in this game are too high to be playing against each other on the side."

"And why would I ever entrust my secrets to this cabal of cowards?"

Kyno met my eyes and did not waver. "We aren't you. The Oracle was right when she judged you. You say all the things a man in your position must not say, you do all the things that you must not do, and as far as I can tell, you are the way you are for the thrill alone. Most men aren't made in your image. And if you want to work with us, you're going to have to live with that."

We stared hard at one another while I bled out on the Heroine's floor. Finally, I tilted my head.

"That day, before we went to see yours, you told me to seek the Scarlet Oracle," I said. He nodded. "When was the last time you saw her or knew someone to have seen her?"

The Heroes exchanged looks.

"Recently," Kyno said at length. "Why?"

"During my brief stroll through the Storm That Never Ceases," I said, drawing my pankration hands back within myself with some effort, "I spoke with each of the Oracles."

"You... what?" Jason asked. Anastasia hummed in interest.

"Seven in all," I continued, "but when I reached the eighth, the oracle of my own home, I found her broken and battered in a crater of melted stone. Can any of you explain that?" By this point Elissa had stopped raging, a pensive frown settling onto her face, and Kyno slowly lowered her to the floor.

Anastasia spoke for the first time since I'd arrived. "That's a question you'd have to ask her successor. Or your master, perhaps."

"Of course." I rolled my eyes and turned, striding back down the hall.

"Wait!"

"You're leaving in that state?"

"Absolutely not."

I glanced down at the marble white hand gripping me by the elbow and holding me in place. On my best day, a Heroine's strength was something I couldn't have shaken. As I was now? I may as well have tried to pull heaven and earth along with her.

"What do you think you're doing?" I asked Anastasia. If the body was weak, then presence would prevail in its place.

Unfortunately, she wasn't fazed. Caustic green eyes burned as they roved up and down my body, and with a distasteful click of her tongue, she pulled me back into the room. I allowed her to do it because my only other option was to resist and fail. She sat me down on one of the lounges next to the table, and I grabbed the remaining jug of spirit wine and downed it in protest.

"'What do I think I'm doing', he asks," Anastasia muttered,

shaking her head in disbelief. With deft movements, she wound her hair into a simple braid and shrugged out of her fine onyx robes, leaving her in a simple peplos that fell to her midriff. "As if I'd let you walk out of here in that state just so you can die. Solus would never forgive me."

I opened my mouth to say something appropriately harsh and shut it just as quickly as she laid her hands on my chest, searing heat sweeping through my body. I jerked back, but she only leaned forward, guiding that heat through the vital channels of my body where the Rein-Holder's marrow dwelled.

So, this was purity.

"You're a healer," I mused, tracing her pneuma as it wound through me, burning away the impurities that it found and cauterizing internal wounds that my rosy hands of dawn couldn't reach.

"That's one of the things that I am," she agreed, her usual conniving smile replaced with focus and intent. In this moment, more than any other that had come before, I bore witness to the Heroine that was Anastasia.

"Teach me," I said.

The Heroine blinked, her pneuma faltering in my veins, and glanced up at me.

"Medicine isn't something that can be learned overnight. It's not some fighting stance to add to your inventory after a few days' practice."

"That's fine," I said. "I'll master it all the same."

"Why?" Jason asked, sitting on the couch opposite the table and leaning forward with his elbows on his knees, visibly forcing himself to lean closer to Anastasia so he could watch her work. "You never struck me as the type. You break, you don't build."

"I am whatever I desire to be," I said. "As for why, this morning has made it clear that I can't rely on others to mend me when things are dire. If I had known how to do it myself, I wouldn't have had to turn back at the precipice of the peak."

"The peak of the mountain?" Elissa cut in.

"He threw you that far?" Kyno asked.

"No," Lefteris answered for me, frowning my way. "Based on the trajectory, you couldn't have landed more than a third of the way into the storm."

"That's true." I acknowledged. "My great-great-grand-master didn't have the courtesy to send me all the way up, so I had to travel the rest on foot."

"You went up the mountain?" Elissa hissed. *"Alone?"*

"Not alone. I made some friends along the way."

"When the Raging Heaven sends initiates up into the storm for their rites, they send all the cult's senior mystikos to guard them," Kyno said with a grave sort of wonder. "There are things in that storm too treacherous for a single cultivator to walk alone."

"The hounds aren't so bad." I lifted my left shoulder in a shrug because the right had stopped functioning hours ago. "Any dog can be disciplined."

"You're serious," Lefteris said. He looked from me to Elissa to Kyno. "He's serious?"

"This is what we were talking about," Kyno said wearily, rubbing at his temples. "So, you braved the trial of tribulation. Official or not, that earns you a right to admittance to the Raging Heaven Cult."

"I didn't make it to the top," I pointed out.

"That just means you wouldn't be inducted as a senior initiate on your first day," Elissa said.

"The higher an initiate makes it up the mountain before breaking or being broken by the storm," Jason explained, "the higher their standing when they first enter the cult. It's a point of pride, as well as their peers' first look at what they're made of."

And I hadn't made it all the way. How annoying.

I sighed. "I suppose I'll have to make up for it when I return with Sol." A beat of uncomfortable silence, punctuated by the crackling hearth.

"Solus... We can't be sure that he'll be coming back," Kyno finally said.

"And why is that?" I asked mildly.

"Look at yourself," Elissa said, gesturing at my admittedly grue-some appearance. By now, she seemed almost too tired to be angry with me. "The Gadfly goes where he wants and says what he wants, and the tyrants of this world allow it, where they would subjugate any other philosopher. Solus may be beyond us, but he certainly is not beyond Socrates."

Anastasia frowned but didn't look up from her work. Jason spoke for her, seeming just as troubled.

"It's not impossible," he said, gripping the upholstered edge of his couch. "Together, under the right circumstances, if we could find him. I owe it to him to at least try. I made a promise that I'd stand by his side."

"And you broke it in under a day," I said, manifesting two pankration hands to clap. "Impressive." He scowled and looked away.

"Enough," said Anastasia, digging fingertips painted black into the juncture between my ribs. I exhaled slowly as an enduring pain in my chest was burned away. "We hesitated, and that was our weakness. It won't happen the next time."

"This is madness," said Lefteris. Sitting beside him, the two boys and their straw hats were staring at me with open curiosity. I stuck my bloody tongue out at them, and they both flinched. "I won't be a part of it," he insisted, beseeching Kyno and Elissa. "And you two shouldn't either. More likely than not we'd be going after a dead man, challenging the Gadfly over a *corpse*. We might as well go charging straight into Tartarus and save ourselves the detour."

The beating of wings sounded from outside the door, cutting the archer off before he could get a full head of steam. Elissa cursed.

"The *door*."

But what swept through her entryway wasn't an ink-black crow, rather a great messenger eagle. Sorea glided into the room, his wings brushing either side of the hall, and he settled himself on the back of my couch with an expectant trill. Lefteris inhaled sharply, recognizing the bird, while his boys stared in wonder. Anastasia, for her part, immediately ceased healing me in her delight.

That delight died a quick death when the messenger eagle disdained her reaching hand, beating his wings and shrieking in her face. She drew back, hurt.

"The bird is wise," I said, holding out a palm. Sorea snapped his beak and heaved, vomiting a handful of black bones as well as a roll of papyrus into my hand. I inclined my head in thanks and opened the message, something primal easing in my chest as I saw Sol's tight, militant script.

I read two lines before I was smiling.

"What does it say?" Jason demanded, leaning over as far as he could to see. I went back to the beginning and read it for the room to hear.

Griffon,

I hope this letter finds you in one piece. You've been due a smack in the mouth, but I won't be able to enjoy it until I know you've survived to be reminded of it. Sorea will wait for you to send back a reply—don't keep him long after you've read this.

I can't rejoin you just yet. I'll be fine where I am so don't come charging after me. I came to this city looking for Aristotle and found his master's master instead. It will have to do. Socrates has identified an aspect of my cultivation in need of improvement, so while he advises me, I'll be behind closed doors in the late kyrios' estate.

Try not to be yourself until I get back. You can tell the others I'm alive, but don't give them the full details. Things have become complicated enough as it is.

Ever,

Solus

"Ah," I said, looking from the assembled cultivators' expressions back to the last paragraph. "I suppose I shouldn't have read this out loud."

The room erupted.

Chapter Sixty-Two

THE SON OF ROME

"Tell me, Solus, what do Romans do for fun?" Selene asked, resting on her stomach in the late kyrios' bed while I paced slowly around the room. Her legs kicked idly behind her. We had been speaking for hours while I waited for Sorea to return with news of Griffon's survival.

The Scarlet Oracle was borderline ravenous for tales of life outside of the Half-Step City. She eagerly listened to my description of the city of Rome as a Roman knew it, chiming in to contrast it with what she had been told of the Republic as a Greek. She didn't hesitate to point out similarities between her own city and mine when she noticed them, and she was even quicker to ask about differences in our ways of life.

I'd had an idea from the start when we first spoke to each other on that plateau—surrounded by initiates of the Raging Heaven Cult and yet entirely alone—that she was an isolated girl. I had assumed that had more to do with her father than anything else, but then I'd found out she was an Oracle. It was impossible not to see once I knew to look for it. Selene was a girl that no common mystiko could hope to approach, even for a casual conversation. Those that could afford to be in her company were, by the nature of their power and influence, far older and far less agreeable than a girl her age needed in a friend.

The more we spoke, the more I found myself sharing the truly painful memories. The ones that stung like fresh wounds because they were small enough that I could afford to not remember them every day. The thousand-thousand little things that made me proud to call myself Roman. The countless shards of a shining, shimmering mosaic that together made up the Republic.

Selene accepted those small remembrances, all but meaningless to someone who hadn't lived them, with genuine reverence. And that made it all too easy to keep divulging them to her.

What did Romans do for fun? I pondered the question.

"Games," I said because it was the first thing that came to mind. "The chariot races were the largest spectacle by far. My father would always reserve the best seats at the corners of the track, where the races were the deadliest. It was considered a dull affair if at least three chariots didn't crash by the final lap."

"I wouldn't have guessed racing to be Rome's favorite pastime," Selene said, interested.

I glanced wryly back at her, bracing half my weight on the raven's bronze spear. "Why do you say that?"

"Well..." She tucked a finger behind her golden veil and lifted it just enough for a single scarlet eye to peer back at me. Her Heroic fire burned mischievously. "I've only met one Roman so far, and you seem to fall in line with the common consensus."

"I enjoy games as much as the next man," I protested. "In fact, I enjoy them *more*." She smiled obligingly and let the veil drop.

"I believe you, Solus. I'm just surprised. I would have expected a more violent game if nothing else."

"It was permitted for chariot riders to whip their opponents," I admitted.

Her smile deepened. "I see."

"Regardless," I said, waving the point off, "the simple things are always enjoyable. A hot bath and a cold bath, an afternoon at the races or a game of dice with friends, and whatever sport happened to be at hand."

"What was your favorite game when you lived there?" she asked, tilting her head. Then, rising up slightly, she added, "Is it a game we could play here?"

I still had my knuckles, and I suspected that the late kyrios would have all manner of board games and curiosities here in his estate—if what Griffon had told me of the man was true. But the question had been what my favorite game *was*.

"My favorite game was *Lusus Troiae*," I said and shook my head. "It's not something two people can play."

"The Game of Troy," she murmured, disappointed and curious in equal measure. "How was it played?"

"Officially? The Lusus Troiae is a maneuvering game, a communal test of skill rather than a competitive one." I paused in my pacing, allowed the distant cadence I had been keeping in the back of my mind to fade, and sighed heavily as the throbbing ache in my left leg came roaring back to the surface of my thoughts. "In honor of victory, in respect for a statesman's passing, or in commemoration of new holy ground, the games were invoked as a remembrance of the present as well as the most distant past—the origin war that birthed the Republic."

"A communal test of skill," Selene mused. "What's it look like?"

I inhaled deeply, tasting the clatter of equestrian steps and the drumbeat of their flawless formations.

The column split apart
As files in the three squadrons all in line
Turned away, cantering left and right; recalled
They wheeled and dipped their lances for a charge.

"Three squadrons of mounted Cavalry, each fifteen strong," I recounted, closing my eyes and seeing it unfold. "Twelve riders, two armor-bearers, and a leader to guide them. Forty-five men and their warhorses in total. We call it the Game of Troy because what they were doing was more than just a drill." I smiled because the wonder was still there. Even the memory was dazzling.

They entered then on parades and counter-parades,

The two detachments, matched in the arena,
Winding in and out of one another,
And whipped into sham cavalry skirmishes
By baring backs in flight, then whirling round
With leveled points, then patching up a truce
And riding side by side.

"They went to war amongst themselves, those forty-five men. They brought the Battle of Troy to life without spilling a drop of blood," I recounted. "During my time as a young patrician in Rome, and later as a young officer in Gaius' legions, I had seen the Lusus Troiae in motion more than once. Each occurrence was as profound as the one that came before. It never got old. It's difficult enough to coordinate forty-five men in such a complex formation. On horseback, in front of the most demanding audiences in the Republic? Incredible doesn't do it justice."

"It sounds impressive," Selene agreed. "But not the sort of thing you can play at a moment's notice. How often did you get to do it?"

I chuckled ruefully. "Never. I was always an observer."

I wasn't old enough, back when I skulked the streets of Rome. And after, I never had the time.

"Your favorite game is one you never played?" Selene asked, frowning severely. "That isn't fair at all. It's also very sad!'"

"I said that was the *official* Lusus Troiae," I corrected her. "And it is one of my favorites to this day, observer or not. But as a boy, my favorite was the *unofficial* Game of Troy. The one that young patricians and street rats alike would play while the adults were away."

"Oh?" She leaned forward, eager.

"Sometime after I met Aristotle," I explained, "the pickpocket that led to our meeting introduced me to the child's Lusus Troiae."

For a moment, the aches and pains were a fond thing, a memory of long afternoons in the alleys and streets of Rome. I shook my head.

"We formed teams of children, one always larger than the other, and where the adults chose to recreate the war in its finest form, capturing the essence of martial ingenuity without any of the bloodshed, the boys of Rome chose to do the opposite. We would draw a line in the dirt, and the larger team would do everything in its power to drag the smaller team across that line. Tactics were minimal—if they were there at all. Bloodshed and broken bones were common occurrences."

Selene hummed, tilting her head. "I think I can guess which of the two teams you preferred to be on."

"To prevail in the face of overwhelming numbers," I mused. "That is the essence of Rome."

"How do you win as the smaller team? Drag the larger team across the line?"

"No, the official game of Troy is an ode to coordination, but the boys' game is the opposite. The only way to win was to be the last man standing on your side of the line."

"And how often did you win, Solus?" the Scarlet Oracle asked me. I glanced back at her, smiling faintly.

"Every time."

We continued on like that, trading stories long into the night while I awaited the return of Socrates or my eagle, whichever came first.

It ended up being the latter, to Selene's delight and my quiet relief. The messenger eagle alighted on the raised butt of my spear, vomiting a message as well as a pile of ink-black crow bones into my open hand. Idly, while I unfurled the papyrus and began to read, I cracked a bone open with my teeth and sucked the marrow out. The starlight strength rushed through the new channels in my body, cascading down towards my left leg and burning horrifically as it began its bloody work. It wasn't an immediate fix, but any help was welcome.

"Solus," Selene said, and I glanced up to find her rising from the bed, veiled face tilted down towards the remaining bones in my hand, "what are those?"

I tossed one to her, and she juggled it between both hands as if it burned.

"Griffon and I believe them to be a fraction of a Tyrant's influence," I explained, spitting the fragments of bone out onto the kyrios' priceless ivory and gold floor when I was done with them. "They taste vile and burn going down, but they're better than hard tack."

The Scarlet Oracle considered the midnight bone in her hand for a moment before slipping it into a fold in her Oracle attire. She sighed softly and shook her head. "You're not going to live a very long life if you keep on like this, Solus."

That was divine wisdom if I had ever heard it.

Sol,

As always, it's a pleasure to hear your voice, even when I'm only imagining it. If I'm being honest, I might even prefer the you that exists within me.

You'll be pleased to know that I took your great-grandmaster's lesson to heart and have since advanced to the second rank of the Sophic Realm. Please, deliver to Socrates my thanks when you get the chance. A bolt of tribulation lightning should convey my gratitude quite well, I think. Failing that, you may instead inform the great philosopher that he's an ugly son of a bitch, and I intend to punch him in the throat when next we meet.

I await your company along with our Heroic friends, whose strength I have long admired. Perhaps while your great-grandmaster is revealing to you the secrets of creation, I might be able to learn a thing or two from these great legends. Assuming they can find the courage in their hearts to face the tyrant known as reality.

Learn quickly and hurry back, worthless Roman master.

Always,

Griffon

I read the message delivered by my virtuous beast, and then I read it again out loud for Selene's benefit. She was giggling by the end of it, and I couldn't deny a bit of exasperated mirth myself.

"This Griffon is your companion that Socrates spoke of?" she asked, and I nodded. "I take it he isn't really your student."

I shrugged. "We grew up in different worlds. I'm not strong enough to stand over him as a mentor, and neither is he to me, but there are some domains where I am the master."

"And some where he is in turn," she finished. I nodded. "I think I'd like to meet him. No, I know I would."

I considered the attire of the Scarlet Oracle, the sunrise silks of dawn. "I think he would feel the same way."

I folded up the missive and dropped it into my shadow, consumed the rest of the ink-black bones and internalized their starlight marrow, and tightened my grip on the raven's bronze spear.

I began to hum another cadence under my breath, walking along the ivory and gold path, and after a moment, Selene joined in. For the first time since we had arrived on the shores, paradoxical as it was to think while crippled and held captive, I relaxed. Tension slipped away and purpose took its place. Things hadn't gone the way that I'd intended, but that was a fact of life I had grown all too accustomed to over the years.

What mattered was that I had found a mentor, and I could begin moving forward towards what Griffon had dubbed my hopelessly grim future. My relentless companion was alive and well, stronger than ever. For the moment, I could shrug off the weight that Olympia had heaped upon my shoulders.

Of course, the legions had taught me early on that such moments rarely lasted.

Sorea noticed the intruder first, shrieking an alarm and fanning his wings out wide in a threatening stance, still perched atop my spear. Selene was by my side in an instant, a spear of her own suddenly in her hand, its shaft a bone-white yew topped by a bronze head, the entire weapon covered in carved depictions of war and tragedy. Her sun ray silks whispered quietly as they fell to the floor, revealing the ornate bronze armor she had been wearing underneath.

I inhaled a wary breath and drew myself up to my full height, forcing my left leg to take my weight. I set aside pain and infirmity, things that an officer had no time for, and faced the archway with severe bearing.

"Come forth," I demanded, and miraculously enough, someone did.

Scythas stepped out of the open air, already three steps inside of the late kyrios' courtyard, and dropped his sword to the mosaic floor. It clattered musically, every jarring impact somehow turning to whistling chimes on their way to my ear.

"Solus," he said hoarsely, and I saw the bags under his eyes. The hazel flames of his heart flickered fitfully, their gold embers dulled to copper. I recognized the look on his face immediately.

It was the kind of exhaustion that sleep couldn't fix.

The Hero of the Howling Wind Cult dropped to one knee, gritting his teeth. He bowed his head shamefully.

"They told me to kill you," he confessed. "I wasn't brave enough to tell them no. But how can I kill you, after you stood by my side? After you were strong for me when I was weak?"

Selene inhaled a slow breath beside me, easing forward a step. She reached out a slender hand, slowly, and laid it upon the crown of Scythas' head. He didn't react when she did, other than to shiver and grit his teeth.

"Beware, cultivator," she said quietly, with sad sympathy. Before my eyes, the curious and vibrant girl I had been introduced to dimmed and became something deeper. "Your heart is not your own."

"Tell me it isn't true, Solus," he begged without meeting my eyes. "Tell me you aren't striking out against the elders. Tell me you aren't the raven that hungers."

Slowly, with care not to betray my pains, I knelt before the Hero of scything wind.

"That night, I wasn't the one that took the first step," I reminded him. Not cruelly. With no particular heat. But he flinched nonetheless, dark brown curls of hair matted with sweat hanging over his eyes. "I only made you aware of injustice in action. I only followed where you led."

"I didn't want to hunt," he protested. "I only wanted to save Jason. I only wanted to save *someone*, for *once*."

I frowned and glanced up, into the sunlight veil of the Scarlet Oracle. I tilted my head back, towards her personal quarters within the kyrios' estate. Her lips pursed. After a long moment, she inclined her head in a nod.

"Why are you here, Scythas?"

"I told you. The Tyrant Aleuas wants you dead—"

"Not here in this courtyard," I said. "Why are you here in this city? What is a Hero doing in the most secure city in the world while there are people out there in need of saving? Monsters in need of slaying?"

When he refused to answer, or was unable to, I gave him my best guess. I voiced the trend that I had noticed among all of our companions. The red thread that connected us all.

"You ran away," I quietly condemned him. Scythas nodded miserably. "You wanted to save someone, to be yourself again. I can respect that. I can even admire it. But it isn't enough to be that man once. You have to be him every day, every hour, every single moment. You can't afford to be less when the world needs you to be more."

He looked up at me, and there were tears in his eyes.

"How can I be?" he asked, tortured. "How can I possibly be a hero now, when I had the audacity to be a coward when I was needed? When I *had to be brave?*"

Just like Jason before, I looked into the mirror's reflection and felt rage at what it showed me. I set my jaw and rose on worthless legs, thrusting out a hand. Scythas stared at it like it was a living serpent.

"You're asking the wrong question," I told him harshly. Those broken eyes snapped up to mine. Belatedly, I felt Selene's hand on my back, steadying me. Always another person's hand holding me up. Always another soul standing beside me in support, helping me do what I should have been able to do for myself.

"The question you should be asking yourself—how can you be anything else?"

Scythas stared up at me, and I saw him teetering on the edge of giving in to despair.

"What do they have on you?" I asked him. The First Spear of the Fifth had told me once that the men didn't need to think you were soft to confide in you. They didn't need to be comforted or consoled. It was enough to know that you'd go to war for them. It was enough to know that you'd tear out throats for those in your care.

"I'm engaged to his daughter."

Ah.

"You care for her," I said. He didn't say yes. He didn't have to. "What else?"

His pneuma rippled and flexed around him. "My brother. They have my brother. They took him into the Howling Wind Cult, into the kyrios' own confidence. They've taken my brother, and every day they strive to turn him against me. They took my *family*, Solus."

"So kill me."

He met my eyes in despair.

"You have two choices," I told him, crushing the part of myself that urged me towards empathy. "You can obey, now and tomorrow and the day after that, and pray every day for a Tyrant's mercy. You can do what they tell you and kill me where I stand. It might even be enough to keep the people you care about safe.

"Or."

I clenched my outstretched hand into a fist and pulled him to his feet with *Gravitas*.

"You can stand," I said fiercely. "You can fight. And you can take back what is yours. You can't live both lives, so which will it be? Will you be a slave? Or will you be Scythas? What does your heart say?"

He stood under his own power. Haltingly, he reached out to me.

"It says I'm lost," Scythas whispered.

"Take heart, cultivator," Selene said. "You may be lost."

I took his hand and gripped it tight.

"But you are not alone."

Epilogue: Old 'Zalus

The room was large but modestly furnished, barren by the standards of most made men. Its floors were polished marble, pure and unblemished by gemstone veins. What furniture that there was, a massive cypress bed frame and side tables of the same wood, was all finely kept but notable for its lack of adornment. There were no paintings, no statues or sacred treasures. It was as humble a home as any man could have.

And yet, that did not change what it was. The lack of overt majesty made it no less potent. No less his. The response to intruders here was just the same as in the most palatial estate.

"I'm going to kill you, Gadfly," Polyzalus promised the man intruding upon his place. It was an insult that no Tyrant worth their title would tolerate. After all.

A Tyrant's domain was the throne of their soul.

"Good evening to you too, 'Zalus," Socrates said, brushing the weight of a Tyrant's displeasure off his shoulders. "I've come to bargain."

The Gadfly, pest among pests, strode into Polyzalus' domain as brazenly as he did everything else, passing by the bed and side tables without a second glance on his way to the wide-open terrace. That he

522

didn't hesitate even for a moment while he passed the woman in the bed was the only reason Polyzalus didn't kill him where he stood.

But the urge was strong. It always was.

"I have nothing to give you, and you have never had anything worth wanting," the Tyrant dismissed the Philosopher.

Idly, in another place and another part of himself, the Rein-Holder listened through the ears of his faithful shadows as they left to do their dark work. These aspects of himself, the shards of the Tyrant that was Scarlet Polyzalus, existed in his perception in the same way that the shadows they epitomized did. Silhouettes without true detail. Impressions and whispered half-truths.

It was enough to know when his crows were on the hunt. The rest would be revealed to him when the shadows of himself were re-gathered to the whole. Assuming, of course, that they were not devoured first.

"Fortunately for the both of us, nothing is exactly what I came here to bargain for," Socrates said, sitting cross-legged on the marble floor with his back to the stone rails of the terrace.

"Deal, then. Now leave."

"That's no way to treat a guest."

Polyzalus paused in his work, and in his far-seeing as well, and he leveled the Gadfly with the pressure of his authority. Socrates met his eyes just long enough to make his worthless point before allowing his head to bow.

"You haven't been my guest in over three hundred years," the true Tyrant of the Burning Dusk said, and his conviction made it so. Within these plain walls and upon this marble floor, the word of the First-to-Burn was natural law.

And yet Socrates found it within himself to reach outside of that new natural order and make a nuisance of himself as always.

"What would our father in heaven think, to hear you cast aside *xenia* so callously?"

Night was falling, casting shadows in the room. Polyzalus reached out with the crystallized purpose of his ravenous soul and from nothing declared something, burning out of non-existence several sunset lanterns that drifted like fireflies into his domain. With his hands, he dipped an unstained cloth into a basin of water and twisted it, gently ringing out the bulk of the moisture.

"There are no gods left to punish such things," he said, taking her arm in his hand and setting to his work with the damp cloth.

"Is that so? Is that what you truly believe?"

"Near enough."

These days, it made little difference.

"Then disregard the pantheon," Socrates said, unwinding sash after sash from around himself and casting them to the wind. "What would you think, three hundred years ago, to see yourself now? To hear your own voice uttering such foul sentiment?"

"I wouldn't think anything meaningful at all. I never did, in those days."

"If not the gods, and not the you of yesterday, then is the you of today truly the sole arbiter of morality? How can you know that the 'Zalus of tomorrow won't disagree? If all the world tells you—"

"Not today," Polyzalus said simply and leveraged the weight of his purpose. Outside of his domain, he would have had to manifest his pneuma for this. But here, seated upon the humble throne of his soul, all he had to do was desire it.

And it was his.

The Gadfly shut his mouth, and it was worth every ounce of ethos that Polyzalus had invoked to achieve it. He dipped his cloth back in the basin of water, wringing it once more.

Alas, it didn't last. "I'll be brief, then."

"Will you?" the first son to burn mused, brushing back golden hair the same shade as his own and wetting her forehead. "Even in my own domain, I never thought I'd see the day."

"I've taken on a boy."

He sneered. "Spare me your personal details."

"I'll be overseeing his development for the near future, so expect to see him around the Raging Heaven. I don't want him pulled into the current schemes."

The damp cloth stilled, resting against her right cheek.

"What is his name?"

"He calls himself Solus. But his companion calls him Sol."

Polyzalus glanced back at the arrogant Gadfly. "You're tempting the Fates, boy."

Socrates scoffed, amused. "Three decades difference aren't what they used to be. We're both old men these days—it's only that I choose to look it."

"Those children took a bite out of my influence," Polyzalus explained, because the world was a strange place, and he had known wiser men to be less informed about more obvious things in the past. "They perverted the nature of my shades and used their stolen strength to do the same to my peers. Even if I were to grant them clemency, the others wouldn't." Especially when these hungry ravens had thwarted all attempts to bring their lost Heroes in line.

Tyrants were greedy existences. It was already the case that they hungered beyond any satiation. Anything that strove to take even more from them would face the same fate regardless of whose heels they were nipping at. What else could a starving lion do when provoked by a scavenger?

"What makes you think that the boys I'm referring to are the same ones tearing down your crows?" Socrates pressed, with his veiled curiosity. He reached out with his poisonous logos as if Polyzalus couldn't see it written in the stars between them.

"I don't think. I know."

He watched with a dim sort of mirth as the logos strengthened, coiled in on itself in preparation. And then he waved his influence through it, brushing it off like sand from his shoulder, and headed off the argument before it could be made.

"You can run your circles all you want in the agora, but not here. Not right now. And especially not in front of my wife." Three times he asserted himself within his domain, and three times it was made so.

He dipped his cloth into the shimmering basin once more and returned to his duty. In the fine feather bed, his wife continued to sleep her dreamless sleep.

"I came here intending to be civil," Socrates said, scowling now, and he reached into a fold in logic disguised as cloth, pulling from it a jug of fine kykeon. The smell of it permeated Polyzalus' domain, and he knew it was no coincidence that this was the exact blend he had served a young man in search of understanding over three hundred years ago. Back when he ruled in the Scarlet City.

Back when the setting sun belonged to him.

"How can a scholar be anything less than civil in the presence of a king?" Polyzalus mused. "But so be it. I'll humor you—where do you intend to keep this boy?"

"It just so happens that an estate has been made vacant recently," Socrates said, shrugging and taking a pull from the wine jug himself. He swallowed easily, savoring the taste.

Then he grimaced in fleeting unease as Polyzalus burnt **Courage** from his soul.

"What?"

"I gave the boy a place to learn some sense away from prying eyes —and the presumptions of men that think they know best."

The damp cloth burnt to ash in his hands, and the ash burnt soon after. Outside of the bedroom, to the farthest edges of his domain, members of the Burning Dusk Cult faction within Olympia dropped anything and everything they were doing and moved. Whether that was to rush towards them or away depended on the individual.

Of course, he'd seen Socrates bring the boy to the kyrios' estate in the heart of Kaukoso Mons. It wasn't an act outside of the Gadfly's usual privileges, confidant that he had been to the late lord of the Raging Heaven Cult. But refuge for the night was one thing, and prolonged accommodation was entirely another. "You intend to keep him there? In the heart of the mountain where the Oracles sleep? With my *daughter?*"

He had promised murder when the Gadfly first walked in—and countless times before today. Perhaps, after all these years, he'd finally make good on that promise.

Socrates raised both hands, with some effort, against his ethos. And he spoke. "I brought no ravens to your doorstep, I can promise you that. Only a boy with more potential than sense. Your daughter is as she's always been. Safe and secure."

"And why should I take you at your word? Why should I accept a young fool's resolve over my own?"

Socrates matched logos to ethos, as he always had, and the sight was as absurd as it had been the very first time.

"Because you're all balancing on the knife's edge, and even a young fool's word could be the difference that places one of you above the rest. And unlike your peers, who are each trying to decide which path best suits their greed, you don't have a choice."

Socrates spread his hands and offered up the truth of Polyzalus' world as he understood it.

"The others can decide. They can go home and reclaim what was theirs before the kyrios took them from it, or they can stay and fight for what the kyrios left behind. But not you, 'Zalus. The only way out for you is through. Nothing remains of you in the Scarlet City. No one is waiting for you there."

No one but Damon Aetos.

Rage warped the sunset domain for a single instant. In the time it took him to reclaim himself, every soul in the Burning Dusk's portion of Kaukoso Mons dropped to the ground, their eyes and ears leaking blood. The only one spared was his wife. As always, **courage** wrapped her in its tight embrace.

"The world is on the brink of being a violent place once again," he finally said, the tightly leashed fury in his voice cracking the marble beneath their feet. "I won't tolerate another threat to my ethos."

"I'll keep them in line," Socrates promised. Them. So he sought to include the other hungry raven in his protection. Polyzalus stared him down, stared through him, sifted through the light of his soul, and didn't find a single answer that satisfied him.

"You said you'd never take on another student," he finally said, reaching into empty air and grasping the jug of wine that Socrates had brought in offering. He drank deeply from it, remembering simpler times. "What changed?"

Socrates sighed.

"Nothing at all."

Polyzalus finished the wine in two more pulls and dismissed the jug from his domain. He turned away from the philosopher, back to his wife.

"Swear to me they won't take another bite out of my influence, and know that if either of them advances on my daughter, I'll tear their mortal threads from the loom and eat their beating hearts."

"I swear. And I understand."

Polyzalus waved an irritated hand. "Fine. Do what you will."

The Gadfly always did.

About the Author

As a long-haul truck driver and a lifelong fan of the ancients, Striker's days are largely spent contemplating glorious antiquity and blasting 80's Synth. He enjoys reading grand scale modern fantasy as well as the classics - of all his favorites, the Epic of Gilgamesh rests highest on his shelf. Striker hopes to one day live in the mountains, subsisting on roasted game and snow.

www.ingramcontent.com/pod-product-compliance
Lightning Source LLC
Chambersburg PA
CBHW030537020726
47494CB00005B/1411